The Silent Accord
Parts I–III

by
Robert Stewart

Cover artwork and the Cosmology graphic were generated by:

ChatGPT using GPT-4-turbo

"There is a silence before memory, and a fire after forgetting.

Those who walk between must carry both.

A raven's shadow, a whisper in flame—

the path unwinds where the living turn back."

— Old Ravkari Proverb

Table of Contents

Introduction

The Silent Accord begins in a different voice than it ends. This is intentional.

Part I, *The Price of Returning*, reads like a legend whispered at the edge of a fire, or a tale etched into the walls of a forgotten temple. It is mythic, fragmented, and poetic—because the story it tells was not passed down in books. It was remembered, distorted, and rediscovered through grief.

This first part invites the reader to drift rather than charge forward. Names emerge slowly. Time folds. What matters most is not what happens, but how it echoes.

By contrast, Parts II and III ground the narrative. They give names to those who once moved like echoes. The characters—Bryn, Nyv, Tassa, Kaerda, and the others—step out of myth and into themselves. The narrative becomes more personal, more immediate, and more structured as their voices and choices take shape.

Think of Part I as the boat sailing on the lake at dawn. Parts II and III are the journey through it's waters—where you begin to see the ripples, the wake, and the wildlife enjoying the stillness.

For those returning to this story, welcome back. For those beginning for the first time, step carefully. The shadow remembers.

Dramatis Personae

Members of the Silent Accord

Bone-Anna

A silent, skeletal companion brought to life through Bryn's magic. Though she does not speak, Bone-Anna expresses loyalty and awareness through gesture and action. Over time, she begins to show signs of independent thought and emotion—becoming a true member of the Accord rather than just a summoned ally. Her Veilstep and quiet vigilance make her a formidable force.

Bryn Lovas

A Shadowbound warlock bound to the Queen of Stillness. Quiet, deliberate, and deeply loyal, Bryn's connection to death is both a burden and a blessing. She commands spectral ravens, bends shadows to her will, and serves as the spiritual heart of the Silent Accord. Her long raven-black hair is worn in space buns, and she wears a bandeau tiara with a small eye in the front. Bryn's artistry and restraint conceal great emotional depth, which slowly unfurls over the course of the journey.

Geoff the Newt

Nyv's familiar. Small, olive-green, and eerily intelligent, Geoff mimics Nyv's movements, posture, and even emotional tone. Many have mistaken him for a mere lizard—but those who watch closely realise that Geoff is something far stranger. He reflects her magic, her awareness, and her bond with the party in ways that defy explanation.

Kaerda Flintward

A dwarven Forge Cleric of Durnach the Forgemaker. Loyal, steady, and proud of her craftsmanship, Kaerda serves as the defensive bulwark and spiritual anchor of the group. She believes in tools, precision, and resilience—and brings radiant might to the battlefield when needed. Though not one for many words, she watches her companions with quiet insight and often sees what they cannot say.

Nyvana "Nyv" Vojta

A pale and determined Ravkari witch with hidden mysterious ancestry blood. Her white hair is always tied in a high ponytail, and her every action is precise. Trained in battle-magic, Nyv specializes in counterspells, illusion, and elemental control. Initially aloof and tactical, she grows emotionally closer to her companions—especially Bryn—unlocking ancestral magic known as Communal Binding. Her familiar, Geoff the Newt, mimics her with eerie synchronicity.

Tassa Emberlin

A halfling sorceress with a golden flame in her blood. Tassa's past is scattered with half-truths and self-protection, often asking questions rather than giving answers. Her fire magic is vibrant and unmistakable—always golden, always ricocheting with a mind of its own. Tassa speaks in riddles and carries the echo of something ancient. Her luck, as it turns out, may be something more than chance.

Other Notable Figures

Dalebar

The innkeeper of Candlecut Hollow in Estavar. Quiet and unassuming, Dalebar rarely speaks unless needed—but when he does, his words cut to the heart. Though he plays a small role, his act of sending for help when the Silent Accord needed it most changed the course of their journey. Bryn recognises his insight and quiet courage, offering him rare thanks in return.

The Druid

A scatter-brained wanderer found deep in the wilds, whose cryptic puzzles and odd behaviour mask an extraordinary grasp of natural magic. Though strange, he is wise in ways the Accord cannot always predict. He recognises truths hidden beneath appearances—including the nature of Bone-Anna and the intertwined roots of Bryn and Nyv. His aid is critical in transporting the group across great distances, though his presence lingers like a riddle left unsolved.

The Lieutenant

A powerful martial commander encountered and defeated by Bryn during a pivotal moment in Part II. Though unnamed, his presence embodied the authoritarian threat pressing in on the Accord. His defeat marked a shift in Bryn's arc—from one who followed to one who stepped forward. Cold, dutiful, and unyielding, the lieutenant served as a grim warning of what might come if power is obeyed without conscience.

Mairadas

A cunning and ancient shadow dragon of the Ashbound steeped in the corrupted currents of the Witherlace. Mairadas is a creature of ambition and manipulation, whose presence twists the land and minds alike. He seeks dominion, legacy, and something even older—an echo of power lost to time. Though terrifying in his full form, Mairadas is even more dangerous in disguise, weaving influence through mortal agents and forgotten ruins.

The Man With No Mouth

A broken and terrifying figure shaped by a flawed attempt to rewrite death. Once a man, now something else entirely, he moves in silence with a face erased and a soul half-pulled from the grave. He is both hunter and echo—an imperfect creation left in the wake of failed necromantic ambition. His presence marks the return of forgotten magic, and his movements ripple with shadow.

The Pilgrim of Durnach the Forgemaker

A wandering devotee of Durnach the Forgemaker encountered by Kaerda in the desert ruins. Though unassuming, his reverence for craft and quiet understanding of the divine forge leave a lasting impression. His words reinforce Kaerda's belief in faith expressed through creation, and his presence helps illuminate the quiet strength she has carried all along.

Selvestar

A silver-robed figure who moves between memory and shadow. Selvestar is quiet and difficult to place—neither fully present nor fully gone. They speak in solemn tones and is drawn to places where grief and time intersect. Their presence hints at a deeper connection to the past and a role not yet fully understood.

Vaelric

A quiet, silver-robed figure the Silent Accord encountered outside the ruins of the Banished City. Though he said little, his presence carried the weight of memory and loss. It was Vaelric who pointed the group toward the path they needed to take—offering direction without demand, as though nudging fate itself. His connection to Vhal'turien remains uncertain, but his guidance arrived when it was needed most.

The Vaulmar Binder

An ambitious necromancer from Vaulmark who sought to rewrite death itself by claiming the power of Vhal'turien. His ritual failed, but its ripple was felt through the land, sparking the events that would draw the Silent Accord together. Though he appears only in Part I, his actions have lasting consequences—twisting fate and inspiring others to seek forbidden power.

Vhal'turien

Once a powerful and enigmatic figure who studied the boundaries between death, memory, and fate. His legacy, preserved in scattered murals and half-buried texts, suggests a being who sought to create something eternal—an escape from the finality of death. The Silent Accord first glimpsed him in a mural in Tharniseth: neither savior nor villain, but a man who chose to wield forbidden magic and paid the price. What remains of Vhal'turien is fragmented, yet his name still shapes the world's most dangerous questions.

Yeldanna

A determined Ravkari woman driven by grief and hope, Yeldanna is the figure Bryn, Nyv, and Tassa accompany in Part I on her dangerous quest to resurrect her son. Her strength lies in quiet conviction, and though the journey nearly breaks her, she remains resolute. It is through Yeldanna that the story first explores the boundaries between memory and death—setting the tone for everything that follows.

Part I - The Price of Returning

In the dark, before the story knew its shape—
there was only memory, and the cost it carried.

Prologue

What Was Left Behind

Setting: The outer keep of a ruined fortress deep in the wilds. The ground is scorched and strewn with broken spears, gnoll corpses, and shattered stone. The air still stinks of blood and smoke. Twilight descends slowly, painting the sky in ash and rust.

Chovee lies motionless near the shattered gate, his body twisted in a final act of defiance—surrounded by fallen gnolls, their black blood soaking the stone. His wounds are mortal. His axe is gone. His pack. The rings from his fingers. Even his boots.

They took everything.

Shadows lengthen across the ruin. Then—

Nyvana Vojta enters the keep, alone. Her black mask is cracked—one lens a starburst of ruin. Her robes are torn and streaked with ash. In one hand she holds a scimitar slick with dried blood. The other glows faintly with healing magic, already spent.

She sees him.

And stops.

Nyv (quietly): "No..."

She walks to him on trembling legs. Her knees hit stone as she drops beside his body.

His eyes are open.

His face is cold.

She doesn't speak at first. She just reaches for the frayed edge of his cloak—the same one he wore when they first met. It's soaked through.

Then she sees it—the tracks of others. Boots. Drag marks. Signs that the rest of his so-called companions had left him. Taken what they could carry. Moved on.

No burial.

No words.

No honour.

Nyv (softly, as if speaking to ghosts): "You bastards..."

She lowers her mask fully, pressing her brow to Chovee's. Her breath shakes. She reaches into her satchel and withdraws the sending stone, still etched with frost-rimed runes.

She closes her eyes.

Nyv (telepathically): "*Yeldanna. It's Nyv. He's gone.*"

"*I found him in the keep. His party left him.*"

"*...I'm bringing him home.*"

"*I'm sorry.*"

The message ends.

Nyv doesn't move for a long time. She just sits there, hand resting on Chovee's chest, as the shadows crawl over them both.

She spots his javelin discarded in the corner of the room.

Finally, she begins to wrap his body.

One breath. One wound. And every memory left behind.

Act I – The Threads of Grief and Duty

The Stone Speaks

Setting: A quiet glade near the edge of the Lethvain Reach, just outside the Ravkari heartland. Snow lies undisturbed beneath tall, silent trees. A thin plume of smoke rises from a small cooking fire beside a bedroll. Yeldanna sits cross-legged on a worn cloak, her armour resting nearby. Her eyes are closed, hands folded, as she meditates in stillness.

Birdsong fades.

The forest goes still.

And then—a pulse of warmth ignites in her satchel.

Her eyes open. The sending stone glows blue in her satchel—warm with magic. She draws it out, listening.

"Yeldanna. It's Nyv. He's gone."

"I found him in the keep. His party left him."

"…I'm bringing him home."

"I'm sorry."

Silence.

The wind moves through the branches above, gentle and cold.

Yeldanna does not cry. Her breath remains even. Her hands still. But her knuckles tighten around the stone until the edges press hard into her skin.

Slowly, she sets it down beside her.

She stands.

Her shoulders sag—just slightly. As if the weight of the world had pressed down all at once.

She kneels beside her armour and runs her fingers over the hilt of a longsword—once meant for her son.

Then she looks to the trees—toward the south.

Yeldanna (to the wind, quietly): "Come home, then."

Yeldanna (softer, after a beat): "And I will make them remember you."

.

The Long Road

Setting: Across valleys, rivers, and frozen trails, the path to Ravkareth stretches long and quiet. Snow deepens by the day. Wolves follow the scent of blood. The trees, ancient and sharp-shouldered, whisper in languages only witches know.

Nyvana Vojta walks alone, wrapped in a bloodstained cloak. A makeshift travois drags behind her, fashioned from broken shield-struts and rope, pulled across snow and stone. Chovee's body, wrapped in thick furs and secured tight, rests atop it—motionless, yet present in every breath she takes.

Each morning, she speaks aloud—

Nyv: "Still with me, aren't you?"

Each evening, she builds the fire and sets her bedroll near him.

She doesn't cry. Not anymore. Grief has cooled—hardened into something quieter. Something sacred.

✦

She passes through a half-buried village, its windows dark, its signs of life faint. Children peer at her from behind curtains. No one asks who she is, or what she carries. Some already know.

The local priest offers shelter. She refuses.

Nyv (flatly): "He didn't rest. I won't either."

✦

She crosses a frozen river, slipping once and gashing her hand. Blood falls in the snow beside Chovee's wrapped form. She stares at it a moment, then presses her palm to his furs.

Nyv (quietly): "Still bleeding for you, you stubborn oaf."

✦

On the sixth day, the snow turns deep and soft. The wolves grow bold.

They circle at night, yellow eyes gleaming just beyond the firelight.

Nyv doesn't sleep. She watches. She waits. One hand on her blade. The other on the javelin—Chovee's javelin. Hers now—by duty, not by blood.

When one of the wolves gets too close, she casts Burning Hands—and doesn't stop until its pelt ignites like oil-soaked cloth.

The rest run.

She looks to the body behind her. Nyv (with steel): "See? Still got it."

✦

On the tenth day, she sees the stone watchtowers of Ravkareth rise over the white horizon.

And only then—when she sees smoke from homeland fires and the distant silhouettes of the Veilwarden temples—does her breath catch.

She lowers the sled's ropes. Her breath catches in her throat.
Nyv: "I kept my promise."

The Weight We Carry

Setting: A frost-covered ridge just beyond the gates of Ravkareth. The forest thins into open tundra, where the mountain winds bite sharper. A single figure stands motionless amid the swirling snow—Yeldanna, clad in full armour, her cloak pinned at the shoulder with a carved silver raven. Her eyes are fixed on the white horizon.

She hears the sled before she sees it.

The soft scrape of wood over snow. The slow, steady rhythm of boots. The breath of a tired beast—though it is only Nyvana, alone, dragging Chovee's body across the frost.

Nyv crests the ridge, and their eyes meet.

No words.
No tears.
Only silence.

Yeldanna walks forward and kneels beside the travois. Her fingers brush back the furs and rest gently against her son's cheek.

She exhales—slow and heavy.

Yeldanna (softly): "He hated the cold."

Nyv doesn't answer. There's nothing to say.

Yeldanna stands.

Yeldanna: "I'll take him now."

Nyv (quietly): "You don't have to."

Yeldanna (firm): "I do."

She steps to the head of the sled, takes up the weight, and begins to pull. Her strength is staggering—not drawn from magic, but from something buried deeper. Grief, made solid.

Nyv walks beside her—the silence between them thick but no longer painful. They pass through the outer gates of Ravkareth—guards bow their heads as they pass. A pair of witches standing in the shadows say nothing—only watch.

Nyv (after some time): "They left him. The others."

Yeldanna (flat): "Then they were never his kin."

A pause.

Nyv: "I was too late."

Yeldanna (glancing at her, then back at the road ahead): "But you came."

That is enough.

✦

Transition: The Temple of the Veilwarden

The temple rises like a crown of ice and shadow—white stone, black spires, and walls etched with runes that shimmer faintly in the twilight. Ribbons of spirit-mist drift lazily through the air—ancestral guardians watching in silence.

Yeldanna steps forward to the heavy doors. They swing open with a slow groan—not from hinges, but from will.

She turns to Nyv.

Yeldanna: "You may enter if you wish."

Nyv (nods once): "I will stand beside you."

Together, they cross the threshold.

And the dead walk with them still.

The Circle Unanswered (Part I)

Setting: The inner sanctum of the Veilwarden temple, a round chamber carved into the earth beneath Ravkareth's oldest standing hill. The walls are adorned with relics of the dead: bones, feathers, etched memories sealed in glass. The air is thick with incense and magic older than names.

At the centre of the room lies Chovee's body, cleansed and wrapped in white ceremonial cloth, resting upon a stone slab engraved with the runes of return. A bowl of dark water sits at his feet. Iron candles flicker at the points of a circle drawn in chalk and ash.

Yeldanna stands to one side of the slab, hands folded, face carved from grief and will.

Nyv stands at her opposite, silent and tense, her eyes darting across the sigils. Behind her, a trio of Veilwarden witches—cloaked in red and black—chant in a language that scrapes like wind through bare branches.

First Witch: "Let his name be called."

Yeldanna (firmly): "Chovee, son of Yeldanna, son of the Ashblade line. Hear me."

The room grows colder.
The candles dim.
A faint ripple disturbs the surface of the water bowl.

Second Witch (chanting): "We call from the roots of Ravkareth. From the river, the sky, the blood, and the flame. Return, if you will. Rise, if you are not yet lost."

For a breath, it feels as though something stirs. A flutter in the candlelight. A pull in the air. Nyv's eyes widen.

Then—
Stillness.
Nothing.

The water stills. The chalk dims. The air grows still and empty.

Third Witch (softly): "He does not come."

A long, breathless silence.

Yeldanna does not move. Only her eyelids close—once—and rise again.

First Witch (gently): "He is too far. His soul has begun to wander."

Nyv (quietly, bitter): "There must be another way."

The witches exchange glances.

Second Witch: "Perhaps. But not within the bounds of life and death as we know them."

Third Witch: "There is... one hope."

They all look to Yeldanna.
The candles flicker again.

First Witch: "The Heart of Vhal'turien."

The Circle Unanswered (Part II)

Setting: The ritual space is silent but for the soft hiss of melting wax. The failed resurrection hangs like incense left too long to burn—clinging to every breath. The flickering shadows cast by the candlelight stretch long across the chamber walls.

Nyv steps forward, her hand instinctively reaching toward the edge of the summoning circle. She stops just shy of the boundary, fingers trembling.

Nyv (quietly): "You said he was strong. His spirit. I felt it."

First Witch: "Strength cannot unmake distance. He is beyond our reach."

Nyv's jaw clenches. Her gaze drops to the still form of Chovee.

Nyv (low, bitter): "I was too slow. I failed him."

Yeldanna (without looking): "No."

Her voice is sharp—controlled.

Yeldanna: "You brought him home. That is more than they would have done."

She meets their gaze—unyielding, clear as ice.

Yeldanna: "What is the Heart?"

The witches remain quiet for a beat, but the weight of Yeldanna's name and legacy is undeniable in this chamber. She is no stranger to Ravkareth's oldest powers—nor one to be dismissed.

The Second Witch steps forward, her voice even.

Second Witch: "It is not a simple relic. The Heart of Vhal'turien is a binding— ancient and dangerous."

Nyv turns, brow furrowed.

Nyv: "You're suggesting something forbidden."

Third Witch (calmly): "We are suggesting something desperate."

First Witch: "You may refuse. You may bury him. That, too, is sacred."

Yeldanna does not move. Her hand rests on the edge of the stone bier.

Yeldanna: "Tell me what it is. Where to find it."

The Breath That Lingers

Setting: The witches glance among themselves. The First Witch raises a hand—one by one, the candles snuff out until only a single flame remains. The circle dims. Shadows gather. The chamber seems to inhale.

First Witch (softly): "Before Ravkareth. Before the Iron Lord. Before the Veilwarden... there was Vhal'turien."

The name hangs in the air like thunder before a storm.

Second Witch: "A Gold Dragon—ancient beyond reckoning. Not a conqueror, but a keeper. He watched the rift between life and death. His breath was said to cure sickness, his voice could call spirits from the far realms."

Third Witch: "When death came for him, he did not resist. He gave his heart willingly. Not to defy death—but to offer a path through it."

Nyv stiffens, her voice low and wary.

Nyv: "You said it was a binding. Not a relic."

Second Witch (nods): "It is both. His heart still burns, encased in crystal and guarded by sacred flame. It houses the breath of resurrection... but only for those whose spirits have wandered too far for mortal magic."

Yeldanna: "Where is it?"

A long pause.

First Witch: "In the ruins of Skarbek Thar, a dwarven stronghold lost beneath the Velthorn Peaks. The dwarves once worshipped Vhal'turien as a divine ally. When the keep fell, kobolds—twisted descendants of dragonkind—claimed it."

Third Witch: "They worship the Heart as a god-egg. They guard it fiercely—without understanding what they hold."

Second Witch: "You must take it. And if it answers you... then perhaps your son will find the way home."

The witches step back from the circle, the ritual complete—even if the soul remains unfound.

First Witch (gently): "You will not return unchanged."

Yeldanna (quietly): "I was changed when I first saw him."

Flame and Feather

Setting: The temple's high threshold, where the spiral stairs meet the wind-swept plateau above the hill. The sun is just cresting the peaks of the Velthorn Peaks, casting long shadows across the frost-glittered stones. The air is sharp—with cold and prophecy.

Yeldanna stands in full armour, her travel cloak pinned with a raven-etched brooch. Her jaw is set, her gaze fixed eastward. Nyv adjusts her satchel, robes still bearing the faint scent of incense. The runes along her sleeves gleam softly in the sunlight.

From beneath her sash, a small movement stirs. A rough-skinned newt, olive green with a bright orange belly, crawls slowly into view. He blinks sleepily and climbs up Nyv's shoulder with practised ease.

Geoff the Newt.

Nyv (without looking): "You slept through the entire ritual."

Geoff the Newt emits a low, unimpressed huff—as if withholding judgment—before curling himself around her neck like a living scarf. His golden eyes narrow against the morning light.

A hush falls as one of the Veilwarden elders approaches—an ancient figure cloaked in crimson and shadow, with long silver hair braided with bone and feather charms. Her voice carries the weight of many winters.

Veilwarden Elder: "You walk into flame and ruin. We cannot walk beside you, but we will not let you leave empty-handed."

Two acolytes appear, bearing a carved wooden box and a pouch of river-smoothed stones. The elder gestures to them.

Veilwarden Elder: "These are Ember Runes. Strike one where fire cannot survive—and fire will come. The stones are spirit-markers—lay them in a circle, and they will shield you briefly from scrying… or worse."

She turns her gaze to Yeldanna.

Veilwarden Elder: "You are strength—but strength alone cannot carry the weight of the dead."

Then she turns to Nyv, eyes piercing.

Veilwarden Elder: "You are wisdom—but wisdom cannot anchor the soul."

Geoff the Newt lifts his head at that, tongue flicking once—as if in subtle protest.

The elder continues:

Veilwarden Elder: "You will need more than what you carry. The mountains hold more than kobolds. The Heart is not guarded by fear, but by belief. And belief burns brighter than fire."

She steps closer and presses a single black feather into Nyv's gloved hand.

Veilwarden Elder: "When the road splits, let this be your sign. It will not lead to safety—but it will lead to trust."

Nyv stares at it for a long moment.

Nyv (dryly): "You witches always speak in riddles."

Veilwarden Elder (smiling faintly): "If we spoke clearly, you wouldn't listen."

Geoff the Newt lets out a quiet, approving *chirrup*.

Behind them, the doors to the sanctum close with a low, rumbling sound. Chovee's body is sealed behind stone—safe, but far from them.

Yeldanna (softly): "Watch over him."

Veilwarden Elder: "We will. The body rests. The spirit waits."

The wind howls briefly, catching their cloaks and feathers both.

Veilwarden Elder (faintly): "Bring us the fire. And bring him home."

Without another word, Yeldanna, Nyv, and Geoff the Newt turn east—toward the peaks, toward Skarbek Thar, and toward the waiting unknown.

Teeth Beneath the Snow

Setting: Five days north of Ravkareth. The Velthorn Peaks rise like jagged teeth from the frostbitten earth. Snow falls in slow spirals, softening the broken ridges and rocky gullies that mark the path ahead. The wind bites. The silence is absolute.

Yeldanna walks ahead, wrapped in furs, her hand never straying far from the hilt of her sword. Nyv follows close, a thin barrier of warding magic pulsing faintly around her against the cold. On her shoulder, Geoff the Newt hunkers beneath her collar, eyes narrowed against the flurries.

The landscape shifts from passable trails to a twisting gorge of jagged stone. The path narrows. Every echo is a stranger's footfall. Even Nyv's bracers feel heavier than they should.

A pair of ravens begin circling overhead, their cries lost in the wind.

Nyv (quietly): "The spirits feel close."

Yeldanna (without slowing): "Let them learn something."

They pass a ruined cairn, old and broken. It bears no runes—only claw marks.

Geoff the Newt shifts, his body tensing as his tiny claws dig into Nyv's shoulder.

Nyv: "He senses something."

Silence

Yeldanna: "So do I."

Nyv crouches, brushing snow from the ground. She reveals tiny tracks, three-toed and deliberate, skirting the edges of the cliffside.

Nyv (frowning): "Kobolds. They're watching us too."

Yeldanna steps back and places a hand on her blade.

Yeldanna: "We press forward."

They continue through the ravine. The wind dies.

And then—

A rock falls from the ledge above.

Yeldanna stops mid-step.

Geoff the Newt hisses.

Nyv (tense): "Trap."

From both sides, movement in the snow—small figures, dozens rise from behind rocks, crawling out of crevices, their yellow eyes glowing, blades drawn. Kobolds.

Nyv: "We're in deep trouble."

Yeldanna draws her sword. Radiant light blooming along its edge.

Yeldanna: "Hold the centre. No retreat."

Geoff the Newt lets out a low warble and burrows tight against Nyv's neck.

The first arrows fly.

Act II – The Fire and the Veil

The Fire and the Veil

Setting: A narrow, snow-choked ravine beneath the Velthorn Peaks. The moon peers through torn clouds as the wind howls between crags. At least a dozen kobold corpses already litter the snow—burned, skewered, or torn apart. But more surge forward—twenty or more—led by a towering kobold shaman cloaked in bones and soot.

Yeldanna, bruised and bloodied but unbowed, stands with her back to a rock wall, sword blazing with divine light. Nyvana crouches behind her, pressing her hand to a bleeding wound at her side. Magic still glows faintly in her fingertips, but her breath is labored.

Yeldanna (gritted): "They just keep coming…"

Nyv (dryly): "You're welcome to tell them to stop."

Above, the shaman raises his staff. Smoke curls from his snout as he begins a chant in Draconic. Flame coils like a serpent in his palm—ready to strike.

But then—

"Naulëth súlëar!"

A flaming orb—no larger than an apple—arcs from the mist above. It strikes a kobold dead-centre—then erupts. Golden fire billows out, leaping from one enemy to the next. Screams pierce the snow.

From the rising smoke steps a small figure: a halfling woman, cloaked in patchwork cloth and scorched leather, golden embers trailing from her fingertips. The sorceress.

Halfling (lightly): "Do they always gather like this? Seems… convenient."

Before Nyv can respond, another presence follows—tall, pale, robed in grey and white. Her eyes are obscured beneath a silver-stitched hood. At her back, a swirling murder of spectral ravens drifts silently through the gloom. In a low voice, some words of power are whispered. Then, with a flick of her hand, she loosed a bolt of inky energy—a raven-shaped blast that streaked toward the shaman and slammed into his chest, sending him staggering. A flicker of silver-white light rippled across the back of Bryn's hand—subtle, like moonlight brushing steel. The feather-shaped mark pulsed once, the Queen's attention settling over her as the silence reclaimed the air.

A shadowbound elf, calm and wordless, steps forward.

Then comes the third—a rattling form of bone and sinew. A skeleton, clad in dark leathers, bow drawn and glowing with eerie green energy. She fires once, twice—each arrow splits in flight and skewers a kobold cleanly.

The tide turns.

Nyv rises, hand glowing. She summons her Moonblade and cuts down two more kobolds that charge from the right. Yeldanna follows with a radiant slash, sending another flying back into the snow.

The shadowbound elf's hand rises again, casting another blast. The halfling launches a final firebolt that detonates behind the shaman, and the skeleton lands her third arrow—splitting the skull of the last charging kobold.

Silence falls.

Only the wind remains.

No words are spoken. The halfling lowers her hand, chest rising and falling.

Bryn watches the horizon, her eyes distant.

Yeldanna: "You're not with them."

Halfling: "Very astute."

Nyv: "But you were following us."

The halfling shrugs, then glances toward Bryn.

Bryn (softly): "We saw the signs. We came to help."

Yeldanna (tight): "We didn't ask for help."

Tassa: "No. You asked to die surrounded."

Yeldanna steps forward, but Bryn lifts her hand calmly.

Shadow-Elf: "Bryn Lovas. This is my companion…"
She gestures to the halfling, still trailing fire from her fingertips.

Bryn: "Tassa Emberlin."

Bryn (pausing briefly): "We're not your enemies."

Nyv (flatly): "That depends on your companion…" She gestures to the halfling, still trailing fire from her fingertips.

Tassa (tilting her head): "Does it matter who saved you, or just that we did?"

The skeleton silently returns to Bryn's side. One of the spectral ravens alights briefly on its shoulder before dissolving into mist.

Nyv (narrowing her eyes): "You walk with death."

Bryn (even): "I serve the Queen of Stillness. This one—" She places a hand on the skeleton's shoulder. "—is Bone-Anna. She protects me."

Yeldanna: "And what do you want?"

Tassa: "Would it sound suspicious if I said… nothing?"

Nyv: "Are you incapable of giving a straight answer?"

Tassa (brightly): "Wouldn't that ruin the mystery?"

She doesn't know how, but she senses this warlock can be trusted—more than logic allows. There's something in Bryn's stillness that draws her in, like silence that waits for meaning.

Nyv (tentatively): "This is Yeldanna, and I am Nyvana. You may call me Nyv."

Bryn glances at the wounded Ravkari warrior. The weight in her eyes shifts— calculating, then steady.

Bryn: "You're not done fighting, are you?"

Yeldanna (quietly): "No."

Bryn: "Then we'll walk with you. At least for a while."

Snow falls gently over the carnage. Somewhere in the distance, another raven calls.

Ash and Embers

Setting: Night has fallen deep. A small campfire crackles near the mouth of the ravine, casting golden light across the stone. Snow melts in a slow ring around the fire. Four women sit close to its warmth, tension still simmering in the cold between them. Bone-Anna stands watch nearby, unmoving. The ravens are gone for now, faded into shadow.

Yeldanna sharpens her blade in slow, deliberate strokes. Nyv is hunched over a steaming tin cup of tea, her wounds mostly healed by her own magic. Bryn sits with her knees drawn to her chest, wrapped in her coat, quietly observing the flames and occasionally, Nyv—watching the way Bryn's fingers turn the tin cup, precise even in exhaustion.. Tassa lies on her back, feet toward the fire, twirling a gold button between her fingers.

Nyv (letting her words spill out like water over a dam): "We're on our way to recover something called the Heart of Vhal'turien. It's in a ruin filled with kobold fanatics who worship it as a god-egg."

Bryn catches a quick flicker of surprise on Yeldanna's face.

Tassa (without looking): "Do you think it is an egg?"

Yeldanna (gruffly): "It doesn't matter. We need it."

She looks across the fire to Bryn.

Yeldanna (slightly lowering her guard): "My son is dead. The Veilwardens say this artifact is the only chance to bring him back."

Bryn nods once, solemn.

Bryn: "And they sent you alone?"

Nyv: "They sent me to help her."

Tassa (with a grin): "That working out for you so far?"

Nyv shoots her a withering look. Tassa only smiles wider.

Bryn (softly): "I'll come with you."

The fire crackles. No one speaks. Even Bone-Anna seems stiller somehow.

Yeldanna: "Just like that?"

Bryn: "There's something wrong near those ruins. I felt it before I saw the ravens. Something old. Hungry."

Tassa rolls over and props her chin on her hands.

Tassa: "Would you believe I'm only going because I'm curious? Or because I heard something call my name in fire?"

Nyv (sighing): "You're both lunatics."

Tassa (brightly): "Isn't that just another word for 'adventurer'?"

Bryn turns to Yeldanna.

Bryn: "You need more blades. More magic. Someone to watch your back when your grief clouds your sword."

Yeldanna tightens her jaw—but doesn't argue.

Nyv: "We don't have time to argue about trust."

Tassa: "Can't trust anyone you don't travel with. That's how it works, right?"

A silence falls again, this time less tense. The fire crackles. Snow melts.

Bone-Anna slowly turns her head toward Bryn—as if waiting for permission—then returns to watch the dark.

Yeldanna looks into the fire. Her hand tightens on the hilt of her sword.

Yeldanna: "Fine. We travel at first light."

Tassa: "And if we're all killed by kobold cultists?"

Nyv: "Then you can haunt me in the afterlife."

Tassa (cheerfully): "Would you like that?"

Bryn (softly, to no one): "Let's make sure none of us finds out."

Second Watch

Setting: Later that night. The fire has died to glowing coals. The mountains are quiet, save for the wind slipping between crags. Yeldanna and Nyv sit side by side, cloaked against the cold, the dying embers casting faint orange glows across their faces.

Above, hidden in the shadow of a crooked pine, a single raven watches—its eyes glowing faintly with borrowed thought.

Yeldanna (low): "The tall one... Bryn. No hesitation. Just offered herself."

Nyv: "That concerns you?"

Yeldanna: "Shouldn't it?"

She pauses. Snow crunches softly in the distance—but it's only the wind, shifting the drifts.

Yeldanna: "She walks with the dead. Commands one."

Nyv: "So do the Veilwardens. It's not death magic that worries me."

Yeldanna: "Then what?"

Nyv (after a pause): "The little one. Tassa. She doesn't speak plainly."

Yeldanna (gruff): "She speaks like she's hiding something."

Nyv (frowning): "Or like she's afraid to know what she's hiding."

They sit in silence for a moment longer. The wind picks up again.

Yeldanna (quietly): "Do you think they're watching us? Judging whether we're worthy?"

Nyv: "They saved us. Shouldn't that be enough?"

A long pause. A soft hush fell over the clearing.

Then Nyv's bag gave a faint rustle. Geoff the Newt crept out from within, blinking at the night like a priest appraising a sacred flame. He clambered along the satchel's edge and, after a pause, tugged out a single object from its mouth—a single black feather—long, unbent, and weightless.

Nyv froze. For a heartbeat, she didn't breathe

She reached out slowly, letting Geoff drop the feather into her hand.

She remembered the Veilwarden's voice—calm and certain: "When the road splits, this may guide you."

She glanced toward the sleeping figures by the fire—Bryn curled beneath her white and grey coat, unmoving. Tassa's robe glowed faintly with ember-coloured threads. In the nearby trees, a lone raven sat watching—eyes glinting in the dark like coins of onyx.

Nyv looked down at Geoff and whispered, "Clever little prophet."

Yeldanna raised an eyebrow. "What is it?"

"A gift. A reminder," Nyv said softly. "The road's already split."

The wind sighed through the branches above, as if acknowledging the truth.

"We need them, Yeldanna. The Veilwarden Elder knew that. Even if we can't trust them fully yet."

Yeldanna (quietly): "I'm tired of carrying this weight alone."

Nyv places a gloved hand over Yeldanna's, eyes steady.

Nyv: "Then let's share it."

They sat in silence for a time. The feather lay between them.

Yeldanna finally nodded. "Then we walk it together."

Overhead, the raven silently takes flight, drifting back toward the camp's edge.

Bryn lies beneath her cloak, unmoving. Her breath is steady—but her thoughts stir. She whispered her thoughts toward the lizard inaudibly, but low enough that only her raven could hear:

"Good call, little one. They chose well."

And though she does not speak it aloud, the thought settles like snow in her chest:

So did I.

Geoff the Newt

Setting: The morning after the kobold ambush. The snow has softened, and the gorge is quiet again. The four companions are preparing to break camp, steam rising from mugs of bitterroot tea.

Bone-Anna stands apart from the others, motionless as ever. Her bow is slung across her back, her skull tilted toward the morning light—as if listening.

From beneath Nyv's cloak, a familiar head pokes out—Geoff the Newt, blinking slowly in the cold air.

He stretches, sniffs the wind, and scampers down Nyv's arm.

Nyv (warning, but fond): "Don't go far, little friend."

Geoff the Newt pads toward the fire, stopping halfway when he spots Bone-Anna. He tilts his head, considering. Then, with purposeful confidence, climbs onto her boot.

Bone-Anna does not move.

Geoff the Newt stares up at her. Then mimics her posture—standing on his hind legs, arms stiff at his sides.

Tassa bursts into laughter.

Tassa: "Is this how lizards flirt?"

Nyv (dry): "He likes strong, silent types."

Bryn (watching with mild amusement): "He's drawn to the dead. That says something."

Yeldanna, checking the buckles on her armour, glances up.

Yeldanna: "Should we be concerned?"

Nyv: "Only if she starts feeding him."

Bone-Anna, in her usual stillness, does nothing. But Geoff the Newt clambers up to her knee and nestles into the hollow of her hip bone, content.

Bryn (quietly, to Bone-Anna): "If you crush him, I'll have to raise him too."

Tassa flops down next to the fire, propping her head in her hands.

Tassa: "So... we have a dead marksman, an orange-bellied newt, a shadow-slinger, a Ravkari paladin, a witch, and a golden fire-slinger who talks in riddles."

Nyv: "You're the only one calling yourself golden."

Tassa (smiling): "Am I?"

Yeldanna rises, ready.

Yeldanna: "Whatever we are, we move after breakfast. We still have mountains to climb—and a god-heart to claim."

Geoff the Newt peeks out from behind Bone-Anna's femur, his tongue flicking at the firelight like a sparkcatcher.

Bone-Anna doesn't acknowledge him. But she shifts—just slightly—giving him space to perch more comfortably.

Bryn, noticing, smiles faintly.

Bryn (to herself): "That's approval. Rare—from her."

The wind stirs the snow, carrying her words away before anyone can hear.

The Unseen Spine

Setting: A frost-bitten pass in the Velthorn foothills. The path narrows between jagged cliffs, snow hardening into crusted ice. The sun is sinking low, casting long shadows over the stone. The wind has stilled. The world holds its breath.

Nyv walks near the front, hood up, hand resting lightly on the hilt of her blade. Perched atop her shoulder, half-hidden in the folds of her cloak, is Geoff the Newt—his olive-green body pressed close against her neck for warmth, golden eyes darting warily.

Geoff the Newt lets out a soft, rasping huff, his breath fogging briefly in the air.

Nyv (without looking): "You smell something, don't you?"

Tassa, a few steps behind, twirls a glowing ember between her fingers.

Tassa: "Is that breathing… or grinding?"

Before an answer comes, the growl intensifies. From behind a jutting rock, a creature lumbers into view—a grotesque fusion—bear bulk, elk limbs, wyrmling hide—its spine warped with jagged ridges and plated bone. A second jaw hangs limp from its chest, twitching with every step.

Nyv (coldly): "That's not born of any womb."

Yeldanna (drawing her sword): "Eyes open. Formation!"

The creature roars and charges.

Nyv's hands ignite with red-gold runes. She lashes out with a spell—spectral chains of light coil around the creature's limbs. It slows—

—then rips through them, snarling louder.

Nyv (muttering): "I hate when they do that."

Yeldanna meets it head-on. Her blade strikes true—but the creature's plated hide deflects the blow, the sword skittering off like steel on stone.

Yeldanna (shocked): "My blade won't pierce it!"

Tassa flicks a flaming orb into the beast's flank, a burst of golden fire lighting the air—but the creature slaps it aside, smoke curling from its unharmed skin.

Tassa: "Would it be rude to suggest running?"

Nyv: "Do you ever suggest anything helpful?"

Tassa (grinning): "Would it change anything if I did?"

Bryn steps into the fray with quiet resolve, eyes locked onto the creature.

Bryn: "There's a weak point—left side, base of the spine."

Nyv: "At that angle? Through the plating?"

Bone-Anna is already climbing the cliff face—silent, swift, without waiting for discussion. She finds her perch, draws her bow, and steadies her skeletal arms.

The creature wheels toward Yeldanna, ready to crush her beneath its bulk.

Yeldanna (bracing): "Now, damn it!"

Bone-Anna fires.

The green-glowing arrow whistles through the wind. It arcs perfectly—spinning like a razor of emerald fire through twilight. It lands exactly where Bryn said— beneath the jagged plating, between muscle and bone.

CRACK.

The beast jerks. Limbs twitch. It collapses, shaking the earth—then lies still.

Geoff the Newt, wide-eyed, leaps from Nyv's shoulder, scurries across the snow, and clambers up Bone-Anna's leg with sudden, exuberant speed. He perches on her shoulder and stares proudly down at the felled creature, tail twitching in approval.

Tassa (awed): "Did he choose her over Nyv?"

Nyv (deadpan): "That hurts more than it should."

Bone-Anna shifts minutely—just enough to let Geoff the Newt settle more comfortably into the hollow of her collarbone.

Bryn (quietly): "She doesn't warm to many. Dead or living."

Yeldanna (to Bryn): "You said she protects you. She protects all of us now."

Bryn nods once, her expression unreadable.

Bryn: "She remembers what it means to be loyal."

The party continues on, stepping past the beast's broken form as dusk thickens. Above them, the ravens return—circling high on the cold wind, watching.

None speak as they walk. Behind them, snow begins to cover the broken corpse.

The Weight We Don't Share

Setting: A cold night deep in the Velthorn range. The others sleep in bedrolls around the dying campfire. Snowflakes drift softly from a still sky. Yeldanna and Bryn sit opposite one another near the embers, taking the second watch. Geoff the Newt is curled near Nyv. Bone-Anna stands at the edge of camp, unmoving.

For a long time, neither woman speaks.

Bryn stirs the fire with a long stick, eyes low. Yeldanna sharpens her blade in slow, silent strokes.

The quiet stretches.

Bryn (softly): "You don't sleep much."

Yeldanna doesn't look up.

Yeldanna: "I can't afford to."

Bryn: "You carry a large burden."

The scraping of the whetstone halts. Yeldanna stares at the blade.

Yeldanna (flatly): "He died alone. They left him. Stripped his body and walked away."

Bryn (quietly): "Nyv found him."

Yeldanna: "Too late."

Bryn knew it wasn't meant as an accusation, just an observation.

The fire pops. A faint wind stirs the edge of Bryn's coat. Her voice is calm— like a still pool that hides its depth.

Bryn: "You hold your grief like a sword. I've seen that before."

Yeldanna (coldly): "Should I hold it like a child instead?"

Bryn: "No. But you don't have to hold it alone."

Yeldanna glances up, finally meeting Bryn's eyes.

Yeldanna: "You think pain shared makes it lighter?"

Bryn: "No. But it makes it *bearable*."

They sit in silence again.

Yeldanna: "He was everything I had left. Every promise I made—every part of me I gave to Ravkareth—was so he could be free. And he still died like... like something discardable."

Bryn watches her.

Bryn (gently): "He died a warrior. He died defending others."

Yeldanna (bitter): "And it wasn't enough."

Bryn: "It never is. That's why we keep going."

Yeldanna's jaw clenches. She stares into the fire.

Yeldanna: "And you? What are you still going for?"

Bryn (quietly): "The same reason you are. Because death doesn't stop the ones left behind."

She leans back slightly, shadows curling faintly at her fingertips.

Bryn: "I walk with death every day. I guide what's lost. I guard what's left. That's how I serve. That's why I'm here."

A breeze caught the edge of her coat. Beneath it, the feather on her hand pulsed softly—neither command nor comfort, but presence.

Yeldanna studies her for a long moment. Her voice is softer when she speaks again.

Yeldanna: "The others look to you, you know."

Bryn (surprised): "They look to you."

Yeldanna: "They look to me to break the wall. They look to you to hold it steady."

A beat passes.

Yeldanna (firmly): "Don't waste that."

Bryn doesn't answer. Not with words.

But she nods—once, deeply.

The fire crackles between them. No warmer—but shared.

And they sit there, two women forged by loss, warming their hands by the same fire.

Act III – The Dragon's Echo

The Breath Beneath Stone

Setting: Late afternoon. The mountains have grown sheer and steep. The snow thins—swept away by wind that howls through the stone like breath in ancient lungs. The path curves into a rocky hollow carved by time and forgotten hands.

The party walks in silence. Even Geoff the Newt keeps low against Nyv's collar, eyes darting. Bone-Anna walks slightly ahead, bow in hand, skull scanning the rocks above.

The ruins are close now. Everyone feels it.

Tassa (softly): "Does the wind always feel... warmer here?"

Yeldanna doesn't answer, but her hand stays on her hilt.

Bryn pauses as they reach the mouth of the hollow. Her ravens circle once overhead, then vanish into the swirling mist. Her voice is hushed.

Bryn: "This place remembers."

The walls around them are carved—not by kobolds, but by ancient tools. Symbols in Draconic, worn by wind, still mark the stone—spirals, wings, fire, and eyes. The rock itself hums faintly beneath their boots.

Nyv (scanning the glyphs): "These aren't kobold etchings. They're older. Dwarven... no—draconic-influenced dwarven. Like a temple."

Yeldanna (tense): "A tomb."

Tassa: "Or a cradle?"

They stop walking.

Bryn turns slowly to look at Tassa, who stares at a scorched section of wall. Her hand hovers near it—not touching, but close. A visible shiver runs through her.

Bryn: "What did you say?"

Tassa (tilting her head): "Isn't that what it looks like? A cracked egg... waiting to open again?"

Nyv's brow furrows. She opens her mouth to speak, then closes it.

A gust of hot wind rolls through the hollow. Unnaturally warm.

Yeldanna's sword glows faintly in response.

Yeldanna: "There's something below. Watching."

Bryn (softly): "Or waiting."

Geoff the Newt tenses, letting out a low rumble that surprises even Nyv.

The group pushes forward, deeper into the ancient cleft in the stone. As they descend the slope, the light dims unnaturally, not with sunset—but with something thicker than shadow.

Bryn's ravens return, circling above in tighter patterns. One lands briefly on her shoulder, then vanishes.

Bryn: "We should make camp before the descent. Whatever lies beneath won't be reached in a single breath."

Yeldanna nods. The others wordlessly agree.

They begin to unpack their gear as the sun sets behind the peaks— leaving only the echo of wind, the weight of stone, and the faint pulse beneath their feet— slow, steady, ancient. A slow, steady rhythm. Something ancient, alive, and waiting beneath the mountain.

Ash and Offerings

Setting: Just past twilight. The wind has died, and the cold has crept into every crack and crevice. The party follows a narrow trail that winds deeper along the cliffside. A strange scent clings to the air—burned herbs, scorched bone, and something sweet beneath it, like rot.

Yeldanna stops suddenly, raising a hand. The others freeze.

Up ahead, nestled in a rock alcove, a crude kobold shrine squats beneath a jagged overhang. It's made from mismatched stone blocks, old dwarven bricks, and scavenged metal.

At the centre of the shrine is a smooth, obsidian bowl filled with grey ash. Around it are draconic effigies—twisted representations of something draconic, all facing inward.

Dozens of golden trinkets have been left among the ashes: buttons, coins, lockets, even a child's ring.

Nyv (crouching): "They're leaving offerings."

Yeldanna: "To the Heart?"

Bryn: "To *what they think* the Heart is."

Tassa steps closer, frowning.

Tassa (softly): "Doesn't it seem strange they know it's here? Or that it calls to them?"

Yeldanna: "Stranger than them building a shrine out of old bones?"

Tassa (more quietly): "*Why gold? Why does it always have to be gold?*"

Bryn kneels at the edge of the circle. Her eyes trace a charcoal pattern etched into the stone: a spiral of flame surrounding an empty core, as if something once rested at the centre—and might return.

Bryn: "It's not worship. It's reverence. Fear. Obsession."

Nyv: "We should destroy it."

Bryn (shaking her head): "Not yet. Let it think we're still beyond its reach."

Yeldanna: "You think it's aware of us?"

Bryn: "It's dreaming. And it's listening."

Nyv's fingers tighten around one of her scimitars.

Geoff the Newt clings tightly to Nyv's neck, his eyes locked on the blackened bowl—unblinking, alert.

Tassa (quietly): "What do you think it's dreaming about?"

No one answers.

But Tassa lingers a moment longer—her fingers grazing a broken locket left in the ashes. She doesn't take it.

Instead, she stares at it with something between recognition and unease.

Tassa (to herself): "What do they see when they look into it?"

Bryn watches her from the corner of her eye—curious, but saying nothing.

The party moves on, leaving the shrine undisturbed. But marked.

Behind them, a faint breeze stirs the ashes in the bowl. The trinkets clink faintly together, like distant laughter.

The Dreaming Flame

Setting: Nightfall. The party has set camp beneath an overhang of cracked stone, a makeshift shelter tucked into the lee of the mountain. The fire crackles low. Snow falls lightly beyond the glow. A strange stillness blankets the area—one that doesn't feel natural.

Nyv paces near the fire, a blackened scrap of parchment between her fingers—scorched, etched with Vaulmar glyphs.

Nyv (sharply): "This is fresh."

Yeldanna takes the scrap, eyes narrowing.

Yeldanna: "Vaulmar Binders don't wander this far north by accident."

Bryn (calmly): "He's not just wandering. He's hunting."

Nyv: "Or binding. That spell residue—it's necrotic."

Tassa, curled near the fire with Geoff the Newt nestled beside her, hums a soft tune under her breath. She doesn't look up.

Tassa (idly): "Do you think he wants the Heart? Or just what's inside it?"

Yeldanna (curt): "They want power. That's all they ever want."

Nyv (muttering): "If one of them gets to the Heart before us…"

She doesn't finish the thought.

Bryn watches the others argue, her expression unreadable. The flames reflect in her eyes—half shadow, half fire.

✦

Later that night, the fire has burned low. The others sleep in shifts.

Tassa stirs. She dreams...

She is a child again—bare feet pressed into the dark earth beneath a harvest moon. In her palm is a golden button, shining too brightly for the darkness around it. An old halfling woman—her caretaker—sits cross-legged by a candle made of tallow and ash, whispering stories.

"We were never meant to last, little spark. The giants had strength. The elves had time. But us? We were clever… and hungry."

The old woman lights the candle with a snap of her fingers. The flame burns gold.

"So we made a deal. Just a flicker of soul for a lifetime of luck. And in return, something watches. Something waits."

In the dream, the flame swells. Wings, eyes, a draconic silhouette form—then blur, just out of reach.

The caretaker leans closer, her voice low:

"It's why fire follows you, girl. Why gold feels like memory. Don't go looking too deep. You might not like what looks back."

The candle's flame replies:

"The Heart knows its kin."

Tassa jolts awake. The fire is out. In her palm, clenched tight, lies the golden button.

She doesn't remember bringing it with her.

✦

The fire is low. Bryn sits on watch, unmoving.

Tassa rubs her eyes and sits up slowly. Geoff the Newt lifts his head sleepily and rests it on her leg.

Tassa (half-whispering): "Is it normal to dream of fire that talks?"

Bryn turns her head slightly. Her voice is soft.

Bryn: "Sometimes."

Tassa: "Should I tell the others?"

Bryn (quietly): "Not yet."

Tassa nods once, not sure why she trusts the answer.

She lies back down.

Bryn watches the fire a moment longer. She doesn't sleep. She never does.

She listens.

"The Heart knows its kin…"

She says nothing.

But her ravens stir in the darkness beyond the firelight.

Threshold of Stone

Setting: Morning. A pale grey light creeps across the peaks. The fire is cold ash. The wind has died, leaving behind a brittle silence. The party stands before a dark, gaping archway half-buried in snow and overgrowth—the sealed entrance to Skarbek Thar.

The massive stone door is cracked just enough to squeeze through. Ancient dwarven carvings spiral along the lintel—some scraped away by clawed hands. Black soot stains the surrounding stone.

Yeldanna (scanning the carvings): "This was no siege. They opened it."

Nyv (touching the scorch marks): "No... they broke something. From the inside."

Tassa crouches low, running her fingers across a patch of melted stone.

Tassa: "Do you hear that?"

Yeldanna: "I hear nothing."

Tassa: "Exactly."

Bryn's ravens circle above, but none enter. One perches at the archway's edge—then wheels away, back into the sky.

Bryn (to herself): "Even the dead keep their distance."

Geoff the Newt climbs up Nyv's arm and nestles on her shoulder, peering into the dark. His bright orange belly pulses faintly—like he's holding his breath.

Nyv: "He doesn't like it."

Tassa (to Geoff the Newt): "What's scarier—what's in there, or what's not? Because I'm leaning toward 'not.'"

No answer—only the creak of cold stone as Yeldanna forces the door wider, revealing a descending stair into pitch darkness.

The air that spills out is warm.

And wet.

Bryn: "It breathes."

The party exchanges glances.

Yeldanna: "We go in together."

Nyv: "No splitting up."

Tassa (smiling faintly): "So we're agreed on one bad idea, at least."

Bone-Anna steps forward first, arrow nocked.

Then one by one, they pass beneath the stone threshold and disappear into the black.

Behind them, the wind does not rise.

And the light does not follow.

The Path of Ashen Faith

*Setting: Deep inside the outer levels of Skarbek Thar. The walls are rough-hewn stone—
ancient dwarven craftsmanship, now defaced with claw marks and smeared pigments. Narrow
corridors wind downward like veins, and everything smells faintly of scorched copper and
melted wax.*

The group moves in formation.

Bone-Anna leads, bow drawn. Yeldanna and Nyv flank Tassa, who walks
slightly ahead, fingers aglow with soft golden fire. Geoff the Newt perches
alertly on Nyv's shoulder.

Bryn walks rearmost, shadowy wisps drifting from her steps, her ravens
nowhere in sight.

They pass old halls lined with broken statues—dwarven warriors with missing
eyes, cracked hammers, and mouths stuffed with blackened wax.

Then they find the first sign of life.

Nyv (whispering): "Blood. Dried."

A trail of dark crimson smears the floor, leading to a collapsed side passage.
Tassa squats near the wall—where a series of shallow carvings spiral around a
broken support beam.

Tassa: "More of their symbols. But these are... *tighter*. Frenzied."

Bryn: "Faith, collapsing into madness."

Yeldanna moves ahead—then halts.

Yeldanna (sharply): "Stop. Tripwire."

The others freeze.

Strung across the hall, just above boot-height, is a thin, nearly invisible wire
looped around a cracked torch bracket.

Tassa follows the wire with her eyes and spots a small trigger plate beneath a
loose stone.

Tassa: "If I were small and scared... I'd load that with something awful."

Nyv (nods): "Explosive glyph. Or poison darts."

Yeldanna carefully disarms the tripwire, her hands steady. It snaps loose with a tiny click. No trap springs.

Yeldanna (grimly): "Clever. Crude, but clever."

Bryn: "They know we're coming. But they still expect us to walk like prey."

They step carefully around the disarmed trap and continue down the corridor.

The air changes again—warmer, tinged with a faint metallic sweetness. The walls begin to glow faintly with red runes, pulsing like veins.

Tassa (quietly): "What if this place isn't guarded?"

They all look at her.

Tassa: "What if it's hungry?"

Silence.

Bryn narrows her eyes toward the flickering hallway ahead.

Bryn: "Then we feed it what it's earned."

The Breathless Hollow

Setting: A natural cavern nestled between carved stone passages. The ceiling arches like a ribcage overhead, veined with glowing red ore. The air is unnaturally still, as if the stone itself is listening.

The party crouches behind a broken outcropping, watching.

Six kobolds move through the chamber in loose formation—but they're wrong.

Their eyes burn from within, scales cracked and veined in molten gold. One drags a melted axe behind it, the metal fused to its hand. Another's jaw hangs open as if unhinged, whispering softly to itself in Draconic.

Nyv (hushed): "Those aren't scouts. They're *sacrifices*."

Yeldanna (low, grim): "Still dangerous."

Bryn: "If they cry out, others will follow."

Tassa: "So we move like shadows?"

Nyv: "We strike. No light. No sound."

They fan out, moving with deadly purpose. Bone-Anna climbs the cavern wall with uncanny grace, bow ready. Bryn's hand glows faintly—then fades, her magic veiled in shadow. Yeldanna signals the count with two fingers.

One. Two.

The battle erupts in a whisper.

Yeldanna strikes silently, her sword cutting through a kobold's spine before it can turn. Bryn's Eldritch Blast is muffled by shadows, hitting like a gust of wind and toppling another. Nyv leaps in with both scimitars, spinning a deadly circle of cold steel and muttered runes.

Bone-Anna's arrow punches through two kobolds in a single shot. They fall without a cry.

Tassa stands still, starting the incantation with her palm out. A glowing orb of fire blooms—then fizzles.

Tassa (whispering): "Too loud. Not yet."

She instead steps in and kicks a stunned kobold into a chasm crevice, letting gravity silence it.

The last one stares at them—mouth wide, pupils vanished. Its chest swells as if inhaling flame—

Yeldanna (shouting in a hiss): "NOW!"

Bone-Anna fires. The arrow hits strikes dead centre. The kobold slumps without a sound.

Silence returns.

Breath catches.

Geoff the Newt peeks from Nyv's shoulder, sniffing the air. He lets out a low rumble, barely audible.

Tassa (quietly): "Did they scream in their minds?"

Bryn: "Let's hope minds don't echo downward—into something listening."

They regroup, eyes still on the edges of the hollow.

The glowing veins pulse once. Then settle.

But none of them are certain if their silence truly went unnoticed.

Runes in the Dust

Setting: Deeper within the ruined stronghold, where the architecture shifts. The halls become smoother. Less dwarven. More shaped. More claimed. Cracks in the walls pulse with unnatural red light, forming runes that were never carved but simply appeared.

The group moves cautiously, steps muffled against soot-covered stone.

Nyv pauses at an archway where the walls are scorched black. Her hand hovers over a rune seared into the stone—not drawn, but branded there with necrotic magic.

Nyv: "Vaulmar. A ritual anchor."

Yeldanna: "He's casting in stages."

Bryn: "Or building something."

They pass a collapsed chamber where a kobold shrine has been overtaken. The old draconic symbols are scratched out—replaced with Vaulmar glyphs, painted in what smells like old blood.

A single warped emblem lies where the gold trinkets once rested—melted together into the shape of an eye within a flame.

Tassa stares at it longer than the others.

Tassa: "Do you think he's... feeding it?"

Nyv (grim): "Twisting it. Corrupting it."

Bryn: "He doesn't worship the Heart. He's trying to own it."

Bone-Anna walks slowly along the wall, trailing her skeletal fingers across blistered stone. Her arrow is still nocked.

Geoff the Newt flicks his tail uneasily and tucks beneath Nyv's collar.

They descend a crumbled staircase into a half-collapsed antechamber. The air is thick—with sulfur, incense, and something unspoken. Above them, the ceiling pulses faintly with red veins—as if the keep is *breathing*.

Yeldanna (tired): "We make camp here. Just long enough to gather strength."

They settle in cautiously, positioning Bone-Anna at the edge of a side passage as lookout. Tassa draws her knees to her chest and leans on her pack, her fire-dappled eyes flickering with unease.

Tassa (softly): "Do you think it still wants to be saved?"

Yeldanna (without looking): "What?"

Tassa: "The Heart. The dragon inside it. Or the memory. Whatever it is. Do you think it's asking for help? Or screaming?"

Tassa's eyes flicker with unease as she watches the slow pulse of the walls.

Tassa (softly): "Do you think it still wants to be saved?"

No one answers.

But Bryn, tending the small, flickering campfire, watches Tassa carefully.

Bryn (quietly): "We'll know when we see it."

Nyv: "Assuming it doesn't see us first."

The Shattered Vein

Setting: Hours after their rest. The party moves cautiously through a massive corridor with fractured stone columns and flickering red runes along the walls. The ground is uneven—once finely tiled, now shattered and warped by magic. The heat is suffocating. The air hums with held breath.

Nyv leads with scimitars drawn. Bone-Anna scouts ahead in silence, arrow nocked. Geoff the Newt huddles on Nyv's shoulder, his tiny body trembling slightly—not from fear, but instinct.

Geoff the Newt lets trills low.

Nyv (narrowing her eyes): "He knows something's wrong."

Tassa slows, her golden eyes flicking from shadow to shadow.

Tassa (quietly): "Would now be the right time to ask who's watching us?"

Yeldanna: "We would've seen them by—"

Too late.

From a side tunnel behind them: a sudden explosion of light and sound.

Twelve kobolds pour in from behind—corrupted, glowing with the same molten-veined madness as before. At their centre stands a tall, robed figure—a Vaulmar Binder, his bald head tattooed with arcane brands, eyes glowing with cruel purpose.

Vaulmar Binder: "They brought it here. And they thought to keep it from me."

Bryn's ravens scatter, shrieking.

Bryn (coldly): "Form up. Protect the centre!"

The kobolds swarm.

Yeldanna charges the left flank, cutting through two—but a third slams her into a pillar.

Tassa raises her hand crosswise, fire coiling around her fingers.

Tassa (forcefully): *"Naulëth sülëar!"*

She hurls an orb of made of flame, fire bursting across the kobolds, but it's absorbed by their twisted scales.

Nyv's blades sing, slicing through the front line, but she's overwhelmed—forced to retreat to protect Tassa.

Bone-Anna's arrows drop kobolds with deadly precision. But even she is forced back as two flank her, blades flashing with clawed savagery.

Vaulmar Binder (chanting): "I claim this breath. I claim this soul. I claim the last fire of Vhal'turien!"

A wave of necrotic energy erupts, throwing the party back.

Tassa is barely conscious. Geoff the Newt scurries beneath Nyv's cloak. Yeldanna is bleeding from a dozen cuts. Bryn's shield arm is numb.

Nyv (shouting): "We're not going to make it!"

The Vaulmar Binder steps forward, raising his staff. The kobolds rally, forming a protective arc around him.

Vaulmar Binder (triumphant): "You die forgotten—"

Bryn (softly): "No."

She steps forward, blood in her mouth, shadows rising from her skin like smoke and promise.

Bryn: "You die *remembered.*"

She raises both hands, shadows curling around her shoulders.

Bryn (whispering): *"Ehte forochel."*

Ice erupts from the ground in a thunderous wave—a clash of glaciers summoned by will and wrath.

The floor beneath the wizard erupts in a line of frost and stone, massive boulders of jagged ice slamming into the kobold line. The temperature plummets. One of the glacier shards pierces the Vaulmar Binder's summoned shield, cracking his staff.

The kobolds scream—four are crushed instantly, the rest scattered.

The Vaulmar Binder stumbles back, snarling. He raises a spell—then vanishes into a portal of burning light.

The survivors are gone. The room is cracked and frozen. The silence returns.

Bryn lowers her arms, nearly collapsing, her breath clouding in the sudden chill.

Yeldanna (panting): "You let him go."

Bryn (steady): "I forced him to leave."

Nyv helps Tassa to her feet. Geoff the Newt pokes his head out, chirping softly.

Bone-Anna emerges from the mist, missing one shoulder pauldron but still standing.

Tassa (weakly): "So... is this the part where we win?"

Bryn (quietly): "Not yet. But we didn't lose."

The shattered runes around them begin to dim. The wizard is gone—for now.

And somewhere beneath them, the Heart waits.

Before the Pulse

Setting: A quiet side chamber, half-collapsed and shielded from the main corridor. The floor is cracked but dry. The ceiling has caved in on one side, forming a wall of stone and old bones. The magical heat from deeper within the ruins has faded. This place is still and cool—like the breath held before a scream.

The party rests in silence.

Yeldanna sits against a wall, eyes closed but alert. Her armour is dented, her knuckles bruised. She cleans her blade slowly, methodically.

Nyv tends to Tassa, wrapping her arm in clean cloth. Geoff the Newt lies across her lap, twitching gently in his sleep. His belly pulses—dim and golden, faintly warm.

Bone-Anna stands by the cave entrance, bow in hand, immobile.

Bryn leans near the fire, shadows curling around her hands like old friends. Her voice breaks the silence.

Bryn: "We're past the breath of the mountain now."

Yeldanna (without opening her eyes): "What does that mean?"

Bryn: "What lies below isn't a place. It's a memory. A wound that never closed."

Nyv looks up from her work.

Nyv: "Then why is it still bleeding?"

Tassa (softly, almost to herself): "Because it was never allowed to heal."

The others glance at her, but she says nothing more.

Yeldanna: "We go down at first light. If there is light here."

Bryn (quietly): "There won't be. Not where we're going."

Nyv conjures a small flame, letting it dance like thought across her palm.

Nyv: "If we see him again... the Vaulmar Binder... we don't hold back."

Yeldanna: "No prisoners."

Tassa: "No mercy?"

59

Yeldanna (flat): "Not for him."

They fall silent again.

Geoff the Newt stirs and opens one eye, staring at the crack in the far wall.

Tassa (watching the wall): "Do you feel it?"

Bryn: "The pulse?"

Tassa nods.

Tassa: "It's louder now."

The others feel it too—deep beneath their feet, a subtle rhythmic thrum. Like a heart. Like breath. Like something awakening after a very long sleep.

Bryn (to them all): "When we go down there, we go together. No split fronts. No lone charges. We protect each other. That's the rhythm. Break it, and we don't come back."

Yeldanna meets her gaze and nods.

No one argues.

The fire flickers. The ravens have returned, watching in silence from above. Around the flames, each of them prepares—sharpening weapons, centring minds, sealing wounds.

They do not sleep deeply.

But when they rise, they are ready.

Tomorrow, they descend.

The Heart of Vhal'turien

Setting: The lowest chamber of Skarbek Thar. The party descends a spiraling stone staircase carved into the cliff wall—ancient, cracked, with no handrail and no guard. The air grows warmer with each step—not like a furnace, but like breath. The only light is from the glowing runes that pulse along the stone in slow rhythm.

At first, the space seems empty.

Then the staircase opens into a vast subterranean chasm, easily the size of a temple. The walls are lined with colossal, fractured obsidian ribs, like the bones of some long-dead serpent embedded in the earth.

And at the centre—floating, suspended in a web of molten-gold strands—is the Heart of Vhal'turien.

It pulses once.

The chamber answers—runes flaring brighter for a single breath, then fading.

The Heart is not stone.

It is not crystal.

It is a shard of memory, burning with layered flame—gold, crimson, and white. It floats four feet off the ground, perfectly still, radiating heat and sorrow and something that could almost be called thought.

Yeldanna (whispering): "That's not a relic."

Nyv (in awe): "It's alive."

Tassa takes a slow step forward, her hand at her side.

The Heart pulses again—once, hard—and for a single breath, its flames twist into the shape of a dragon's eye, staring directly at her.

Tassa stumbles back, breath catching—as if she'd touched something forbidden.

Tassa (quietly): "Did it see me?"

Bryn (softly): "It knows you."

Geoff the Newt, clinging to Nyv's shoulder, lets out a tiny, warbling growl. The sound reverberates through the chamber and fades like a bell. His eyes do not leave the Heart.

Nyv: "This isn't just magic. This is... memory given form."

Bryn steps forward, her ravens circling the perimeter in silence.

Bryn: "We made it. But this is only the edge of memory."

Tassa (watching the emberlight): "It doesn't just burn. It remembers."

Nyv: "Runes hold knowledge. Enchantments preserve will. But this... this place feels older than either."

Bryn (quietly): "Because it is. The Heart isn't just a forge or a relic. It's memory—given form."

Tassa (half-skeptical): "You mean like a library that hums?"

Bryn: "No. I mean it responds to what we carry. What we've lost. It echoes what matters most."

Yeldanna (softly): "Then it's not power he's after. It's proof. Proof that even the dead can be rewritten."

Bryn: "But the Heart doesn't serve those who demand. Only those who remember."

Yeldanna (steeling herself): "This is where it begins."

The Heart pulses a third time—hard sudden. The flame-like strands snap and reform, drifting upward into the dark. A wind rises, from nowhere, smelling of ash and wildflowers and something impossibly ancient.

Bone-Anna draws her bow without being asked.

The adventurers stand, ringed in flame-shaped shadow, their faces lit by golden fire.

And far below the stone, something stirs.

Act IV – The Price of Returning

Echoes of Flame

Setting: The chamber of the Heart. The stone breathes around them—slow, rhythmic pulses of heat and light rolling outward from the Heart like waves. The chamber floor is smooth and blackened, cracked with golden veins. Overhead, the stalactites glow with internal fire, like stars caught in mid-fall.

The Heart of Vhal'turien hovers before them, suspended in tendrils of gold and emberlight. It turns slowly—though no wind moves it. Each pulse throws soft illumination across their faces, highlighting fear, reverence, and the silence of something eternal.

No one speaks at first.

Yeldanna stands motionless, arms at her sides. Her gaze is locked on the Heart—but her mind is somewhere else. A battlefield. A cradle. A memory she hasn't spoken aloud in years.

Nyv slowly circles the chamber's edge, touching nothing, but noting every glowing rune etched into the walls. Her voice breaks the quiet.

Nyv: "These aren't protective. They're… binding. It's not just sleeping. It's sealed."

Geoff the Newt presses himself against her neck, trembling—not with fear, but tension. He won't look directly at the Heart.

Bone-Anna stands watch at the far edge of the chamber, arrow drawn, body poised. She does not flinch at the heat. She doesn't need to blink.

Tassa steps forward, drawn despite herself. Her voice is low.

Tassa: "Would you believe me if I said it's whispering?"

Yeldanna (tense): "Whispering what?"

Tassa (without looking back): "That I'm late."

A heartbeat later, the Heart pulses again—and the flames shift, just for a breath, to form the shape of a golden eye—narrowed in recognition, fixed on her.

Bryn steps beside her. She doesn't pull Tassa back. She simply observes, her voice calm and certain.

Bryn: "It knows you. More than we do."

Tassa tears her eyes away from the Heart, startled—but not frightened.

Tassa (to Bryn): "What would it take... to hold something like that?"

Bryn: "A soul strong enough to burn and not be consumed."

They walk the perimeter together now. Near the base of the floating Heart, ancient inscriptions are carved into the stone—partially buried by centuries of ash. Bryn kneels and brushes the soot aside.

Bryn (reading, translating): "*We gave it our breath. It returned to us flame. We gave it our name. It gave us silence.*"

Nyv: "That's a funerary script."

Bryn: "I think it's an offering."

The chamber tightens around them. The heat rises—not dangerously, but intimately. The flames along the walls begin to hum.

Tassa: "Do you hear it?"

They all do.

Not a voice.

Not words.

Just emotion—regret, longing, the echo of something broken and unfinished.

Yeldanna (steady): "We came to bring a soul back."

Bryn: "And we're standing in the remains of one."

The Heart pulses again—more slowly this time.

A single tendril of flame trails toward Tassa and curls around her wrist, hovering just above her skin. She doesn't flinch.

It doesn't burn her.

Tassa (softly): "Why does it feel like... it's waiting for me to finish something?"

Bryn (barely above a whisper): "Because you are."

But the flame doesn't bind. It only lingers—hesitant, like the Heart itself is unsure. Not of her. But of the weight still clinging to its edges.

The Second Coming

Setting: The Heart chamber, still glowing and humming with power. The group stands beneath the pulsing light. Shadows crawl along the walls—but not from the Heart.

They come from behind.

A roar—not beastly, but arcane—shakes the chamber. A portal of swirling red flame tears open across the far wall. A wave of corrupted kobolds marches forth—twitching, warped, their eyes blazing with unnatural light.

Behind them steps the Vaulmar Binder.

He is changed.

His tattoos burn like open wounds. His robes float as if caught in some internal storm. The staff he carries pulses with runes not born of Vaulmark.

Vaulmar Binder: "You took what was mine. But I have walked farther through death than you ever will. And now I take it all."

Bryn (cold): "You walk in borrowed power."

Nyv (stepping forward): "Then let me return it to the dirt."

The kobolds charge, a flood of shrieking bodies. Yeldanna, Tassa, Bryn, and Bone-Anna form a line, blades and spells lashing out.

Bryn drops them one by one with pinpoint Eldritch Blasts, her ravens swirling like sentinels in flight. Tassa's eyes flick from Nyv to the flickering pouch at her belt. She rips it open and lets the Ember Runes tumble into her palm. They glow with soft, buried heat.

Tassa (low): "Alright. Let's see if you're still listening."

She grips the stones, channels the spell through her other hand, and shouts—

"Naulëth sülëar!"

The fire surges brighter than before, tearing through the charging kobolds in a sweeping arc. Ash and sparks scatter like leaves.

Yeldanna fights like a storm, shield and blade a blur.

Bone-Anna stands firm, arrows flying with inhuman calm.

The chamber smells of ash and charged air.

Nyv exhales once—vanishes into mist—and reappears before the Vaulmar Binder.

He reels back, surprised.

Nyv (low, burning): "This is for Ravkareth."

Her blades sing—Shimmerstrike carving across his chest, the Moonblade pulsing with righteous wrath. Sparks fly as arcane wards falter.

He begins to cast—but Nyv speaks a word of breaking. Her blade severs the forming glyph mid-spell.

Vaulmar Binder (spitting blood): "You filthy peasant—"

Nyv (cutting him off): "I'm your reckoning."

He raises a hand to retaliate—and Geoff the Newt leaps from her shoulder, biting into the exposed flesh just above the wizard's bracer.

The wizard screams. The spell unravels.

Nyv steps in, slams her shoulder into his chest—and drives her Moonblade through his heart.

Nyv (whispering): "Vaulmark burns with every name you forgot."

The wizard collapses. Magic bleeds out of him in flickering embers.

As his ashes fall, the Heart flares once—violent and bright. But instead of rage, the flames recoil, spiraling away from the space he once occupied. A low pulse follows, softer than before—as if the chamber itself is exhaling. The runes dim. The heat shifts. The Heart no longer resists.

Behind her, the kobolds falter. The Heart pulses once—and a wave of golden fire sweeps through the chamber, dissolving the remaining enemies, and the corpses of their fallen comrades, in silence.

Only the adventurers remain.

Geoff the Newt, panting, climbs back up to Nyv's shoulder and settles there, utterly calm.

Tassa (blinking): "Did the lizard just... help?"

Bryn (grinning faintly): "He always knows where to bite."

Tassa (shrugging): "For the record, I didn't know the runes would do that."

Yeldanna (raising a brow): "Then why throw them in?"

Tassa (with a grin): "They were humming. And I've learned to listen to things that hum."

Yeldanna lowers her sword.

Yeldanna (to Nyv): "You carried us."

Nyv (quiet, exhausted): "I carried Ravkareth."

Then—the Heart pulses again. Stronger.

It listens.

What We Leave Behind

Setting: The Heart chamber, silent in the wake of battle. The Vaulmar Binder's remains are already fading, drawn into the veins of the stone like ink in water. The flames of the Heart burn brighter now—no longer chaotic, but expectant.

Yeldanna stands at the edge of the platform, staring into the shifting fire. The shape of the Heart pulses slowly. With every beat, the heat deepens. But it does not threaten. It calls.

Tassa (quietly): "Is it done?"

Bryn: "No. This was never just about stopping him."

Nyv, arms still trembling from battle, sheathes her blades. Her eyes do not leave the Heart.

Nyv: "It wants something now."

Tassa: "What kind of something?"

Bryn (soft): "A price. Not for power—for return."

The flames swirl and coalesce into a shape: a dragon made of fire, its wings spread wide, its eyes empty. In the centre of its chest, a hollow space—waiting.

Bryn (quietly translating the magic): "*A soul can be called. But not freely. This place was built on sacrifice. That law still holds.*"

Yeldanna steps forward. Her voice is clear. Unwavering.

Yeldanna: "What does it want?"

Bryn: "Not life. Not blood. Memory. The piece of you that holds him close."

Silence.

Tassa (a whisper): "A memory of Chovee."

Nyv: "Yeldanna, you don't have to—"

Yeldanna: "I do."

She closes her eyes. Breathes deeply.

Yeldanna: "When he was born... he wouldn't cry. The priestess panicked. But then I touched his face—and he grabbed my finger. Tight. So tight. And he looked at me like he already knew me. Like he was waiting."

She opens her eyes.

Yeldanna: "That's what I'll give."

Tassa: "But you'll forget."

Yeldanna (softly): "I already carry too much. Let him have this."

She walks to the Heart.

Bryn raises a hand in ritual.

Bryn: "Do you give this memory freely?"

Yeldanna: "Yes."

The Heart pulses once.

Gold and white flame flare around her.

The moment hangs in eternity.

And then—it is done.

Yeldanna gasps.

Yeldanna (blinking): "I... what was I saying?"

She looks around, confused, her hand drifting to her heart as if searching for something she can't quite recall.

No one answers.

The Heart's flames dim—leaving behind a single glowing ember, floating gently down into Bryn's waiting hands.

Bryn: "This is him. Not yet restored... but no longer lost."

Geoff the Newt sniffs the ember and chirps once. It glows a little brighter.

Tassa (softly): "Does it ever end?"

Bryn: "Now we take him home."

The Ember Rises

Setting: Ravkareth, beneath the dawn sky. The wind carries the chill of the Velthorn Peaks, but the ground is soft with spring thaw. The Veilwarden temple stands atop a hill woven with ancient runes, draped in ribbons and warded mist. At its centre waits the chamber of soulbinding—the place where life may be returned... for a price already paid.

The party approaches in silence.

Bryn walks at the front, the ember of Chovee cupped in her hands like sacred fire. The ravens circle above, silent and slow.

Yeldanna walks with steady steps. She no longer remembers the warmth of her son's grip—but something in her heart still aches with love.

Nyv and Tassa flank her, and Geoff the Newt clings to Nyv's shoulder, still oddly alert. Bone-Anna remains by the gate, watching over the path behind them.

At the temple doors, three Veilwardens step forward. Their eyes fall on the ember—then shift to Tassa.

Their expressions still.

They say nothing.

But one—the eldest—lowers her head. Not in greeting, but in quiet deference.

Tassa (half a whisper): "Did anyone else see that?"

Nyv: "They know something."

Tassa (quietly): "So do I."

Tassa swallows. For once, she doesn't make a joke.

As they enter the soulbinding chamber, Bryn slows.

The space is circular, its walls lined with shadow-glass and symbols that glimmer faintly in Tassa's presence.

She pauses, reaching toward one glyph.

It glows beneath her fingers—not red, but gold.

Tassa stares. Her reflection stares back—almost hers. But almost entirely.

Behind her eyes, something shifts. Not memory. Not voice.

Instinct.

"*You were broken*," a thought whispers—not hers, but within her.

"*But not undone.*"

Bryn watches her closely.

Bryn (softly): "You feel it, don't you?"

Tassa nods. No jokes. No riddles.

Tassa: "I think I always did. I just didn't have a name for it."

Bryn: "You still don't. That's what makes you dangerous."

Tassa turns back toward the ritual.

The ember hovers now—centred in a web of runes drawn in Veilwarden ink and memory.

The witches chant softly. The flames grow brighter.

Yeldanna kneels, head bowed.

The ember breaks—not with sound, but with light—unfolding like wings across the chamber.

And when it dims—

Chovee stands.

Alive.

Confused. Breathing.

Whole.

Yeldanna (eyes shining): "You're back."

He smiles at her, uncertain.

Chovee: "Have… we met?"

She flinches—but nods. She holds him close, her cheek pressed to his hair. And wraps her arms around him.

Yeldanna (quiet): "You will."

✦

Later—

Tassa stands alone outside the temple, the breeze tugging at her coat.

Geoff the Newt climbs to her shoulder and rests there without hesitation—quiet and steady, as if he has always understood more than he lets on.

He simply looks at her—*knowingly.*

Tassa: "What do you think I am?"

Geoff the Newt, as ever, says nothing.

The mountains shimmer on the horizon, a soft haze of light curling around their peaks.

Tassa (softly): "Maybe that's the wrong question."

Bryn steps beside her, hands folded in her sleeves.

Bryn: "You don't have to know yet."

Tassa (with a half-smile): "Will you tell them?"

Bryn: "Not unless they ask the right question."

They stand together.

One born of shadow.

One born of flame.

Epilogue

Embers Beyond the Fire

Setting: Three days after the ritual. Ravkareth is still. The peaks of the Velthorn Mountains blur beneath a veil of spring fog. Wildflowers bloom cautiously along the trail leading out of the Veilwarden temple grounds. A wind rustles the birch trees, as if whispering farewell.

Chovee sleeps beneath heavy furs in the temple's central hall. His breathing is steady. His memories—fragments. Faces, not names. Feelings, not stories.

Yeldanna sits beside him.

She strokes his hair in silence.

She no longer remembers how he looked when he was born.

But she loves him still.

And that is enough.

✦

Outside, beneath the pale morning sun, Bryn, Nyv, and Tassa prepare for the road.

Geoff the Newt scurries across Nyv's shoulder to inspect their travel packs. He opens a buckle, climbs into a pouch, and settles in without permission. As always.

Nyv (muttering): "He's not *helping*. He's *judging*."

Tassa (smiling): "Is there a difference?"

Bryn adjusts the strap of her satchel in silence. Overhead, her ravens circle— like drifting thoughts in a windless sky.

Yeldanna approaches. Her face is calm, but her voice carries the weight of goodbye.

Yeldanna: "I can't go with you."

Bryn: "We didn't expect you to."

Nyv: "You gave more than anyone."

Yeldanna places a hand on Bryn's shoulder.

Yeldanna: "He'll need guidance when the memories stop returning. The witches will tell him... tell him I always knew he'd come back. Even if I can't remember why."

She watches them go until they vanish into the trees. Then she turns, alone—but not lost.

Bryn nods.

There are no grand farewells. Just quiet understanding.

The kind between warriors.

The kind between women who've carried too much for too long.

✦

Later, at the edge of the forest, the three younger women stop.

The road forks—one path winding south, toward the Merishan frontier, where rumors stir of tombs opened by unnatural flame. The other, westward, vanishes toward Narfell, where a rift in the Worldthread was said to swallow a village whole.

Tassa (tilting her head): "Which mystery are we chasing?"

Nyv (firmly): "The one that needs us more."

Tassa (smirking): "Is that a guess or a prophecy?"

Nyv: "Both."

They look to Bryn, who gives only the faintest nod.

Bryn steps forward first, silent and certain. The others follow.

They walk south.

The ravens rise. Geoff the Newt snorts in approval.

As the forest swallows them, Tassa turns once—just briefly—to look back toward the mountains.

She doesn't speak.

But for a heartbeat, her eyes burn brighter than the sun.

✦

Somewhere deep beneath the world...

The embers of Vhal'turien stir.

And something very old begins to dream again.

Part II – Veil and Vow

Trust forged in shadow, sealed without words—
a bond stronger than steel, quieter than faith.

Prologue: What Should Not Rise

The desert had no name. Not anymore.

Once, there had been roads—stone-cut and sun-bleached—marked by brass signposts and temple bells. Now, there was only sand. Sand, and the hollow sound of wind scraping bone.

At the edge of a forgotten necropolis, a figure knelt. Robes the colour of dried blood clung to their frame. Their hands, bare and cracked, traced symbols into the dust—one after another, until the ground beneath them pulsed with warmth.

The heat was not from the sun.

The sun had fled this place long ago.

A low rumble shivered through the crypt stones. The sand hissed. Beneath the kneeling figure, a half-buried obelisk groaned—and then, without warning, cracked open, breathing for the first time in centuries.

From the split rose a coil of black flame. It moved like smoke. But it burned without light, casting shadow instead of heat. The figure did not look away. They opened their mouth, and the flame entered.

Their eyes boiled white. When they spoke, their voice was not their own:

"Flame remembers the bone.

"Bone remembers the name.

"Name remembers the Gate."

And somewhere far beneath the earth, something stirred.

● ● ●

In the days that followed, the towns nearest the desert began to fall silent.

Messenger birds returned with nothing.

Merchants came back whispering of graves that burned from within.

Children spoke of a man with no mouth and too many eyes.

Clerics dreamed of a bell tolling beneath the earth—muffled, but growing louder.

No one knew where it began.

No one could say what it meant.

Only that the dead were not resting.

And something ancient was helping them remember why.

Chapter 1: The Ember-Marked

The path curved along a granite ridge, etched with old runes long faded by time and wind. Sparse pine trees clung to the slopes, their twisted shapes half-drowned in mist. Somewhere below, the valley breathed out its morning fog, silver curling through frost-bitten ferns.

It was Nyv who noticed the smoke—thin and even, the kind wildfires never make.

They followed it without speaking. Tassa squinted into the light, chewing a blade of dry grass as her boots kicked loose shale over the edge. Bryn said nothing, only adjusted the strap of her satchel and let her raven spirits drift ahead into the curling cloud. Bone-Anna followed at a quiet distance, her skeletal frame making no sound as she moved, bow strapped to her back, one empty eye socket catching the morning light.

When they reached the ledge, they saw her.

The forge was built into the mountain, nestled beneath a carved overhang blackened by years of soot. No banner. No sign. Just an anvil sunken into stone, and a low hearth glowing soft with orange coals. Above it, chiseled into the granite wall, was a circle of etched names—rows of dwarven script spiralling outward like a sunwheel, each no more than three letters long.

A woman stood at the forge.

She wore a long leather apron over chainmail, the sleeves of her tunic rolled to the elbow. Her skin was the colour of embered clay, her arms thick with quiet strength. Around her neck hung a loop of iron medallions, each no larger than a coin, some inscribed, some scorched. Her hair was braided tightly into a crown around her head, with soot marking the tips of her temples.

She didn't look up when they approached. She dipped her tongs into the coals, drew forth a faintly glowing strip of metal, and laid it flat against the anvil.

ting... ting... ting

The hammer fell softly. Not for war. For memory.

● ● ●

There was no welcome. But neither was there wariness.

Nyv was the first to approach the carved wall, eyes trailing over the spiral of names. "What is this place?" she asked.

The dwarf spoke without pausing her work.

"A forge for what remains."

Tassa tilted her head. "What does that mean?"

The woman did not answer.

It was Bryn who stepped forward next. She knelt before the offering table—a stone shelf nestled to the side of the forge, crowded with old tokens: splinters of bone, rings without stones, weathered feathers tied with twine. She reached into her pouch and withdrew a small carving—a raven formed from whalebone, wings folded, its eyes closed.

She set it gently among the others.

The flames in the hearth seemed to breathe, just once.

The dwarf's voice came quieter now. "She watches over them, you know. Even if they don't rise."

Bryn looked at her. "You mean Durnach the Forgemaker?"

"I mean all the ones who remember the names."

There was silence again.

Nyv's fingers brushed the edge of the offering table. After a long moment, she pulled a black cord from her sash. Attached was a tiny charm—obsidian glass in the shape of a teardrop. Without explanation, she placed it beside Bryn's raven.

Bryn glanced at her, but said nothing. Nyv didn't look up, but her lips curved slightly—as though she'd expected Bryn to notice.

Tassa hesitated. She had no such tokens. No fragments of the past she was willing to give. Eventually, she reached into her coat and withdrew a scorched coin—burned nearly black, but still glinting with golden edges. She tossed it onto the stone with an odd mix of defiance and reverence.

"Do they… mean anything?" she asked. "Or is it just for the sake of ritual?"

The dwarf finally looked up.

Her eyes were pale silver. Not blind, but seeing something far deeper than what stood before her.

"They mean that someone remembered," she said. "And didn't let the remembering get burned away."

Tassa's jaw tightened, but she didn't reply. Instead, she turned slightly and found herself face-to-face with Geoff the Newt, who had scampered up her arm and now perched on her shoulder, blinking. The little lizard looked toward the dwarf, then slid down Tassa's sleeve, scampered across the stone with slow, deliberate steps, and with deliberate calm, crawled up onto the anvil.

Kaerda didn't flinch.

She paused her work, met Geoff's eyes, and gently touched her soot-darkened fingers to her brow in quiet acknowledgement.

Geoff gave a faint, dismissive huff and hopped down, curling beside the coals.

Nyv's eyes narrowed. "…He doesn't do that often."

Bryn tilted her head toward Nyv, murmuring just loud enough to be heard:

"Perhaps he knows she remembers the right things."

● ● ●

They shared no fire that night. Instead, they stayed near the forge, wrapped in their own cloaks, the warmth of the hearth pulsing gently beside them.

The smith said little. But she let them stay. Even brought out dried meat and thick-cut bread, smoked with lavender. They ate in silence, except for Tassa's occasional questions: Why metal instead of stone? Why no prayers? How do you choose which names to carve?

Most were left unanswered—though the smith did pause once and respond softly:

"Stone is for what endures. But steel… that's for what changes hands."

When the bread was gone, Bone-Anna moved to the edge of the firelight and stood watch without being asked. The smith didn't question the undead sentry, nor the strange shadows that danced more deliberately than fire ought to.

Eventually, Bryn asked the question they all hovered around.

87

"What's your name?"

"Kaerda," she said. "Flintward. Of the Firevault line."

"And are you staying here?"

Kaerda shook her head. "I keep moving. Only stop when there's enough memory to melt."

Nyv's gaze lingered on her. "Are you hunted?"

"No."

"Are you lost?"

Kaerda turned to her. "Not anymore."

● ● ●

Later, when the others drifted into a kind of uneasy rest, Bryn sat up beside the coals and watched Kaerda work. The dwarf had drawn out a small steel disc, no larger than a thumbnail, and was etching something into its surface with a fine chisel.

"Whose name is that?" Bryn asked softly.

Kaerda paused. Looked over. "Yours."

Bryn blinked. "But I'm not—"

"Not dead," Kaerda finished. "I know. Still. I make them for those I think I'll need to remember."

There was no threat in her voice. Just truth, shaped like steel.

Bryn looked at the disk, then at her own hand. The feather mark was faint tonight. She could feel the Queen's attention elsewhere, drifting through the skeins of sleep and shadow. But this place—the forge, the tokens—it felt like her. Like a whisper of approval.

"She'd like you," Bryn said. "You don't trap memories. You let them cool—take shape."

Kaerda smiled, just barely. "They never stay molten forever."

● ● ●

By dawn, the trio had made their decision.

They didn't say it aloud—not yet. But something had shifted—an understanding not spoken, but felt. They walked with Kaerda when she packed up her tools. They lingered at her side as she doused the coals. They offered nothing, demanded nothing.

Just walked.

And Kaerda walked with them.

Not because she was needed. But because, for the first time, all four of them felt something deeper than need:

Accord.

Chapter 2: Hallowden

The path downward from the mountains narrowed into a thin spine of shale, flanked by pine and crooked ash trees. Mist clung to the roots, and the ravens that accompanied Bryn circled overhead in slow, watchful arcs. The party walked in near silence, save for the occasional jangle of Kaerda's tools and the clicking of Bone-Anna's bony gait behind them.

Below, nestled in the hollow where the trees thinned, lay the village—Hallowden.

It did not look like a place that wanted to be found. The buildings were low to the earth, their thatched roofs dark with age and weather. Wisps of chimney smoke barely rose above the rooftops, and a faded wooden post bore a half-cracked sign:

Candlecut Hollow – Warm Beds, Quiet Fire.

"Warm sounds nice," Tassa muttered, adjusting her belt. "Quiet I'm less fond of."

Nyv said nothing. She studied the layout of the village with practised eyes, noting the narrow paths, the stone well at its centre, the closed shutters—even in daylight.

Kaerda paused beside her. "No bells," she said. "Not even a shrine bell. Odd, for a town this old."

Nyv nodded once. "Let's see what they're hiding."

● ● ●

Inside the Candlecut Hollow, the tavern glowed with flickering amber light. Candles sat in stone recesses carved into the walls, their flames barely stirring in the still air. The scent of cider, smoke, and something faintly metallic lingered in the room.

The innkeeper, Inevin Dalebar, gave them a slow once-over from behind the counter. His eyes lingered a moment too long on Bone-Anna before he gave a subtle nod and gestured toward a booth near the hearth.

"You'll want the corner," he said. "Good sightlines."

Tassa grinned. "Now *you* speak my language."

As they settled in, Kaerda removed her pack with careful precision, setting it beside her without letting the hammer strapped to her back so much as clink. Bryn stood a moment longer, her eyes sweeping over the tavern's patrons. No one stared—but no one met their gaze, either. She sat last.

The drinks arrived with little conversation. Just the quiet hum of murmurs, the creak of wood, the soft ring of a spoon in a cup.

"Friendly place," Tassa muttered.

"Cautious," Bryn corrected. "Not unfriendly."

"They've reason," Kaerda added. "This far out, small towns don't have room for risk. Or mercy."

Nyv leaned back, cradling a mug of mead. "Let's listen a while."

• • •

The rumors came in fragments, caught between sips and shadow.

Two siblings in hunter's leathers sat near the window, their voices low and fast, overlapping. Locals called them Veyden and Ril Harthorn—they hadn't ventured into the hills since returning from a failed hunt. Bryn sent one of her ravens to perch nearby, and the group listened.

"Colder than snowmelt, and not just the air. The stone *bit*."
"Saw a carcass halfway devoured, but no blood. Not a drop."
"We shouldn't have gone near the crypt. Something watches from *underneath*."

At the bar, an elderly halfling woman with braids like dry grass clinked bone charms together while muttering to herself. Tassa leaned closer to catch the words.

"Lightless fire on Barrowrise. Burned in pulses. Like breathing.
Not flame. Not right."

Later, they watched as a pale, drawn priest entered the tavern. Cairl Renvar, the village cleric. He ordered wine and sat alone. When Bryn approached and politely asked whether he might speak of the dead, his expression fell like a crumbling altar.

He said nothing at first.

Then he drank, deeply.

"Spring burials. Three of them. Gone now.
Graves torn open—from the inside. I tried to rebury them. Prayed. The rites…
they don't work anymore. It's like light fades before it reaches them."

He pressed a trembling hand to his temple.

"Don't follow the cold. It's not natural. It's not *death*—not really."

Bryn's face was unreadable in the candlelight. She placed a silver piece in front
of him, then turned away without another word.

● ● ●

Back in their room above the inn, the party gathered around a table cluttered
with wax-dripped bottles and one empty bowl of stew. Bone-Anna stood at the
door, unmoving. Geoff the Newt perched on a bedpost, blinking slowly.

"I vote we leave in the morning," Tassa said, cracking her knuckles. "Weird fire,
cold crypts, empty coffins—sounds like they planned a welcoming party."

Kaerda sat cross-legged on the floor, polishing one of her medallions. "I don't
like the bit about the rites failing. That's not something you lie about when
you're sober."

"He wasn't sober," Tassa said.

"Didn't matter," Bryn replied. "He was afraid."

Nyv was silent a long moment, her mask resting on the edge of the bed. She
turned it slowly in her hands before speaking. "The Harthorns didn't lie. That
cold wasn't weather—it was presence. If something is disturbing the threshold
between life and death, we should know what."

She glanced toward Bryn.

"We *should* act."

Bryn gave the smallest of nods. "Not because the town needs us. But because
the Queen will want it answered."

Kaerda gave a grunt of agreement. "Then we'll go see what shouldn't be
moving in the cold."

Tassa stretched her legs out in front of her. "And if there's something worth punching in there, I call dibs."

Geoff the Newt let out a soft click that sounded suspiciously like approval.

●　●　●

At midnight, Bryn stood alone near the window, watching the shadows drift across the quiet street. One of her ravens returned and landed silently on the sill, tilting its head toward her.

There were no words exchanged.

Only understanding.

Tomorrow, they would follow the cold.

And perhaps uncover what should not rise at all.

Chapter 3: The Weight of Whispers

The morning broke without ceremony. A pale sun crept over the ridgeline, its light thin and reluctant, as if even the sky doubted the day. The streets of Hallowden remained still, disturbed only by the gentle crunch of frost underfoot and the occasional flick of raven wings as Bryn's flock surveyed the path ahead.

They gathered just beyond the Candlecut Hollow, cloaks drawn tight. Kaerda tightened the straps on her pack, her armour quiet beneath her layered wool. Nyv adjusted her mask, then moved instinctively to Bryn's side, not needing a word. They rarely spoke when preparing to leave—but they always moved in sync. Tassa bounced slightly on her heels, eyes scanning the fog-draped horizon. Bone-Anna stood motionless beside Bryn, and Geoff the Newt clung to Nyv's shoulder like a silent green badge of quiet approval.

"So," Tassa said, blowing warm breath into her gloved hands. "Crypt first, yeah?"

Kaerda nodded. "If it's the one the twins and priest spoke of, it won't be far."

Bryn extended a hand, and one of her ravens landed lightly upon her wrist. She whispered a brief word in Elvish. The bird rose and darted east.

"We'll follow."

● ● ●

The walk took them past the outer edge of the village, where tilled soil gave way to knotted weeds and half-rotted fence posts. Beyond lay a small grove that sloped gently upward toward a low hill crowned in stone.

At its crest stood the crypt.

It was dwarfed by the land around it, half-sunken into the earth, ringed by headstones so worn they bore only hints of names. Its door—a single slab of granite etched in flaking silver script—hung slightly ajar.

"This isn't abandoned," Kaerda said as they crested the hill. "Just avoided."

Tassa moved first, her hands resting lightly near her weapons. She pushed the door open with one boot.

The cold hit them immediately.

Not wind. Not the chill of altitude. This cold had weight. It clung to the skin like wet cloth, settled deep in the joints, and made breath feel unwelcome.

Nyv stepped to the threshold and paused. "The light doesn't carry."

It was true. The morning sun reached the doorway but did not enter. The darkness inside was absolute.

Bryn touched the edge of the frame. Her fingers came away with a dusting of frost.

"This place is claimed."

• • •

Inside, their footsteps were muffled. The air tasted stale and metallic. Bryn let her ravens spread through the space in cautious spirals, and faint echoes returned through her senses: old stone, something cracked, something weeping without tears.

The chamber was simple. A central slab. Niches lining the walls. Bones, still arranged. No sign of rest. No sign of peace.

Kaerda approached one of the walls. She ran a gloved finger over a long-dormant lantern hook and frowned. "Recently touched. Not recently cleaned."

Tassa crouched by the central slab. "No writing. But this isn't an altar. It's a lid."

Nyv crouched beside her. Her eyes flicked across the seam where the stone met its base.

"It's been moved. Look here—see the scrape? Someone opened it."

Kaerda turned. "Then closed it again. But why?"

Bryn stood near the far niche, fingers brushing an empty socket where bones once lay.

"Because something walked out. Or was taken." She turned slowly, her voice dropping. "And it didn't leave alone."

• • •

They searched for an hour.

In the corner, Nyv found dried wax near a cracked tile—ritual markings in a tongue even she couldn't name. Bryn pocketed a shard of the wax, murmuring that it would be safer outside the crypt. Kaerda found drag marks in the dust, too faint to follow. Bone-Anna remained silent throughout, bow drawn and ready.

Eventually, they emerged into the light.

It felt no warmer than when they had entered.

● ● ●

That night, they gathered again in their room at the inn. The candlelight flickered across weary faces.

"Cairl wasn't lying," Nyv said. "Graves *are* being disturbed. But it's not theft. There was no looting. No signs of grave robbers."

Kaerda leaned forward, her fingers tracing the grain of the table. "Then it's something else. A calling."

"A summoning," Bryn whispered. Her eyes were distant. "They weren't raised. Or bound. Just… awakened. And returned."

Tassa looked between them. "So someone opened a crypt, invited something back, and then what? Just let it walk away?"

Nyv folded her arms. "Or followed it."

The room fell silent.

Geoff the Newt shifted on Nyv's shoulder, letting out a small, uncertain chirp.

Kaerda reached for her medallions.

"We need to keep moving. The flame Noma spoke of, the frost the hunters felt—they're symptoms. Not the cause."

Bryn nodded slowly. "East. Always east. That's where the stories lead."

"And the silence," Nyv added.

Bone-Anna turned toward the window, gaze fixed on the night beyond.

Something moved in the dark.

● ● ●

In a place far from Hallowden, beneath stone that remembered no sunlight, the man with no mouth and too many eyes stood before an altar of bone. His fingers twitched. His eyes did not blink.

He saw a raven take flight in the west.

And deep in the dark, he smiled without lips.

Chapter 4: Ash on the Wind

The road east of Hallowden was less a road and more a memory. What had once been a narrow trade path had long since surrendered to root and vine, leaving only a shallow depression winding between frost-hardened trees. The forest grew stranger as they pressed on: bark split by unknown heat, patches of earth scorched black, and long, jagged furrows in the ground where something large had passed.

Bryn knelt beside one such mark. Her ravens circled above, silent.

"Not a wagon. Not hooves. Claws."

"Something fleeing," Kaerda added, studying the crushed underbrush. "Not hunting."

They moved on. The sun never fully pierced the canopy, and even Tassa—who usually found ease in open air—stayed close to the centre of the group.

By midday, they reached a ruined homestead.

A single cottage, roof half-collapsed. A fence trampled flat. Plates still on the table, weathered by wind and rain. No blood. No bodies. Only absence.

Nyv stood in the doorway. "No sign of struggle. Whatever happened, it wasn't a fight."

"They ran," Kaerda murmured. "But not from bandits."

In the yard, Geoff the Newt sniffed at a blackened circle in the dirt, then scurried up Nyv's arm without a sound.

Tassa unslung one of her crossbows. "I don't like how quiet it is."

Neither did the trees.

● ● ●

The attack came with no warning.

A crashing wall of motion tore from the treeline—a shape half-bird, half-bear, all rage. The owlbear's feathers were ragged, its eyes wide with panic. It barreled toward them not as a predator, but as a creature driven too far for too long.

Kaerda stepped forward before anyone else could move. Her shield rose in a flash, and the owlbear's claws met steel with a brutal, scraping shriek.

"Hold!" she barked.

Tassa rolled aside and fired a bolt into the earth near the beast's feet. "We doing this the loud way or the clever way?"

Nyv didn't answer. She reached into her pouch and withdrew a pinch of powdered root, murmuring a calming incantation. Bryn followed with a gesture of her own, weaving violet threads of shadow through the clearing. **Geoff the Newt** clung tighter.

The owlbear swiped again, furious but uncoordinated.

Kaerda stood firm, shield raised, her stance immovable. "It doesn't want to fight. It's afraid."

Bryn moved beside her, palm open. A shimmer of shadow flickered outward— a barrier between them and the beast. "Then we calm it. Not kill it."

It took time.

And patience.

But slowly, the creature's breathing eased. Its stance dropped. The fire in its eyes dulled into exhaustion.

Kaerda lowered her shield.

Nyv stepped forward just enough to be seen and opened her hands.

The owlbear stared a moment longer. Then it turned, clumsily, and vanished into the trees.

Silence returned.

"Well," Tassa muttered, reloading. "That was new."

Kaerda exhaled and let her shield rest against her leg. "Not everything twisted by this is lost. Some things are just... displaced."

Bryn nodded. "And some things might still be spared."

● ● ●

That evening, they made camp beside a shallow stream. The trees here bent away from the water, as if wary.

As they sat around the fire, Kaerda re-checked her armour while Tassa carved idle symbols into the dirt. Bryn took a small bone token from her pouch and placed it by the stream, whispering a quiet offering to the Queen.

"We still don't know what could drive a creature like that west," Nyv said. Her tone was calm, but edged.

Kaerda stared into the fire. "Something bigger. Something old. It didn't attack until it was cornered."

"We go farther east," Bryn said. "Follow the scorched trails. The marks on the trees."

Geoff the Newt let out a quiet chirp and lifted his snout toward the horizon.

Tassa chuckled. "Looks like the little guy agrees."

They followed his gaze.

A thread of smoke rose in the far distance, barely visible against the dusk.

Something was burning in the dark.

And it was waiting.

Chapter 5: The Smoke That Stays

The smoke thickened as they drew closer.

It clung low to the earth, curling around their boots and drifting between the trees in lazy spirals. The air had an acrid bite—burned wood, yes, but something beneath it too. Something older. Charred rot. Magic spent too violently.

By midmorning, the trees broke, and they stood at the edge of a hollow where a village had once stood.

The buildings were nothing but blackened skeletons. Stone chimneys stood like sentries amid heaps of collapsed timber. Shattered glass glittered in the ash. There were no sounds of insects. No wind through shutters. No birds.

And no bodies.

Tassa was the first to speak. "No corpses. Not even bones."

Nyv stepped forward, her boots sinking into a layer of soot. She passed what remained of a well, now half-caved in, and crouched beside a scorched wall.

"Burned quickly. Uniformly. But not wild."

Kaerda stepped past her and lifted a beam from the ruins. The underside was seared in a clean line—not merely blackened by flame, but etched with runes.

Bryn joined her. "The same symbols as the wax in the crypt."

She looked skyward. Her ravens wheeled overhead, silent and watchful.

"This wasn't a raid. This was a ritual."

• • •

They moved through the village in careful formation. Bone-Anna remained by Bryn's side, bow in hand. Geoff the Newt watched everything from Nyv's shoulder, tail flicking with uneasy rhythm.

Near the centre of the village, they found the town square—a scorched ring in the stone plaza. What might once have been a fountain now lay shattered, its basin cracked and empty.

But in the centre, a single standing stone remained. Blackened. Unbroken.

Kaerda approached it slowly, shield raised.

"More runes," she said. "But deeper here. Ritual carvings."

Nyv studied them, tracing her fingers just above the surface.

"The same patterns... but layered. These were done over time. This didn't happen in a single night."

Tassa paced a slow circle. "Then where are the people? Even if they were raised, there should be something. A boot. A belt. A mistake."

Bryn crouched and placed her palm against the stone. Her eyes narrowed.

"They were taken. Not just from life. From memory."

The wind stirred.

Kaerda turned. "Something was here. Not long ago."

● ● ●

They camped at the edge of the hollow that night, unwilling to rest within the ruins.

The fire burned low.

"Undead don't coordinate like this," Kaerda said. "Not unless they're under command."

"Or guided," Nyv said softly. "Subtly. A suggestion. A hymn. A voice from beyond."

Tassa looked out at the village, eyes hard. "Whatever did this... it knew exactly what it wanted. And it left nothing behind."

Geoff the Newt clung tight to Nyv's cloak.

Bryn stared into the fire. "Something is building. Not just death. Purpose."

She reached into her pouch and withdrew another token. This one, unlike the others, was blank.

She placed it in the fire.

It burned with violet flame.

● ● ●

Far from the hollow, in a forgotten chapel beneath a dead city, the man with no mouth and too many eyes walked between rows of open tombs. He did not speak. He could not.

But his thoughts sang.

He remembered fire. He remembered the village that should not have resisted. He remembered how they sang as they burned.

He was not done.

He was never done.

Chapter 6: Between Ruin and Pursuit

They left the burned village behind as the morning sun struggled through a sky smudged with ash. None of them spoke for some time.

Not even Tassa.

It was Bryn who finally stopped walking. She turned to the others, her cloak trailing in the soot, and pointed toward a low rise just beyond the village's edge.

"We should mark them. Even if no names remain."

Kaerda nodded without a word and began gathering stone. Nyv joined her, tracing faint spirals into the rocks with powdered chalk. Bryn produced one of her bone tokens—simple, round, its face uncarved—and placed it atop the cairn they built together.

Geoff the Newt crawled down Nyv's arm and perched at the base, his small body perfectly still.

Tassa crossed her arms, expression unreadable. When Kaerda glanced her way, Tassa finally moved. She found a jagged shard of glass and wedged it into the cairn, facing east. It caught the light for just a moment.

"So they can see the way out," she muttered.

Bryn placed a hand on the topmost stone. No names. No prayers. Just remembering.

● ● ●

Later, they rested beneath a weathered outcropping. A cold stream trickled through the stone, and the only sound was the slow clink of Kaerda unbuckling her gauntlets.

Bryn sat apart, fingers curled in prayer, her voice no louder than the wind.

When she opened her eyes, the vision came.

Not a message.

Not clarity.

Only a bell—vast, suspended in blackness, unmoving.

Chains coiled around its crown, vanishing into the void.

And far below, like a whisper carried too late, a single raven feather falling through shadow.

She gasped.

Nyv was beside her in an instant. "What did you see?"

Bryn shook her head slowly. "Nothing useful. And yet... everything."

● ● ●

The decision to continue east was quiet, but unanimous.

They followed the traces left behind—not footprints, but wounds. Trees split down the middle. Scorch marks shaped like veined hands. Stones rearranged in spiral patterns too deliberate to be natural.

Kaerda, walking second from the front, glanced back at Nyv.

"You're different when it comes to death. Not afraid of it. But not drawn to it either."

Nyv replied with a dry smile. "In Ravkareth, we live alongside it. We believe the dead watch what we do with the days they no longer hold."

Kaerda considered that. "In my temple, they taught us to forge memory into steel. To keep the names alive. I think we would have liked your ways."

Nyv nodded once. "I think we still might."

Geoff the Newt squeaked quietly.

● ● ●

By evening, they reached the crest of another hill.

Bryn narrowed her eyes. "Smoke."

Tassa sighed. "That's three days in a row."

Kaerda stepped forward, frowning. "No fire. Just smoke."

The trees below shifted in the wind, and for just a moment, they saw it—a flicker of black ash rising where no fire burned.

Bryn said nothing, but her hand drifted toward her spellbook.

Nyv spoke first. "We follow. Whatever this is... it isn't done."

Bryn turned.

"No," she said. "It's only just begun."

The ravens took flight, circling once, then veering east.

They followed.

And behind them, unseen in the gathering dark, something followed.

Chapter 7: When the Silence Breaks

They smelled the dead before they heard them.

It was the stench of rot without flesh—a hollow reek, like mold clinging to dry bone and something older underneath. A scent that didn't belong to decay, but to stillness. To memory. To graves left open too long.

Tassa froze mid-step. "That's not campfire smoke."

Kaerda raised a fist. The group halted.

They were on a narrow ridge path, looking down across a shallow basin below. There, where the trees thinned, the party saw them.

Hundreds.

A slow-moving tide of bodies in varying states of death. Some were fresh, their clothes still bearing the soot of burned villages. Others had been dead for months—eyes gone, limbs twisted wrong, fingers raw from clawing free of soil. They moved without sound, without leader. Yet their march had rhythm. Purpose. They did not stumble. They advanced.

Bryn's ravens screeched and scattered, pulling sharply back from the edge of the basin.

"That's not a horde," Nyv said, her voice low. "That's a procession."

Geoff the Newt burrowed deep beneath Nyv's cloak, trembling.

● ● ●

They retreated from the ridge and dropped into cover behind a thicket of gnarled birch. Bryn motioned for Bone-Anna to stay hidden. Shadows coiled around the skeleton as she faded into the brush.

Tassa gritted her teeth. "We can take a few dozen. Not that."

"We won't," Kaerda said. "We hide. We move on."

But the ground beneath them betrayed their intent.

A low cracking of roots. A shift in the earth. And then, a shriek—not from a creature, but from the land itself.

A raven fell from the sky.

The procession turned.

Heads rose. Eyes—some hollow, some glowing faintly with sick light—fixed on their thicket.

And the dead began to run.

• • •

"MOVE!" Kaerda roared, stepping into the open, shield up.

Tassa fired a bolt into the lead corpse, dropping it, but another took its place.

Nyv whispered a spell, casting a haze of warding air around them. Bryn summoned twin ravens of shadow and hurled them into the crowd, but it was like flinging birds into a storm.

They were surrounded in moments.

Kaerda braced herself against three incoming attackers, her shield flaring with divine light as she absorbed blow after blow. Tassa kept firing, but her quiver would not last. Nyv burned a half-circle of radiant energy into the ground, buying seconds. Bryn called on her Queen's power, shadows screaming from her hands—but even she knew it would not be enough.

Geoff the Newt hissed and flared orange along his belly.

Tassa fell back toward Kaerda, bleeding from a clawed shoulder. "Any more clever ideas?!"

Nyv opened her mouth to respond.

And then the world went still.

• • •

A sound like a *bell* without metal rang through the clearing. Not in the air—in the bones.

The dead stopped.

Every corpse froze in place. Fingers inches from Kaerda's throat. Teeth bared near Nyv's face. The air thickened.

And then parted.

From the treeline stepped a figure robed in silver-grey, with armour that shimmered like starlight beneath a travel-stained cloak. A tall, androgynous form with skin pale as marble and hair that hung like loose threads of firelight. Their eyes glowed softly—not gold, not blue, but the colour of skies before a storm.

A **lantern** hung from their belt, casting no light.

The dead shuddered.

Then, without command, they began to *fall*. One by one, as though strings had been cut. No fire. No fury. Just collapse. Bone to dirt. Cloth to ash.

The figure stepped forward, hand outstretched.

A gate of radiant shadow tore open behind the party, called forth by figure's presence alone.

They were pulled backward.

● ● ●

The world snapped back into sound and motion. They landed on cold stone, winded but whole.

It was a cave. Dark, dry, distant. Safe.

Kaerda was already on her feet, shield up. Bryn knelt beside Nyv, checking her wounds. Tassa rolled her shoulder with a wince.

The figure stood over them.

"You were marked," they said.

Their voice was soft, smooth, and filled with something like grief.

"Marked?" Nyv asked.

"By the innkeeper. Dalebar."

Bryn looked up. "Inevin?"

The figure nodded. "He has not forgotten what heroes can be. He saw what walks behind you. He asked me to watch."

113

Tassa narrowed her eyes. "So you *can* stop them. Why didn't you sooner?"

"I cannot stop what has already been set in motion. Only preserve what must endure."

Kaerda lowered her shield. "Then who are you?"

They bowed their head slightly.

"I am Selvestar. I serve balance. I am not your weapon. I am your warning."

They turned to leave, shadows curling around their feet.

Bryn stood. "Will we see you again?"

Selvestar paused.

"Only if you are very lucky. Or very unfortunate."

They vanished.

● ● ●

The group stood in silence for a long while.

Geoff the Newt emerged slowly, blinking.

Tassa gave a shaky laugh. "So. That was dramatic."

Kaerda exhaled. "But effective."

Bryn looked toward the cave mouth.

"Something wanted us dead. Not just undead. *Us.*"

Nyv nodded. "And someone wants us alive. Which means this isn't random. This is a game. And now... we're on the board."

Outside, the wind shifted.

And far away, the procession marched on without its prey, but not without purpose.

Something had marked them.

And now, something greater was watching.

Chapter 8: What the Eyes Remember

He did not dream. There was no sleep in him—
not anymore.

But there were visions.

Images clawed at the inside of his mind, endless and repeating: a cracked bell. A burning city. A boy with white hair staring at him through a shattered window. He did not know the boy. Or the window. Or the city.
But he *remembered* them.
That was all that mattered.

He walked.

Each step was a prayer.
Each footfall a drumbeat in the silence between death and what follows.
The dead did not speak to him.
They followed.
That was enough.

He stood now upon a rise of charred stone, looking eastward across the river valley. Below, a village began to stir. A mill turned. A dog barked. A woman opened a window and tossed out a pan of water.

His head tilted.

He did not remember his name.

But he remembered purpose.

Behind him, they waited. Not merely a horde—an echo of forgotten lives. The bones of generations left unburied, ungrieved, unnamed.

The air shimmered behind him. A ripple. A presence.

He turned to face it.

A figure stood there, robed in shadow. No face. No form. Only pressure—cold and ancient.

He did not kneel. He only bowed his head.

"Soon," the pressure said, without voice. "Velkhar."

A map unfolded across his mind. Not ink and parchment—memory.
Streets he had never walked.
Walls he had never touched.
And yet, he knew every brick.

"There are still the marked ones," he thought. Though he had no mouth, the words carried.

The pressure pulsed.

"They walk in shadow. They delay. But they cannot stop.
You are the door."

He raised a hand—bone-white, slender, unnatural.

At his gesture, the bones of a nearby corpse shuddered and rose. A woman. Once a mother. Now only a vessel.

She stood. Silent.

He pointed, and she turned north.

Others would follow.

He turned again to the east. Toward Velkhar.
Where the living forgot their dead.
Where names had become numbers.
Where pride still held the gate.

He smiled without lips.

And walked on.

● ● ●

Far behind him, in a forest smothered by silence, one of Bryn's ravens watched from a blackened tree.

It turned. Took flight.

And flew as fast as shadow could carry it.

Chapter 9: The Whisper Beneath the Veil

The fire burned low. No one slept.

They had travelled far from the battlefield, from Selvestar's cave, from the cold death-march that nearly claimed them all. Yet distance brought no comfort.

Tassa stared into the flames, her brow furrowed. "That was just one group. One branch. And it almost killed us."

Kaerda sat cross-legged, hammer across her knees. "We can't fight numbers like that. Not without something more."

Nyv nodded slowly. "They weren't even looking for us. Not yet. What happens when they are?"

Geoff the Newt chirped quietly and nestled deeper into Nyv's cloak.

Bryn sat apart, the soft glow of her spellbook illuminating her face. Her eyes hadn't moved from the page in nearly an hour.

"We cannot outrun this," she whispered.

Bone-Anna stood behind her, silent and still.

Nyv rose. "Bryn. What are you thinking?"

Bryn closed the book. Looked up.

"I am going to ask Her."

● ● ●

They travelled two more days, away from the roads, following whispers only Bryn could hear. The landscape changed with each mile. Trees bent away from a forgotten trail, and moss grew in strange shapes across ancient stone. Somewhere in the foothills of the Dragonjaw Mountains, they found it.

A clearing in the forest. Perfectly circular. At its centre stood a structure of black slate and silver-veined stone—an altar, long buried and now cracked open by time.

Bryn stepped into the circle. The others watched from the edge, wary.

She knelt. Drew a raven feather from her satchel—a gift from her Queen long ago—and held it to her lips.

"If you hear me," she murmured, "I ask not for power. Only a way forward."

The feather caught in an unseen wind and vanished.

Shadows spilled from the altar.

A soft warmth curled along her hand. The mark shimmered—faint, but awake. The Queen was listening.

The world dropped away.

● ● ●

She stood in a place that was not a place.

The air was weightless, heavy with silence. Beneath her feet, feathers. Above her, darkness. In front of her—

A figure. A woman made of memory and grief, crowned in shadows.

The Queen of Stillness.

Her face was ever-changing. Sometimes Bryn's mother. Sometimes herself. Sometimes no one.

Bryn did not speak. She could not.

The Queen raised a single hand. And pointed.

A ruin appeared.

A temple, long lost, swallowed by roots and time. Deep within it, a chamber. And within the chamber, two books. One open. One bound shut with chains of blackened bone.

A whisper coiled through Bryn's mind:

"You may read the one that echoes. Not the one that binds. Not yet."

The mark shimmered coldly as Bryn stepped into the chamber—its light no longer warm, but pale and watchful. The Queen was near. Not close enough to guide. But close enough to witness.

Then she was falling.

• • •

Bryn awoke with a gasp.

The others had already stepped into the circle, drawn by the shadows that had curled upward in her absence. Bryn stood, her eyes clearer than they had been in weeks.

The feather mark on her hand glowed with the faint sheen of ink and frost—memory made light. The Queen had spoken, and part of her remained.

"I know where to go."

• • •

The ruin took another day to reach. Half-buried in a ravine, its upper floors long collapsed, it rose like a broken tooth from the forest floor. Vines clung to its surface like veins.

Inside, they passed murals long faded. Statues broken at the neck. Names scratched from altars. And finally, beneath the sanctuary, a door sealed in ice.

Before they could approach, six stone faces carved into the wall beside the door spoke in unison. The voices were hollow, layered in time.

"Six truths from six mouths. Only one must lie. Choose the false, or remain outside."

Below each face, an inscription appeared:

"The Queen loves only silence."

"The dead do not feel pain."

"Undeath is freedom."

"Grief is weaker than rage."

"Names bind souls."

"Memory fades even in death."

The group stood silently, reading the inscriptions. Tassa scowled. "Well that's comforting."

They took time. Debated. Each truth carried weight—but also danger. They circled the inscriptions, offering interpretations and counterpoints. Nothing leapt out clearly as false.

Nyv muttered, "One lie among them."

Kaerda crossed her arms. "Grief is weaker than rage? That feels false. Grief can drive you to anything."

"But rage burns hotter," Nyv countered. "It moves faster."

Tassa pointed at the first. "The Queen loves only silence? That feels like a riddle. But... it might still be true. She is the goddess of memory, yes—but memory lives in stillness. In reverence. She's not a deity of songs or praise. She values quiet, the acceptance of death. Silence isn't absence to her. It's devotion."

Bryn studied the fifth inscription. "Names bind souls. That... that one feels true. It's ancient magic. Names always mattered."

Kaerda shook her head. "Then what about number two? 'The dead do not feel pain'? That sounds like it's meant to comfort, but it's shallow. We've seen the way some of them move, the way they *scream*. Not just sound—for some, it's almost like memory. They reach for old wounds, or recoil from certain spells. That inscription assumes pain is only physical. But undead feel something deeper. Not pain through nerves—pain through memory, compulsion, regret. Pain leaves a shape, even after death. That shape moves them still."

Tassa looked at the fourth again. "Grief and rage are twins. Neither is weaker. Just different."

Nyv nodded toward the sixth. "And this one—'Memory fades even in death.' That's hard. But I think it's true, too. We've seen spirits lose themselves. Seen undead that don't even remember their own names. The soul tries to hold on, but it unravels. Death is silence. And silence forgets."

Kaerda added quietly, "It's why we forge names into steel. Because without something to bind memory, it bleeds away, slow and quiet."

Tassa frowned. "And 'Undeath is freedom'... that's the one that doesn't sit right. It reads like propaganda."

Nyv nodded. "It's a promise made to justify a curse."

Bryn stepped slowly forward, her mind lingering on every argument, her hand hovering over the third.

"Undeath isn't freedom. It's theft. It takes choice, memory, and will."

She placed her palm against the third face.

The stone cracked. The ice on the door hissed and receded, melting away.

She spoke a word in Elvish. The last of the frost dissolved into mist.

They entered.

● ● ●

The chamber was circular, with six pillars surrounding a single stone dais.

Upon it rested two books.

The first lay open. Its script danced across the pages like drifting smoke.

The second was bound in sinew and sealed with bone. It pulsed faintly when Bryn approached.

She reached out. Touched the open one.

Knowledge poured into her. A ritual. A whisper.

Walking With The Dead: Place a copper beneath the tongue. Speak the Queen's hidden name. Step beyond sight. For one hour, no undead shall mark you—so long as no hand is raised, and no magic cast.

She staggered back.

"I can do it. We can pass them."

Tassa tilted her head. "And the other book?"

Bryn moved toward it. Reached out.

The room dimmed.

A tension filled the air, like the breath before a scream. A voice—not heard but felt—brushed her soul.

121

"Not yet. When the silence becomes sanctuary. When the end begins. Then, child."

Though the book remained sealed, she took it.

Kaerda stepped beside her. "Then let's take what we can now. And earn the rest."

They left the ruin together.

And the book pulsed behind them, waiting.

● ● ●

That night, Bryn sat alone by the fire, whispering the new ritual to herself. She felt no triumph. Only resolve. And the weight of the path ahead. She closed her eyes and bowed her head briefly, silently thanking the Queen of Stillness for her guidance.

Bone-Anna watched from the treeline.

And far away, beneath the soil, something else listened.

Chapter 10: The Silent Watch

Kaerda rarely took second watch, but tonight she had offered without being asked. The others had retreated into a makeshift camp tucked beneath a crescent of moss-covered stone. Bryn slept with one hand resting on the ritual book. Tassa was snoring lightly. Nyv's mask lay beside her bedroll, her expression peaceful—for once.

The night was still. The forest hushed. Only the low crackle of the fire broke the silence.

Kaerda stood at the edge of the firelight, hammer across her back, arms folded. Her eyes swept the treeline. Then, as if something unseen whispered to her, she turned.

Selvestar stood just beyond the fire's glow.

Kaerda didn't reach for her weapon. She simply inclined her head.

"You walk softly."

Selvestar gave the faintest nod. "I walk only where I must."

They stood in silence for a long moment.

Then Kaerda asked, "Is it time again?"

"Not for me," Selvestar said. Their lantern—still dark—swayed gently, its movement whispering like distant bells. "But for you... yes."

Kaerda said nothing. She waited.

Selvestar stepped closer, and the shadows bent away from them.

"You know now what walks. You've seen its reach. Hollow cities. The organised dead."

Kaerda's jaw tightened. "I've also seen how little we can do against it."

Selvestar regarded her, storm-lit eyes unreadable.

"And yet you're still here. Still choosing to face it."

"We protect what we can. We always have."

Selvestar reached into their cloak and produced a folded strip of parchment. They offered it to Kaerda.

She opened it. A map. Markings. A river crossing. A town circled in silver ink.

"What is this?"

"The next to fall," Selvestar said. "The horde marches for it—three days at most. Not yet in full force. But their scouts have come. Rituals are stirring. Defences are thinning."

Kaerda frowned. "And you're telling me because…?"

"Because you can reach it first. Prepare it. Turn the tide—not with strength. With strategy. With memory."

Kaerda folded the map. "Why us? Why *me*?"

Selvestar's voice softened. "Because you haven't lost your purpose. Not to rage. Not to fear. You build. That is rare. And it is needed."

Kaerda exhaled—long and quiet. "We'll go."

Selvestar nodded. "You'll have to use the ritual."

"*Allowing us to walk with the dead?*"

"Yes. Use it well. The veil will hide you—but it is thin."

Kaerda looked toward the camp.

"Do they need to know you were here?"

"Only what matters."

She turned back—but Selvestar was already gone.

Only the map remained in her hand.

● ● ●

Morning came with mist and silence. Kaerda passed the map to Bryn without a word. The others gathered quickly.

"We're heading here," Kaerda said, pointing to the silver-ringed town.

Nyv studied it. "That's Estavar. Riverfront trade post. Decent walls."

"Three days," Kaerda said. "We'll beat the horde there. We prepare, defend—and when they arrive, we end them."

Tassa grinned. "Finally."

Bryn nodded, voice low. "We'll use the ritual. Pass through their shadows. Prepare the light."

Geoff the Newt raised a tiny fist.

Bone-Anna strung her bow without comment.

And together, The Silent Accord turned east.

Toward Estavar.

Toward the first place the dead would march on—and fail.

Chapter 11: The Tide We Choose

The spell was cast in silence.

Bryn knelt in a crumbling shrine outside Estavar's eastern wall, the townspeople watching from a respectful distance. She placed a copper piece beneath her tongue, whispered the Queen of Stillness's hidden name, and released the ritual's magic. One by one, she placed her hand over each companion's chest, then Geoff the Newt's tiny snout. Shadows curled around them like ink in water.

The veil settled.

They were dead to the undead. For now.

But there was an unexpected side effect. Bone-Anna, too, could no longer see them. Though her hollow gaze swept over the area without recognition, she still moved as if tethered by instinct to Bryn's presence. Wherever Bryn led, Bone-Anna followed, as if guided by memory alone.

They moved quickly.

Through forest and field, bypassing a trio of shambling scouts. At the riverbank, they watched a robed figure plant bone sigils beneath the surface—preparations for the coming ritual. They marked the site.

By dusk they stood atop Estavar's inner wall, the ritual fading. Bryn's breath shuddered.

"We have a few days now before we need to cast it again. Let's make every moment count."

Kaerda nodded. "We will."

● ● ●

The town of Estavar was not large. No garrison. Just a fishermen's militia and aging veterans. But it had a natural moat: the River Telwin split the town in two. Only one stone bridge connected the halves.

They built their plan from that.

Nyv and Tassa worked together to rig the bridge with magical traps: glyphs hidden beneath cobblestones, delayed fire sigils etched into the masonry.

Kaerda reinforced the east-facing palisades and trained the militia to form shield walls. Bryn marked the graveyard with protective wards and consecrated the shrine.

Bone-Anna climbed the bell tower each morning to observe.

And they waited.

● ● ●

The dead came on the third night.

Hundreds.

They moved like water, surrounding Estavar with a silent flood. The townsfolk quailed. But Kaerda stood tall atop the gate.

"We will not fall," she said. "We will not feed their hunger."

The undead advanced.

The first wave hit the palisade—and Glyphs of Warding detonated in cascades of flame and force. Bodies flung skyward, limbs blown apart. Tassa raised both arms and cast a wall of fire, a searing curtain erupting across the outer street, funneling the charging undead into a narrow corridor between burning barricades.

"Now!" she shouted.

Bone-Anna, perched in the bell tower, loosed arrow after arrow into the compressed ranks. Her shots were cold, precise, and ceaseless. Though she could not see the group, she followed Bryn's intent like a phantom tether.

Bryn and Nyv stood just behind the inner gate. With a shared nod, they raised their hands in unison.

"*Rakae*," Bryn intoned.

The air trembled. A thunderous pulse cracked the ground, shattering bones and splintering skulls Like a kernel of corn becoming popcorn. Psychic screams filled the night—not from fear, but from the tearing of existence itself. The undead reeled.

Another pulse erupted to their right, launched by Nyv, as she shouted, "*Rakae!*" The combined force collapsed an entire wave of the assault, their broken remains skidding across the cobblestones.

Tassa hurled a fire-charged auric ember. The sphere blazed with red-orange flame, struck a dense cluster of enemies—and rebounded, arcing to another, and another. Each bounce triggered an explosion of fire and bone. Twelve corpses dropped in a chain of detonations before the spell finally flickered out. It struck a dense cluster of enemies—and rebounded, arcing to another, and another.

She blinked in surprise. "That never happens. I mean—twelve? That was lucky."

Kaerda, at the breach, shouted over the roar. "Hold the gaps! They're thinning!"

Elsewhere, the townsfolk proved their mettle. A squad of militia led by a wiry old fisherman named Halen held the north alley—armed with spears reinforced by Kaerda's instruction and lit torches. When a smaller contingent of undead tried to flank the town, the militia held firm. With a coordinated shove, they forced the corpses into a dead-end lane soaked in lamp oil. A spark from a trembling young woman named Calira set the trap ablaze, turning the alley into a pyre. When the flames died, only smoke and bone remained.

Their victory wasn't just borrowed from the adventurers—it was earned in sweat and steel.

Bryn launched another clash of glaciers down the main thoroughfare, icy boulders crushing the advance and leaving behind a slick path where the undead faltered.

Bone-Anna never stopped firing.

Their line held.

The bridge became the final choke point.

Kaerda shouted, "Now!"

Nyv triggered the last fire glyph. The bridge collapsed in an explosion of fire and ice, sweeping a third of the horde into the river.

Those that remained turned to scatter. But the townspeople, emboldened, pressed the line.

And the undead faltered.

They had not expected resistance.

They had not expected strategy.

They had not expected hope.

● ● ●

Dawn broke over a broken field.

The battle had raged for hours, stretching through the dead of night into the grey hush of morning. Estavar had become a crucible of fire, frost, and willpower, where the tides of death were turned back only by the relentless resolve of those who refused to fall.

The undead were ash and ice, their sigils shattered, their scouts hunted. Estavar held.

But the cost had been steep. Bryn's fingers trembled as she turned the ritual book's pages, her reserves nearly spent. The glow around Nyv's bracers had dimmed, her spells cast into the marrow of the fight. Tassa had no more orbs prepared, her magic flickering at the edges of exhaustion. Even Geoff the Newt looked weary, his fire-dappled belly dulled to a quiet orange.

Kaerda's shield was notched, her arms bruised from the force of undead strikes. The townsfolk's arrows were nearly gone, their shields splintered and spears worn. Bone-Anna's quiver was empty, though she remained silent, her bowstring frayed and thin.

This was a victory won with every last breath, spell, and arrow.

Kaerda surveyed the aftermath, blood on her armour, breath steady.

Bryn sat with the open ritual book in her lap, watching the wind scatter bone-dust across the grass.

Tassa leaned on her crossbow, grinning. "Well. That worked."

Nyv, quiet, just nodded. Geoff the Newt peeked from her hood and gave a satisfied chirp.

Bone-Anna remained in the bell tower. Watching the eastern road.

"This was only one," Kaerda said.

"Yes," Bryn replied. "But it was *ours*."

● ● ●

Far to the east, the man with no mouth stood on a cliff above a rising tide of his own.

He stared toward the smoking hills.

His thoughts seethed. His will sharpened.

They had resisted.

They had won.

And something ancient beneath him stirred—angry, and no longer content to wait.

The next wave would not be so kind.

Chapter 12: Ashes and Echoes

Estavar held.

But it did not celebrate.

The morning after the battle was filled with labor. Shovels struck earth. Prayers were whispered, not sung. Bryn, Tassa, and Bone-Anna remained behind to help the town bury its dead. Bryn walked among the makeshift graves with solemn grace, whispering rites beneath her breath. Shadows gathered briefly over each burial mound as she placed a single raven feather beside each marker.

Bone-Anna stood watch at the perimeter. Though she was not asked to, she never left her post. When the children of Estavar looked at her with quiet awe, Bryn simply said, "She remembers what it means to guard the living."

Tassa, ever uncomfortable with stillness, helped with repairs to the eastern wall. Between hammer strikes she taught a pair of young militia how to spot arcane traces and explained—through half-hearted grumbling—why not all orbs explode the way hers did.

Meanwhile, Nyv and Kaerda departed to the north with a fisherman named Deylen, who had once served as a river guide. Geoff the Newt rode Nyv's shoulder, tiny claws hooked into her cloak.

They began with Tern Hollow, a sleepy village nestled beneath river cliffs. When Nyv approached the town square in her Veilwarden robes, silence fell. Farmers and weavers bowed their heads; an elder knelt and offered a sprig of wolfsbane.

"We did not know the Seidra walked these lands again," he said. "What spirit guides you?"

"The one who watches from behind the veil," Nyv replied.

They met with the council and detailed Estavar's survival. Kaerda brought out sigils and maps, and Deylen spoke of the unnatural silence that preceded the assault. The villagers agreed to build new defences. A young tanner volunteered to ferry warnings upriver.

In Linas Bridge, a larger town built along the split-current banks, Nyv entered the temple square and was greeted by a hush. A Veilwarden was not seen as mere adventurer here. She was law. She was legacy. Children were ushered back, and a priest offered her the town's ceremonial torch.

She refused it gently.

"Not fire for fire's sake. But to hold the dark at bay."

Kaerda spent the afternoon training the guard. Geoff the Newt offered unprompted bursts of flame as punctuation. In the tavern that night, a group of locals asked to rename their square the Accord Yard.

Gorse-by-the-Reeds was harder. Suspicious. Closed. But when Kaerda placed a half-burned undead sigil on the table before the village chief and said, "This floated down your river. Will you wait to see what else follows?"—they listened.

In every town, they left behind not fear, but *resolve*.

Prepare. Organise. Build traps. Call for aid. The dead are not mindless. They are *led*.

● ● ●

Three days passed. Nyv, Kaerda, Geoff the Newt, and Deylen were still a day's journey from Estavar when the confrontation began. They returned the next morning, greeted by the uneasy hush of a town still reeling. Though the battle had ended hours before, the air remained heavy with echoes of what had passed, and Bryn stood pale but tall beside Bone-Anna. The signs of conflict had not marred the streets, but something heavy lingered in the air.

Before that moment, Tassa had left the town centre at Bryn's suggestion to aid with rebuilding the river dam that powered Estavar's mill. She had laughed it off—"Sure, I'll go plug a hole with magic"—but in truth, the work mattered. It fed the town. And she'd earned the trust of its engineers. It meant Bryn stood nearly alone when the undead arrived.

"It worked," Nyv said. "Some are readying themselves. Others need more time."

"They won't get it," Bryn replied softly. She stood atop the bell tower, her eyes scanning the horizon.

A wind passed through the streets. Cold. Unseasonable.

And then he came.

He did not arrive with an army.

He walked alone through the eastern gate, and the townsfolk felt it first—not fear, but a suffocating wrongness. Children were pulled inside. Elders bowed their heads, though they didn't know why. The guards froze, unsure why their hands would not move to weapons.

He was tall. Gaunt. Pale as raw parchment. Robes of grey and bone hung from narrow shoulders. His eyes were gold coins sunken in shadowed sockets.

And he *spoke*.

Not aloud, but within the minds of everyone present.

"*You are late, little raven. The Queen turns her face, and you speak her name in vain.*"

Bryn descended the tower slowly.

"You should not exist."

He smiled without warmth.

"*And yet, here I am. Memory stitched into flesh. Thought bound to rot. Her silence gave birth to something... purer.*"

A member of the town militia raised their crossbow.

"*Shoot and you doom your town,*" the creature warned, smiling wider. "*I came to see. To learn. Not to burn.*"

Kaerda was not there. Tassa was gone. Bryn stood alone with Bone-Anna at her side, and the townsfolk could only watch, unable to speak, as if the air itself held its breath.

The creature tilted its head. "*I already have. You cannot stop the tide, only ride it.*"

Bryn raised her hand. Shadows curled around her fingers.

"Then come ride it through me."

He laughed—a hollow, brittle sound like bones knocking in a chest.

"*Soon. Not today. Today, you bury hope. Tomorrow, you bury flame.*"

No one knew what he meant. But the words did not leave them.

And then, without so much as a step, he vanished.

Not gone. Just *elsewhere.*

Bone-Anna notched a new arrow anyway.

Bryn stared at the space he left behind.

"That was no ordinary undead."

Nyv and the others returned the next morning, their arrival marked by quiet embraces and sombre nods. The townsfolk had told them everything.

As Bryn finished placing the last feather over a grave, Nyv approached. She exhaled. "What was he?"

Kaerda's brow furrowed. "Where did that power come from? What force makes a thing like that?"

"An abomination," Bryn said. "Something that should not think. Should not speak. Should not remember."

Kaerda looked east.

"He will come back."

Bryn shook her head. "Could be any of the gods of death. Maybe something older, something quieter. I don't know for sure yet."

She looked toward the east, toward the road they'd all feared they'd take.

"I'm tired of being forced to react. We'll go to him."

Geoff the Newt chirped softly.

The wind rose.

And the silence felt like a warning.

Chapter 13: The Trail Beyond the Flame

They departed Estavar before dawn, silent and shadow-bound.

Bryn walked at the front.

She said little, but her presence was enough. Shadows licked at her heels like watchful dogs, and her ravens circled high above the forest path. Each step carried intention. The others followed without question.

Behind her strode Kaerda, heavy pack over one shoulder, shield slung across her back—occasionally glancing at the terrain with a soldier's eye, marking disturbances and subtle trails. Nyv and Geoff the Newt brought up the centre, the little lizard alert and restless. Tassa, begrudgingly awake, toyed with the remaining gems for her next orb, muttering about the wrong kind of dew on her boots. Bone-Anna, silent as ever, trailed them like a wraith.

They left the safety of Estavar's reach and followed what little the lieutenant had left behind: traces of necrotic energy, disturbed soil, and whispers among the trees.

That evening, Nyv gave them direction. Standing among the roots of an ancient elm, she knelt and pressed both palms to the moss-covered earth. Her voice lowered into a chant, soft and musical, invoking *Commune with Nature*. The winds shifted. The trees seemed to listen. The world held its breath.

After several long minutes, her eyes opened—burning faintly with silver light.

"He passed through here," she said. "East by southeast. Two days ahead. Undead. Walking. Thinking. Twisting the land with every step."

Bryn gave a solemn nod. "Then we're on the right path."

Something twisted lingered in the air.

● ● ●

They reached a hill by midday, and Bryn called a halt. She knelt at the crest and pressed her fingers into the earth.

"It's here," she said.

"The trail?" Kaerda asked.

"The echo. It's faint, but he passed through. Recently."

137

Bryn removed a small bone token from her satchel—one she had carved back in Kaerdahl Hold. Whispering a prayer to the Queen of Stillness, she placed it at the base of a crooked tree. Shadows curled inward.

From the darkness emerged a form—not flesh, but memory.

A spectral image of the lieutenant passed silently across the glade.

"That was him," Nyv said, eyes narrowed. "But where was he going?"

The image turned, paused, and though incorporeal, seemed to lock eyes with Bryn—aware, deliberate—before dissolving into mist.

Tassa muttered, "I hate when dead things notice us."

"East," Bryn said. "He's circling something. Not heading straight for Velkhar."

"A staging ground?" Kaerda asked.

"Or a ritual site," Bryn replied.

• • •

The path led them into the Weeping Marshes.

No maps covered the region in detail. Locals claimed the dead whispered through the reeds. Now, those whispers had become screams.

The fog thickened. Light dimmed.

"I don't like this," Tassa said, hurling a pebble that vanished into the mist with a plop.

"You're not meant to," Nyv replied. "This place remembers."

Geoff the Newt hissed and flattened against Nyv's collarbone.

A half-drowned stone circle emerged from the mist, its standing stones covered in old elven script. Bryn stopped short.

"This was sacred once. I think... it still is. But corrupted."

At the circle's centre lay a corpse, pinned to the earth by bone stakes. Kaerda moved first, inspecting it.

"He was a priest. Of Elunara, by the markings."

The body shuddered.

A breathless voice rasped, "He walks... on borrowed light... she... she knows not... he remembers... too much..."

Then silence.

Bryn closed the man's eyes and took the bone stakes. She examined one briefly. Its carvings matched the style etched in the ruined village. A pattern was forming.

"He was a message. Left for me."

"Deliberately?" Kaerda asked.

"Yes."

• • •

They made camp in the circle that night, unable to move further in the mist.

Kaerda took first watch. Bryn joined her for a time.

"You've changed," Kaerda said.

Bryn didn't look up. "How so?"

"You lead now. And not just because others follow. Because they *should*."

Bryn didn't smile, but her voice softened. "I'm tired of waiting. Of watching people die."

Kaerda nodded. "Then we'll stop them. Together."

• • •

By the third day, they reached higher ground overlooking a long valley.

The sight robbed them of breath.

Below lay a sea of motionless figures. Undead—hundreds, perhaps thousands—stood in eerie stillness. At the far end of the valley, a ruined fort pulsed with a low red glow. Ritual fires burned along its walls. Something *massive* moved in the shadows behind them.

Nyv lowered her spyglass. "They're not marching yet."

"They will," Bryn said.

Tassa exhaled. "How do we even scratch that?"

"Not with force," Kaerda replied. "With patience. And precision."

"With faith," Bryn said. "He's not unreachable. He's just hidden. And now—we have a trail."

Geoff the Newt raised a claw dramatically.

Bone-Anna stood beside Bryn.

They looked out over the valley as the sun dipped behind the mountains.

Bryn whispered, "We find the cracks. We break them open. And then...

We burn the rot from the inside."

Chapter 14: The Spark That Burns

They did not wait long.

As night cloaked the valley, the party gathered beneath the boughs of a fallen pine just above the ridgeline. Below, the ruined fort pulsed with low red fire, and the undead stood in patient silence, as if dreaming upright.

Bryn laid the plan out carefully. "We only need him to leave the safety of the fort. Once he's alone, I'll face him. But there's something darker waiting ahead. I can feel it. We can't spend everything on him."

Kaerda frowned. "Worse than him?"

Bryn nodded. "The man with no mouth. This one is his sword—not his shadow."

They each nodded grimly.

• • •

The distraction began an hour before dawn.

Kaerda led a team of Estavari scouts to the northern ridge, lighting a string of decoy campfires in a pattern the undead might interpret as a second militia force. She struck flint and whispered prayers over each fire, her shield catching stray moonlight like a silent beacon.

At the same time, Nyv stood at the edge of the lower marsh, invoking minor illusions of movement, torches, and low whispers carried by the wind. *Commune with Nature* had told her where the fog would flow—so she shaped it with subtle winds to veil their tricks.

Geoff the Newt scampered across the edges of a dried creek bed, sparking flares of elemental light and echoing footfalls. His little limbs moved fast, and his trail mimicked a dozen soldiers.

The army stirred. Dozens of undead split from the core and began marching toward the false activity—just as planned.

• • •

Tassa, meanwhile, waited until the first sliver of sunrise. Perched in a pine overlooking the southern edge of the fort, she whispered a soft string of words into her *Chromatic Orb*, then hurled it like a comet.

It struck a spire of bone and charred stone—one of the pylons that marked the edge of the lieutenant's ritual perimeter. The blast lit the hill in a wash of molten fire and orange light. Chunks of the pylon rained down, cracking the outer defences.

"That should do it," she grinned, vanishing into the trees.

● ● ●

But the most critical piece moved alone.

Bone-Anna had left at midnight, walking without breath or heat. She passed the first ranks of undead without so much as a glance. Her presence stirred no reaction—they saw only kin.

She crept among broken towers and gutted barracks, slipping between sentinels and walkers. The fortress stank of old blood and cold ash. She counted hundreds in silent formation, each one tethered to the lieutenant's dark will.

She moved to the heart of the camp.

At the base of a shattered altar, where a statue of Lemvor had once stood, now corrupted and broken, Bone-Anna knelt.

In her hand, she carried a small, hand-carved token of bone: a raven in flight, its wings etched with broken chains and flame.

The token pulsed faintly with energy. Bryn had carved it with a mixture of bone dust, charcoal, and her own blood. It held no explosive power—but it was a message.

It whispered defiance. It echoed the Queen of Stillness's grief and fury. It was a death sentence wrapped in devotion.

Bone-Anna placed it at the foot of the broken god.

Minutes later, the lieutenant arrived.

He walked in silence, parting the undead like fog. His golden eyes burned in the dim, and when he reached the corrupted altar, he paused.

His gaze fell on the token.

He knelt slowly, as if unsure what he was seeing—then plucked it from the stone and turned it in his pale fingers. The raven etched in flight. The broken chains. The flame.

Recognition flickered in his eyes.

Then—rage.

His fingers clenched around the token with such force it cracked, but he did not break it fully. Instead, he held it up toward the eastern trees.

"Your Queen is dying in silence," he whispered, voice like gravel dragged across bone. "And still her little carrion things bite at my ankles."

He rose.

"So be it."

He tucked the token into his belt—*a trophy and a vow*—and turned toward the ridge.

It would be his undoing.

His anger.

His pride.

His choice to come alone.

● ● ●

Atop the hill, Bryn stood waiting at the edge of a long-forgotten battlefield—not consecrated, but scarred by memory. It was here she would stand.

Moments later, Bone-Anna emerged from the trees.

And in the far distance, a shape began to move.

The lieutenant walked alone.

Drawn by the flame.

Drawn by the insult.

Drawn by the Queen's mark.

143

Bryn whispered, "Let him come."

As Bryn raised her eyes to the figure before her, the feather mark on her hand flared—brighter than it had in days. Even without hearing the Queen's voice, she felt the presence settle around her like a cloak. Not command. Not power. Just presence.

The ground trembled.

And the shadows held their breath.

Chapter 15: The Duel

He stepped into the clearing with the silence of death, the broken bone token still tucked into his belt like a talisman of vengeance. Bryn stood twenty paces away, one hand lifted and outstretched, shadows licking at her heels. Her space-bun hair was wind-tossed, her silver-etched coat rippling with ghost-light.

"You should have stayed behind your wall of corpses," she called.

The lieutenant gave a slow, mechanical bow. "And miss the honour of carving down the last flicker of her will?"

With a whisper of force, Bryn uttered the arcane words for her eldritch blast—"*márna rúvína*"—as her hand snapped forward. A raven-shaped burst shrieked across the clearing, dark with violet fire. The lieutenant twisted, and it clipped his side, sending a spray of necrotic ash into the air.

He lunged forward.

Bryn moved. With a flicker of shadow, she teleported twenty feet to the left, reappearing behind a moss-covered stone. Another raven-shaped blast struck his chest as he turned, Bryn's voice still echoing: "*márna rúvína!*"

He snarled. "Cowardice in motion is not courage."

"You confuse distance with fear," Bryn replied. "And anger with strength."

He charged, blade drawn—a massive weapon of rusted metal and fused bone. Bryn ducked behind a crumbling pillar, uttering the arcane words, "*gwâth thúrín.*" Instantly, her form blurred, wrapped in flame-like darkness.

The lieutenant swung wide, striking a stone slab and cleaving it in half.

Bryn emerged from the gloom, her voice sharp and clear: "*ehte forochel!*"—bringing the force of a glacier to bear. Icy boulders surged across the ground, crashing into his legs and knocking him off balance. He roared, breaking free in a burst of necrotic power.

He reached her.

With a grunt, he slammed the hilt of his blade into her ribs. Bryn cried out, stumbling backward. Blood slicked her side. Her magic faltered.

He raised his blade for the killing stroke—

An arrow struck his shoulder.

Bone-Anna, perched on a ridge beneath a half-collapsed tree, drew again. Her skeletal fingers moved with precision born of both memory and magic. The second arrow found its mark in his side, forcing him to adjust his balance. He glanced toward the source—then dismissed her. She wasn't one of the living. Not a threat.

A mistake.

The force of her next arrow—an elemental shaft infused with poison—drove him back a full step and spoiled his timing. It bought Bryn the moment she needed to recover.

Bryn rolled, hand glowing with defiant magic. "*márna rúvína*!" The eldritch blast flew—then another, and a third, each shaped like a raven streaking with force and shadow. The lieutenant snarled and charged again.

This time, he was faster.

His blade slashed low, catching her across the thigh. Bryn cried out and nearly fell, blood soaking through her boot. He raised the blade again—slow, heavy, certain. But she gritted her teeth and lifted one trembling hand.

"You don't—"

Whatever he meant to say was lost.

A circle of pure black opened beneath him. "*dúil pórth*!" Bryn cried—arcane Elven words meant to summon a portal below him first, followed by another above him.

The lieutenant vanished in a rush of air and force—and a moment later reappeared high above, falling fast.

He crashed through a skeletal tree, snapping branches that hissed with necrotic residue, and struck the earth with a jarring, echoing crack. Dust exploded outward. A ring of frost marked the spot where he landed, and pieces of scorched earth curled like old paper beneath him.

He struck the earth hard, landing on his back with a bone-crunching thud. Dust rose around him. He groaned, momentarily stunned and vulnerable.

Bryn stood, favouring her wounded leg thirty feet from where she had been, breath ragged. Her magic reserves were nearly gone; the energy around her shimmered with exhaustion. Her vision blurred at the edges, colour draining from the world like ink in water. Her shadow curled protectively around her, its tendrils beginning to unravel, fraying as though barely holding their form. Still, she stepped into her final stance, whispering thanks to the Queen she could no longer hear—but still trusted.

The lieutenant began to rise—but too slowly.

He turned wildly, searching.

"Where are you?!"

Her voice came from behind him: "Exactly where you led me."

He turned—and took the final strike.

Bryn's hand plunged forward, a burst of force erupting from her palm. The raven-shaped blast tore through his chest. The token on his belt cracked and fell apart.

He staggered.

"She will abandon you. Just as she did me."

Bryn stepped closer, eyes calm. "You never waited."

The light faded from his golden eyes.

He fell to his knees, then collapsed.

Silence.

Bryn sank to the ground, clutching her ribs.

Bone-Anna approached, bow lowered. She crouched beside Bryn, skeletal fingers resting lightly on her shoulder.

Bryn whispered, "We won."

She looked down at his broken form, then leaned closer and added, just above a whisper, "Your rage made you predictable. My Queen taught me patience."

But the wind whispered through the battlefield, and the ravens circled above.

Not in celebration.

In warning.

The true threat had yet to arrive.

Chapter 16: Lines in the Ash

They buried the lieutenant's body beneath a cairn of stone and frost. Bryn said no words. None felt necessary. Whatever man he once was had died long before she delivered the final blow. Bone-Anna stood sentinel beside the mound until the sun reached its highest point, then silently turned and followed Bryn back down the ridge.

By nightfall, the rest of the Silent Accord had returned.

They gathered in a small grove near the stream that fed Estavar. The air still carried the scent of ash and broken magic, but it was quiet now.

Nyv was the first to speak. "Three villages on the western tributary have fortified. Gorse-by-the-Reeds is holding drills. Tern Hollow is reinforcing bridges with warding charms. But they're scared."

Kaerda nodded. "Linas Bridge had a message carved into a tree just outside their fields. No tracks. Just... words burned into the bark. 'The mouthless one remembers. He sees beneath skin.'"

Tassa rolled a smooth fire-gem between her fingers. "Estavar's scouts found a dead tree with no bark and no leaves. Every knot and groove carved into eyes. Dozens of them."

Bryn's voice was low. "We've heard whispers. We've seen echoes. But this... this is a message, not madness."

"And it's spreading," Kaerda said.

Nyv looked to Bryn. "What do we do next?"

Instead of answering immediately, Bryn reached into her satchel and removed her ritual book. She flipped past familiar pages until she came to the one inked in her own blood.

"We use our newly discovered ritual to blend in. It won't stop them. But it will let us move through them."

Kaerda furrowed her brow. "And then what? Once we're inside their ranks, what do we do? We still don't know how to kill something we don't understand."

Bryn hesitated.

The second book—the one still bound by her Queen's silence—rested quietly in her pack. Its power hummed, locked away. Not yet.

"We get closer," she said finally. "We find out how far this rot has spread. We watch. We listen."

Nyv's voice was steady, but low. "And if we're discovered?"

Bryn looked up, her eyes clear. "Then we don't run. We make them afraid."

Geoff the Newt, perched on Nyv's shoulder, gave a small, approving chirp.

Tassa cracked her knuckles. "So when do we start?"

Bryn closed the book.

"Two days. We prepare. We rest. We make sure nothing watches us. Then we vanish into the dead."

● ● ●

And in the dark, the wind turned colder.

Far to the east, beyond hills thick with fog, unseen eyes blinked open.

And watched.

Chapter 17: The Eye of the Watcher

It began with a whisper.

In the hours before dawn, Nyv stood watch at the edge of camp, eyes scanning the treeline. Geoff the Newt stirred on her shoulder, and a prickle ran along her neck—a subtle pulse in the Worldthread.

Whispering an incantation, she cast *detect magic*.

Her eyes widened. A trace of divination shimmered faintly in the air above Kaerda, who slept near the fire.

Nyv stepped lightly across the clearing and knelt beside Bryn, shaking her gently awake.

"We're being watched. Divination magic."

Bryn rose quickly, breath shallow, and whispered, "He sees us."

She reached into her coat, retrieved a sliver of cold moonstone, and spoke the words *sharn eledeth*, granting her shadowlight vision to see what is hiding.

There, suspended in the moonlight above Kaerda's head, hung a fist-sized orb of soft light. Silent. Watching.

"A sensor," Bryn whispered.

Her hands moved again, this time weaving the pattern of *dispel magic*—but as the incantation neared completion, her voice caught.

A pressure built in her mind.

Something pushed back.

A will.

It didn't speak. It *pressed*. A silent hunger. A formless message: *You are seen.*

Bryn clenched her jaw and pushed harder, her voice growing louder, stronger.

"Your gaze ends here."

The pressure cracked. Light flared. The orb collapsed into itself and vanished with a faint pop of displaced air.

Bryn staggered.

"Are you alright?" Nyv asked, steadying her.

"I saw him," Bryn murmured. "Not clearly, but enough. A man—or what was once a man. No mouth. Eyes where they don't belong. Layers of skin drawn tight like parchment. He's somewhere far east, in fog. Mountains in the distance. He was using something of hers—Kaerda's. A shard of armour or a strand of hair."

Nyv's brow furrowed. "He's watching us through what we leave behind."

"Then we stop leaving anything," Bryn said. "And we burn what we can."

She turned back toward the dark east, her expression hardening.

"He'll know I saw him. He'll feel the break."

And in the fog beyond the mountains, unseen eyes blinked. And for the first time, they blinked in pain.

● ● ●

By midday, the party had gathered and set protective wards around their camp. Kaerda carved sigils into stones; Nyv whispered to the wind; Tassa created small bursts of flame to check for magical interference. It didn't take long.

Bone-Anna found it.

Near a fallen pine, nestled between roots, sat a small, eye-shaped stone. Perfectly round, the iris carved in spirals, its centre hollow.

Nyv's expression tightened. "That's not Vaulmar. It's older. Feral magic."

Kaerda's hand hovered over the stone. "It's cold. Too cold. Not just watching us—listening."

"And linked," Bryn said. "To him."

"Then we break it," Tassa said, raising her boot.

"No," Bryn interrupted. "We don't destroy it here. It's a tether. If we just sever it, he'll know we found it."

Nyv nodded. "We need to remove the root—not just the branch."

Kaerda glanced at the stone again. "So this stone—it isn't the same as the sensor?"

Bryn shook her head. "No. The sensor was a spell—temporary, distant. This is older. It's a crafted tether, embedded into the land itself. He didn't just want to see us. He wanted to *listen*. To *lurk*."

Nyv added, "It's like a buried ear, or an open wound. Destroying the sensor blinded him. This might be what *lets* him keep finding us."

● ● ●

The villagers had spoken of a place north of Estavar—Harrowfen, a grove long sealed off by bramble and superstition. It was said to twist the minds of those who entered and trap spirits that couldn't move on.

"That's where it's linked," Bryn said. "We remove it there, at the source. We do it right."

● ● ●

The journey took half a day. The forest grew silent as they approached, birdsong falling away into stillness. Geoff the Newt clung to Nyv's collar, eyes narrowed.

The trees arched unnaturally in Harrowfen. As if grown to deny sunlight. The path led them to a hollow wrapped in brambles. At the centre stood a stone well with no rope or bucket. Only shadow.

Bryn took the eye-shaped stone from Bone-Anna and stepped forward.

"Ready?" Kaerda asked.

"Not even slightly," Bryn replied, then dropped the stone into the well.

The effect was immediate.

The earth trembled. Black fog surged upward from the well's mouth, curling around the party. Images flickered: ghostly eyes in trees, the lieutenant's broken voice, Estavar in flames.

The magic surged to overwhelm them.

Bryn dropped to her knees and pressed a bone token to the ground. "He has no claim on us."

Kaerda raised her shield, her holy symbol of Durnach the Forgemaker glowing. "We forge our path. Not him."

Nyv cast a warding veil, wrapping them in natural stillness.

Tassa hurled fire into the mist, carving it away.

And Bone-Anna—silent and fearless—stood in the centre, her hand resting on Bryn's shoulder, a sentinel of bone and memory.

The darkness shrieked.

Then it broke.

Light spilled upward from the well. The tether was gone.

For a moment, silence fell like snowfall. The oppressive weight that had lingered at the edge of their thoughts lifted, as though a curtain had been drawn back. Bryn felt the shift first—her breath coming easier, the shadows no longer tugging at her nerves. Nyv blinked in quiet surprise as Geoff the Newt let out a soft chirp and settled. Even Kaerda, always the anchor, let out a breath and lowered her shield, her shoulders easing with the weight gone. It wasn't just the absence of magic—it was the return of clarity... one they didn't know they lacked.

● ● ●

That night, they returned to camp. The pressure was gone. No presence in their minds. No whispers.

"He can't follow us now," Bryn said, exhaustion sinking into her voice.

Kaerda stared into the flames. "If he could see and hear us... why didn't he stop us at Estavar? Or pull his lieutenant back from that duel?"

Nyv answered first, her voice quiet behind her mask. "Hubris. The powerful don't always believe what they see. Maybe he thought it was a trap for us."

Bryn nodded slowly. "Or maybe he wanted to watch us try. To see if we'd succeed, or break."

Tassa kicked a stone toward the fire. "Or maybe he thought Selvestar wouldn't dare intervene. Didn't count on us being worth the trouble."

"Either way," Kaerda muttered, "he won't underestimate us again."

Tassa grinned. "So in one more day, we walk into his house wearing dead skin and smiles."

Kaerda nodded. "And he won't even see us coming."

But Bryn looked eastward, toward the growing dark beyond the hills.

"No. This time he'll *feel* us."

And far away, in a place where fog thickens and names are forgotten, a watcher blinked—and for the first time, felt doubt.

Chapter 18: The Road Before Shadows

No one looked back toward Estavar. What had been saved now rested behind them, but the cost still echoed in their bones.

The party set out at dawn, leaving the village of Estavar behind. The sky was the colour of tarnished steel, clouds hanging low and heavy. A narrow path wound through low hills and tangled wood, carrying them eastward toward the outer edges of undead territory. The trees grew thinner. The laughter of birds was gone.

Still, for now, it was only silence. And silence was survivable.

They walked without speaking for hours, the mood pensive but not grim. Bryn and Nyv flanked the group, their eyes always watching the trees. Kaerda kept to the centre with Bone-Anna, and Tassa scouted ahead with a half-smirk, flicking small sparks from her fingertips whenever the path felt too dull.

That peace was broken by the rustle of undergrowth ahead.

Tassa held up a hand. "Company."

From between the trees stumbled a strange mix—three goblins in tattered leathers, a broad-shouldered half-elf with a too-shiny sword, and two human men with patchy armour and rotted boots. Highwaymen, by the look of them, though barely more than scavengers.

One of the humans grinned. "Well now, what luck. Road's a dangerous place, friends. Undead crawling all over the borderlands these days. Travellers vanish. Whole wagons found overturned with no sign of a fight. But we're happy to keep it safe—for a donation."

The half-elf smirked and gestured lazily with his blade. "Let's call it... a toll."

No one moved.

Nyv took a step forward, cloak shifting like smoke. Her voice came low and quiet. "Step aside."

The goblins looked at one another.

The man with the shiny sword chuckled. "No need for threats, little lady. We're professionals."

Nyv's eyes narrowed behind her black mask. Shadows curled at her feet.

"Professionals don't wear scrap metal and demand coin from ghosts."

One of the goblins shifted nervously. Another took a step back.

Bryn stepped beside Nyv. Her voice was soft but carried like ice cracking underfoot.

"You've mistaken us for people who will hesitate."

Geoff the Newt mimicked her stance from Nyv's shoulder, arms folded like a tiny judge. His bright orange belly pulsed with irritation.

The lead goblin, noticing Geoff, blinked. "Is... is that thing glaring at me?"

Tassa, still to the side, called out with a grin. "Careful. That one bites."

Kaerda said nothing. She only adjusted her shield and took a step forward.

The would-be robbers looked at the silent skeleton standing beside her. Bone-Anna, still as death, notched an arrow.

The goblins froze.

The lead one squinted, doubling-down while trying to puff himself up. "Maybe we don't care who you are. Maybe we take your coin and let you breathe."

Nyv tilted her head. "Maybe you try."

One of the humans raised a shortbow halfway. Kaerda's shield came up in a blink.

"Not smart," Kaerda said evenly. "Not today."

Bryn stepped forward just enough to let her shadow stretch long across the dirt road. It writhed, unnatural in the soft daylight.

"We bury things now," she said. "Not always the dead."

Geoff the Newt, still perched on Nyv's shoulder, mirrored her exact posture—head slightly tilted, arms crossed, tail twitching like a blade.

The lead goblin's confidence cracked. "Okay—wait—what is that thing *doing*?"

"Copying," Nyv answered, not looking at him. "And judging."

Tassa, now leaning lazily on a branch, smiled. "I once saw him do that just before we set a troll on fire."

The half-elf took a step back. "Alright. Fine. No gold. No toll. No trouble."

"Good choice," Bryn murmured.

Now the goblins turned.

"Yup. No gold here. Definitely not worth it."

One human muttered, "Are they all warlocks?"

"Worse," Bryn said. "We're out of patience."

The half-elf backed away, blade lowered. "No harm meant. Just a misunderstanding."

The group scattered into the trees without another word.

Just before they vanished, Nyv called after them, voice like cold iron. "He may want payment."

One of the goblins paused, glancing back.

"Who does?"

Geoff the Newt slowly raised one clawed hand and pointed.

Right at them.

The goblin blinked once—twice—then turned and ran like the trees were on fire.

Tassa clapped once. "Newt tax. Reasonable."

For a few moments, silence returned.

Then Tassa laughed. "That's the most fun I've had in days."

Nyv raised an eyebrow. "They'll probably tell stories about the murderous newt."

Geoff the Newt gave a self-satisfied blink and stretched on Nyv's shoulder.

Bryn allowed herself a small smile. "Let them."

And onward they walked, toward the dark that waited just beyond the next rise.

Behind them, the forest slowly swallowed the path—and the story of the scariest newt ever to judge a band of fools.

Chapter 19: Unlocked

The forest gave way to fog-draped fields and half-rotted fences, silent but watchful. The edge of undead territory loomed just beyond the rise. The air hung heavy, as though even breath dared not trespass.

The party made camp at the base of a crumbling watchtower—long abandoned, its stones pitted with age. The skeleton of an ancient tree leaned over it like a sleeping sentinel.

They spoke in low tones around the fire.

"We know how to get in," Kaerda said, tracing a path in the dirt. "The *Walking With The Dead* ritual will buy us time."

"But not forever," Nyv added. "Once we're in, what then? We still don't know what he's building… or what we're walking into."

"We can't carry out an attack inside," Kaerda said. "We'd be outnumbered a hundred to one."

"So we observe," Bryn murmured. "And wait for an opportunity."

But even her voice wavered with doubt.

They drifted to rest in twos and threes. Bryn took the last watch, seated alone beside the fire's embers, the ritual book in her lap. The second book—the one she still could not open—lay just beside it.

Then came the shift.

A breeze that stirred no flame. A sudden, aching hush in the trees. The scent of snow where none had fallen.

The shadows around her bent inward.

And a voice, colder than death and laced with pride, brushed against her ear.

You are not forgotten.

Bryn's eyes closed. Her heartbeat slowed. She let the fire dim, and when it guttered low, the dream took her.

She stood on a field of bone and starlight. All was still. The wind whispered like a thousand wings in mourning.

The Queen of Stillness stood before her.

Her face was veiled, shifting with sorrow and memory. Shadows clung to her like silk. In her hands—she held the second book.

You have served with silence. With grief. With purpose, the Queen said. *Your hand has not faltered.*

Bryn lowered her head.

You are ready.

The Queen opened the book, and with it, the space between worlds seemed to still. A pulse of magic surged from its spine, and symbols scrawled in shadow and light burned themselves into Bryn's mind.

What was sealed will answer now, the Queen whispered. *You may read the one that binds. But the one that burns... is not yet yours.*

Bryn opened her eyes.

The second ritual book sat before her, no longer cold. Its clasp had fallen open. The pages fluttered slightly, as though exhaling.

She opened it.

The ritual burned into her vision—a sacred consecration. A declaration. A warding of ground so strong it would strip the undead of their power. It would keep them out. Or trap them in.

Hallow.

She smiled faintly and whispered, "Thank you."

Dawn broke.

And with it, their plan solidified.

Now, they had a way to end it.

By the morning fire, they gathered close, the ritual books between them and maps scratched into old parchment.

"We go in under the cover of *Walking With The Dead,*" Bryn said. "Straight through the camp—silent, unseen."

Nyv nodded. "We'll head for the centre. There must be a command hub. Or something he uses as a sanctum."

Kaerda leaned in. "That's where we cast *Hallow*."

Bryn tapped the page. "Two hours. That's how long it takes. The moment I begin casting, the invisibility drops."

Tassa frowned. "So we need to find a place out of sight. A ruin. A building. Something with cover."

"Something with walls," Kaerda added. "And only one way in."

"We trap him," Bryn said. "The ritual will bar his minions from crossing its threshold. If we time it right, we bait him in and close the door behind him."

"And then we hit him with everything we've got," Nyv said. "All spells. All steel."

Bone-Anna stood beside them, silent but watching. Her fingers flexed around her bow.

Geoff the Newt blinked slowly, then mimicked Nyv's determined posture.

Kaerda looked around the group. "It's not the best plan."

"No," Bryn agreed. "But it's ours."

And they began to pack.

At twilight, they would walk unseen into the lands of the dead.

Chapter 20: The Hallowed Battle

The ritual wrapped the party in quiet shadow, their steps muffled and their presence erased from undead senses. They passed through the enemy camp like whispers on wind, ghosts among corpses. Fires crackled, sentinels stood idle, and the dead wandered in restless patterns—but none turned toward them.

Near the centre of the camp, they found it: a burned-out house, blackened beams curled like ribs around a scorched floor. The walls still held, barely, but it was tucked behind a collapsed barn and sheltered by low stone fencing. It would do.

Bryn stepped inside, her fingers already brushing the ritual book's cover. "Here. This is the place."

Kaerda, Nyv, and Tassa formed a loose perimeter, weapons and spells ready. Bone-Anna climbed the collapsed barn, her skeletal bow strung and steady, watching for patrols.

The casting began.

Minutes passed. Then an hour.

Then—footsteps.

A small group of undead patrols veered dangerously close. Nyv held her breath. Kaerda raised her shield.

But Bone-Anna moved. A pebble, tossed with careful aim, struck a beam near the patrol's flank. The undead turned, distracted by the faint sound, and wandered away.

Bryn never looked up. Her hands moved steadily, her whispers a steady chant in the gloom.

When the final sigil was inscribed, the earth responded.

A pulse of sacred energy surged from the floorboards. A sphere of bright light radiated outward, illuminating the ruined house and the ground within a 60-foot radius. Shadows hissed and burned away. The undead outside reeled.

And Bone-Anna cried out—not in pain, but as if the wind had been pulled from her non-existent lungs.

She was forcefully pushed from the barn roof and landed just outside the glow, flat on one knee. She reached a hand toward Bryn but could not cross the threshold. Her bow trembled in her grip. Bryn's eyes met hers.

Bryn's breath caught in her throat, panic flashing through her. Bone-Anna had been by her side for so long—closer than even her shadow. *What if she couldn't return? What if the Queen's light kept her out forever?* She swallowed the fear. "I'm sorry," Bryn whispered. "I think it has to be this way."

Bone-Anna nodded once and stood, silent and patient as ever. She would wait.

All around the glowing boundary, the other undead surged. Clawed hands scraped at the invisible barrier. Mouths gnashed and groaned without breath. Some hurled themselves against it, howling as they were repelled by the divine magic. The sound was relentless—a steady, pounding noise of desperation and rage.

Only Bone-Anna remained still among the chaos. She stood apart from the frenzied dead, her form unmoving, her bow idle at her side. Watching. Waiting.

From the far edge of the field of light came a voice—not spoken, but carved into their minds:

You ran from my eyes.

You severed the root.

And now you think walls and spells will stop me?

The man with no mouth stepped into view.

He stood at the edge of the warded space, the undead behind him hissing like waves on rock. He did not walk—he glided, his motion unnatural. He wore no armour, only layered black cloth and skin stretched taut across his face, where too many eyes blinked with hunger.

He lifted a hand, and the ward pulsed.

I will peel your name from memory. I will wear your regrets like a cloak. And I will burn your Queen's house to the marrow.

Bryn stood tall. "Then step inside."

He did.

The ward didn't stop him—but it closed behind him with a sharp *snap*, trapping him in with the living.

The fight began.

Kaerda charged first, her shield deflecting the first burst of necrotic flame. Nyv shouted a command, summoning a flurry of arcane blades around the intruder's form. Tassa raised her hands and shouted, "*naur ram!*", penning him in with a wall made entirely of fire, while Bryn shouted "*márna rúvína!*" and sent a raven-shaped blast that struck one of his many eyes.

They pushed him back. Each hit staggered him—but not for long.

Then Nyv raised her arms and shouted into the storm of battle. Her voice summoned not fire, not shadow—but the strength of the wild itself.

She called out, "*gwaur naurwen!*"—invoking the wrath of the wild.

The ground trembled. Roots burst from the soil. Blackened trees twisted upright, their limbs animated by vengeful spirits. Vines slithered toward the man with no mouth, coiling around his legs and arms, dragging him to one knee. Stones from the ruined walls launched skyward and hammered into him, one after another.

He howled—not with a mouth, but with his mind.

The party pressed their advantage. Tassa shouted "*corma losta!*" as her chromatic orb ricocheted through the chaos. Kaerda struck hard and fast with her hammer, driving him back toward the burning boundary. Bryn unleashed another blast, searing his torso with violet flame.

And then... he laughed.

A terrible, echoing pulse radiated outward.

You think this is my end? he said in all their minds. *This is my beginning.*

His body cracked. His arms split at the seams, shadow bleeding from within. Skin gave way to plates of bone. His many eyes burned violet. Wings of sinew and rot tore from his back as horns curved from his temples.

He rose—a new form. Demon-made. Demon-born.

Nyv's breath caught. Kaerda swore under her breath. Even Tassa took a half-step back, her flames flickering in hesitation. The battle had shifted—and they all felt it.

The ritual barrier shuddered—then shattered. A wave of corrupted force radiated outward, and the invisible threshold meant to hold back the undead flickered, then collapsed.

With a cry, the undead surged forward, no longer kept at bay. Clawed hands tore at the remnants of the burned-out house. The holy ground still held its light, but now the tide of the dead pressed close from every side.

Inside the ward, the party reeled. Nyv staggered backward, her spell faltering. Kaerda was thrown against a wall. Tassa's fire faltered and died.

Chapter 21: The Burning Moment

And from the edge of the battlefield, something stirred.

Bone-Anna.

Freed from the divine ward that had held her at bay, she stepped silently through the chaos of the undead horde. They ignored her, parting like mist around her skeletal frame. She moved with purpose, bow already strung, eyes fixed on the demon.

But she was not alone.

Geoff the Newt, singed but determined, clung to a broken beam near her perch. He looked at the demon, then at Bone-Anna, and gave a low, guttural trill—his version of a battle cry. Then, mimicking Nyv's earlier casting gesture, he pointed a tiny claw toward the enemy.

Bone-Anna adjusted her aim.

The shot loosed with perfect silence.

The arrow struck the demon's side, piercing one of the unnatural plates of bone that had begun to form. The demon staggered, grunted, and turned his head slightly, many eyes sweeping over the battlefield—but seeing nothing he deemed a threat. Bone-Anna remained still, just another corpse among the horde. That was his mistake. As with so many others, he had dismissed her. Just as he dismissed the witch, the smith, the flame-sorcerer. And most of all, the one who bore the mark of the Queen. His undoing had already begun. It wasn't a killing blow—but it staggered him, just enough to halt his momentum.

Inside the burning ruin, Bryn and Nyv moved as one.

Bryn unleashed another raven-blast of shadow, crying, "*márna rúvína!*" while Nyv summoned thorn-covered roots from the floorboards to grip the demon's legs. Together, they forced the demon back. He snarled in fury, his many eyes pulsing with dark light.

You delay nothing, he whispered in their minds. *Your Queen is absent. Your doom is chosen.*

Bryn's reply was a second blast—followed by a third.

Nyv gritted her teeth and poured more magic into the roots, but the demon began to tear free, one limb at a time.

Outside, Kaerda raised her shield and called upon Durnach the Forgemaker, casting a divine ward that repelled the pressing horde with radiant force. The dead shrieked as light washed over them.

Tassa, her hair wild with sweat, flung a fireball into the densest part of the crowd. It exploded with a roar, sending scorched bodies flying.

"I need more space!" she shouted.

Kaerda slammed her shield into the ground, channeling divine magic again. "Buy us seconds! That's all we need!"

But inside the house, the balance began to shift.

The demon tore free.

He lunged forward, striking Bryn with a blast of necrotic force. She staggered, vision swimming.

Nyv tried to shield her, but the demon swept his arm wide, knocking Nyv aside with supernatural strength.

The light of the hallow ritual dimmed. And though none could see it yet, high above the field, the ravens paused in their circle, waiting.

Fall, the demon whispered. *Fall in silence.*

Bryn fell to one knee. Her breath hitched, a moment of stunned silence stealing the battle from her senses.

"I'm sorry," she whispered, voice barely audible over the roar of battle. "I wasn't strong enough."

And the wind shifted.

The fire no longer crackled. The screams fell away. Time stretched.

In the hush that followed, a single breath brushed Bryn's ear—soft, cold, and full of purpose.

Now, child. Burn what does not belong.

The air ignited—not with flame, but with purpose. A thousand ghostly ravens burst from the ground around Bryn, their wings trailing shadows made of memory. They circled her in a cyclone of midnight feathers and gleaming silver eyes. Each beat of their wings echoed with the screams of the forgotten and the vow of vengeance.

Bryn rose.

The mark on her hand flared to life—a feather-shaped mark glowing white-hot. Her coat lifted in the unseen wind, her hair rippling like ink in water.

She lifted her palm, and the shadows surged forward.

The demon snarled—but his voice faltered.

From Bryn's hand erupted a tide of burning shadow, not fire but pure, sanctified oblivion. It washed over him in a cascade of violet-black flame, its edges etched with flickering runes of the Queen of Stillness's tongue.

The ground cracked beneath him. His wings shriveled. His armour of bone shattered.

The undead horde wailed as the light spilled across the field, searing them from existence. The wave of sanctified shadow obeyed only one truth: what did not belong, would burn.

Bone-Anna stood untouched, her bones catching the glow like moonlight. The sanctified power washed over her but did not burn—only recognised.

Geoff the Newt raised a tiny claw in salute, eyes wide with awe. Nyv, coughing and battered, managed a tired smile, watching him with quiet pride.

And when the light faded—

The demon with no mouth was gone.

Ash drifted where he had stood.

● ● ●

When Bryn next opened her eyes, the battlefield was gone.

She stood in a place of silence and velvet dark, where the stars pulsed like slow heartbeats and memory whispered with every step.

The Queen of Stillness stood before her.

Her form shimmered with sorrow and storm, veiled in flowing shadow. The eyes beneath her hood held no malice—only recognition.

"Why?" Bryn asked, voice soft. "Why now? Why this?"

The Queen of Stillness's voice was wind and hush and gravity. *Because you were faithful. Because you listened. Because you waited.*

Bryn lowered her head. "I thought I had to do this alone."

Not alone. Not always. You carry silence and shadow. But He brought hellfire to your door. And so I answered in kind.

The Queen lifted a hand, brushing two fingers across Bryn's cheek.

Balance, my child. That was all. Now, rest.

The starlight swirled. The Queen vanished like smoke on the wind.

And Bryn fell into waking. The battlefield waited for her return.

Chapter 22: Ash and Memory

The silence that followed the battle was unlike any the Silent Accord had known. Not the quiet of waiting, nor the breath held before violence—but something sacred. Something emptied.

The field was scorched black and still smoking. Where once a demon had stood, there remained only a brittle, fractured imprint of charred ground and drifting ash.

Kaerda was the first to move, limping across the ruin with her shield still raised, until she stood at the place where the demon fell. She lowered to one knee, pressing her hand into the cracked earth. "It's over," she said softly. "For now."

Tassa stood nearby, sleeves torn and smoke trailing from her fingertips. She winced, rolling her shoulders. "I hate that I almost ran out of fire," she muttered. "Almost."

Nyv crouched beside Bryn, who had collapsed into a sitting position against a broken beam. Her eyes were open but unfocused.

"She's breathing," Nyv said. "But barely."

Bone-Anna approached and knelt beside them. She gently placed one skeletal hand over Bryn's heart—then nodded once. Still here.

Geoff the Newt scampered up Nyv's arm and nestled under her collarbone, peeking at Bryn's face with a worried blink.

Moments passed.

Then Bryn stirred.

She sat up slowly, her face pale, her eyes wide—not from fear, but reverence. "She was there," she whispered. "She answered."

They didn't press. Not yet.

● ● ●

By morning, they had a direction.

Estavar—the last place they had truly rested, and the town that had fought beside them. The people there had proven themselves brave, resourceful, and loyal. And after what had just occurred, the Silent Accord needed time to recover and somewhere to plan.

They turned west.

As they walked, Bryn looked back only once.

"Estavar will believe us," she said. "And once they do, the rest will listen."

No one disagreed.

Their next war would begin from a place that had already learned to stand its ground.

• • •

Later, they gathered at the edge of the battlefield, near a stream where the water still ran clear. They washed blood and ash from their skin and armour.

Tassa glanced toward the ruins. "Where did he get that kind of power? That wasn't just undeath. That was something older. Bigger."

Bryn looked up from the water, her voice quiet. "I don't know. Not exactly. It could have been Orcus. Maybe Vecna. There are others who claim dominion over undeath—some older than names carved in stone."

Geoff the Newt trilled softly.

"But whoever it was," Bryn continued, "he had their favour. That much is certain."

Nyv rested her hands on her knees, gaze narrowed. "If he saw everything we did—Estavar, the lieutenant, all of it—why didn't he act? Why let us win?"

Kaerda exhaled. "He didn't see us as a threat. That's what undid him in the end. Not his magic. Not our strength. Just his arrogance."

Tassa gave a tired smirk. "I hope he remembers that. Wherever he is now."

Bryn added quietly, "Even when he was watching us, he never really saw us. Not Bone-Anna. Not Selvestar. Not the people of Estavar."

Nyv nodded. "He underestimated everything that wasn't darkness."

And only when the sun dipped low did Kaerda speak again.

"If that was just one of his chosen," she said, staring at the curling smoke, "what else waits behind him?"

Nyv was quiet for a long moment. Then, "We'll find out. And we'll be ready."

Tassa sat cross-legged beside the stream, idly flicking embers from her palm. "We should send word to Velkhar. And Ravkareth. Maybe even Merishan. Someone out there should know what's rising."

"They'll doubt us," Kaerda said.

"Maybe," Nyv said. "But they'll listen after the next one falls."

● ● ●

Bryn stood a little apart from the rest. In her hand, she held a shard of blackened bone—the only fragment left of the demon. She turned it over once, then knelt and buried it beneath a tree.

"Let him have no name," she said. "No remembering. Only the grave."

Bone-Anna stood beside her. Watching. Guarding.

Night settled gently over the fields. The silence held. Not the end of war—but the space where memory begins.

Epilogue: The Foundation

Estavar welcomed them—like kin long feared lost.

The battered gates swung wide, and familiar faces ran to meet them. Children who once fled in fear now waved to Bone-Anna. A fisherman laid out bread and cheese at the Silent Accord's feet. Old women placed their hands over their hearts as Bryn passed, whispering blessings. They had not forgotten who stood for them.

Mayor Aelric met them in the square. He said nothing at first—only embraced Kaerda in the way of old soldiers. Then, turning to the rest: "The house above the east ridge is yours. We'll keep watch below."

Within days, Estavar changed. Not by command, but by resolve.

The people built higher walls.
They formed night patrols.
Children learned the sound of undead—and the shape of silence.

The Silent Accord did not rest idly. They helped raise defences. They taught. They listened. They wrote.

Nyv sent letters, sealed in ash and wax, to the highlands of Ravkareth. She trained three village youths in minor wards. Geoff the Newt leapt from stool to stool, nodding solemnly whenever a student got it right—his approval now a badge of honour.

Kaerda crafted wards of faith to bless the wells and crossroads.

And Bryn carved tokens.

This time, they were not for the dead.

They were for the living—small, polished bones shaped into feathers, etched with a single word: *remember*.

Villagers wore them proudly around their necks.

● ● ●

A few nights after their arrival home, Bryn slipped out alone. She made her way back to the edge of the square where Candlecut Hollow stood quiet and unassuming, as it always had.

Dalebar was behind the counter, polishing a mug that didn't need polishing. He didn't look up when she entered.

"You sent for help," Bryn said simply.

His hand stilled. "Didn't know if it would matter."

"It did."

He nodded once. "Good."

She stepped closer. "Why?"

He finally looked at her—tired eyes, steady voice. "Because you looked like the sort who wouldn't ask."

Bryn smiled faintly. "Still. Thank you."

Dalebar gave a quiet grunt and returned to his polishing. "Don't make a habit of needing saving."

"We hope not to," she said. "But sometimes… it's good to know someone sees you."

The next day, the first of the riders came. Not enemies—but messengers. From Velkhar. From Merishan. From Ravkareth.

They had heard.

What comes next will stretch beyond Estavar. Beyond memory.

Now, the world watches.

And the Silent Accord is ready to be heard.

Part III – Where the Thread Fails

The thread may break before we reach the end.
Still—we choose who we carry with us.

Prologue – The First Feather

The forest was quiet, and that was how Bryn knew something sacred was about to begin.

It wasn't the hush of predators, nor the solemn stillness of dusk. This was different. The trees seemed to hold their breath. The wind stirred only enough to shift the moss on the stones. Ravens circled overhead—silent. Waiting.

Bryn stood barefoot on the glade's soft loam, her raven-black hair tied back in a ribbon braided with shadow thread. Her mother had told her to keep her eyes open. "You shouldn't lower your gaze when the Queen sees you," Nera had said.

And now, Nera stood beside her.

The older elf's cloak rustled faintly as she knelt, pressing one hand to the earth. Her face—marked with age only in spirit—held the same stillness as the forest. "It's time," she said, voice barely above a whisper.

Bryn swallowed. "I don't feel anything."

"You will."

They stood beneath a half-fallen arch of blackroot trees. Around them, the Lethvain Reach opened in soft spirals of fog and moonlight. Nera had led her here without explanation—only a knowing look, and the soft certainty of a mother who had once stood here herself.

"I knew it would come for you," Nera said. "But I never wanted to choose it for you."

"I know," Bryn replied, quieter still.

Nera turned to her daughter, brushing a loose strand of hair from Bryn's cheek. "This isn't a ceremony. It's a threshold. You don't walk through it unless you're ready to leave something behind."

A single black feather drifted down between them.

Nera looked up. "She's near."

Then, as the silence deepened, Nera spoke again, this time with a softness threaded in memory. "When I was your age," she said, "I waited at the edge of a frozen river for three days. I thought the Queen had passed me by. But on the

----

third night, I dreamed of a star falling into the water. When I woke, the river was gone—and I stood on a path made of feathers. She doesn't speak when we want. She speaks when we're quiet enough to hear."

Bryn's eyes shimmered. "Did you speak back?"

"I didn't have to. I listened. And listening is its own kind of answer."

The wind changed.

It came not from the trees but from within them—like breath drawn from the roots of the world. Bryn's heart slowed. Her breath caught. Shadows lengthened across the moss as the ravens above turned in unison, wheeling into a slow, perfect spiral.

A voice came—not from above, not from Nera, but from the marrow of the stillness itself.

"Do you come with silence?"

Bryn did not speak. She nodded.

"Do you carry memory?"

She closed her eyes. Her father's laughter. The bones of a small animal buried beneath a riverstone. A story carved into birch bark. Yes.

"Will you take the veil?"

Bryn hesitated.

Then she lifted her hand.

A burn—sharp, cold, absolute—etched across her skin. She gasped and dropped to her knees. The mark had already formed, shaped like a raven's feather. It glowed briefly, then dimmed to black.

The wind stopped.

Silence fell.

And then, the raven came.

It landed lightly on a branch just above her, its feathers half-translucent, eyes like the void beneath roots. It did not caw. It only watched.

Bryn rose, her legs unsteady.

Nera approached slowly, reverently. "She sent a companion."

Bryn nodded. "She's accepted me."

"She didn't choose you. You chose her. And she answered." Nera touched her daughter's shoulder. "You're hers now. But you'll always be mine, too."

Bryn looked at her hand, then at the raven. It dipped its head—once.

Tentatively, Bryn stepped forward. The raven tilted its head at her approach, its eyes meeting hers without blinking.

"What's your name?" Bryn asked softly.

The raven blinked once. A single black feather detached from its wing and drifted into her outstretched hand. A whisper followed—not in sound, but in shape and memory. One word, pressed gently into her mind like a name she had always known.

"Morwen."

Though Nera had heard no words, she saw the change in her daughter's face— the quiet awe of someone who had heard a truth meant only for them.

"You spoke with them," she said, not as a question.

Bryn nodded. Then she smiled, her voice low. "Then I'm glad to meet you, Morwen."

Morwen was no ordinary raven. Bryn could feel him—not just his presence, but a shared tether of thought and soul that pulsed quietly beneath her skin. It wasn't speech, not truly, but a deep mutual awareness. They were bound, not as master and servant, but as companions. She sensed the weight of his purpose: to guide, to watch, and to remain. The Queen of Stillness had gifted her more than a symbol—she had gifted a soul to stand at her side. The first of many.

But it wasn't the only gift the Queen had left her. Bryn could feel it—beneath her breath, behind her eyes. Something inside her had changed. The forest smelled different. The shadows seemed to listen. She couldn't name the transformation, but she knew it was good. She was still herself... but more. A threshold had been crossed, and she had not crossed it alone.

The feathers began to fall again. Not many. Just a few. But enough to mark the veil had been drawn.

Behind her, the forest exhaled.

And Bryn Lovas, nineteen years old, turned away from childhood—and began the path toward shadow, sacrifice, and memory.

She stood quietly a moment longer, watching Morwen vanish into the trees. Then she turned to Nera, who waited with a patient, steady expression.

"It feels... like something broke open inside me," Bryn said softly. "But not in a bad way. Just... bigger. Like I can hear the wind clearer. Feel the roots underneath."

Nera nodded. "That's what it feels like when you're given more than most are ever asked to carry. Most people spend their lives rooted in place—never called, never marked, never leaving the line of their village trees. But you? You've been handed a path."

Bryn glanced down at her hand, flexing it slowly. "And that path goes far beyond here, doesn't it."

"It does," Nera said. "But you don't walk it alone. You have Morwen now. And me, for as long as you need me. And perhaps, someday, another—someone who hears the same stillness you do, and chooses to follow it beside you, just as I found my friends and later your father. Just as I stood shoulder to shoulder with those who helped me stop the enemy from unraveling the planes. We didn't succeed because we were powerful—we succeeded because we shared the burden."

Bryn's throat tightened. "What if I don't? What if I fail?"

Nera stepped closer, brushing Bryn's shoulder with her hand. "Then fail with honesty. Rise with purpose. The Queen doesn't ask for perfection. She asks for truth. For memory. For silence when it matters most."

Bryn looked toward the glade again. The moss shimmered in the moonlight, and the air no longer felt heavy, but sacred.

"Then I'll carry it," she whispered. "Whatever it is she's given me, I'll carry it."

"Good," Nera said. "Because now, it begins."

She paused then, as if remembering something long tucked away. Slowly, she slid a ring from her finger—a modest band of dark silver chased with violet etching. The metal shimmered faintly with age and use.

"I bought this in Muckels," Nera said, holding it out. "Years before you were born. The gnome who sold it to me said it would find its way to the one who needed it most. I never knew what he meant until now."

Bryn took the ring with trembling fingers, hesitating as it sat in her palm. Then, as if sensing her, the metal warmed faintly.

"You're not just walking into a new life, Bryn," Nera continued. "You're continuing a legacy. This—" she gestured to the glade, the raven, the shadowy stillness, "—this is yours now. A place, a purpose—and a beginning. Your first step beyond the veil. And you'll shape it in your own way."

Bryn slipped the ring onto her finger. It settled like it had been waiting for her all along.

Chapter 1 – The Quiet After

Years had passed since Bryn Lovas stood beneath the blackroot arch in the Lethvain Reach and felt her soul burn into shape. The world had turned many times since then, and so had she. The Queen of Stillness had spoken—rarely, but unmistakably—through silence, through ravens, through dreams Bryn could never quite forget.

The others had come in time—Kaerda, quiet and unshakable; Tassa, restless and fire-born; and Nyv, whose stillness mirrored Bryn's own. Together, they became something more than adventurers. Estavar knew them by the name the townsfolk whispered: the Silent Accord. A band not bound by words, but by what went unspoken.

Estavar held its breath beneath a grey spring sky. Smoke curled from chimneys, carts rolled lazily through the market lanes, and snowmelt sang soft songs beneath bridges that arched like the backs of sleeping cats. It was not the silence of danger, but the silence of something paused—like a city waiting for a page to turn.

Bryn stood near the edge of a shallow canal, her coat folded neatly over one arm, her boots resting on a dry stone path. The morning air bit gently at her ankles. Her fingers moved slowly over a strip of dark cloth, wrapping it around a sliver of dried lavender and obsidian. A small ritual—nothing more than a centring charm. But she liked the quiet it brought.

A few feet away, Nyv knelt beside a cluster of purple-stemmed herbs growing from the cracks in the cobbles. She murmured something to herself—perhaps to Geoff the Newt, who blinked slowly from her shoulder. The newt's orange belly glowed faintly in the cool light.

Bryn didn't interrupt. Instead, she waited until Nyv rose, dusting her palms clean. The Seidra witch looked calm, but there was a furrow in her brow that hadn't been there weeks ago.

"You found it?" Bryn asked softly.

"Vennroot," Nyv replied. "The real kind. Didn't expect it this far west."

Bryn nodded. She didn't say she had been watching Nyv work for the better part of ten minutes, drawn, as always, to the way the Seidra's fingers moved—with practised care, yes—but also with something else. Intention. Grace.

Something Bryn hadn't yet dared to name. She didn't have to. They moved back toward the stone bench they'd claimed without speaking further.

They weren't alone in Estavar, but this morning it felt like they were.

● ● ●

Back at their house in Estavar, Kaerda Flintward was repairing the strap of her shield with careful, deliberate strokes. Bryn and Nyv sat together at the table nearby, each absorbed in their own quiet task—Nyv grinding dried herbs into a small ceramic bowl, Bryn thumbing through a thin, rune-marked notebook.

Tassa Emberlin sat on the windowsill, her legs swinging idly as she read through a scroll held sideways. Every now and then, she asked a question no one answered.

"Is it really stealing if the item is cursed?"

Nyv's lips twitched, but she didn't look up. Bryn simply raised an eyebrow, flipping a page.

"Does fire magic count as divine if the flame was part of a sacred relic?"

"Or," she added with a sigh, "if a riddle kills you before you solve it, is it still considered a test?"

Still nothing.

Tassa clicked her tongue. "Philosophers are cowards."

Kaerda looked up, one brow lifting in slow, deliberate judgment. "Philosophers don't usually face trolls."

"Exactly."

● ● ●

That afternoon, the Silent Accord ventured through Estavar. Not as warriors or legends, but as neighbors. Kaerda helped repair a mill wheel with the town's blacksmith, her hammer ringing in time with the younger apprentice beside her. She offered few words but left behind a set of reinforced braces that would outlast the season.

Tassa taught three children how to shape harmless flame into floating dragonflies, much to the chagrin of a worried father. She only grinned and promised, "They'll never forget how to call warmth when it's needed."

Nyv assisted the apothecary in sorting rare herbs salvaged from melted snowbanks. Her quiet explanations and deft fingers soon drew a small crowd of older villagers—those who remembered Ravkari spells and asked careful questions in low voices. Bryn wandered nearby, offering charms in exchange for stories: a bit of woven shadow for a lost name, a polished stone for a memory of song. Her path curved just close enough to pass where Nyv knelt among the apothecary's herbs, and without meaning to, Bryn glanced toward her. Only for a second. But the way Nyv's hands moved—steady, precise—caught her breath the way it always did when she wasn't expecting it.

They shared bread with the bakers and news with the guards. They listened to rumors and laughter. Children pointed—not out of fear, but awe. Even Bone-Anna earned a kind of reverent silence from a group of teenagers who watched her shadowless steps as if witnessing myth.

By the time dusk fell, the Accord had walked every street without lifting a weapon. They were not only protectors of Estavar. They were part of it.

And Bryn, standing near the square with Nyv at her side, felt the weight she carried shift. Not disappear. But redistribute—into laughter, into murmured thanks, into hands that would lift with hers when the time came."

● ● ●

Later, Bryn sat cross-legged on the floor of their shared room, slowly trimming the wick of a ritual lantern. Nyv was writing by candlelight, her letters careful and slanted—written in the Ravkari script. A stack of half-folded parchment lay beside her.

"Sending messages home?" Bryn asked, her voice just above the soft scrape of wick against knife.

Nyv didn't look up. "Yes. The Elders should know what we've seen."

Bryn paused, then reached into her satchel and pulled out a smooth stone, polished black with a faint grey ring around the centre. She had chosen it two days ago and hadn't said why—but she'd known Nyv would need it. She handed it to Nyv without comment.

Nyv accepted the stone, fingers brushing Bryn's palm briefly. She turned it in her hand once, then smiled—faint, but genuine. "Good weight. Smooth edges. This will work well for sending."

Nyv turned back to her letter. She didn't explain further—she didn't need to. Bryn knew the primary stone waited in the Veilwarden temple, always listening. It was a Ravkari practice, old and quiet: craft a tether-stone, speak your message, and trust the magic to carry it—so long as the elders heard it in time. The stone would hold a message for a day or two—long enough to reach Ravkareth, if the place magic held.

She looked at Bryn for a beat longer than needed. In that glance lingered something thoughtful—an appreciation not just for Bryn's attentiveness, but for the way she respected the invisible things, the unseen threads Nyv believed in too. "You've gotten good at picking the right stones."

"You taught me well."

They returned to their tasks without another word.

● ● ●

The evening brought soft rain. Kaerda prepared a stew near the hearth, humming an old dwarven hymn. Tassa conjured dancing flames in the shape of small animals, sending them skittering across the floor for Geoff to chase. Geoff sprang into motion with theatrical reluctance, chasing the flickering creatures like a cat that knew it was being watched—and enjoyed the game all the more for it. Bryn sat near the window, eyes tracing the outline of the rooftops through streaked glass. A single raven—one of hers—rested on the sill, wings folded, head tucked beneath its body. It stirred only when she did.

"They're quiet lately," Nyv said from behind her.

"They're watching," Bryn replied. "Even when I'm not."

"Is that comforting?"

Bryn didn't answer right away. "It used to be. Now it's... more like a weight I'm still learning how to carry."

Nyv stepped beside her. Not close enough to touch, but close enough that the distance between them felt intentional. The old magic they both bore— different in origin, yet similar in weight—seemed to recognise itself, and neither woman dared disturb it. Nyv said nothing at first. She watched the raven on the sill for a breath longer than necessary, as though it, too, understood the weight they carried. In that stillness, she found herself thinking how rare it was to stand beside someone who treated power like a trust instead of a weapon. Bryn never tried to command the magic. She listened to it—and it listened back. Nyv made a quiet note of it, not with envy, but intention. She would try to do the same.

"When power this old finds a vessel," she said softly, "it doesn't sit lightly."

Bryn turned slightly toward her and nodded once, slow and thoughtful.

They stood together, saying no more. Not out of distance, but because reverence needed no echo.

The raven lifted its head and blinked once—slow and deliberate. Outside, the rain deepened into rhythm.

At some point, Geoff seized a spoon from the stew pot and brandished it like a sword, triumphant and oblivious.

Kaerda reached for some pot holders and picked up the stewpot. "Dinner's ready, everyone."

● ● ●

In the dark, after the fire had dimmed and the others drifted to sleep, Bryn lay awake beneath her cloak, her eyes on the rafters. One raven rested above, and Morwen—always Morwen—stood guard beside the door. He was the oldest of her ravens, the first companion gifted to her by the Queen.

Across the room, Bone-Anna stood sentry near the hearth, her skeletal frame nearly still. She kept to the edges, as always, watchful but unobtrusive. No one asked her to stand guard. She simply did.

She looked toward Morwen. He tilted his head slightly in response, as though he'd been waiting.

"Do you remember when we pulled Splug out of that ruin?" she whispered. Her voice barely stirred the air.

Morwen blinked once. The room around her remained still, but the echo of that memory rose—sunlight flickering through broken beams, the hiss of undead closing in, and Splug's battle cry faltering just before Bryn and Morwen arrived.

"He would've died if we hadn't found him."

Morwen hopped once, then returned to his stillness.

Bryn smiled faintly. "You saw it before I did. I don't think I thanked you."

A quiet pressure settled in her chest—warm, steady. She reached up and rested her hand lightly against her ribs.

"You're not just my eyes, are you?"

No answer came. There didn't need to be.

● ● ●

Earlier, before the fire dimmed, Tassa had leaned backward in her chair and balanced herself on two legs while sipping from a steaming mug.

"I wonder if Geoff's secretly the Queen's chosen and we're all just side characters in his story," she mused aloud.

Kaerda didn't look up from her notes. "Then why do we always clean up after him?"

"Classic chosen-one misdirection."

Geoff the Newt burped softly and knocked over a spoon.

"See?" Tassa grinned. "Power move."

Nyv, who had been quietly preparing her ink and scrolls nearby, glanced over. "If he starts glowing, I expect a full Ravkari coronation." In Ravkareth, familiars who displayed powerful signs were sometimes believed to carry ancestral spirits—silent watchers of the coven line.

Kaerda exhaled slowly through her nose. "If he starts glowing, I'm walking into the nearest volcano."

"Fair," Tassa said. She raised her mug. "But admit it—if he did start glowing, you'd forge him a crown and call it destiny."

Kaerda gave her a look. Then, after a pause: "Only if he asked nicely."

Bryn chuckled from across the room, not looking up from her ritual. "He'd ask. And he'd want a spoon as a scepter."

Chapter 2 – Echoes of the Heart

Tassa awoke with a start, her breath sharp in her chest, as if the very air around her was charged with the weight of a distant storm. The night had been restless. The dream—those burning flames, the eyes of a dragon—lingered in the corners of her mind, refusing to fade. There was a gnawing feeling deep within her that she couldn't place, a growing awareness of something she couldn't quite touch. Her heart still thundered from the vividness of it.

The house was quiet in the morning gloom. Estavar had gifted it to them after the siege—an act of gratitude wrapped in cedar beams and hand-mended windows. It had only two bedrooms, so they shared in pairs: Kaerda and Tassa in one room, Bryn and Nyv in the other. It was small, but it was theirs: a hearth, a roof, and rooms with beds instead of dirt. For Tassa, it was the first place she'd ever called home that didn't come with conditions.

Tassa rubbed her eyes, sitting up in the bedroll. Something tugged at her, and she crawled to the side of her pack and retrieved a small lacquered jewelry box tucked deep beneath her spare tunic. It was old—simple, but lovingly carved, with faint star patterns etched along the lid. A boy from her village had given it to her when they were both thirteen, carved it himself with a whittling knife and more hope than talent. She'd kept it, not because the boy had meant anything in the long run, but because the gesture had been sweet, and over time, it became the only box she owned that didn't carry someone else's story. It creaked softly as she opened it.

Inside were a few scattered items—a tarnished brooch shaped like a sunburst, a bent silver chain with a shard of sea glass still looped on it, and a carved wooden button from a jacket she'd outgrown years ago, though she couldn't quite recall why she'd kept it. Maybe for the feel of it. Maybe for the shape the memory made. Nestled among them was the ring.

She hadn't worn it in years. It had always been too mysterious, too weighty. But now, in the quiet that followed the dream, it felt different. She slipped it on slowly, turning it on her finger as if waiting for it to burn.

It didn't. Not with heat. But it felt... awake in a way it never had before. She had worn it once or twice in the past, more from curiosity than meaning. But those times it had been just metal—dull, indifferent. Now it seemed to pulse faintly, as if it recognised her in return. As if it had been waiting for something to change.

It was the only piece of her past she carried with her, the only connection to a family long lost. Her father's ring—given, not explained. Small, unadorned. Heavy with something she hadn't yet understood.

Tassa lay in her bedroll, staring up at the low beams of the ceiling. The soft crackle of the fire from the common room filtered through the door. She could hear Kaerda's even breathing on the other side of the room, the familiar rhythm of her calm sleep. She thought she heard Nyv's quiet, steady breath through the adjoining wall—a calm presence she could feel even without seeing her. A quiet shuffling from Kaerda's cot told her the dwarf had turned over. Kaerda murmured something under her breath, a fragment of what might have been a prayer to Durnach the Forgemaker.

Kaerda had seen the shadows under Tassa's eyes the night before. She had paused mid-polish of the stew pot, wiping her hands on her apron as she watched Tassa from across the room. Normally, mornings were full of noise—Tassa teasing Kaerda about her hammer's new shine, Geoff stealing pieces of fruit, the scent of Kaerda's porridge bubbling just a little too long. But not today. Geoff hadn't played or pounced. Tassa had barely spoken. Bryn and Nyv sat in near silence. Even Kaerda's cooking was quieter somehow, as if the warmth had dimmed.

She hadn't said anything, but she noticed. She always noticed. Her faith didn't offer answers, but it taught her to notice the weight others carried.

Tassa walked to the window, the first rays of dawn barely breaking through the clouds. The familiar sight of Estavar—narrow streets, mist-cloaked rooftops—felt quieter today, as if the city itself was holding its breath.

Tassa closed her eyes for a moment, willing herself to breathe deeply, to still the churning in her stomach. But it was no use. The dream had unsettled something deep within her. It was more than just the fire, the dragon's eyes. There was a sense of destiny, something pulling her toward a path she wasn't sure she was ready to walk. She reached for her journal, the worn leather cover smoothed by her fingers, and began writing.

She didn't write sentences so much as fragments—half-thoughts wrapped in heat. *Wings, not flame. Not wings—memory. The roar wasn't sound. It was knowing. Why gold? Why fire? Was it watching me, or was I watching it?* She paused and scribbled again. *I don't want to be a piece in someone else's prophecy.*

Her fingers hovered above the page, then wrote one more line:

What if it's not waking up inside me? What if I'm waking up into it?

● ● ●

Meanwhile, Bryn walked the edge of the yard behind their house in Estavar, her thoughts heavy with the weight of a missing raven. Not Morwen—he had returned, circling distantly overhead earlier that morning. But one of the others, a younger raven she had not yet named. It had flown out before dawn, as usual, but this time had not returned. The absence was subtle, yet unmistakable. She felt it like a distant echo—like a thread pulled too tight and about to snap.

She moved toward the edge of the garden path, her boots crunching lightly over the damp stone and soil. Her fingers brushed the air in front of her, trying to reach for the familiar sense of the raven's presence. She could feel the soft tug of the bond, but it was faint, as though something had dampened the connection.

"What's happening?" Bryn whispered to herself, though she knew no answer would come. Each of her ravens carried a piece of her Queen's will—souls made loyal through memory and grace. She felt their presence as a chorus, a flock of quiet thoughts always nearby. The loss of even one pressed into her like a bruise. Morwen may have been her first and closest, but the bond to the others was no less real. And this one... this one had simply vanished.

Her eyes flickered back toward the fire pit near the back of the house. Nyv stood near it, a shawl wrapped around her shoulders, watching Bryn with those quiet, knowing eyes. Perhaps the dream had roused her too—or perhaps she had simply noticed Bryn's absence and followed the same instinct that always seemed to lead her where she was needed. Bryn's gaze met hers, and for a fleeting moment, the weight of their shared silence hung between them. Nyv said nothing, but the understanding in her expression was enough. It was the same look she had given Bryn after the battle with the undead in Estavar—the one that turned the tide and earned them this quiet home—the look of someone who had felt the weight of Bryn's heart and understood it without words.

Nyv's presence was a balm, even in this unsettling moment, and Bryn appreciated the unspoken solidarity between them. She nodded to Nyv and then turned back to the shadows, the dark edge of the forest beyond the clearing drawing her in.

• • •

As the morning passed, the tension that had settled over the house thickened.

Earlier, there might have been laughter—Tassa's teasing, Geoff's antics, Kaerda grumbling good-naturedly over a pot of nearly burned oats. But not this morning. Geoff hadn't so much as flicked his tail. Tassa had paced without aim. Nyv had gone quiet, her brow drawn as if listening for something far off. Kaerda moved through the kitchen like a smith tending a forge in mourning. Even Bryn, usually the first to draw them gently into ritual or rhythm, had withdrawn into silence.

The house had not been this still in weeks.

Even Bone-Anna, who normally sat sentinel by the window or moved with quiet, eerie purpose, remained completely still. She hadn't stirred since just before dawn, her bow resting across her lap, her skull tilted slightly as if listening for something only she could hear. Geoff the Newt, usually quick to mimic Nyv or leap to her shoulder in jest, stayed pressed beneath her collar— wide-eyed and still. It wasn't fear, exactly—it was anticipation. A held breath shared between them all.

Whatever was coming, none of them needed to speak to feel it pressing at the edge of the day.

From their windows, a few early risers in Estavar stared at the shifting clouds with furrowed brows, their morning routines slowed without reason. A baker who normally hummed through sunrise kneaded dough in silence. A city guard at the southern watchtower paused mid-step, one hand resting on the stone rail, eyes fixed on the horizon. No one said anything aloud—but in the way they moved, in the quiet between words, something was changing.

The unease wasn't just within the Silent Accord. It was spreading—quietly, intuitively—through the bones of the city they had fought to protect. Tassa, her restless energy a contrast to Bryn's quiet contemplation, couldn't shake the unease. She paced, unable to settle, the weight of her dream gnawing at her every step. She felt disconnected from the group, as if there was something more she should be doing, something pulling her that she didn't yet understand.

As noon approached, the air inside the house turned heavier still. Tassa joined Bryn and Nyv around the fire, trying to focus on the task at hand. But her thoughts kept returning to the dream—the dragon's eyes, the flames, the

----

suffocating heat of it all. She felt her connection to fire magic pulsing in her veins, but it was a reminder that something ancient, something buried, was waking inside her.

"You're quiet today," Nyv remarked as Tassa sat beside her. Nyv's voice was soft, almost a whisper, but it carried the weight of understanding.

Tassa looked at her, a small, forced smile curling her lips. "Just thinking," Tassa said, though the weight in her voice made it sound like more.

Bryn, who had been staring into the fire, glanced up. "About the dream?"

Tassa nodded, her smile fading. "Yeah. I can't shake it. It's like a part of me that I didn't know was there is... waking up."

Bryn's eyes softened, a knowing look passing between them. "Power has a way of doing that. It doesn't always come when you're ready."

Tassa sighed, her shoulders slumping. "I just wish I knew what it wanted from me. I'm not sure I'm ready for whatever it is."

"None of us are," Bryn said quietly. "But we'll face it together."

There was a long pause, a moment of shared silence that spoke louder than words ever could.

● ● ●

As the sun reached its zenith, the peace of the morning shattered with the faint, eerie call of the wind. It had started as a soft gust, but now the wind began to whip through the trees, and with it came the scent of something unsettling.

"It's coming," Nyv said, her voice barely above a murmur.

"What is?" Kaerda asked, stepping into the clearing, her tone sharp with concern.

"The storm," Nyv replied, standing up and scanning the horizon. "It's not just wind. There's something darker about it."

Tassa's eyes widened, a strange realization passing through her. "The storm... it's not just natural, is it?"

"No," Bryn said, her hand gripping the hilt of her sword. "It's connected to something—something that's been following us since we left Estavar."

The tension in the air was palpable now, thick with the certainty that something beyond the storm was approaching.

Even Geoff the Newt had gone quiet. He clung to Nyv's collar, his normally vibrant belly dimmed to a deep rust-orange, his pupils wide and fixed toward the shifting sky. Birds wheeled overhead in uneven spirals, flying lower than they should. The town's animals—normally so lively in the late morning—were nowhere to be seen.

Bryn glanced up at the trees. The branches bent in slow arcs, not with wind, but as if leaning away from something unseen. Her breath caught. There was a taste to the air—iron and smoke and something colder underneath.

"This isn't weather," she said. "This is warning." And whatever it was—it wasn't far now.

Chapter 3 – The Return of Yeldanna

The knock came just after breakfast, when the quiet of the house still clung to the walls like morning mist. Kaerda stirred a pot of barley tea, the wooden spoon clinking faintly. Nyv was bent over her spellbook, fingers tracing old Ravkari script. Tassa sat cross-legged on the floor, a single flame flickering above her palm—not practised, just absent-minded. Even Bryn, still wrapped in her morning shawl, had settled into a hush that didn't feel heavy for once. Bryn's eyes lifted at the first knock. Not alarm, not exactly—but something like recognition. She was already rising before the second knock landed. Kaerda set down her tea and moved to the door, her boots silent on the stone. When she opened it, she found herself face to face with a stranger—taller, travel-worn, and carrying something in her eyes older than the road.

"Hope I'm not too early," the woman said, voice low and weathered by distance.

Kaerda didn't answer right away. She studied her the way a smith sizes up a blade—measuring weight, use, and balance in the space of a glance.

"Kaerda Flintward," she said finally.

The woman gave a nod, not of deference, but recognition. "Yeldanna of Ravkareth."

It wasn't a handshake they shared, or even a smile. Just an understanding. One warrior meeting another.

Kaerda stepped aside without ceremony. She returned to the kettle, pouring a second cup without asking, and handed it to Yeldanna as she stepped inside. The older woman accepted it with a quiet nod.

Bryn was already on her feet before Kaerda opened the door. Nyv gave a small nod and set her spellbook aside. Tassa, still seated, gave a two-fingered wave without looking up from the fire. No one rushed to greet her—but there was ease in the way the room shifted around her, like they'd simply been waiting for her to arrive.

"You're just in time," Kaerda said. "Barley tea. It's not fancy, but it's warm."

Yeldanna inhaled the steam before taking a sip. "It's perfect. Gods, I haven't had quiet in weeks."

They gathered around the low table without ceremony. Nyv gently closed her spellbook.

"Did you spend time in Ravkareth?" she asked, her tone careful but curious.

Yeldanna nodded slowly. "Long enough to leave signs. I didn't speak to the Seidra directly, but I sent word they would feel. Messages in the old ways." She glanced toward Nyv, then Bryn, her expression unreadable. "They know you're well. And they sense the bond that holds your group together."

Nyv tilted her head slightly. "What kind of bond?"

Yeldanna gave a small, enigmatic smile. "The kind the Veilwarden used to whisper about when we thought no one was listening. The kind that doesn't need spells to hold. Especially between people who've chosen each other in silence. Some bonds are collective, born in shared struggle. Others are quieter— threaded between two who understand without speaking. The Seidra can sense both." Bryn, still wrapped in her shawl, passed Yeldanna a small bowl of dried fruit. Tassa poked at the fire with a poker longer than she was tall.

"You came from the south?" Bryn asked.

Yeldanna nodded. "Passed through two villages I used to know. One of them's gone now. Not burned, not broken. Just... emptied. Not like what you faced here. This is something quieter. Slower. Like the land itself is forgetting the people who lived there." She didn't elaborate. "There's a shadow out there. Not the kind you can fight with steel. People sense it, but they don't talk about it. They just leave."

A silence fell over the table—not heavy, just thoughtful.

Nyv's eyes drifted toward the corner where the javelin rested. So did Bryn's. It had been Chovee's—his favoured weapon in life, now kept close by Nyv since the moment she took it from his fallen hand. Hers now, by duty, not by blood. She had placed it in the corner, not to forget it, but to keep it from haunting every glance. Until now, it had gathered only dust and memory.

Neither of them said anything, but the corner seemed darker than it had been that morning.

And then she stopped walking.

The silence stretched a heartbeat longer than it should have.

"That javelin," Yeldanna said, her voice sharp with sudden clarity. "Chovee's javelin. I remember it." Her eyes flicked to Nyv, then back to the glow. "It's glowing."

All eyes turned to the far corner of the room where the javelin rested, tucked against the wall behind a tall shelf of ritual books and bundled scrolls. Nyv had placed it there months ago—her way of keeping it close, but not too close. It had rested in silence, untouched, until now.

But it was glowing. Softly, unmistakably. A deep amber hue, as if lit from within.

Tassa frowned, taking a hesitant step closer. "That thing's watching me," she muttered—not quite joking. Then, louder: "Has it done that before?"

"No," Bryn murmured.

"It's only glowing because of her," Yeldanna added, her gaze never leaving Tassa. "It didn't light up when I entered. Or when Kaerda stood near. But the moment you moved close..." She didn't finish the sentence.

Tassa's brow furrowed. "It's a weapon. Not a lantern."

Bryn stepped a half pace closer, eyes fixed on the faint amber light. Something about it stirred the back of her mind—not with alarm, but with a sense of wrongness. To the others, it might look like simple radiance, but to her, the glow pulsed not with light but with a thin veil of shadow threaded through its centre. It felt... misplaced. Not the Queen's. Not her own. Something that didn't belong, but had learned to hide.

She didn't speak yet. Only watched.

Yeldanna stepped closer, narrowing her eyes. Her expression changed—not alarmed, but deeply focused. "There's something clinging to it," she said quietly. "Not a curse. Not divine." She extended one hand toward the javelin but didn't touch it. "It feels like shadow—not yours, Bryn. Not Hers. Something old. Residual. Like it brushed against death and didn't quite let go."

Bryn moved toward it slowly, Nyv mirroring her path from the other side of the room. The others hung back as the two of them approached the javelin in silence, drawn by the quiet pulse of light. They didn't hesitate. Whatever lay within the javelin, it was part of Chovee's truth now. And that made it theirs to carry.

They reached for it at the same time. Their hands hesitated for the briefest moment, then Nyv's fingers wrapped around the haft first followed closely by Bryn's hand closing over hers. Their eyes met—steady, but something deeper flickered beneath. The moment lingered, and neither pulled away. Bryn pulled her hand back, quickly but not harshly, her gaze flicking down, a flush rising to her cheeks. Embarrassed—not by the touch itself, but by how long she'd let it last.

Yeldanna watched, saying nothing. Her eyes shone knowingly—not at the javelin, but at their hands.

The javelin pulsed again—brighter this time, the glow catching along the curve of Nyv's palm and Bryn's knuckles where they touched. A faint vibration passed between them, like a word unsaid.

Yeldanna's voice broke the silence, low and certain. "You may have found more than your coven after all."

Nyv blinked. "You mean all of us, right?"

But her voice was softer than before, and a flush bloomed faintly beneath her eyes—an unspoken realization stirring just below the surface. She didn't look at Bryn, but her thoughts clearly did.

Yeldanna didn't answer. But she smiled—just slightly. The kind of smile an older woman gives when she sees a truth two younger ones haven't yet dared name. Her quiet approval, folded into silence.

The smile faded from Yeldanna's face as her gaze returned to the javelin.

"That glow isn't just reacting to presence or magic. It's signaling something. It's why I'm here. Chovee's spirit is restless—caught between two states, struggling to remain in either. And something has changed—enough to make it react to Tassa."

The silence lingered after Yeldanna's words, thick with unspoken realization snapping Bryn and Nyv back into the moment. The javelin continued to pulse faintly, its amber light a quiet reminder of the unrest that was growing, unseen.

Yeldanna stood, her hands clasped loosely behind her back. "The path to understanding this... this unrest," she said slowly, "won't be found by sitting here waiting for answers. You'll need to travel—to find someone who can help you cross between worlds. Between life and death. There is someone who may be able to help, a powerful, but selective druid"

Bryn looked up, her expression unreadable. "Where is this druid?"

Yeldanna hesitated. "There's a grove, far from here—hidden deep within the forest. But it's not just a matter of distance. This druid, he does not simply offer his aid to anyone. He only helps those who seek him with purpose—and with strength. He may not welcome you, but you will need him to move forward. To see what comes next."

Tassa, still caught in the quiet intensity of the moment, shifted on her feet. "What kind of 'purpose' do we need? We're already... in this. Isn't that enough?"

Yeldanna smiled faintly. "Purpose isn't just about why you've come this far. It's about how you'll choose to walk forward. You all have different reasons—different strengths. But only by aligning those strengths will you be able to handle what's coming."

Her eyes met Nyv's for a long moment. There was no surprise in the Seidra witch's gaze—only a quiet understanding, as if she had known this connection existed before they had even realised it. Nyv, usually so reserved, offered a slight, almost imperceptible nod, as though acknowledging something unspoken. Yeldanna's lips curled in the smallest of smiles, but it was not one of joy—it was the smile of someone who had seen what was coming long before anyone else.

"What exactly is this 'unrest' you're speaking of?" Bryn asked, her voice steady but laced with uncertainty.

Yeldanna glanced at the javelin again. "Chovee's spirit is still tethered to this world, and it's trying to pull others with it. His unrest isn't just about peace or vengeance—it's about a force that seeks to alter the balance. You're already tied to it, whether you wish to be or not. That javelin is no longer just a weapon. It's a marker. And the longer it glows, the closer you come to what it signifies."

Kaerda cleared her throat. "So, we travel to this druid. And then what?"

"Then you let him guide you," Yeldanna replied simply. "But be careful. His ways are not kind to those who do not understand the land. The forest will respond to your presence in ways you cannot predict. And what awaits you... might be more than any of you bargained for."

The weight of her words settled over them all. None of them spoke for a moment.

Tassa was the first to break the silence. "Then we need to go. The sooner, the better."

Bryn nodded, and even Kaerda, who rarely spoke without first considering the words carefully, seemed resolved.

Yeldanna set the empty cup down and looked to each of them in turn. "We've lost enough time already. You'll need to leave at first light. There's no telling what's already gathering behind the veil."

She crossed to the table, where a map lay, worn but well-kept, and spread it out before them. The parchment crackled faintly in the still air. "The path I'd suggest isn't the easiest, but it's the safest. The wilds between here and the druid's grove are thick with more than just trees. There are forces in play that you'll want to avoid, and others you'll have to face head-on."

Tassa leaned forward, a finger tracing the routes Yeldanna marked on the map, her brow furrowed. "What kind of forces?"

"Elementals, ancient spirits. Some corrupted, others just... wild. But there's a village here," Yeldanna tapped a spot further along the map, "that can help you. Once you reach it, the druid will sense your approach."

Bryn nodded slowly. "And how do we get there? You mentioned avoiding the shadow?"

Yeldanna's gaze softened for a moment, almost like she was remembering something distant. "You'll need to travel by day and hide by night. Keep the fire low and your voices softer than usual. The land has ears, and not all of them are friendly."

Nyv, who had been silently studying the map, spoke up. "How will we know when we're near the druid?"

Yeldanna met her gaze and smiled faintly, an expression that held both wisdom and mystery. "You'll know. His grove speaks only to those who truly seek it. And when you find it, it will find you in return."

The group settled into a quiet rhythm as Yeldanna continued marking their path. By the time the last sliver of light faded from the sky, the map was dotted with notations, and the plan was set. The Silent Accord had their route. They packed their gear in the dim light of the hearth, moving quietly, each absorbed in the preparations, but there was a shared feeling that hung in the air—a tension, but also a unity.

As they gathered by the door, ready to rest before the journey ahead, Yeldanna stood in the doorway, her cloak already wrapped around her shoulders. "Sleep now," she said. "You'll need all the strength you can muster for what comes next."

With that, she left them to their preparations. They didn't need to say it aloud. The journey had already begun.

Chapter 4 – Roots and Rumours

The hills east of Estavar were soft with spring, but the air hadn't decided whether to be kind or not. One moment warm with birdsong, the next sharp with wind that carried the scent of loam and rain. The party travelled in near silence, following no road, only Yeldanna's memory and Bryn's instinct. Somewhere ahead, tucked among root-veined stones and sleeping groves, was the man who might be able to fix what none of them could name.

Kaerda took the lead without speaking, her shield strapped across her back and her eyes scanning for signs more ancient than trails—scorched branches, moss turned the wrong way, stones that rang hollow. Tassa trailed a few steps behind, bouncing a small ember-orb between her hands like a juggler with a secret. She was humming, but only just.

Bryn walked alongside Nyv.

For a long time, they didn't speak. It wasn't uncomfortable—just shared quiet. Nyv carried Chovee's javelin across her back, wrapped in cloth, its glow hidden. She looked forward with a sense of purpose that never fully left her, even in the stillness. Bryn kept pace easily, letting her shadows drift a step behind her like smoke unbothered by wind.

They reached a small village near dusk, the kind that looked like it had grown accidentally rather than been built. Narrow footpaths wove between crooked homes, and chickens crossed wherever they pleased. The locals didn't seem unfriendly, but they weren't open either. They watched with the caution of people who'd survived things they weren't ready to name.

Nyv stepped forward first.

She didn't flash her spellbook or invoke her title. She simply asked, in a quiet, even voice, whether anyone had seen a druid pass through—or vanish near the southern groves.

No one answered directly.

But an old woman sitting near the well spat once and muttered, "Trees shift near the ridge path. Don't grow right. Something keeps birds from nesting."

Nyv nodded her thanks and placed a silver coin in the woman's bowl without ceremony.

"I hope this druid can help Chovee," she murmured as they turned to leave. It wasn't a declaration—just a thread of hope she didn't want to lose.

As the group prepared to move on, Bryn lingered at the edge of the square, watching Nyv speak to a weathered farmer. Nyv's hands moved in that calm, practical way of hers—gesturing, not commanding. A child clung to the man's leg. Nyv knelt to speak to the girl too, voice low and sure.

Bryn didn't realise she was smiling until Tassa leaned in behind her and whispered, "You watching the trees or something else?"

Bryn didn't answer. Just stepped forward and kept walking.

They left the village just before full dark, following the ridge path toward the southern groves. But as the last light faded, they stopped short of the trees and made camp in a clearing below the canopy's edge. Yeldanna's warning lingered in their minds: the forest didn't like to be walked after dark.

● ● ●

They kept the fire small and the camp tighter than usual, ringed with stones and faintly warded by Bryn's sigils drawn into the earth. Shadows shifted among the trees beyond the clearing, but none came close. Not that night.

Nyv took first watch, sitting with her back to a fallen log and her eyes on the treeline. She didn't call her familiar—Geoff had curled into her cloak hours ago—but she whispered quietly to the forest, as if the trees might answer. Geoff stirred once as the wind shifted, lifting his head with slow, deliberate motion. His eyes flicked toward the trees, unblinking. Then he ducked deeper beneath the cloak—not out of fear, but something quieter. Wariness, perhaps. Or recognition.

Bryn relieved her without words. As Nyv settled into her bedroll, Bryn lingered by the fire, half-lit and still. She didn't glance down as Nyv passed, but their shoulders brushed—unintentional, unspoken.

Later, Kaerda stirred in her sleep and muttered something about hammer strikes echoing in stone. Tassa, dreamless, snored softly under a heap of her cloak.

Bryn didn't wake them. She just watched the trees breathe.

Bone-Anna stood at the edge of the firelight, unmoving. She didn't need rest, but she stayed near, her bow slung across her back like memory waiting.

• • •

They rose at first light. The air was cool and damp, the fire long gone to ash. Bryn scattered the coals and whispered a word to the ravens circling above. The ravens didn't immediately follow her whisper. They wheeled once overhead, then perched along the treeline, silent and watching. Even they seemed unwilling to cross into the woods before morning. Then they moved on—quiet, focused, and alert.

The ridge path mentioned by the old woman was narrow and badly overgrown. It rose steadily into a low wooded shelf, then dipped into deeper groves where the trees seemed too old for the soil and too still for the wind.

The first sign came as a hush—not silence, but the absence of all familiar sound. No insects. No birds. Even their footsteps seemed muted. The air thickened, carrying the faint smell of crushed pine and something sweeter beneath it, like rotting mint.

"Something doesn't want us here," Kaerda murmured. "But it's not trying to stop us. Just... watching."

They passed a tree whose bark curled in spirals too perfect to be natural. Another had long vertical cuts along its trunk—smooth, even, deliberate. Tassa reached out toward one, but Nyv caught her wrist.

"Not that one," Nyv said softly. "It remembers being hurt."

Tassa glanced at her, puzzled, but withdrew her hand without argument.

Farther along, a fox crossed the trail in front of them—its fur pale and mottled, its eyes an unnatural green. It paused, looked directly at Nyv, then trotted off the path and vanished behind a copse of underbrush.

"I think that was an invitation," Bryn said.

"I think it was a warning," Kaerda muttered.

Still, they followed.

• • •

They emerged into a clearing marked by a single standing stone, no taller than a person and covered in moss. Around its base, the ground was bare—no grass, no leaves, no insects. Just earth.

A thin man with a hooked nose and layers of damp scarves was already there, kneeling by the stone with a chipped bowl in one hand and a carved pipe in the other.

"Are you the druid?" Nyv asked.

The man looked up, startled. "Me?" He snorted. "Gods, no. I sell roots and stories, not magic. But I saw something, if that's what you want."

He gestured vaguely to the standing stone. "That's new. Wasn't here last week. Then again, neither was the wind that talks or the stag that bowed at my door."

He leaned back on his heels and tapped the side of his pipe. "There was a squirrel once—grey as ash, with one red eye and one made of glass. It came down from the north and dug a hole beneath the alder roots, whisperin' names it didn't own. One day it left a pine cone on my doorstep, perfectly carved with a pattern no one could read. That's when the stone showed up."

He looked at them expectantly, then blinked as if surprised they hadn't understood. "Anyway. Not my business. Roots and stories, that's all."

He laughed to himself and went back to his bowl.

They left him behind, but not without exchanging glances.

"Not him," Tassa said.

"No," Bryn agreed. "But someone wanted us to speak to him."

Not long after, they stumbled into another clearing—this one thick with mushrooms clustered in a perfect spiral pattern, no wider than a cartwheel. The mushrooms were of several types: bone-white caps, orange wrinkled stalks, and one that shimmered faintly blue. None of them had seen anything like it.

Kaerda crouched beside the formation. "This isn't natural. Or if it is, it's not accidental. My grandmother used to say mushroom rings were faerie tricks— step into one, and you forget your name."

Tassa tilted her head. "A message?"

Nyv frowned. "Or bait."

They circled the spiral once, careful not to disturb it. Bryn said nothing, only stared at the blue one.

"What does it mean?" Tassa finally asked.

No one answered.

After a long silence, Kaerda straightened. "It means we're wasting daylight."

They moved on.

● ● ●

As the path narrowed again, the underbrush grew thick and thorny. A deer trail wound east, away from the old road, and the scent of fresh water wafted from that direction.

"Do we follow the signs or the water?" Kaerda asked.

Tassa gestured toward the deer trail. "That fox came from that direction. Same shimmer to the trees."

"But the stone was near water," Kaerda said. "And the mushroom ring was damp beneath. That blue one almost pulsed."

Nyv folded her arms. "We can't assume every oddity was meant for us. But we also can't treat them like nothing."

Bryn stood very still, eyes drifting between the paths. Her voice was low. "This place isn't just showing us things. It's reflecting us—choices, impressions, memory. The question isn't which path is safer. It's which one is expected."

Tassa frowned. "So... we should take the one that makes less sense?"

"No," Bryn said, stepping toward the deer trail. "We take the one they want us to take."

Nyv glanced at her. "And what if that's the trap?"

"Then we spring it together," Kaerda said simply, already moving.

The others followed.

The forest swallowed them without a sound. Even the ravens followed, silent on their wings.

211

As the Accord readied their weapons and spells, Bryn glanced down. The feather on her hand had begun to glow again—not brightly, but steadily. It wasn't power the Queen offered now. It was trust.

Chapter 5 – The Druid's Puzzle

The forest pressed in on them from all sides. No longer the wild, open spaces of the previous night, the trees now gathered densely, their branches clawing toward the sky like the fingers of a forgotten god. The air smelled of damp earth, wildflowers, and something else, something far less pleasant—decay, perhaps, or the faint sting of ash.

"Do you hear that?" Kaerda asked, her voice low.

The others paused and listened. In the distance, the steady hum of something ancient seemed to vibrate in the earth beneath their feet.

Bryn's eyes narrowed as she scanned the treeline. The Queen of Stillness's presence was strong here, but she could not discern whether the hum was a signal from the Queen or another trick of the land.

"It's him," Nyv said, her gaze shifting between the trees. "We're close."

A sound like a cracked branch splintering underfoot reached their ears. A massive snail, its shell streaked with lichen and old runes, crept into the clearing. It paused, antennae twitching, and then began to ripple with a strange shimmer—its form contracting, collapsing inward.

Before their eyes, the snail twisted into something upright—legs sprouting, moss falling away in folds, until what remained was a thin, reed-like man.

Geoff the Newt, who had been perched tensely on Nyv's shoulder, let out a low chirp and visibly relaxed. His small claws unclenched, and the ridge of tension along his spine smoothed. He blinked slowly, his orange belly dimming to a calm amber, and nestled closer to Nyv's neck as if reassured by the transformation.

The man's gaze drifted lazily across the group, and when it settled on Bone-Anna, something in his posture shifted. He tilted his head, as if listening to a distant tune.

"That one's not natural," he said, more to the grove than to them. "But she's not wrong, either."

The moss at her feet curled inward, but did not recoil. The forest allowed her.

He nodded, almost respectfully. "Some things return because they must. Not all memory decays."

Whatever this strange druid was, Geoff did not sense danger—and that alone shifted the group's tension.

The man's skin was pale, but it wasn't entirely the colour of flesh. There was something more unsettling about him—his eyes glowed faintly, like living embers in the dark.

"Well, well. It's you," the druid said in a voice that sounded both amused and confused. His eyes flickered over them, though it seemed like he was trying to focus on something else entirely. "Not many find their way here without a nudge from the wind or a whisper through root."

Nyv stepped forward, her tone measured but calm. "We're looking for guidance."

The druid's gaze finally locked on Nyv, and for a moment, she felt an odd sensation—a pull of recognition. She didn't understand why, but the sensation passed quickly—like remembering a dream just out of reach. A name nearly spoken. A voice she might've known once, long ago.

"Guidance?" the druid mused, his smile crooked. "That's a word people use when they're afraid to ask for help. But help, see—that's a vine with thorns. Always tangles. Always costs. Maybe a puzzle's kinder. At least it tells you when you're wrong."

He turned with no further explanation and walked into a clearing ringed with ancient stones. The clearing was perfectly round, lit by sun filtering through thick green canopies above. Strange flowers bloomed here in defiance of the season—out-of-place wildflowers and plants that should have wilted long ago. The stones were etched with faded spirals, and in the centre, a low bowl of dew sat on a flat altar of moss.

"One flower for each of you," he said, gesturing lazily. "But not of your choosing. The garden remembers. Plant the seed that best matches who you are, not who you pretend to be. If the flower blooms, the way opens. If not... well, that's just the way of it."

Kaerda stepped toward the seeds, but Bryn lifted a hand, her gaze drifting over the stones. "This is a test of memory. Of attunement. Let's proceed thoughtfully, rather than in haste."

Nyv was already kneeling by the bowl. The seeds shimmered faintly. "They resonate. Look—if I hover my hand here, it warms. Just barely."

"Try another," Bryn said softly.

Nyv shifted her hand. The glow dimmed.

Tassa leaned over. "So what happens if we pick the wrong one?"

The druid grinned. "Nothing blooms. Nothing opens. Nothing moves. You just sit here. Forever, maybe."

Kaerda muttered, "Charming."

But as they began to approach, the druid lifted a single finger.

"Ah," he said, tilting his head. "You'll want to tread carefully. She watches."

The moment his voice fell silent, the clearing itself responded. The moss thickened around the edges of the stones, creeping upward like wary fingers. A low hum began beneath the earth—a gentle, melodic resonance that tugged at the chest. The bowl of dew shimmered, and the seeds rose slowly—weightless, as if lifted by breathless memory.

Then, they scattered.

With a faint burst of silver light, the seeds embedded themselves in the earth around the stones, hidden now from sight.

Tassa took a step back. "Was that supposed to happen?"

The druid shrugged. "She likes surprises."

Nyv narrowed her eyes, already scanning the moss. "It's not about finding the right seed—it's about knowing where it went."

Kaerda exhaled slowly. "And planting it again?"

"No," Bryn murmured. "Calling it back."

She knelt beside one of the stones, closing her eyes. Around the others, the forest seemed to grow quieter, more still. Each companion understood: the puzzle wasn't just to choose, but to remember. To feel. To draw the right part of themselves into the earth and coax it to respond.

Only then could the flowers bloom.

One by one, they began the ritual.

Bryn and Nyv went first—and together. As Bryn extended her hand toward the moss, Nyv's fingers brushed her own, and both paused. They exchanged a glance.

"That one," Bryn whispered.

Nyv nodded, finishing the thought. "It smells like breath after grief. Like something let go."

They reached for the same seed.

For a moment, neither moved. Their hands hovered side by side above the moss, fingertips almost touching. There was no need to speak—something had clicked into place, something deeper than understanding. A shared stillness passed between them, not romantic, not yet, but unmistakably intimate.

Tassa, watching from her stone, raised one eyebrow and smirked, exchanging a look with Kaerda. Kaerda said nothing, but her brow lifted slightly—just enough to mark the moment, then softened into the smallest of smiles.

Bryn and Nyv, still knelt together, didn't notice. Or if they did, they didn't let it show.

Instead, they pressed their palms gently into the moss together, and the earth responded—not with light, but warmth. A hum. A whisper that only they seemed to hear.

The others watched as each companion stepped to a stone and planted a seed into the mossy surface. Tassa's flower bloomed in a burst of fire-orange with flickering petals like tongues of flame. Kaerda's flower came forth in embered bronze—warm, sturdy, unshaken by the wind. Bryn's bloomed midnight violet, veins of silver streaking across petals shaped like raven wings. Nyv's was the last—a pale blossom with a gold centre and teal-tipped edges, humming faintly.

The druid clapped once, vaguely.

"Well, I'll be," he said, approaching each flower with a tilt of his head. "She remembers. Look at this..."

He crouched beside Tassa's flame-lily first. "This one burns loud. Reckless. Hungry. But it blooms because it knows when to yield to softer winds. That's fire tempered by choice."

Then Kaerda's. "Embered bronze. Sturdy and loyal. This flower wouldn't bloom for someone seeking glory—it blooms for those who endure. Who carry memory like a hammer carries its strike."

He moved next to Bryn and Nyv's stones. He paused longest here.

"These two... well now. Not just in tune. Interwoven. Look here—silver veins in hers, gold edges in hers, and the roots below the soil have tangled."

He looked between them, one brow arching. "Not something you see often. The land saw fit to answer both at once. That means more than either of you knows just yet."

Tassa rolled her eyes but smiled. Kaerda simply nodded, arms crossed—knowing.

Bryn and Nyv exchanged a look, but said nothing. A quiet smile passed between them—half curiosity, half comfort. They chalked it up to time spent together, to battle-tested familiarity. Of course they'd chosen the same seed. Of course they'd moved in sync.

They didn't see what the others did. Not yet.

To them, it was another shared moment. A coincidence. Nothing more.

The druid stood, brushing moss from his knees. "That's the mark of true accord. Or the beginning of it."

The druid didn't move toward the tree just yet. Instead, he folded his hands behind his back and turned to face them once more.

"You're going to a place few remember," he said. "A place that doesn't want to be found. But it remembers her—your Queen. And what was taken from her."

Kaerda's brow furrowed. "What's there?"

"Remnants. Clues. Maybe regret, if you're not careful."

Nyv took a step forward. "Then that's where we need to be."

The druid nodded once, slowly. "East of the stormline lies the boundary of what's waking. Beyond the bones, the land shudders with things thought long buried. Something twisted slumbers there—a thing that drinks memory and gnaws on forgotten names."

He tilted his head. "You'll need to pass through the fractured places. Where the wind forgets direction. Where even the Worldthread goes quiet." He paused, and a strange flicker passed behind his eyes. "And where the lightning forgets its name."

Tassa crossed her arms. "Sounds inviting."

The druid chuckled. "Don't worry. You've already proven you remember what matters. That'll get you through the first gate."

Then the druid paused again—his head turning slightly, as if listening to something the others could not hear. A hush fell over the clearing, deeper than before.

He turned slightly toward Nyv but did not speak aloud. Then, as if plucking a thought from the wind, his voice came not through sound but through presence—pressed into Nyv's mind like moss through stone.

"The winds spoke just now, as they sometimes do. I do not choose to speak this—only to pass it on. You'll face a moment soon, daughter of Ravkareth. When the light bends and the shadow bleeds. You will have to choose—follow the logic you've lived by... or the feeling you fear. One will keep you safe. One will save you both."

Nyv blinked, startled by the intrusion, but the druid had already turned away. The others hadn't noticed.

A few heartbeats passed. Then he turned to them as a group once more, speaking aloud—his tone lighter, as if the moment had never happened.

"And where the lightning forgets its name," he added, almost as if to himself.

Then the moss parted. A hollow tree behind him cracked open with a sudden groan, revealing a dark passage lit from within by faint green light.

"There you go," he said. "She'll take you far. Not all the way. But far enough. East of the stormline. Beyond the bones."

He turned, humming to himself as he vanished into the wood.

They stared at the tree.

Bryn looked to Nyv. "Ready?"

Nyv hesitated.

The druid's words echoed quietly—*logic or feeling, safety or salvation*—like ripples beneath still water. She didn't fully understand what they meant, but the weight of them lingered behind her ribs, a pressure she couldn't name.

She looked to her companions. Kaerda stood calm and ready, like stone that could bend but not break. Tassa adjusted the straps on her gear, already humming a battle tune under her breath. And Bryn—Bryn was watching her. Not questioning. Just waiting.

That look, simple as it was, threatened to tip the balance.

Nyv swallowed and turned away before it could.

The wind shifted through the trees.

She drew a breath, steadied her shoulders.

"Together," she said—to all of them.

And stepped through the threshold, into the waiting dark.

Chapter 6 – The Wind That Eats

The storm was waiting.

They were flung from the gnarled trunk of a nearly dead tree—twisted and half-buried in a dune of grey sand, its bark scorched and peeling like old parchment. It was the only living thing in sight, and barely that. The spell had clung to its last breath of life to deliver them through. No transition, no time to adjust—just a sudden, howling violence that clawed at their cloaks and pulled at their breath. The earth here was broken, crusted in dried salt and glassy ridges. The sky, if there was one, had been replaced by a churning bruise of cloud—black and violet, pulsing with lightning that never reached the ground.

Kaerda was the first to recover, raising her shield instinctively as sand slammed into it like thrown daggers. Bryn's coat flared behind her, silver embroidery catching strange flashes of light, her body low and still. Nyv raised an arm to shield her face. Geoff the Newt ducked deep into her collar.

Tassa hit the ground in a controlled tumble, springing back to her feet with a grimace. "Is this where the air forgets how to breathe?" she shouted over the wind.

"Stay together!" Kaerda barked, already forcing herself forward against the wind's push. She planted her hammer in the ground and began muttering prayers to Durnach the Forgemaker beneath her breath, drawing symbols in the air that dissipated too quickly to hold.

The wind didn't howl so much as *speak*—a fractured cacophony of voices pulled from other places, other times. Nyv froze as one of them slithered past her ear in her own voice:

"You left her behind."

She turned sharply, but saw nothing. Only the storm.

"Kaerda!" Bryn's voice cut through the gale. "We need shelter!"

"I know!" the dwarf snapped, teeth clenched. "It's like trying to forge with steam—nothing's holding!"

The ground beneath them shifted again, cracking open to reveal a trench—too shallow to swallow them, but deep enough to scatter their footing. Tassa stumbled. Bryn caught her. Nyv's eyes flicked toward Bryn—not in alarm, but in that quiet, measuring way she always did when Bryn moved too close to danger.

"I can't... I can't feel the roots," she said, half to herself, half in alarm. "The ground is wrong."

Bryn moved to her side, steadying her. "Then we trust stone and shield."

Kaerda let out a sharp breath, dropping to one knee. "Durnach the Forgemaker preserve us," she whispered—and for a moment, the symbols she traced sparked against the air like molten metal cooling. She struck her hammer against her shield and shouted:

"Karun beldor!"

A dome of golden flame surged outward and held—thin and flickering, but solid enough to encase them in a bubble of relative calm. The wind still howled outside, but inside, the storm became a dull roar.

"Not perfect," Kaerda said, slumping slightly. "But it'll hold."

Geoff poked his head from Nyv's collar, blinking. Tassa let out a soft laugh and dropped onto the ground.

Then the ground trembled.

From the swirling dust beyond the dome, shapes emerged—tall, scaled, and twisted. Lizardfolk, but not as they should be. Their eyes glowed faintly with stormlight, and their bodies were marked by jagged black veins. They moved like things that remembered how to be hunters, but had forgotten what they once hunted for.

Kaerda lifted her hammer again. Bryn's shadows stirred.

"Here we go," Nyv murmured, drawing her scimitar.

The wind screamed again.

And the fight began.

Tassa's hand ignited with flickering red-orange energy even as the barrier trembled. "Let's see how storm likes fire," she muttered, hurling an *Auric Ember* through a crack in the dome. The orb exploded against the chest of the lead lizardfolk in a burst of flame—then ricocheted mid-air, catching a second target in its arc. Both screamed as fire bloomed across scale and shadow. The storm swallowed the sound, but not the light.

Bryn stood just opposite Nyv, her movements quiet and precise. As Nyv traced her sigils, Bryn's hand lifted in near-perfect timing. *dúil pórth*, she whispered—six black portals spiraling outward beneath the enemy line, their shadows interlacing with the ghostlight flicker of the Ravkari spirits forming at Nyv's shoulders. Two of Bryn's portals held, dropping startled lizardfolk into the void below—just as Nyv's Ravkari spirits surged outward from her in the same breath, battering and burning the enemies nearest to them. Shadow and spirit collided with storm-born flesh in perfect tandem. It was not rehearsed. But it moved like trust made manifest.

Kaerda braced against the dome's edge, shield raised high. "They'll break through soon," she growled.

Outside, a scaled figure climbed the dome, claws raking over the curve. It leapt and crashed down atop them. The barrier held—but it shuddered.

The group moved as one. Two lizardfolk vanished through Bryn's portals, their snarls cut off mid-scream.

One of the lizardfolk—larger, adorned with broken storm-totems and crude runes—raised its clawed hand. The wind shifted, compressed, and rushed toward Nyv in a concentrated gust meant to knock her from her feet.

But Nyv did not move.

The wind curled around her, parted like water around stone, and rushed past. She blinked but did not stumble.

Geoff let out a low chitter of approval from within her collar.

Bryn stepped to the same side as Nyv now, their shoulders nearly aligned—one wreathed in shadows, the other in flickering ancestral light. They moved without speaking, covering each other's blind spots instinctively.

The dome collapsed—not shattered, but shed. Kaerda released it with a grunt of focus, freeing the group to strike.

Bryn surged forward first, cloaked in *Queens Mantle*, flames of darkness licking the space around her limbs. The shadows pulsed outward as she advanced, and the nearest lizardfolk recoiled too late. One snarled as the shadows seared into its scales—necrotic veins spidering across its flesh, the magic burning without flame.

Kaerda was close behind, shield raised, hammer glowing with divine flame. Her roar echoed across the wind-scoured field.

Tassa wove between them, a blur of fire and motion.

Nyv stepped into the chaos, Ravkari spirits still circling her, scimitar raised, eyes locked.

"We need to break them," Kaerda shouted, staggering as a claw raked her shoulder.

Bryn's voice rang out, calm and certain. "Now."

Nyv met her gaze, and for a heartbeat, the space between them stilled. Bryn's presence was not loud—it was *anchoring*. Nyv inhaled, lifted her hands with renewed purpose, and whispered with breath and force, *venor alashi!*

The ground split with a roar, and a massive *Wavebind* erupted, drawing power from the storm itself. It pulled nearby storm-fused lizardfolk into a spiraling tower of churning water. Their roars twisted into gurgles as the surge drowned them. Around them, the storm faltered—its rhythm broken, wind patterns disrupted by the sudden surge.

Kaerda exhaled, steadying herself. The tide had turned.

Only one lizardfolk remained. Wounded, unbalanced, it turned to flee.

Bryn stepped forward. Her shadows writhed, her gaze cold. She raised her hand and whispered, *márna rüvína.*

From her outstretched fingers, a violet bolt surged forth, shaped like a raven in full flight—its wings of force edged in shimmering light, its core pulsing with arcane fury. It screamed through the air, trailing shadow, and struck the fleeing lizardfolk between the shoulder blades. The creature was thrown forward with a sickening crack, its body folding mid-step before crumpling into the dust, smoke curling from the impact.

The storm quieted.

Kaerda lowered her shield with a deep, steadying breath. Nyv released the final thread of her magic, and the Ravkari spirits faded into mist. The massive pillar of water collapsed in a rush of steam.

For a long moment, nothing moved.

Then, silence returned.

Kaerda was the first to move again. She stepped forward slowly, scanning the dusted horizon, hammer still gripped tightly in one hand. "We need shelter," she said, her voice low and hoarse. "This quiet won't last."

Bryn nodded, eyes still on the horizon where the last lizardfolk had fallen. "We're too exposed."

Tassa exhaled, letting her flames recede with a flick of her fingers. "I vote for anywhere with a roof."

Nyv stepped beside Bryn. "There was a shape—half-sunken, maybe a ruin— before the last gust hit. I think I saw it to the east."

No one argued. They gathered what they could, checked for wounds, and set out in silence—moving cautiously through the scattered remains of battle, heading toward the direction Nyv had indicated.

The storm didn't return, but it loomed—circling above, watching.

As the sun began to dip behind the bruised sky, they reached the edge of a collapsed stone structure—walls half-swallowed by sand, its top lost beneath the dust.

Kaerda stepped forward first and tested the stone. It held.

"This'll do," she said, more quietly than usual.

They descended into the ruin, finally stepping out of the wind.

Only then did they begin to speak again.

As they set down gear and checked wounds, Nyv moved toward Kaerda, who had slumped against a low wall. Blood darkened a tear in her armour near the shoulder.

"Let me see," Nyv said softly.

Kaerda hesitated, then gave a small grunt and allowed her to kneel.

Nyv peeled back the armour just enough to inspect the wound. Her fingers were quick, careful. A soft chant under her breath—nothing grand, just a thread of old Ravkari charm—slowed the bleeding.

Kaerda grunted again, this time with approval. "Didn't know you had a bedside manner."

"Only for people I trust," Nyv replied, her tone dry but warm.

They shared a small nod.

Then the party settled in around the ruined chamber, breath beginning to even, the weight of the storm still clinging to their clothes.

Kaerda removed one gauntlet and crouched near a portion of the exposed wall, brushing away sand with a reverent hand. She pressed her palm to the stone and closed her eyes, muttering softly. The others watched in silence.

"This stone wasn't carved by surface folk," she said finally. "Too fine. Too seamless. And this—" she tapped a faint groove in the wall "—isn't Dwarven. It's arcane. Purpose-built. Velthari work, most likely."

Tassa leaned back against a column fragment. "So… we're in the desert?"

Kaerda nodded. "Vharask Dunes. Has to be. That druid flung us halfway across Núvarien."

Bryn crossed her arms, thoughtful. "Which means we're near the bones of what used to be Veltharyn. That explains the storm... and the shadow-bleeding lizardfolk."

Nyv, still standing near the entrance, looked back toward the horizon. "We may not know exactly where—but we know enough to plan."

Kaerda nodded once. "We rest here tonight. At first light, we start searching the ruin. There's more buried here than sand."

● ● ●

Later, under the fractured remnants of a ceiling that barely kept the cold wind out, Bryn and Nyv took the first watch while the others slept.

Geoff nestled quietly beside Bryn's boot, his eyes half-lidded.

Before settling into her watch, Nyv moved quietly across the chamber and knelt beside Tassa. The halfling murmured in her sleep, brow furrowed. Her blanket had slipped to one side. Without a word, Nyv adjusted it gently over her shoulders, then rested two fingers briefly at Tassa's temple—a gesture of calm more than healing.

Tassa stilled, the furrow smoothing from her brow.

Then Nyv rose and returned to Bryn's side. Tassa lay with one arm draped across her chest, the soft glow of residual ember magic fading at her fingertips. Kaerda snored softly, her hammer across her lap.

Bryn sat just inside the archway, one knee drawn to her chest. Nyv sat beside her, adjusting the wrapping on her scimitar's hilt.

"That waterspout... I've never seen you cast anything like it before. It was incredible," Bryn said, the admiration plain in her voice.

Nyv glanced up. "Neither have I. The spell—I don't know, it felt like the storm helped me. Like something old in it knew me."

They were silent a moment, listening to the wind press against the ruin walls.

"You and I," Bryn said, "we moved like we'd trained together for years."

Nyv smiled faintly. "We've fought side by side long enough."

Bryn's expression softened. "Still. It felt different today."

"Yeah," Nyv murmured, after a moment. "It did."

Neither pursued the thought. The silence that followed was not uncomfortable.

They kept watch like that—side by side, eyes on the storm.

And the wind, for once, did not speak.

Chapter 7 – Shadows in the Stone

The first light of dawn pressed dimly through the fractured ceiling—not true sunlight, but a faint golden haze, filtered through the thinning veil of storm above. It painted softened streaks across dust and ruin. Bryn stirred first, rising without sound. Her coat was already on. Nyv followed, rubbing the sleep from her eyes as Geoff the Newt crawled from the folds of her bedroll and stretched with a quiet chirp.

Tassa grumbled, curling tighter in her blanket. Kaerda, already sitting upright with hammer across her lap, grunted and stood.

"We should search the rest of the structure," Kaerda said, glancing toward the partially collapsed corridor leading deeper underground. "There might be something useful. Food. Maps. Anything that tells us where we are—or what else was buried here."

"Agreed," Bryn said softly. "And we don't know what the storm will do next."

As they gathered their gear and ate a quick ration, the wind outside remained quiet—too quiet. Not stillness, but tension held just beyond the threshold.

They moved cautiously into the ruin, descending cracked steps choked with sand and moss. Faint traces of arcane light glowed in sigils too old to decipher.

Kaerda moved with a careful reverence, one gloved hand brushing along the stone walls. "This wasn't just carved," she murmured. "It was shaped. Layered through enchantment. Built to endure, but not to be remembered."

Nyv paused to examine a pillar etched with long-faded symbols. "It's wrong," she said. "My magic doesn't read the stone. It's like trying to feel with numb fingers."

Further in, the air grew colder. Columns rose like ribs from the floor, and the light dimmed unnaturally—shadows clinging where they shouldn't.

"This is Velthari," Kaerda said at last, halting near a fractured arch inscribed with faintly pulsing glyphs. "I've seen similar structure lines in ruins near the Sunset Mountains. Same magical threading. But this place... it's different."

Kaerda stepped forward again, more deliberate this time. Her brow furrowed, her eyes focused like a smith inspecting flawed metal. She crouched low, running her fingers along the faint seams in the floor and walls, her gloved hand moving from groove to groove with practised care.

"This wasn't made for aesthetics," she muttered. "It's precision. Every angle set to direct flow—magic or memory, maybe both. Look here—see this hairline split? It's a memory conduit. I've only ever seen work like this in artifacts, not architecture."

Kaerda crouched by a cracked wall just beyond the final chamber. Her fingers brushed faint etchings in the stone—worn by time, but deliberate. "This isn't a guard post," she muttered. "They weren't defending from within. They were sealing something out."

She scraped away the dust and retrieved a sliver of obsidian etched with a faded insignia—two concentric circles around a jagged tower. Her brow furrowed. "I've seen this seal before—Banished tactical glyphwork. Elite corps. Not loyalists. These ones defected."

Bryn stepped closer, brow tight. "Defected?"

"Tried to lock something away. Memory maybe. Or knowledge. Something they weren't willing to let their masters have."

Nyv ran her hand over the air, sensing lingering threads. "Then whatever was here wasn't just a threat to them—it was sacred enough to die for."

The silence that followed was not of fear, but reverence.

She shifted, tapping an indentation nearly smoothed by time. A faint hollow sound echoed back. "They wove memory into the stone itself."

She sat back on her heels, gaze still fixed on the wall. "Nothing enchanted here. Not anymore."

She ran her fingers over a hairline seam in the wall. "This wasn't part of the original empire. This is from the Banished City—the one that was banished by Vharion the Final Warden. They were sent into Umbraveth, some refer to it as the Shadowlands, and stayed there for centuries."

Tassa frowned. "And then what?"

"Then they came back," Kaerda said grimly. "Not as scholars. As conquerors. Altered by their time in the dark they found a way to return. They served Nhalis, who they called the Veilmother. Not Vessara, the Keeper of Magic as most users of the arcane had done. But their return was imperfect. The landscape had changed since they left and when they returned, there was nothing to tether the city to the now sunken landmass far below them. The entire city fell."

Nyv looked around. "The people who built this place… they weren't just powerful. They were hungry."

Kaerda nodded. "The Banished. The name of the city's gone from me, but everyone knew it as the Banished City."

They stood in silence, the enormity of the place settling around them.

They found the mural near what must have once been a gathering hall—its walls half-collapsed, ceiling broken in places, the remnants of a once-vaulted ceiling now choked with rubble. Much of it was obscured by rubble and dust, fractured stone concealing large portions of the surface.

Kaerda, Nyv, and Bryn worked in near-silence to shift a few of the larger fallen stones. Even Geoff the Newt paced curiously along the mural's lower edge. As more of the wall was revealed, the true scale of the artwork emerged: nearly fifteen feet across and at least eight tall, rendered in pigments that had darkened but not faded. The figures were unmistakable now—dragons. One gold, radiant even in decay. One shadowy-blue, sleek and sharp, lightning arcing faintly from its open mouth. They soared above a shattered landscape that bore the hallmarks of magical ruin.

There was reverence in the brushstrokes, but something else beneath it— something that shimmered just below the stone, waiting.

Tassa approached first, drawn without thinking. As her hand lifted toward the edge of the painting, something shifted.

The mural pulsed.

Not visibly—but in her mind. A thread of shadow pulled taut. The others froze as the air around them stilled.

The gold dragon turned, slow and majestic, its scales glowing with memory and pride. The blue followed just behind—familiar, trusted. There was no sound, yet Tassa *felt* it. Wind and sky. Heat on her wings.

Then—without warning—lightning surged from the blue's jaws. It struck her—*the gold*, but also *her*—through the wing and into the ribs. The sensation wasn't pain alone; it was betrayal. Shock. A helpless, spiraling fall. And in the periphery of her mind, a voice echoed:

"There is no room for weakness."

The gold dragon fell, twisting in the air, its light dimming.

The blue did not roar or chase. It kept flying, straight into a yawning black sky that folded inward like a wound. And then it too was gone.

And then the vision was gone.

The silence that followed wasn't real. Not yet. It echoed too loud inside her.

Tassa gasped and stumbled backward, one hand clutching her chest, the other bracing against the wall. Her eyes were wide, unfocused.

"Are you alright?" Bryn asked, her voice low but alert.

Tassa shook her head. "I… it was just a mural. I thought it moved."

Nyv studied Tassa for a long moment. "You saw something."

"It felt… familiar," Tassa whispered. "But not in a way I can name."

They gave her space. Only when her breath had steadied did Tassa describe what she'd seen—the gold dragon, the betrayal, the fall.

Kaerda leaned against a fractured pillar. "A gold dragon brought down by a blue? I've never heard of that. Not in any of the old epics."

Bryn's expression was unreadable. "Dragons betray each other. But this… it sounds personal."

Nyv frowned. "It wasn't conquest. From Tassa's description, it was cruelty."

No one had an answer. But the mural, quiet now, seemed to listen.

Kaerda broke the silence, her voice thoughtful. "If this mural was made before the city disappeared, when the inhabitants still lived here, before becoming Banished—and that city crashed over a hundred years ago—then this painting is nearly two-thousand years old. But it's depicting something older. Much older."

Bryn nodded slowly. "A memory passed down? Or preserved in the stone the way the rest of this place was."

Kaerda crossed her arms. "We haven't seen anything else like this. No other memory triggers, no similar enchantments. The painting itself was likely created in line with the rest of the structure—but the embedded memory was added later. By someone... or something."

Nyv's voice was low. "Either way, someone thought it was important enough to remember—maybe so we wouldn't forget the cost of betrayal. And something embedded in it has stirred up our Tassa."

Bryn lingered a moment longer by the mural, her gaze tracking the shadow dragon's arcing silhouette. Then she stepped back, allowing the shadows to settle.

Nyv touched the edge of the wall lightly, her palm flat against the stone. There was nothing—no sensation, no pull. Her magic couldn't read it. The stone felt as hollow as silence.

Behind them, unseen by the party as they moved on, the faint outline of the shadowy dragon in the painting shimmered subtly—etched just beneath the surface of the stone, as if the memory had left a shadow behind.

Chapter 8 – The Gilded Lock

The corridor narrowed with every step, its edges uneven and unfinished. Dust coated everything. Whatever had once passed through here had not done so in ages. The torchlight flickered over rough-cut stone, broken tile, and wind-scattered debris. Kaerda moved slowly at the front, her hand grazing the wall with each step.

"We've passed four collapsed hallways," Tassa muttered from the rear. "How do we know this isn't another dead end?"

Kaerda didn't answer. She had that look again—the one that meant she was listening to something only she could feel.

Bryn watched her closely. "She knows stone," she said quietly. "Let her lead."

They came to a stop in a narrow alcove where the air seemed colder, denser. Kaerda crouched, running her palm along the floor's edge. The stone changed here. Less fractured. More deliberate.

"There's something off," she murmured. "This wall doesn't belong."

At first glance, it was just another section of ruin—tall, sheer, and impassable. But under closer inspection, its surface was different: not dull and aged like the rest, but dark and smooth. Obsidian.

Kaerda stood and pressed her palm to it.

"No seams," she muttered. "No door frame. But this was placed, not carved. I can feel the echo where it connects to the foundation."

Bryn stepped forward, examining the edge under the light. "It's too clean," she agreed. "Too perfect."

Nyv nodded once. "Then something's behind it."

Tassa tilted her head. "Locked tight with no lock."

Kaerda's eyes narrowed. "Then we make a key."

She knelt again, this time bringing her face closer to the glossy surface. Pulling a small chisel from her belt, she tapped it gently against the base of the obsidian wall—once, twice—listening, not for sound, but for resistance.

"There," she said, almost to herself. "Not a flaw. A hollow."

She scraped delicately at the edge, clearing dust with the side of her hand. A faint groove emerged, no wider than a thread, so seamless it would never have been seen under less focused hands. She followed it upward, fingers reading the shape by touch alone.

And then, halfway up the wall, her gloved fingers paused.

Kaerda blew gently against the stone. A fine layer of grime swirled away, revealing a recessed mark no bigger than a coin.

"A keyhole," she confirmed softly. "But you'd never see it. Not unless you were listening through the stone."

Kaerda remained crouched before the wall a moment longer, tracing the recessed mark with the edge of her glove. "The size is smaller than I expected," she murmured. "Shallow insertion, narrow stem. But there's weight to it—whatever this unlocks, it wasn't meant to be opened often."

Bryn stepped beside her, crouching to examine the groove. She withdrew a small jeweller's pick from her pouch, probing gently. "The key will need a tapered end," she said. "Flat, not toothed. Almost like a tuning pin, not a blade. Precision over complexity."

Kaerda nodded. "And dense enough not to warp."

Bryn looked up and met her eyes. "We'll only get one chance."

Kaerda rose and reached for her pack, drawing out a small bundle wrapped in oiled cloth. She unwrapped it with care, revealing a short ingot of pale, silver-steel alloy etched faintly with dwarven runes. "Forge-bonded," she said. "Meant for sacred work. I never thought I'd need it out here."

She set it onto a stone slab and withdrew her travel hammer and a pair of thick-handled tongs. "I can shape the frame, but it'll need detail. Precision."

Bryn stepped forward. "I've worked finer pieces," she said, her voice quiet but sure. Her fingers hovered above the alloy. "With your strength and my finesse, it may hold."

Kaerda nodded once, then knelt and began to heat the alloy with a soft flame summoned from her palm. The metal glowed slowly, shifting to orange, then gold. Bryn knelt opposite her, eyes fixed on the forming shape.

Together, they worked—Kaerda striking with practised rhythm, Bryn guiding the shaping with whispered shadows that cooled and carved as needed. Tassa and Nyv stood back, watching in silence, the only sounds the soft tap of hammer, the hiss of shadow cooling hot metal, and the quiet breath of trust passing between them.

What emerged was simple—no ornament, no flourish. Just a key, perfectly shaped to fit a lock no one else would have found.

Kaerda took the finished key in hand, its weight undeniable despite its size. She stepped toward the obsidian wall, breath steady, and inserted it into the hidden slot. It slid in cleanly—too cleanly—and as she turned it, the key didn't click. It vanished. Melted into the stone like a drop of ink into still water.

The wall remained still. Then a tremor passed through it—a pulse of sound, low and harmonic.

Lines of soft white light traced outward from the keyhole in precise geometry, blooming across the obsidian surface in a spiderweb of shifting shapes. A rising tone echoed in the corridor—pure, crystalline, and unfinished. It hovered there, unresolved.

Tassa flinched. "That's not a door. That's a chord."

Bryn's eyes narrowed. "A lock that sings."

A small panel slid open beside the wall, revealing a set of five obsidian tiles arranged in a line. Each bore a faint glyph and a subtle groove, as if they could be pressed or slid.

Kaerda exhaled slowly. "The key turned. Now we tune it."

There was a long silence.

Then a sound—a hum, soft and low—drifted from the rear of the group. Tassa, still leaning lightly on her staff, tilted her head and began to match the tone that echoed from the wall. The hum rose in pitch, brightening with the harmony that floated through the corridor.

Nyv blinked. "You're... humming it?"

Tassa didn't answer. Her eyes were half-lidded, fingers trailing over the nearest tile as if feeling for vibration rather than sight.

"Third and fifth," she murmured. "The second is flat. That's why it won't resolve."

Kaerda raised an eyebrow. "How do you know that?"

"I don't," Tassa said cheerfully. "But my ears do."

One by one, she adjusted the tiles—pressing one down slightly, sliding another into alignment. Each movement gave a soft chiming note. The tone shifted, drawing closer to harmony.

"Almost," Tassa whispered. Her voice was low, focused. "One more..."

She touched the final tile and gave it a gentle press.

The suspended chord resolved.

The obsidian wall shimmered like water—and then erupted into motion.

A bloom of golden light burst outward from the centre glyph, casting radiant veins across the surface like cracks in glass. The wall fractured—not with destruction, but precision—as if each shard were a pane of reality sliding aside.

Arcane runes flared to life in the air, spinning like constellations. The folded segments of obsidian rotated in silent sequence, overlapping and dissolving into mist. The air grew heavy with the scent of ozone and ancient magic—Velthari, unmistakable and near-perfect.

A final pulse rippled through the chamber, and with it, the entire wall vanished.

Beyond it lay a chamber of impossible scale—its ceiling vaulting far beyond the architecture of the ruin above, as if reality had stretched to accommodate it. Gold gleamed in precise formations—not scattered, but stacked like altars or libraries of coin.

The group stepped cautiously into the chamber. Their boots made no sound on the polished stone floor, and the air within felt untouched—dry and reverent, as if the space itself were holding its breath.

Kaerda scanned the architecture with quiet awe. "This isn't just a vault," she murmured. "It's a sanctum."

Shelves of treasure rose in measured arcs from the floor to the far wall—meticulously placed coin, polished ingots, and decorative urns that shimmered with arcane sealwork. Nothing was disturbed. Not a single scrap of dust.

Tassa's breath caught in her throat.

"It's beautiful," she whispered. "Not greedy. Just… glorious."

She stepped forward, drawn by the golden light that reflected off her cheeks and collarbones. Her fingers hovered over a particularly ornate bowl etched in spiraling flame patterns.

"It feels warm," she said, almost in a trance.

Nyv watched her carefully. "Don't touch anything yet."

Tassa didn't move closer. But she didn't step back either.

Her fingers trembled slightly as she gazed at the mountain of gold.

"It's not just beautiful," she murmured, more to herself than to the others. "It feels like it's waiting. Like it knows me."

Kaerda shot her a glance, wary. "That's not comforting."

But Tassa shook her head, almost smiling. "It's not bad. It's… familiar."

She stepped between two arched mounds of coin, her boots brushing against their polished edges. "My people taught that gold remembers fire," she said. "And I always believed it. There's a warmth to it. A memory. I don't want to take it. I just want to know it's real."

Bryn's voice was quiet behind her. "You've got dragon blood, Tassa. It's possible it's not just memory—it's instinct."

Tassa stopped near the centre of the chamber, eyes wide. "Maybe a little greed too," she admitted, her tone soft with honesty. "But not the stealing kind. The wanting-to-keep kind."

None of them saw the subtle tremor ripple through the nearest heap of coin.

Tassa's fingers brushed the rim of the flame-etched bowl. Just a touch—barely more than contact. Not to take, not to claim, only to feel.

The reaction was instant.

The golden heap beside her surged upward like a wave, coins scattering into the air in a gleaming arc. A limb of treasure struck toward her with the force of a thrown anvil.

Nyv moved before thought, shoving Tassa aside with a burst of strength that sent them both sprawling. The impact struck where Tassa had stood a heartbeat earlier, shattering part of the stone floor.

The pile collapsed again, gold cascading back into place like a breathing thing returning to stillness.

Kaerda raised her hammer. "That wasn't random."

Bryn narrowed her eyes, scanning the mounds. "It's hunting us."

Another strike came from a different heap—this time aimed at Bryn. She twisted away, shadows erupting to block the worst of the blow.

The creature never stayed visible. Each strike came from a new direction—gold erupting from silence, vanishing just as quickly.

"We can't hit it," Nyv hissed, crouched behind a stack of broken urns. "It disappears too fast."

"We wait," Bryn said, her voice low and steady. "We watch. Next time it strikes, we strike back."

A shimmer of motion flickered to Nyv's left. Her eyes widened—too late.

A storm of coins surged toward her, forming a blade-like crescent. Nyv shouted an incantation: *vheran kishel!* A translucent barrier snapped into place just in time. The golden arc slammed into the magical shield with a deafening ring, then burst apart, coins raining harmlessly across the stone.

"Now!" Kaerda roared, swinging her hammer toward the heap that had animated.

Tassa raised her staff, flame flickering from its tip. "That one—it moved!"

The group lashed out, striking toward the mound. Bryn's blast of shadow pierced its forming torso, and Kaerda's hammer crashed into the core just before it faded. The golem's form coalesced for a heartbeat—a shifting figure of coin and power—shuddering as their attacks struck home, before retreating again into the floor.

Kaerda cried out as the blow landed squarely against her side, sending her crashing into a column of urns. Gold and ceramic clattered around her. But as the strike connected, Nyv whipped a blast of wind in response, and Tassa hurled a flare of fire at the heap from which it had launched. Their retaliation struck true—just as the mass began to dissolve once more. The sound of breaking pottery echoed through the chamber.

She grunted, forcing herself up. "That one hurt."

Then it struck again. This time, the blow came faster and heavier—its form almost fully revealed for a heartbeat before lashing out. The heap of gold convulsed into the shape of a massive limb, hurling itself like a wave at the group. Kaerda braced, Bryn shouted a warning, and Tassa raised her staff in defence.

The group reacted as one. Nyv summoned a blast of wind to redirect the arc. Bryn's shadow magic raked across the exposed limb, carving deep through its golden form. Tassa's fire found the joint of its motion, exploding in a flare of molten light.

For the first time, the golem faltered. Coins scattered—hundreds of them—rolling away in all directions. A shimmer at its core, a sigil of control long buried, flickered and dimmed.

The heap collapsed in on itself, reforming—slower this time. Uncertain.

Across the chamber, Geoff the Newt stilled. Where he had been mimicking Nyv's posture moments ago, now he crouched low, head tilted, unblinking.

Nyv noticed. "Geoff?"

He didn't move. His bright orange belly pulsed slowly as he took a cautious step toward the nearest pile of treasure.

Tassa looked up from where she crouched. "Is he... tracking it?"

"No," Nyv said slowly, her voice taking on a hushed reverence. "He's not afraid of it."

Geoff stepped onto a coin, then another. His tiny feet made no sound, but the air around him shifted.

"He knows it's not evil," Nyv murmured. "He doesn't sense hate. Just pain. Just purpose."

Bryn's gaze sharpened. "It's not attacking out of rage. It's defending. Reacting."

Kaerda wiped blood from her lip. "So what do we do? Let it keep striking?"

Nyv turned toward the others, her stance calming. "No. We show it we understand. We stop moving. Stop threatening. We give it space."

One by one, the members of the Accord eased back. Kaerda lowered her hammer. Tassa extinguished the flame at the tip of her staff. Bryn let the shadows fade from around her shoulders, exhaling slowly.

The room grew still again.

From within the largest mound at the centre of the chamber, the gold shifted—not to strike, but to settle. The coins that had surged outward began to roll back into place, piece by piece, as if being drawn inward by memory.

The pile quivered once more, then went still.

It had not fled. It had not retaliated. It had simply… returned.

A silence deeper than before fell over them. The golem had recognised their restraint. It no longer saw them as thieves, but as something else.

Kaerda spoke first. "It's standing down."

Tassa nodded, eyes wide. "Because we did."

Geoff the Newt turned in place once, then padded back toward Nyv's boot with casual grace.

Kaerda looked down at her hammer, then at the scattered coins still rolling to a stop. "I struck it without knowing what it was," she said, voice low. "It wasn't mindless. We just didn't ask."

Bryn stepped beside her. "We reacted before we tried to understand. But it listened when we finally did."

The hoard glistened under the arcane light—unchanged, unclaimed, untouched. A treasure not meant to be taken, but witnessed.

But then, from the apex of one of the central mounds, a single gold coin rolled free.

It did not fall or scatter—it rolled in a perfect arc, curving down the steps of the stacked treasure, clinking once, then again, before coming to rest at Tassa's feet.

No one spoke.

Tassa crouched slowly, picking up the coin with reverent care. It was warm—not hot, not enchanted, but *warm* in a way that echoed her words from earlier. Familiar. Alive.

She looked at the mound, then at her companions. "I didn't ask for it," she said softly. "But I think… it knew."

She turned back to the vault and bowed her head slightly.

"I'll close the door behind us," she said. "No one else needs to wake it."

Tassa approached the tiles, humming softly again—the same melody as before, but inverted, richer, more deliberate. Somehow, the tune was even more beautiful in reverse. Her fingers danced lightly across the stone, and one by one, the tones descended into silence.

As the final note faded, the golden glyphs dimmed. The vault shimmered, then folded closed—not with violence, but with reverence. The wall reassembled, black and whole once more, as if no one had ever passed through.

Kaerda followed in quiet rhythm. She stepped to the side panel near the entrance where the obsidian tiles still waited. She placed her hand gently against the wall where the key had vanished. A moment passed—and then, faintly, the outline of the key reappeared, pressed outward from within. She drew it free with a careful tug, inspecting the metal with a frown of respect.

"I'm not leaving this behind," she muttered. "Not for someone else to find—and not when we might need the alloy later."

The treasure remained untouched.

And the guardian, at last, went back to sleep.

Chapter 9 – Fire in the Mirror

They made camp just before the sun dipped past the western edge of the ruin. The wind was still dry, but calmer now, and the silence between them was more restful than strained. Their fire crackled low in a circle of broken stone near the ruin entrance—the same ground they'd slept on the night before. It felt older now, like the place had shifted beneath them.

Tassa sat with her knees drawn up, the gold coin glinting between her fingers in the firelight.

"You're sure it's not cursed?" she asked for the third time.

Kaerda gave a grunt that might've been a laugh. "If it were, you'd know by now."

Bryn sat opposite her, a silver circle of thread and bone fragments carefully arranged before her. A faint wisp of smoke curled from the centre as she whispered the final words of the ritual.

When her eyes opened, they were glossy and distant for a heartbeat.

"It's not cursed," she confirmed. "And it's not... ordinary. Not enchanted in the usual sense. It's old magic. Dormant. Waiting."

Tassa frowned. "Waiting for what?"

Bryn tilted her head. "That part, it didn't say. But... it feels like a ward. A memory, locked in gold. Protective in nature. If someone were to carry it—truly carry it, not just pocket it—they could draw on it in a moment of need."

She looked at Tassa, the firelight dancing in her eyes. "It wouldn't stop a storm. But it might turn one blow. A moment of protection, drawn from a bond or memory the bearer holds. It's not commanded. It's felt."

Tassa turned the coin over in her fingers, expression unreadable. As her skin made full contact with its surface, a faint pulse of light shimmered across the etched sigil. The coin warmed in her palm—not burning, but insistent, like recognition.

She looked up sharply.

Bryn blinked once, then offered a soft smile. "I don't think it's waiting anymore. It seems to have found who it was looking for."

245

Tassa stared at the coin, then nodded slowly.

Geoff the Newt blinked up from Nyv's knee, then curled tighter into a spiral.

No one spoke after that. They ate in silence, the gold coin resting in the space between them like a question no one wanted to ask aloud.

The fire burned low by the time they bedded down. Normally, one of them would have taken first watch, but the days behind them had been long, and the fight in the treasure chamber had drawn more than just strength. Tonight, even Kaerda didn't argue when Bryn murmured, "We'll take turns tomorrow."

Bone-Anna stood at the edge of the firelight, unmoving, her gaze fixed on the darkness beyond. She needed no sleep, and in truth, no one guarded better. The others slept.

Time passed—silent, still.

Then Geoff blinked once, rose, and walked past the slumbering women. His little feet made no sound as he padded beyond the circle of firelight.

Bone-Anna's head turned with eerie smoothness, eyes tracking his every step until he faded into the gloom. She did not move otherwise, only watched. When he was gone, her gaze lingered for a moment longer—then returned to its original, fixed position.

He moved like he was following something. Or someone.

And then he was gone.

A forge, suspended in darkness. No floor, no sky—only a black void surrounding a glowing anvil and the steady rhythm of a hammer.

Kaerda stood alone, sleeves rolled up, hands calloused and sure. She struck the metal before her—glowing, endless, unfinished. Every blow echoed, not through air, but through memory. With each strike, a face appeared in the metal. Some she recognised. Some she did not. Some were lost. Others still lived. None of them blamed her.

She kept working.

Molten strands spilled off the sides of the anvil, not falling, but curling into unseen framework—something larger. Something necessary.

Geoff watched from the edge of the void, perched on an invisible surface. He did not speak—not at first.

Then, as Kaerda paused to wipe her brow, he blinked.

"Not all strength is steel," he said.

Kaerda didn't flinch. She simply nodded, set her jaw, and brought the hammer down again.

● ● ●

A grove of white-trunked trees emerged from the haze.

Nyv walked barefoot across a bed of soft moss. The air was damp and cool, heavy with the scent of water and wind. Around her, the trees swayed with no breeze. Fog clung low to the ground, and beyond a few paces, everything dissolved into shadow.

She moved forward, eyes sharp but heart uncertain. Something pulled at her— not her limbs, but her thoughts. A thread, silver and fine, shimmered ahead of her, winding between the trees.

She followed.

As she walked, faint whispers stirred—half-familiar voices from memory, old incantations spoken in haste, the laughter of comrades after battle. But the further she went, the more the whispers stilled. The grove grew silent.

And there, in the heart of the fog, stood a figure.

Bryn.

She wasn't facing Nyv. She stood at the edge of a mirror—tall, wide, ringed in flickering silver flame. Her reflection was visible, but only when Nyv drew close. Nyv stepped forward, reaching for Bryn's hand and in that instant, both their reflections resolved—shimmering and clear.

The shadows retreated from the grove.

At her feet, something stirred—small and warm. Nyv glanced down and saw Geoff weaving between the tree roots, tail flicking once before he paused near the mirror. He looked up at her and said quietly, "You tried walking the grove alone. It has served us well for now, but perhaps… we were meant to become more."

● ● ●

Bryn walked alone along the edge of a black pool, the sky above her starless, the trees skeletal and still. There was no wind, but her cloak drifted behind her like it remembered how.

She looked down and saw no reflection in the water—only darkness, shifting but empty.

Then Nyv appeared beside her. Not from the forest, not from the path—but as if she had always been there, only now seen, her hand in Bryn's.

The water changed.

Where before there had been only black, now there was light—soft silver, like moonlit silk—and in it, their reflection stood together. Their faces calm, uncertain, and yet at peace.

Bryn didn't speak. She simply reached forward, fingertips brushing the water's surface.

It rippled, and for a moment she saw something more—something vast and golden burning just beneath.

From the corner of her vision, just before the reflection shattered, Bryn saw Geoff standing calmly on the surface of the water. He wasn't watching her—he was watching the reflection.

"Some hearts cast no shadow," he murmured, "but they draw others in."

Then the reflection shattered, and she was gone.

● ● ●

Tassa stood before a wall of golden flame.

It roared without sound, endless and alive, stretching beyond the horizon of the dream. It wasn't heat she felt—it was recognition. The kind that sinks deep into the bones and of floating glass and shadowwhispers that you've stood here before, in another life or in some echo of memory. The flame pulsed, not with anger or danger, but with invitation.

She took a step closer. Her boots left no imprint. Her shadow flickered behind her in strange shapes—wings, smoke, curling horns—but never settled.

The fire shifted.

From its heart emerged a mirror—not silver, not glass, but liquid gold rimmed in fire. It floated just above the ground, and in its surface she saw not her reflection, but *versions* of herself. One fierce, eyes burning. One broken, kneeling in ash. One radiant, aflame from within.

The mirror asked no question aloud, but the message was clear.

Will you become? Or will you break?

She stepped closer. Her hand trembled—not from fear, but awe. The fire didn't burn her. It *answered* her.

Geoff appeared beside her, blinking once, his eyes reflecting the golden light.

"Tassa Emberlin," he said, voice clear and steady. "You were never outside it. Only asleep."

He turned once, eyes glowing faintly. "Tharniseth remembers you."

The name struck her with force—not the sound, but the weight of it. The truth in it.

She reached toward the mirror. Her hand began to glow—not with flame, but with memory. The coin pulsed in her pocket, echoing the heartbeat of the fire.

Then the dream fractured—like glass catching sunlight—and everything fell away into light.

● ● ●

Geoff stepped back into the camp without fanfare. One moment he wasn't there, and the next, he was padding softly past Bone-Anna on his return to the fire.

Her head turned to track him, just as it had before, following his silent approach. She didn't move otherwise—only watched. When he curled once more beneath Nyv's cloak and settled into stillness, her gaze lingered a moment longer, then returned to the dark.

The fire still burned low. The Accord still slept.

But something in the air had changed. Like the last echo of a note held too long finally fading into silence.

Chapter 10 – The Pilgrim's Flame

Morning came gently, as if the desert itself had softened overnight. The fire had long since burned to embers, and the shadows that clung to the edges of the ruins no longer threatened. The Accord stirred one by one, the stillness of the night broken only by the quiet rustle of cloaks and the clink of gear being packed.

No one spoke of their dreams at first. It wasn't discomfort, only reverence—the kind of silence that follows something profound.

It was Tassa who broke it.

"I had a strange dream last night. No, it wasn't just a dream," she said, still wrapping her bedroll. "It was... something else. I remember it. I *feel* it."

Kaerda paused, her hand stalling on a strap. "A forge with no walls..." she said slowly. "I thought it was just me. But I've never dreamed something that clear. Or that true."

Nyv nodded slowly. "The mirror in mine didn't reflect anything... not until someone stood beside me." She glanced at Bryn.

"I saw you too," Bryn said, quietly. "In a grove. You brought the light."

That earned a look between them—long, steady, and full of things unsaid. They both hesitated, then looked away almost at the same moment.

Neither spoke of the hand they had reached for. Or the warmth in the reflection.

Instead, Bryn murmured, "Geoff was there. In mine."

Tassa straightened. "Mine too. He *spoke* to me."

"He told me something," Kaerda added, eyes narrowing. "It didn't feel like a dream then."

Nyv was the last to respond. "He always sees more than he lets on."

Geoff the Newt blinked from his spot on Nyv's shoulder, tail flicking lazily. He made no sound.

Only Bone-Anna knew the truth of it. But she remained as she always was: silent, still, watching the horizon.

Without further word, they broke camp and turned east—toward whatever lay beyond the ruin's edge.

For the first time since arriving in the ruins, the storm had fully passed. The sky was clear, a pale expanse stretching uninterrupted above them. The ground crunched beneath their boots—sand and stone still dry, but no longer shifting in the wind.

They moved in silence at first, eyes scanning the horizon. What they had mistaken for distant dunes now revealed themselves to be towers—shattered spires half-buried in sand, their angles too sharp, too deliberate to be natural.

Bryn slowed, raising a hand. "There," she murmured. "Ruins. A city?"

Tassa squinted ahead, her brow furrowing. "Tharniseth," she said under her breath.

Kaerda stopped cold. "What did you just say?"

"Tharniseth," Tassa repeated. "I... I don't know why. It just came to me. Actually, it came from the dream version of Geoff last night."

The Accord turned to look at Geoff, who blinked once and gave the faintest shrug in response.

Kaerda looked toward the horizon, her eyes narrowing. "That was the Banished City's true name. Before it vanished into Umbraveth. Before the fall."

Bryn turned to face her. "You're certain?"

"I've only ever seen it in books." Kaerda's voice was quiet, reverent. "But yes. We're closer than we thought."

The morning grew warmer as they walked, and the hard-won clarity of the dream faded into the long grind of desert travel. The sun beat down on their hoods and shoulders. Even without the storm, the sand was no easier to cross—deep enough to swallow each step, soft enough to make progress slow.

Conversation thinned to necessity. The rhythm of travel took over: Kaerda moving in quiet intervals, scanning stone and structure; Nyv pausing now and then to press her hand to the ground, reading the shape of the land with her magic; Tassa drifting near the front, eyes always half-lost in thought. Bryn and her ravens, as ever, kept to the centre—watching them all, one eye to the ruin ahead, the other to the Accord. Bone-Anna trailed watching their flank without complaint.

No birds called. No wind stirred. The only sounds were their footsteps and the shifting hush of sand giving way.

By midmorning, the broken towers on the horizon grew clearer. Still far, but real. The skeleton of a city long buried, half-drowned by time.

They stopped for lunch in the shadow of a broken arch jutting from the sand like a fractured tooth. Kaerda cleared a space with practised efficiency while Nyv coaxed a small flame to life with magic. Bryn's ravens, circling high above, gave a sudden call—sharp, insistent.

Bryn stood, shading her eyes. "We have company."

Tassa looked up quickly. "Friend or threat?"

"I don't know," Bryn said. "But they're alone."

A solitary figure approached across the dunes, walking with the uneven gait of one used to rough roads. A patchwork cloak fluttered around his knees, layered in dust and threadbare cloth, but his posture was upright, and the gear at his side was well-kept. A thin staff was strapped across his back, and his sandals bore the sigil of Durnach the Forgemaker—the Flamefather.

Kaerda rose slowly. Her expression didn't shift, but her eyes narrowed. "He's a pilgrim."

The figure raised a hand in greeting as he neared, but didn't call out.

When he reached the edge of their circle, he paused, his voice quiet but firm. "Mind if I share the shade?"

Kaerda studied him for a moment, then gave a short nod. "If you've come this far with nothing but dust and gears to your name, you've earned it."

The pilgrim smiled, lowering himself to the ground with the slow ease of one who has learned not to rush. He unslung a battered satchel and produced a compact roll of bread, some dried fruit, and a small wooden tool kit he kept within reach.

"My thanks," he said. "I'm Auren. A tinker-priest from the Forgehold of Talanthus."

Kaerda's brow lifted at that. "Talanthus? I spent a season there. Worked the western kiln."

Auren brightened. "Then it's true. You're Kaerda Flintward."

At her startled glance, he reached into his satchel again and withdrew a folded, oil-stained cloth. From within it, he revealed a thin sheet of hammered brass etched with precise mechanical lines.

"This," he said reverently, "is your hammer design. I studied it during my apprenticeship. Master Relduhn called it the 'Balanced Flame.' Said it was the only war hammer that could double as a sacred instrument."

Kaerda took it from him with care, her rough fingers ghosting over the etchings. Her voice was softer now. "I left that behind when I took to the road."

Auren nodded. "Maybe. But you left echoes behind too. Builders always do."

Kaerda smiled faintly. "Do you remember the forgemaster's dog?"

Auren's grin widened. "Oh, don't tell me you were there when it chewed through the bellows straps."

Kaerda raised an eyebrow. "Chewed straight through. Nearly collapsed the entire western venting channel."

"Master Relduhn was halfway into a blessing rite," Auren added. "Had his robes singed at the hem and cursed so colourfully we all learned new words."

They both chuckled.

"But I thought it happened during a night shift," Kaerda said.

"It did," Auren replied. "But it was the northern kiln."

Kaerda paused. "You're sure?"

He nodded. "I was the one sent to fetch more straps. It took half the night. And Relduhn made me recite the schematic oath five times as punishment."

Kaerda shook her head. "We must've had the same disaster. Just… different kilns."

Auren leaned back. "Or maybe that dog just hated forges more than we knew."

Their laughter overlapped this time, the kind that travelled further in a quiet desert than it had any right to.

Auren leaned forward again, his tone shifting from amused to awed. "They still talk about what you did during the pressure valve collapse. When the shielding failed on the central core, they say you stepped in while the others fled. Held the mechanism in place with your bare hands until the override could be reset. Said the glow off the forge didn't burn you—just clung to you, like it knew who you were."

Kaerda said nothing for a long moment. Her expression didn't change, but her grip tightened just slightly around the edge of the etched schematic.

Auren lowered his voice. "Relduhn used to tell us, 'Some clerics preach with fire. But Kaerda Flintward? She *builds* with it.'"

He stood, brushing the dust from his robes and re-tightening the strap of his satchel. "Thank you for the company—and the memory. It's good to know some stories walk the world still."

Kaerda inclined her head. "Travel safely. And keep building."

The Accord watched Auren as he departed, his staff tapping softly against stone and sand as he made his way back into the shimmering heat.

They resumed their journey in silence, the moment lingering like warmth from a forge.

By midafternoon, the city had grown closer, but the monotony of the terrain began to wear on even the most patient among them. The sand remained soft underfoot, deceptively exhausting. Every dune looked the same.

Tassa, walking near the front, began humming softly. Then louder. Then faster.

Her tune drifted upward, starting with the melody she had used to open the treasure vault, then curling backward into the slower, softer cadence she had used to close it. As she hummed, she shifted between those original refrains and playful new variations—some bright, some strange, all her own. The song had changed in her mouth, no longer a puzzle to solve, but a rhythm to pass the time. When no one responded, she tossed a small rock in Kaerda's direction— just enough to get her attention.

"Who wants a game?" she called out. "We guess cloud shapes. First person to spot one wins."

Nyv glanced up. "There aren't any clouds."

"Exactly," Tassa replied, grinning. "It's a challenge."

They crested a low ridge an hour later, and there—sprawled like a broken mirage—was the edge of Tharniseth. Jagged walls and sunken plazas, the remnants of once-proud towers half-swallowed by time and sand. The air grew heavier here, as though memory itself clung to the stones.

Bryn's ravens wheeled above and then scattered—spooked, but not screaming.

At the base of a ruined column, a figure waited.

He wore travelling robes of midnight blue, and though the dust clung to his boots, his presence carried no fatigue. A pack lay beside him. His posture was calm, attentive, almost as if he had been expecting them.

"Greetings, travellers," he said as they drew near, his voice smooth and cultured. "I'm Vaelric, seeker of lost places. You look like you've come far."

Tassa tilted her head. "We have."

Vaelric smiled. "Then may I offer a moment's company? The shade here is sparse, but the company, I hope, is not unwelcome."

He offered a wineskin, poured a cup of water, and gestured toward a scroll unfurled beside him. It depicted fragments of old Velthari glyphs— recognizable, but incomplete.

"I've been mapping the edge of the city," he said. "Trying to determine where the upper terraces once stood. Most of it collapsed during the fall."

Kaerda crouched to glance at the scroll but said nothing.

Bryn offered a polite nod. "We've seen signs of the collapse ourselves."

Vaelric nodded solemnly. "It's said the city bled its memory into the stone as it fell. Some of it lingers. Some of it listens."

The Accord exchanged uncertain glances. Vaelric's tone was pleasant, but his words felt... pointed. Observant.

Nyv's eyes narrowed slightly. Geoff the Newt had crept halfway up her shoulder by then, gaze locked on the man. He didn't blink.

But Vaelric didn't vanish immediately. He lingered as they took a brief rest, asking polite questions—where they had come from, how they found the ruins—and offering observations in return.

"There's a network of channels beneath the southern span," he said casually. "Collapsed in on itself decades ago, but you can still see the intent in the slope of the brick."

He traced a faint diagram in the sand beside them, marking crumbled passageways and speculated choke points. It was thoughtful, precise—and ultimately unhelpful. Every note he offered described places already buried or long since unapproachable.

Yet he spoke with such easy sincerity that the Accord found themselves nodding along.

Bryn, sensing no immediate threat, offered their reason for being there in a measured voice. "We're not here for stonework. We're tracking a threat—one buried deep."

Vaelric looked up from his drawing. "Ah. You seek the one who calls himself Mairadas."

The name hung in the air, unfamiliar yet heavy with implication.

Tassa blinked. "The dragon?"

Vaelric nodded slowly. "He has many names, but that one is his oldest. Be careful with it."

There was a pause then, drawn and quiet.

"May your steps remain light," Vaelric said at last, rising smoothly. "And may the halls ahead forget your passing."

With a parting nod, he turned and disappeared into the ruins without a backward glance.

The Accord stood in silence.

Tassa broke it first. "Well, that wasn't ominous at all."

They continued walking until the light began to stretch long across the sand, and even the promise of the city's edge could no longer hide the ache in their legs. Bryn called a halt beneath a leaning slab of ancient masonry, its shadow just deep enough to shelter a cookfire.

They set camp with practised silence. Kaerda assembled a windbreak from half-buried stone. Nyv drew a faint ring of protective wards into the dust. Bone-Anna took position atop a nearby rubble pile overlooking the campsite, her posture unchanged from morning to dusk.

Dinner was simple: dried fruit, travel bread, and water warmed beside the fire. No one complained.

They took turns on watch. Kaerda first, then Nyv, then Bryn. Tassa volunteered last, claiming she could sleep through anything if it wasn't her turn.

The night passed without trouble. No dreams followed them.

Only the hush of shifting sand and the slow breath of the Accord at rest.

Chapter 11 – The Covenant Within

The edge of Tharniseth rose like the ribs of a buried giant, half-sunken and broken by time. Even from the ridge, the scale of the ruined city was impossible to ignore. Cracked towers leaned like toppled sentries, their blackened stone shimmering faintly under the desert sun. The air felt thinner here, as though what remained of the city's breath was held somewhere beneath its foundations.

The Accord descended slowly, boots crunching over shattered stone and black sand. No voices disturbed the silence. Bryn's ravens flew in wide, uneven arcs overhead, circling but never calling. Even Geoff the Newt clung tightly to Nyv's shoulder, his usual curiosity replaced by watchful stillness.

They passed what might once have been a small temple—its pale stone different from the obsidian ruin around it. Weathered carvings of moons and soft-lit stars still traced its crumbled archway, worn but not erased. A symbol of Elunara, the goddess of the moon and fate.

Kaerda lingered as they passed, glancing back. "That was here before the city fell," she murmured. "Before it vanished into shadow."

Tassa paused beside her. "How can you tell?"

"The stone. The way it's shaped, the joinery. It doesn't match the rest." She touched the broken wall lightly, almost reverently. "It was built in light. Everything else here was reshaped by darkness."

Bryn gave a small nod, her eyes lingering on the faded symbol. "We'll remember this spot. It may offer more shelter than the rest."

As they pressed deeper into the ruin, the stillness thickened. The echoes of their footsteps seemed to reach too far, then vanish too soon. Even Nyv's magic felt muffled when she reached for the land beneath her.

Kaerda slowed again, her brow furrowing. "There's a forge here. Deeper in. I can feel it. But… it's hollow. Like it remembers fire, but not purpose."

Bryn met her eyes. "We'll find it. When we're ready."

They emerged into a wide plaza framed by the leaning bones of towers. What should have been open space felt tight, compressed—as if the buildings still remembered their heights and pressed inward with invisible weight. Cracked stone underfoot shimmered faintly, not with magic, but with memory. Every surface caught the light strangely.

Mosaics still clung to some of the walls, but their shapes were distorted—figures with too many limbs, or eyes where none should be. Murals seemed to ripple when not directly looked at, holding scenes that shifted with the angle of the viewer.

"I don't like this place," Tassa murmured.

Bryn nodded once. "Stay close."

Reflections flickered in broken window glass and pools of still water—shadows of people walking, speaking, pausing in gestures too smooth, too rehearsed. A woman wringing her hands. A man falling to his knees. Children running in tight circles before vanishing into the stones.

Nyv narrowed her eyes. "These aren't just echoes."

"No," Kaerda said. "They're stitched in. Like the city's trying to remember itself... through us? Did our presence activate this?"

They moved through the plaza slowly. Every few steps, the light shifted unnaturally—too bright, then too dim. The air carried a smell not of dust, but of old parchment and ash. And still the reflections watched.

Geoff let out a quiet hiss, his gaze fixed on a mirrored corner where a figure stood staring straight back at them—but when Bryn turned to look directly, the space was empty.

"They're bound here," Bryn whispered. "Whatever they are, they don't leave this place."

But none of them asked the real question yet: what happens when the memories stop watching—and start to move?

The change was slow. At first, the reflections kept to their broken surfaces—pacing, mimicking, reenacting scenes that belonged to another time. But then they began to falter in their loops. The woman who had been wringing her hands turned her head to follow Nyv's motion. The kneeling man now looked up as the party passed, mouth moving without sound. The children stopped running.

And stared.

Reflections that once flickered like light on water now stood still, heads tilted, eyes tracking the Accord from within every shard of glass, every glimmer of shadow.

Tassa stepped closer to Bryn. "They've noticed us."

Bryn's hand drifted toward her spell focus, jaw tight. "No sudden movements."

Kaerda exhaled through her nose. "Group up. They do not like us."

The reflections did not wait.

They stepped forward—from mirrored panels, from the smooth skin of blackened pillars, from the shimmering puddles of shadow pooled in the cracks. They peeled themselves away from the surfaces like silk tearing loose, and as they moved, they changed. Shapes solidified. Echoes became forms. Faces once blurred grew eyes. Mouths. Teeth.

Tassa was the first to act, hurling a bolt of flame at a figure that looked like a noblewoman from an age long past. It passed through her—but not without effect. The creature shimmered, staggered—and then screamed.

A dozen more emerged.

The Accord unleashed their spells, thinking to end it quickly. Bryn opened with a devastating clash of glaciers, shards of ice barreling through the centre of the square. It split several of the figures in half—only for their pieces to stitch back together and resume advancing.

Nyv cast Spiritsworn, a ring of spectral defenders lashing out at the enemies that drew close. It worked—at first. But the reflections were insubstantial one moment, solid the next. The guardians often passed through them uselessly.

Kaerda's hammer slammed into one of the creatures—only to strike air. Then the thing retaliated, a clawed hand swiping across her shield arm, leaving an ice-cold burn beneath the metal.

They pressed the advantage, briefly. Bryn's portals trapped three of the creatures in a sudden ripple of inky black, pulling them into the void—only two reappeared, twisted and malformed. Tassa followed with a barrage of twin fire bolts, one of which ricocheted off the mirrored walls and struck another creature from behind. Kaerda crushed one against a stone column, and it shattered like porcelain, silent as dust.

For a moment, they thought the tide might break.

But the illusion-creatures were not mindless. They adapted. They split apart mid-strike, reformed behind defences, and circled without sound. Nyv's guardians faltered against their flickering forms. Bryn's magic began to show strain—her casting hands trembling, her voice rasping with each incantation.

The plaza became a shifting nightmare of strike, retreat, and warding spells. The creatures adapted to their tactics, appearing behind them, changing shape mid-attack.

And still they came.

Tassa's breath grew ragged. Her flames grew less precise. Kaerda bled from a cut near her temple, too deep for a glancing blow. Bryn's ravens screamed above as she cast spell after spell, her voice hoarse with effort.

Then it happened.

A creature—not the largest, but the swiftest—broke through their formation. Bryn turned to face it, her hand lifted for a warding spell. She was too late. The strike hit her cleanly, driving her to the ground.

"Bryn!" Nyv's voice broke the rhythm of the fight. She reached her, blocking the next blow with a blast of force—but Bryn didn't rise. Blood seeped through her tunic, and her eyes were closed.

Panic flickered across the group. Their spells slowed. Kaerda went more defensive. Tassa hesitated.

They had misjudged the enemy. Every tactic they'd used was fraying.

And still the echoes came.

Bone-Anna fired steadily from a high perch on a ruined balcony, her arrows loosed with eerie precision. Each bolt passed through one target, rattled another, or embedded in mirrored stone—but little slowed their approach. Her presence offered some covering fire, but even her deadeye accuracy barely dented the tide.

Tassa, desperate to slow the advance, cast one of her newest spells—a cluster of flaming spiders that burst from her hands and scurried toward the illusions. They crawled over the surface of one figure, igniting its robes with supernatural flame. It shrieked as it fractured—but the next was already there.

Spell by spell, the Accord spent their strength. Nyv had already used her strongest wards and her healing magic once. Kaerda had exhausted the last of her divine channeling to fortify their footing and buy them breathing room. Even Tassa, always so quick with magic, was leaning heavier on physical cover and minor blasts.

Only Bone-Anna remained fully upright, her eerie calm never breaking, but even she was beginning to run low on arrows.

They were holding—barely—but the cost was rising with every breath, every scream, every step back.

Then one of the illusions—thin, fast, and unnatural in the bend of its limbs—lunged through Nyv's perimeter. Geoff, perched low on Nyv's arm now, let out a shrill, urgent hiss and launched himself toward Bryn. He collided with the creature's leg mid-lunge, not enough to stop it, but enough to slow the attack. The blow landed hard, tossing her limp body a half-step to the side, blood smearing across the stone.

Nyv screamed—not from fear, but fury. Her arm swept wide, shielding Geoff as much as striking the creature, and the next blast from her hands shattered the thing into ribbons of light and ash.

Geoff limped back to her, breathing fast, the edge of his hide scorched where the echo-creature's form had clipped him. Nyv cradled him briefly against her neck, murmuring thanks she couldn't put into words. He curled tighter against Nyv, drained.

But the message was clear now. They wouldn't survive another wave.

They had to retreat—or Bryn, and likely all of them, would die here.

"Cover me!" Tassa shouted, and planted her feet. Her hands flared with molten light as she summoned the last of her magic. From the ground, a wall of flame erupted—arching high between the Accord and their assailants. The creatures recoiled from the blaze, hissing through mouths that hadn't existed moments before.

"Go!" Kaerda barked, hoisting Bryn's unconscious form across her shoulder without hesitation.

Nyv turned sharply, eyes scanning the ruins. "There—there was a temple," she said breathlessly, already moving. "Elunara's enclave. We passed it near the ridge."

Tassa ran beside her, fingers twitching from magical strain. Bone-Anna dropped from her perch, moving with quiet, unnatural grace, loosing one last arrow behind them as they fled.

The flames roared higher behind them, crackling with arcane heat. It would not last long.

But it was enough.

As they crossed the boundary of the plaza, Kaerda glanced back—expecting pursuit.

But the illusion-creatures didn't follow. They gathered at the edge of the flame, flickering in place like half-forgotten thoughts. None stepped beyond the plaza's shattered border. Kaerda narrowed her eyes.

"They're tied to that place," she muttered. "Bound to it. Like they can't exist beyond what the city remembers."

The Accord didn't slow.

They reached the temple in silence, the pale stone façade of Elunara's enclave still standing in partial grace. Inside, the air was cooler, quieter—less heavy with memory.

But relief did not come.

Kaerda laid Bryn down with care, but the blood kept coming. Nyv dropped to her knees, hands shaking as she checked the wound.

"I have nothing left," she whispered. "Not enough for this."

Tassa leaned back against the wall, breathing hard. "If we'd pulled back sooner..."

"We didn't," Kaerda said, voice low. "We gambled. And Bryn lost."

The silence that followed was not empty—it was heavy with regret, with helplessness.

Kaerda pressed a hand to Bryn's side, whispering the last of her divine magic. A faint light shimmered beneath her fingers—gentle, steady—but not enough.

"I've done what I can for now," she said, quietly. "The next part will be up to her."

Chapter 12 – The Weight of Silence

The light inside the temple was dim, filtered through high cracks in the ceiling that once held stained glass. Now, the beams fell in soft, slanted shafts that barely reached the centre of the ruined sanctuary.

Bryn lay on a makeshift bed of cloaks and rolled packs, her skin pale, her breath shallow. The blood had been cleaned from her tunic, but the wound beneath remained deep—too deep for comfort. Nyv knelt beside her, one hand resting lightly on Bryn's wrist, feeling the slow, uncertain rhythm of her pulse.

The rest of the Accord moved with quiet necessity. Kaerda sat a few paces away, rewrapping a long gash along her forearm, the dried blood flaking from the edge of her bracer. Her brow was furrowed in concentration, but her eyes flicked toward Bryn more than once.

Tassa leaned against a pillar, legs stretched out, a faint ember hovering between her fingers. She let it dance above her palm, flickering weakly before dimming. Her magic was nearly spent.

Bone-Anna stood in silence near the shattered doorway, her form outlined in dim light. She hadn't moved since they arrived.

Geoff lay curled beside Bryn's side, his small body rising and falling with shallow breaths. One of his hind legs bore a faint scorch mark, but he made no sound. His small head rested gently against Bryn's ribs, as if he could will her to heal with closeness alone—like a wingless tressym, determined to give what strength he had left. Occasionally, his tail flicked, restless even in rest.

Nyv adjusted the bandages again—not because they needed it, but because her hands had to do something.

She paused.

Let her fingers still.

The silence stretched. The silence pressed in, not heavy, but reverent. Every movement echoed.

She didn't speak yet. Not aloud. Not yet.

Only the sound of distant wind moved through the ruined walls.

When she did, it was in a whisper, barely enough to carry beyond the space between them.

"You always hated when I hovered," she murmured, adjusting the corner of Bryn's cloak. "Said it made you feel like a patient. Said it wasn't necessary. But I don't know what else to be right now."

Bryn didn't stir.

Nyv looked down at their joined hands, her thumb gently brushing over Bryn's knuckles. "You'd probably tell me to rest. That I'm overthinking. That I need to ration my strength. But I can't sleep while you look like this."

A breath. Shallow. Steady. No change.

She hesitated before continuing. "I should've said something. Before. When it was just the two of us keeping watch. Or maybe back in the ruins. Or… I don't know. I kept waiting for the right moment, but the right moment never came."

She swallowed, eyes fixed on Bryn's still form.

A long breath passed. She let it carry the weight she hadn't yet spoken aloud. "And now I'm terrified the last thing you'll remember is that I stayed silent."

Geoff shifted slightly, pressing closer.

Nyv reached for the water skin and moistened Bryn's lips. "You asked me once if I ever feared silence. I told you no. That was a lie."

The temple remained still. The others kept to their places, distant but near—giving Nyv space without needing to ask. Kaerda had finished binding her arm and now sat cross-legged in quiet prayer, her smith's hammer resting across her knees. From time to time, she glanced toward Bryn, her lips moving silently.

Tassa had drifted closer to the fire, a single flame flickering between her fingers—no spell, just a lingering habit. Her expression was unreadable, but she didn't look away from Bryn for long.

Bone-Anna remained at her post. Her silhouette never shifted, yet something in her posture was sharper, more attentive than before. At one point, her skeletal frame gave the barest, involuntary shutter—as if a thread had pulled taut within her. It passed as quickly as it came, but Kaerda noticed. So did Nyv.

They didn't speak of it. But they knew what it meant.

Bryn's death would unsummon her. Bone-Anna was feeling the veil tremble.

Still, she remained. A silent sentinel, she stood between the Accord and whatever still haunted the ruins outside.

Geoff shifted again, resting his small chin on Bryn's side. His eyes had begun to close, but every so often they flicked open—to check, to listen, to stay.

Nyv's gaze drifted across the temple—toward Kaerda, then Tassa, both wrapped in their own silence. Her sisters in all but blood.

She looked back to Bryn.

"The Accord are my sisters," she whispered, voice tight. "But you... you are more. I cannot lose you. Not now."

No one spoke.

Stillness expanded.

Yet the silence between them felt whole, as if they were all listening to something just beyond the edge of sound.

Nyv closed her eyes.

The memory returned with quiet clarity—the druid's voice, not heard but felt, slipping into her mind back in the moss-ringed glade. She would need to make a choice:

One will keep you safe. One will save you both.

At the time, she hadn't known what it meant. She had assumed it referred to strategy, to sacrifice. But now, sitting in the stillness beside Bryn's failing light, the meaning struck with sudden precision.

It wasn't about choosing between action and inaction. It wasn't about the mission. It was about Bryn.

Nyv reached out and took Bryn's hand again. Her fingers were cold, but not lifeless.

"I understand now," she whispered.

She squeezed gently.

The quiet seemed to answer—not with sound, but with permission.

"I choose the one who saves us both. I choose you, Bryn," she whispered. "I always have."

As Nyv's whisper hung in the quiet air—"I choose you, Bryn. I always have."—the mark on Bryn's hand brightened, just faintly. A soft silver shimmer, as if the Queen herself acknowledged the words with a quiet touch.

Bryn's eyes fluttered open.

There were tears in those eyes—not many, just enough to glisten at the corners. Her gaze found Nyv's at once. She didn't speak. She only smiled, the faint curve of her lips full of recognition and quiet joy.

Chapter 13 – The Covenant Within

Nyv leaned toward her friend, her companion lying in the bed. For the first time she let herself feel it. The kiss was soft, trembling, yet fierce. A moment of surrender after so much restraint. For Bryn it was the answer to every unspoken question. For Nyv it was everything she had never let herself believe she had needed. But this wasn't just a kiss. It was a promise, a covenant. Something worth fighting for.

Bryn's eyes re-opened slowly. Her breath was shallow, her skin pale from the blood she had lost, but there was a light in her gaze that hadn't been there before. She managed a small smile.

"You chose," she whispered, her voice a thread.

Nyv sat beside her, brushing a stray strand of hair from Bryn's brow. "There was never really a question. Just fear."

Bryn's smile deepened, and she reached for Nyv's hand. Their fingers laced together, gently.

Nyv dipped the cloth into the water again, gently pressing it to Bryn's brow. The quiet between them wasn't uncomfortable—it was grounding, like moss under bare feet.

Her mind drifted to the druid's words, still echoing days later. *"Follow the logic you've lived by... or the feeling you fear."*

She thought of the fox—the pale creature with glowing eyes that had looked right through her on the edge of the grove. She hadn't spoken of it then. Not to the others. Not even to Bryn.

But she remembered the look. Not just animal instinct. Recognition.

And now, as she watched Bryn's breath steady, as she felt the weight of her own choice settle deeper into her chest, Nyv realised:
The fox had not been a warning. It had been an invitation. A beginning.

Her fingers found Bryn's once more—not tightly, just enough to feel the warmth. The stillness between them held steady.

"I'm glad," Bryn murmured. "I choose you too. Before I ever opened my eyes."

Bryn's fingers tightened ever so slightly around Nyv's.

"I saw you," she murmured.

Nyv turned to her, eyebrows raised.

"In the dark," Bryn continued, her voice soft, fragile around the edges but steady in the middle. "When I was bleeding out and everything was slipping away... I wasn't alone. I was standing in a place I didn't recognise. Cold, endless. A place where even memory was quiet. And She was there."

Nyv said nothing, only listened.

"She didn't speak to me, not exactly. But I knew who She was. I've known her shadow since I was small." Bryn's eyes fluttered half-closed. "She let me choose. She let me remember. Not just the duty. Not just the mission. She showed me your face. The way you stood over me. The way you looked like the world was ending. And I knew—before I ever opened my eyes—I knew what you had done."

Bryn turned her head slightly on the pillow to meet Nyv's gaze again. Her lips curved faintly.

"I woke up with these tears in my eyes because it was beautiful. Because I was still here. Because she told me the truth—your truth. That you'd chosen me. And that was all I needed to return."

Nyv blinked, breath caught in her throat and used the cloth to dab the tears from Bryn's eyes.

Bryn smiled again, faint but full. "You were the tether. You always have been."

They sat together in silence, the weight of the storm outside and the stillness between them finally at peace.

Later that morning, while Bryn rested, Nyv stepped quietly into the side alcove where Kaerda and Tassa were preparing gear. The light was dim, filtered through the worn stone. Kaerda was adjusting the straps on her shield harness. Tassa sat cross-legged on a crate, idly spinning a copper piece between her fingers.

Kaerda looked up first. "She's stable?"

Nyv nodded. "Sleeping. Healing."

Tassa's eyes flicked up, curious. "And you?"

Nyv hesitated, then crossed her arms. "I think... I made the right choice."

Tassa flipped the coin once more. "You always do. Eventually."

Kaerda stepped closer, her tone gentle. "We saw it, Nyv. You don't need to explain anything. But if you want to, we're here."

Nyv's shoulders relaxed a fraction. She sat down on the edge of the bench near them, fingers steepled.

"It wasn't sudden," she said quietly. "It's been growing for a long time. We move together in battle. Think together. Fill in each other's silences. I don't know when it became... this."

Kaerda offered a small nod. "Some roots grow quiet and deep. You only see them when the storm comes."

Nyv smiled faintly at that.

Tassa leaned in. "And now that you've chosen, what happens?"

Nyv looked toward the door, where Bryn still lay beyond. "Now? We fight harder. For each other. For all of us."

Kaerda placed a hand on her shoulder. "Then we're with you. Both of you."

Tassa gave a theatrical sigh. "Ugh, love and loyalty before breakfast. Fine. Just don't get sappy on patrol."

Nyv laughed softly. "I'll do my best."

They sat together a moment longer—an accord, quiet and sure.

Nyv stood and stepped away briefly, moving back through the corridor to check on Bryn. She adjusted the blanket over her shoulders, brushed a few strands of hair from her face, and placed a fresh waterskin within reach. Bryn stirred faintly and murmured something Nyv couldn't catch, but the smile on her lips was enough. Nyv's own smile lingered as she returned.

Tassa watched her reenter. "You're different," she said simply.

"I feel different," Nyv admitted, settling back into her seat.

Kaerda looked between them. "It's not just affection, is it? What you two have—it's built out of something deeper."

Nyv nodded. "We're different, but… we fit. She lives in memory. I live in presence. I ground her. She gives weight to everything I do."

Kaerda offered a slow nod. "You root the moment. She remembers the cost."

Tassa tilted her head, as if seeing Nyv anew. "It's a strange thing, isn't it? You, who call to the land and pattern it with nature's will—and her, a child of silence and shadow. But somehow it works."

Nyv smiled faintly. "We aren't opposites. We're a balance. I shape what lives. She guides what's gone."

Kaerda's tone turned thoughtful. "That's what makes it right. She doesn't pull you from your path. You don't ask her to leave hers."

Nyv stood again, making a quiet check back toward Bryn. She offered a few whispered words, a gentle hand on her shoulder, then returned.

Tassa glanced toward the hall. "You know the Queen of Stillness doesn't give blessings easily."

"I don't think she gave one," Nyv said, thoughtful. "I think she saw who Bryn needed—and left the door open for me."

Kaerda's eyes softened. "Then it seems you walked through it."

Nyv nodded. "Gladly."

They sat in stillness once more, the three of them grounded not in uncertainty—but in understanding.

And above them, the air held still, as if the world itself was waiting.

Nyv made one last trip to Bryn's side. She knelt by the bed, whispering a few quiet words, then adjusted the edge of the blanket again, even though it didn't need it. She brushed her fingers against Bryn's wrist, checking the pulse she already knew was there, steady and warm. Only then did she return to her bedroll, lowering herself in silence, folding her legs beneath her.

She closed her eyes, not to sleep—but to centre herself. And in that moment of calm, something subtle stirred.

Her breath slowed. Her heartbeat softened. Inward she turned—into the silence, into the pulse of the stone beneath her, into the memory of warmth and shadow intertwined.

She stood in a place between sleep and memory, between presence and potential. Around her, the darkness was neither threatening nor empty. It was fertile. Like soil turned in spring.

And in the hush of that imagined grove—its trunks dark as obsidian, its canopy dappled with moonlight—Nyv felt them.

Bryn's presence, steady and solemn, like the hush before a storm. Kaerda's strength, humming like iron beneath earth. Tassa's flicker, erratic and bright, like fire catching wind.

They weren't there, not truly—but she *knew* them. Their shapes, their rhythms, the way they moved around her and beside her. The way they trusted her to shape the path forward.

Memories bloomed like roots beneath her feet.

Bryn standing shoulder to shoulder with her at the bridge in Estavar, holding the line against the undead. Kaerda reaching for her arm in the frost cavern after Nyv collapsed, whispering a Ravkari prayer she should not have known. Tassa pulling her into the alley to dance out the tension before the assault on the watchtower, singing her nonsense songs with fierce, hopeful eyes.

Each memory twined with the next. None of them asked her to lead. But all had followed.

She opened her eyes with a breath—and the air shimmered, briefly, as if recognising the shape of what had just passed.

She said nothing. But she knew.

Her magic didn't feel stronger—just wider. Once it had coiled tight around her, protective and singular. Now, it rippled outward, stretching gently like a canopy. She could feel it—like the subtle change in air before a storm, or the way wind shifts through branches before a snowfall. It could extend now. Not just to shield herself, but to *cover them*. Kaerda. Tassa. Bryn.

It would move as one. A single motion, a shared current. Not power granted, but power acknowledged.

When the time came, she could cast for all of them. Because this was her coven. Her Accord.

Chapter 14 – Beneath the Pale Lanterns

Morning broke over Tharniseth with a sky the colour of ash and rose. It wasn't warmth that greeted the Silent Accord, but stillness—and in it, strength. They rose quietly, gathering gear and preparing wards without urgency, but without hesitation either.

Bryn moved more slowly than the others, but on her own feet. The worst of her wounds had closed beneath Kaerda's steady hands and a night of true rest. Her voice had returned, and with it, a sharpness behind her eyes that hadn't been there since the fall.

They didn't speak much as they left the camp. There was no need. What needed to be said had already been spoken—or understood in silence.

Still, just before they crossed into the ruins proper, Kaerda paused and turned to Bryn.

"You sure you're ready for this?" Her tone wasn't doubtful—just steady. Grounded.

Bryn nodded. "I'm not whole yet. But I'm steady. That's enough."

Nyv's gaze lingered on her a moment longer, searching for any sign of hesitation. "If you falter—"

"You'll catch me," Bryn said, a faint smile ghosting across her lips. "You always will."

Tassa rolled her shoulders. "Then let's agree—no splitting up, no lone heroics, and if the memories start screaming again, we leave this time."

Kaerda grunted. "Agreed."

Nyv gave a quiet nod. "Together."

The Accord stepped forward as one, into the waiting mist.

Mist clung to the stones like breath that wouldn't let go.

The Accord stepped cautiously beneath a fractured archway, where pale lanterns hovered like suspended moons—unmoving, unflickering, and cold. Each glowed with a faint blue-white light, casting long, narrow shadows that didn't match the forms of those who walked below.

Bryn slowed first.

"They're the same," she said quietly. "Same light. Same air."

Kaerda nodded once, her shield already strapped to her arm. "Feels like Tharniseth's watching us again."

Tassa narrowed her eyes at one of the lanterns, her fingertips twitching just above a prepared spell. "They didn't float like that last time. Did they?"

"No," Nyv said. Her voice was calm, but she was scanning the shadows ahead. Geoff clung tighter to her shoulder, unblinking. "But the air's the same. Thin. Quiet. Like it's holding its breath."

They moved forward slowly, boots scuffing against the time-worn plaza. Around them, broken structures loomed—shattered spires and walls whose stones still bore a mirror sheen. Faint reflections blinked in and out along the surfaces. Nothing moved. But nothing felt still, either.

Kaerda stepped closer to Bryn than usual, her eyes always scanning the corners. A silent promise, unspoken but felt.

A few paces behind, Bone-Anna mirrored the motion. The skeletal archer shifted her path to align just behind Bryn's right side, bow already unslung. She made no sound, no gesture of warning—only presence. The way she moved now, protective and poised, made it clear: if anything reached for Bryn again, it would pass through Bone-Anna first. Bryn didn't seem to notice the actions of either of her protectors—her gaze remained fixed upward, watching the lanterns. One drifted slightly as they passed beneath it. Not from wind. There was no wind here.

Nyv watched the lantern, then looked to Bryn. "Do you think they're marking something?"

"Not marking," Bryn murmured. "Remembering."

She didn't elaborate, but the others felt it too. This place wasn't empty—it was echoing.

They passed a narrow alley where thin figures flickered in the stone—too vague to be seen, too present to ignore. A soldier pacing. A girl skipping. A figure with a book clutched tight to their chest.

No one spoke. But they moved closer together.

They had seen this before. And last time, it nearly killed them.

The figures did not vanish.

Instead, they grew clearer.

Across the plaza, the same looped motions began to play out. The soldier turned to march back down the alley. The girl lifted one foot to skip—but never brought it down. The figure with the book opened it to a page that did not exist. The loops reset. And then began again.

"They're performing," Kaerda said softly. "Like last time. But they haven't noticed us yet."

"Yet," Tassa echoed, watching the girl flicker.

Bryn took a careful step closer to one of the walls, eyeing a surface where multiple figures paced behind a shimmer of pale stone. She didn't reach out. Not yet.

"I think they're stuck," she whispered. "Not hostile. Not yet. But fraying."

As if in response, the soldier's movement stuttered. His foot caught. His shoulders jolted—just once—then reset into the same motion.

Nyv murmured, "This is exactly how it began before. The loops broke. They saw us."

"And then they came out," Kaerda finished grimly. "All at once."

The lanterns above flickered—not with motion, but with breath. One pulsed slightly, then another. Then silence.

No one moved.

Then the girl in the wall—so faint they weren't sure she had eyes—turned her head.

And looked directly at Tassa.

Geoff let out a low chirp.

"I vote we don't wait this time," Tassa muttered, raising her hand toward a spark.

But Bryn's voice cut gently across the square.

"Wait. They're not all looking. Not yet. This might still be... salvageable."

The figures hadn't emerged. Not fully. They remained within the glass, the stone, the shimmer. But they were faltering.

Bryn turned to the others. "If we repeat what they're trying to do—maybe we can complete the memory. Close the loop before it collapses."

Nyv's brow furrowed. "You want us to reenact their deaths?"

"No," Bryn said. "Their lives."

She hesitated, then added, more quietly, "Last time, I didn't listen. I just reacted. I fought what I didn't understand."

Her gaze swept across the mirrored figures. "The Queen teaches memory. Not rage. These echoes aren't just remnants—they're stories left unfinished. I think that's what we missed. Let's try to honour their stories rather than invade or interrupt them."

Kaerda adjusted her stance. "Then how do we start?"

Bryn looked to the nearest echo—a nobleman seated at an invisible table, his hand hovering as if toasting unseen guests. "We give them what they're missing."

She stepped forward slowly, shadows flickering at her heels. From her satchel, she drew a small object—a polished stone etched with an old sigil of greeting. With practised subtlety, she infused it with minor illusion: a glimmering goblet, just for a moment, suspended in his hand.

The noble's head turned. His form shimmered.

And he raised the goblet in silence.

Then he vanished.

Tassa blinked. "Did that just work?"

Bryn nodded once. "It's not about power. It's about memory. They're reaching for something that once was."

Nyv moved to the echo of the skipping girl. She knelt and whispered a Ravkari lullaby under her breath, then tapped a small stone—a rhythmic knock that mimicked the cadence of play.

The girl completed her step.

And disappeared.

Kaerda's eyes narrowed, watching the soldier reset his march. "Alright," she muttered. "Let's finish this."

She approached slowly, her armour quiet, respectful. The soldier's boot caught again. This time, Kaerda stepped into his path—not to block it, but to steady it. She raised her shield slightly in an old saluting gesture from dwarven training halls, one a soldier might recognise.

The echo paused. Met her eyes.

And moved past her, straight-backed and whole. Then it, too, faded.

Tassa, emboldened by the others, turned toward a woman who stood frozen mid-spin, hands lifted as if mid-dance. Her expression was blank, but Tassa tilted her head and snapped her fingers, conjuring a flicker of flame-light that spun in a slow arc beside her. With a second snap, the flame pulsed to a rhythm—a heartbeat echo.

The woman's hand lowered. She completed the turn. And vanished.

Even Bone-Anna stepped forward, eerily silent. She knelt near a figure hunched over what looked like a ruined violin, its strings broken in the reflection. Bone-Anna drew a shard of glass from her pouch—carefully, reverently—and placed it before the echo, as if offering a string.

The figure straightened. Its bow hand rose. And it disappeared in a soft shimmer.

One by one, the Accord answered memory with presence. With kindness. With recognition.

And one by one, the memories passed on.

Bryn found one more echo near the edge of a half-fallen colonnade—a woman kneeling as if in prayer, though her lips didn't move. Bryn watched for a moment, then reached into her pouch and withdrew a small, feather-carved charm. She laid it gently at the woman's feet, then closed her own eyes and whispered a benediction under her breath: not in the Queen of Stillness's tongue, but in her mother's.

The kneeling woman bowed her head at last.

And vanished.

Nyv drifted toward a scholar seated on a broken step, an open book resting on their lap. The figure's hand hovered over the page, unmoving. Nyv knelt beside them, removed a length of silver thread from her satchel, and gently laid it across the edge of the reflection—like marking a page in trust. Then she placed her hand beside the book and whispered a name. One she hadn't spoken in years.

The figure blinked once.

And disappeared.

At the far edge of the courtyard, a flickering child crouched in the shadow of a collapsed step, one hand outstretched. Not to the Accord—but to something long gone. The shape beside them was faint and formless—only a ripple in the stone.

Geoff stirred.

Without prompting, the newt slid down Nyv's arm and padded silently toward the figure. He paused before the child, then raised one foot, mimicking the still pose. His body shimmered faintly—orange belly glowing against the grey ruin.

For a heartbeat, nothing happened.

Then the shimmer beside the child took shape: a small dog, tail wagging slow and unsure. The child smiled. The dog licked their face.

And together, they vanished.

Geoff returned to Nyv's shoulder without a sound, settling beneath her collar with a single, satisfied blink.

But not all echoes faded.

Near the edge of the broken plaza, one figure remained. It had not moved during the others' passing. It had not flickered or looped. It had simply stood—watching.

It was a young man. Or the memory of one. His features were half-formed, his limbs too long, too thin, like an unfinished sketch. In his hands, he held a shattered mask. Not decorative—protective. The kind worn by alchemists or mages. Something important, once.

Kaerda spotted him first. "We missed one."

Nyv followed her gaze and took a step forward—but the figure turned before she could approach. His face twisted, not in malice, but in desperation. He staggered forward, the broken mask clutched to his chest like a shield.

Bryn raised a hand. "Wait—he's not—"

The figure lunged.

Fast.

Not violent, but erratic. Like memory refusing to die.

Bryn braced for impact—

And in an instant, Nyv was between them.

vheran kishel!

The spell flared from her hands without thought—an arcing, shimmering Shield that enveloped Bryn and flickered outward in a dome, catching the others in its reach. The figure struck it—and rebounded, harmlessly.

He landed hard. But did not rise again.

Instead, he knelt. Trembling. The mask in his hands glowed faintly.

Bryn stepped forward, her hand slowly lowering.

"He wasn't attacking," she said softly. "He was remembering. The mask. It meant something."

She approached him, one slow step at a time, and knelt.

Bryn's fingers brushed the floor as she knelt, head bowed. "I'm sorry... I didn't see what you were trying to show us." Her feather mark pulsed gently in response, silver light catching in the dust like a memory stirred awake.

She reached out—not to take the mask, but to place her hand beside it.

The figure looked at her once.

Then vanished.

For a breath, all was still.

Then—movement.

From the walls, from the fractured stones, from beneath the ground itself—more memories stirred. Dozens, then hundreds of flickering echoes emerged, not lunging, not hostile, but drawn. They stepped from reflections, from cracks in the architecture, from fading murals and shattered statuary. A wave of memory, not of war, but of longing.

Like moths to the flame of remembrance, they converged—drawn not to the Accord, but to the space the group had made possible. Each one carried a gesture unfinished—a goodbye, a gift, a dance, a word—and completed them on their own.

A knight bowed over a vanished oath. A mother reached for the child no longer there. A priest lit an unseen candle and vanished with the match still glowing in his hand.

None required help. None approached the Accord.

One by one, they found closure.

And one by one, they blinked into the lanternlight above.

The glow brightened—not with heat, but with thanks. As the final echo vanished, one lantern descended—slowly, deliberately—until it hovered before Bryn.

It pulsed once. Then again.

And began to drift, not up, but forward, casting its soft light across a narrow side street half-lost to ruin.

Bryn watched it a moment. Then nodded.

"It's showing us the way."

No one questioned her.

Together, the Accord followed the lantern's glow deeper into the city of memories.

None of them spoke, but the silence wasn't uncertain—it was reverent. Bryn glanced once more at the hovering light.

"This wasn't chance," she murmured. "Someone left it for us."

Kaerda nodded slowly. "Lantern-paths like this... they were used by memory-keepers in the old cities. Not just to light the way, but to preserve intent."

Nyv's voice was quiet, but firm. "Then we're not the first to walk this path. Just the first to be remembered by it."

Bryn lingered a moment longer. Her eyes followed the drifting light, but her mind was elsewhere—drawn back to a different lantern.

One that had cast no glow at all.

Selvestar's.

The silver-robed figure who had saved them from the man with no mouth's undead in the forest—vanishing without explanation, leaving only questions and a lantern that bent the shadows inward.

She hadn't thought of that moment for some time, but now it echoed—sharp, clear. That lantern had pulled shadow to it, not driven it away. Had bent memory inward rather than forward.

"Different kind of light," she murmured to herself. "But maybe the same purpose."

She didn't explain. And the others didn't ask.

The lantern pulsed once more—steady, guiding. And they continued forward.

None of them saw the shimmer that lingered behind them.

A half-formed echo, brighter than the others, remained in the far archway—a figure that had never emerged during the release. It did not blink or fade. It only watched.

When the last of the group disappeared from view, it turned.

And followed.

Silent.

Unseen.

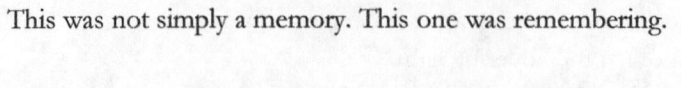

This was not simply a memory. This one was remembering.

Chapter 15 – The Forgotten Barracks

Mist gave way to stone.

The lantern's glow drifted ahead of them, weaving through a narrow pass of leaning walls. Here, the architecture shifted—gone were the sweeping arches and ceremonial columns of the memory district. In their place rose thick bastions of dark stone, low ceilings, and metal-stripped thresholds. This was no place of worship or reflection.

This was a barracks.

Tassa was the first to say it aloud. "We never would've seen this from above."

Nyv nodded slowly, eyes scanning the low corridor. "The lantern wanted us to see or find something here. Or something behind it did."

Kaerda's boots scraped against the stone as she crouched to examine an abandoned helmet. Its shape was strange—too angular, with notches carved for devices long since rusted away. "I don't think this was lost to battle. This was left behind. Deliberately."

They followed the path deeper, past fractured bunk rows and half-sealed doors. Bryn ran her fingers along one wall, where runes flickered faintly beneath layers of dust and oxidation. "There was power here once," she murmured. "Something disciplined. Controlled."

Bone-Anna took point without command, her silent steps never echoing. Geoff the Newt pressed low to Nyv's shoulder, his tail flicking in uneasy rhythm.

Kaerda paused at the edge of what must once have been a training chamber— now a hollow ruin choked with collapsed beams. She pointed toward a broken mural carved in relief across one wall: a formation of soldiers, marching with their backs to a massive forge.

"I know this seal," she said quietly, brushing away debris. "It's a tactical mark. Dwarves use similar ones to designate forward-operating outposts. This wasn't a garrison. This was a staging ground."

Tassa gave a low whistle. "So what were they staging for?"

No one answered.

The lantern pulsed once more, casting long shadows across the stone floor.

Nyv looked to Bryn. "Whatever's ahead—we wouldn't have found it without help. This place... it was meant to be hidden."

Bryn nodded slowly. "And now that we've found it, I think it's meant to show us something."

They stepped into a larger chamber—half strategy hall, half armoury. Scorched tables lined the walls, their surfaces carved with map grooves and arcane notations. Weapon racks stood empty, the dust undisturbed—these had been cleared long ago. Whatever arms once hung here were removed in order, not haste.

The group spread out, silent.

Kaerda drifted toward a collapsed bookstand, its shelves long broken but its base still intact. She knelt beside it, retrieving a splintered metal plate from beneath a fallen beam. "Could've been used for spell-focus training. The surface is etched with deflection patterns."

Nyv examined the far wall, where several panels had partially slid away over the years. She ran her hand along a shallow groove cut into the stone. "This was for storing something heavy. Armour or arcane batteries."

Bryn lingered near the centre, her eyes drawn to a faded crest carved into the floor—an emblem surrounded by a circular path, like a ritual but built for movement. "This room was never meant to rest. It was meant to prepare."

Tassa, meanwhile, wandered along the raised platform in the middle, her gaze flicking across the space with growing wariness. The scent of charged metal prickled her nose, and her boots tapped against the floor with just enough echo to feel intrusive. "Does it feel warmer in here to anyone else?" she muttered.

Kaerda turned, brow furrowed. "Something's changing. Slowly."

Bryn stepped closer to the platform, shadows tightening slightly around her. "There's pressure building. Not arcane casting—something structural. Old magic, trying to wake."

Nyv crouched near a wall and touched her fingers to a faint rune. "This sigil wasn't just for containment—it was part of a layered field. Watchful."

The group shifted unconsciously closer together.

Tassa hesitated near the platform, then reached out to brush aside rubble for a better look.

"Careful," Kaerda said, already eyeing the etchings. "That's a control sigil. Old, but charged."

Nyv stepped closer, crouching low. "I don't think it's active. If it were, we'd see feedback in the walls—or worse, feel it under our feet."

Bryn's brow furrowed. "Not yet."

Tassa moved to the edge of the platform to get a better look, brushing aside more loose rubble. Her hand brushed one of the runes—just enough to disturb the pattern. It wasn't recklessness, just bad luck. Unlucky fingers on an old trigger.

A hum surged through the floor.

The runes flared white-blue, then darkened to violet.

"Well, it's active now." remarked Nyv.

"Move!" Bryn shouted.

Lightning cracked through the walls, snaking like veins.

A deafening sound exploded through the chamber—part thunder, part grinding stone, part arcane feedback. It wasn't just noise—it was pressure, like the air itself had snapped. The walls trembled with it. Dust rained from the ceiling in a sudden, choking wave. From the far corners of the chamber, stone panels slid open with grinding protest. Within them—folded in darkness—six figures stirred.

Golems.

Angular, sleek, and inlaid with metal etched in storm-script. Their limbs unfurled slowly, creaking loudly, like statues waking from long slumber. Where their eyes should be, coils of lightning flickered.

Kaerda raised her shield. "We've seen this kind of blend before—shadow and elemental. Constructs. But not ones I've studied."

Nyv backed up beside Bryn.

The first golem stepped forward, and the floor beneath it cracked from the charge in its feet. The others followed, silent, synchronized.

Bryn raised a hand. "Not a summoning ward. A defence grid. We just triggered the barracks' final command."

● ● ●

The first golem surged forward in a blur of crackling motion, its plated arms unfolding into curved blades that shimmered with stormlight. It struck the ground where Kaerda had stood only a moment before—stone exploded upward in a burst of kinetic force as she rolled clear, shield raised.

"They're fast!" she barked.

Another construct blinked. One instant it stood at the back of the chamber— then with a jolt of inverted shadow, it was directly behind Tassa.

"Left!" Bryn shouted.

Tassa ducked low and rolled, hurling a bolt of flame that struck centre mass. The fire scattered harmlessly across the golem's outer shell. It didn't slow.

"They're phasing," Nyv said, voice tight. "Blinking between light and shadow."

"It's not teleportation," Bryn added, eyes narrowed. "It's Witherlace fracture."

Two golems charged in tandem, aiming for Bryn. Kaerda intercepted one with a hammer strike, the blow ringing like a bell but barely staggering the construct. The other closed the distance.

Nyv reached out with both hands, her voice sharp and clear—"*Résh ákîr!*"

A surge of energy rippled out from her like a pulse of wind. Communal Element Bind shimmered into place around the group—a flickering veil of dampened silver light encasing their forms.

The golem's strike landed—an arc of lightning so fierce it lit the room white— but the magic held. The electricity slammed into Nyv's outstretched hands, surging into her with blinding force.

She gritted her teeth and bent with the flow of it, not resisting—channeling. The absorbed magic spiraled down her arms, then coiled like a storm seed in her core.

With a cry, she swept her hand outward, unleashing the stored energy as a bolt of radiant force transformed by instinct into a blast of sharpened wind and crackling ozone. The elemental fury sheared across the room and slammed into one of the golems, staggering it back into the wall with a hiss of rupturing sigils.

Smoke poured from its frame. It twitched, disoriented.

Nyv exhaled sharply and shook the static from her arms. "Didn't just catch that one," she muttered. "I returned it."

Bryn didn't hesitate. Her voice cut low—"*dúil pórth.*"

A black portal shimmered open beneath one of the golems, swallowing it in silence.

For a moment, the room seemed to settle—then a surge of displaced air burst overhead. The golem reappeared twenty feet above—but it wasn't alone. Another had stepped into the spot where it had vanished, drawn forward by the battle's flow.

When the portal reopened near the ceiling, the first crashed down on the second with brutal force. Their metal bodies collided in a shower of sparks and collapsing limbs. One screeched as its arm twisted beneath the other's falling weight. Both hit the floor in a heap of sparking ruin.

Neither rose again.

The fight turned in rhythm now—not shouted commands, but instinct. Kaerda and Bryn moved in parallel: one shielding, one casting, their steps mirroring each other across the battlefield.

"They're not invincible," Bryn said, panting. "But they adapt."

"They're learning," Kaerda agreed grimly. "So we stop giving them time."

Nyv's wards bent light around the others, responding before the strikes came—anticipating instead of reacting. She circled behind Kaerda once to deflect a bolt meant for Tassa, then spun to anchor a quick protective weave around Bryn mid-incantation.

Tassa fell into the rhythm without words, fire blooming only in the moments when her allies shifted clear. At one point, she banked a fire bolt off Kaerda's angled shield, striking a golem squarely in its throat joint.

Even Bone-Anna, silent and apart, adjusted her vantage after Nyv's blast exposed a weakness in the ceiling, giving her a clear line to support the others.

The Accord fought as one—moving not in formation, but in harmony.

Bryn vanished in a ripple of shadow, reappearing above a golem mid-leap and landing atop its back, whispering a curse as black feathers scattered around her. Her blade drove deep, disrupting the golem's runes before she launched back into the air, her *Fly* spell suspending her just above the chaos.

Tassa's hands burned gold as she whispered the command for *Heat Metal*, directing the searing spell into one of the golem's jointed limbs. It staggered, smoke pouring from its knees as molten etchings glowed bright along its seams.

Kaerda dropped to one knee near a downed column and struck the floor with her hammer—invoking a ward of deflection that shimmered outward. The next blow aimed for Bryn bounced harmlessly to the side.

Nyv's hands moved in a weaving pattern, calling upon the ancient magic of her homeland. *Chains of the Veilwarden* lashed from the ground, binding a golem's legs mid-stride. It pitched forward and collided into a second, sending both crashing to the floor in a tangle of limbs and sparking runes.

They pressed their advantage. No shouts, no orders. Just movement—fluid, relentless, unified.

One golem struck at Bone-Anna. She didn't dodge. She vanished.

A second later, from the upper balcony, her arrow struck true—piercing one golem's shoulder seam, lightning spilling like fluid from the gap.

● ● ●

The last golem collapsed with a sound like breaking glass and thunder rolled into one. It hit the stone floor in pieces, not shattered but... released. The arcane light behind its eyes flickered, then faded entirely.

Kaerda stepped forward cautiously, shield raised. "That's all of them. For now."

Tassa exhaled hard and leaned against a broken pillar. "I hate quiet after fights like that. It always feels like an ambush waiting to happen."

Nyv moved to Bryn, checking her form—not for injury, but for strain. Bryn gave a faint nod, still catching her breath. "I'm alright. The portals held."

Geoff chirped softly and climbed up her arm as if in confirmation.

Bone-Anna descended the stairs from the balcony, her bow held low. She said nothing. She didn't need to.

Tassa glanced at her, then at the balcony. "How did you even get up there?"

Kaerda raised an eyebrow. "I didn't see her climb."

Bryn gave a small, knowing smile. "She didn't."

Nyv tilted her head. "You think she stepped?"

Bryn nodded. "A gift, maybe. From the Queen. Like mine... but rarer. Or more limited."

Kaerda grunted. "Wouldn't mind seeing that again. Preferably when it doesn't end with lightning in my teeth."

Kaerda wandered through the ruined chamber slowly, one hand trailing along the wall as she passed collapsed columns and scorched banners. Her eyes scanned the broken edges of the architecture—looking for seams, not symbols.

Near one of the shattered walls, she crouched to inspect a collapsed archway. "Help me with this," she said, gesturing to Nyv and Bryn.

Together they pulled away debris—splintered wood, fallen stone, rusted lattice. It took time, and sweat, and no small amount of care to avoid triggering any more sigils. But eventually, beneath a warped metal panel once hidden behind layers of plaster, Kaerda found the edge of something carved—ancient stone, clean and purposeful.

As Tassa and Nyv cleared space around it, Bryn provided a gust of wind across the surface. Dust flew away.

It was a map. Etched into the wall with the precision of a master smith.

A tactical record.

Bryn's eyes narrowed as she stepped closer. "That's no battlefield layout. It's a movement route."

The map showed a network of corridors and halls beneath the city, etched in fine, straight lines with branching arcs toward an area marked only by a symbol: a stylized flame surrounded by a broken circle.

Tassa peered over Kaerda's shoulder. "That... looks familiar. Isn't that like the forge seal you pointed out earlier?"

Kaerda nodded slowly. "It's not a seal. It's a mark of crafting intention. A place where something wasn't just forged—but repurposed. Reinvented."

Nyv ran her fingers along the path on the map. "This forge... it's deeper in, but not far from this room. And based on these alignments—it's tied to shadow architecture. The kind we've only seen near ley fractures."

"This wasn't just defence," Bryn said quietly. "They were preparing for something."

Kaerda's voice was steady. "Or someone."

The Accord stood in silence for a moment, the weight of the city pressing in around them once more.

Then Bryn spoke again. "The lantern brought us here for a reason. This map— it's the next step."

● ● ●

The chamber was still hot. Not from fire, but from arcane residue—the scent of scorched stone and charged copper clung to the air. The golems had fallen, but the energy of their assault lingered in every crack, every faintly humming rune buried beneath the floor.

Kaerda leaned against the wall and slowly removed one gauntlet, flexing her fingers. "That shielding ward took more than I expected."

Tassa rubbed her shoulder, then offered a canteen to Nyv, who accepted it with a quiet nod. "You lit that one up with its own lightning," Tassa said. "Poetic."

Nyv exhaled, still rolling out the last tingles of feedback through her palms. "Felt like the whole spell was waiting for a reason."

Geoff nudged a bit of scorched metal with his snout and then chirped once— something between approval and curiosity.

Kaerda returned to the map, eyeing the flame symbol with renewed focus. "We've seen this before. Not just the seal—but the arc pattern around it. Remember that collapsed vault under the hollow stair?"

294

Bryn nodded. "Same stylization. Same spacing between ley points."

Nyv tilted her head. "If it's still partially powered, we'll feel it before we see it. Shadow energy doesn't sleep—it hums."

A pause stretched between them as the implications settled.

Kaerda let out a long breath and slid down to sit fully against the wall. "Before we follow anything, we're taking a break."

No one argued. Within minutes, packs were opened, rations pulled free, and the gear that hadn't been shattered or singed was set aside. The chamber—though still warm—was quiet now. Safe, for the moment.

Tassa unwrapped a bit of salted fish and tore it in half, handing the larger piece to Nyv without comment. Bryn took only a little and sat cross-legged near the edge of the room, tracing her finger through the dust, occasionally glancing at the faint glow still pulsing beneath the floor.

Geoff claimed a warm patch of floor near Kaerda's boots and sprawled out flat, tail twitching lazily.

Bone-Anna didn't sit. She stood near the doorway, still as stone, her bow resting at her side. But something in her posture was easier now. Looser.

The break wasn't long. But it was enough. A moment to breathe, to eat, to share silence that wasn't full of tension or fire or footsteps.

When they rose again, it was together.

"Now we follow it," Bryn said. "We follow the hum."

Chapter 16 – The Chain That Waits

They walked single-file beneath the city's skin.

Gone were the cathedral echoes and broken towers of the upper levels. Here, the stone closed in—tighter, colder, but still refined. The walls were lined with polished obsidian inlays, their surfaces dulled by dust but unmarred by time. Even this deep beneath the city, the architecture bore the hallmarks of the Velthari drive for perfection—symmetrical corridors, elegant archways, and magic woven into every seam. The air shifted slowly, like it hadn't stirred in decades. Each step forward was matched by a faint, rhythmic hum beneath their boots.

"This is it," Kaerda said softly, glancing at the wall-etched map. "The path curves just ahead."

Nyv reached out to brush her hand along the stone. "It's not carved. It was melted with unnatural fire. This was reshaped. With purpose."

They passed through a low archway choked in soot. The corridor opened into a wide chamber—broad and circular, lined in cracked obsidian tiles. Black veins of burned sigils ran up the walls, their edges pulsing faintly with residual magic. The air was too still, like breath caught in a long-held silence.

In the centre of the room stood a forge.

Or what was once a forge.

Its basin was fractured, but its once-beautiful form remained evident—runes carved with obsessive precision, edges still gleaming faintly beneath soot. The anvil had been etched with patterns of power and elegance, now marred, as if defaced by purpose rather than decay. Nearby, a half-formed construct of copper and stone rested in the shape of a large serpentine vessel—hollow, lifeless, but waiting.

Tassa stopped walking. Her gaze locked on the vessel, her breath caught in her throat.

"I've seen this shape before," she whispered. "Not here. In a dream. Or something like one."

Kaerda stepped to the edge of the forge and knelt. Her fingers hovered above the cracked stone.

"It's not cold," she said. "It feels angry?"

The forge flickered. Not with flame—but with something darker, coiled deep within. Something broken trying to remember what it once was.

Kaerda didn't speak immediately. She moved slowly, stepping away from the forge to begin circling the chamber. Her fingers brushed against wall seams, rune clusters, fractured masonry. She traced the flow of the room with a smith's eye—reading the wear on the floor, the heat scoring on distant stone.

"Nyv," she called softly, "see if you can feel the leyline distortions near that corner. There's something off—like the flow got tangled."

Nyv knelt where Kaerda indicated, palms flat to the stone. "You're right. The magic here isn't just damaged—it's folding in on itself."

Kaerda nodded once and kept moving.

She paused at a low stone recess half-buried in collapsed debris. "Geoff," she said gently, crouching. The newt perked up from Nyv's shoulder and scurried down, tail twitching. "Can you slip in and see if anything's humming in there?"

Geoff vanished into the narrow gap with practised ease. A few heartbeats later, he chirped twice, then again—sharp, insistent.

Kaerda frowned. "There's still active current in the lower conduit. Shadow-bound, but stable."

"Tassa, do you hear anything? From inside the vessel?"

Tassa stood near the cracked construct, eyes narrowed. "There's… a tone. Faint. Like wind through a broken horn."

Kaerda returned to the forge at last. She rested her palm against the lip, her gauntlet scraping softly. She didn't flinch—but she did still. Her eyes closed.

The others fell quiet.

Divine magic didn't roar through her like it might in battle. This was subtler. A conversation, not a command. The whisper of Durnach the Forgemaker was not a voice but a memory of motion—hammers falling, fire rising, the steady breath of something being built for a purpose greater than its parts.

Her brow furrowed. "This forge wasn't broken. It was turned inside out. Someone reversed the flow."

"Reversed?" Nyv asked.

Kaerda nodded, eyes still closed. "The energy that should have flowed outward was redirected inward—like a forge trying to fold fire into itself instead of shaping it into steel. That soul-vessel... it wasn't meant to be filled. It was meant to hold something that didn't belong."

Bryn stepped closer, her expression tightening. "A prison?"

Kaerda opened her eyes. "A vessel. To hold a soul. Or maybe something bigger. Something draconic."

Tassa didn't speak, but her eyes were locked on the broken shell across the chamber.

Kaerda stood slowly, brushing soot from her knees. "This wasn't abandoned. It was stopped. Whatever they were trying to bind here—failed."

● ● ●

Bryn circled the edge of the forge slowly, fingers trailing through the dust that lay thick in the cracks. "We can't banish what's left of it. Not like this. Shadow doesn't leave—it just shifts."

"So what do we do?" Tassa asked, arms crossed, gaze still flicking to the soul-vessel like it might move again.

Kaerda stepped forward, wiping her hand against her tabard. "We give it something else to shape. Something honest."

Nyv looked up. "Reforging?"

Kaerda nodded. "We light the forge the way it was meant to burn. And we use it—not to unmake—but to create. Something with purpose."

Tassa tilted her head. "Like a counterweight. Reset the balance?"

"Exactly," Bryn said. "Corruption feeds on absence. If we fill that absence with something grounded, something real—it might overwrite the damage."

Kaerda stepped back, scanning the chamber. "We'll need to do it together. Not just with magic—with intent."

"What are we making?" Nyv asked.

Kaerda smiled faintly. "Something small. But meaningful."

No one moved right away. The forge's broken light flickered faintly as if listening.

Kaerda turned back to face the group fully, her voice lowering. "This isn't just some dormant pocket of corrupted magic. It's tethered to the same current we've been feeling across the city—same distortion patterns, same resonance. It's worse now because he's awake. The shadow dragon's return has emboldened whatever residue still festers here. We're not just facing old shadow magic. We're facing a fragment of his influence."

Nyv's expression darkened. "Then what you're saying is—this forge isn't just misaligned. It's actively resisting correction."

"Exactly," Kaerda said. "If we try to brute-force it, it'll collapse. Or worse— flare."

Tassa muttered, "Great. So we're going to try something delicate in a box full of volatile magical feedback. What's our odds here?"

Kaerda didn't smile. "Low. Very low."

"So what's the plan?" Bryn asked.

Kaerda knelt again beside the basin, inspecting its fractured heart. "We'll need to stabilize the core while it's still fighting us. I'll take the forge controls. Nyv, you'll anchor the pattern into the stone with your place magic. Tassa—sustain the heat. Not flame, but true forge fire. Something alive."

Tassa stepped closer. The golden light that flickered along her fingertips was already stirring. "I want to help with the shadow, too," she said quietly. "My flame—it's not just heat. It's old. Tied to what I am. If the shadow dragon's magic made this worse… maybe mine can soften it."

Kaerda looked to Bryn.

Bryn studied Tassa for a long moment, then nodded. "A golden buffer between shadow and corruption," she said. "That might be exactly what we need."

Kaerda's voice was calm but clear. "Then we keep the forge fed with opposing forces—heat and dark, memory and purpose. We don't fight the shadow. We wrap it. Rein it in. Don't remove it. Just keep it contained while we overwrite it."

Bryn gave a slow nod. "Tassa and I can do that. Just don't ask for subtlety."

Kaerda looked around the chamber once more, drawing a deep breath. "This will burn. Maybe all of us. But if we pull it off, we'll leave something behind that corruption can't claim."

• • •

The ritual began in silence.

Kaerda took her place at the forge's core, her hammer laid across her knees as she whispered the old oaths of Durnach the Forgemaker. Bryn and Tassa stood opposite one another, hands outstretched, shadow and gold coiling through the air like twin ribbons held in tension. Nyv paced slowly in a spiral, tracing ley patterns into the ash-covered floor with chalk and whispered Ravkari verse.

The forge groaned.

A flicker of violet-shadow flared along its broken runes. The chamber seemed to pull inward, the air growing heavy, bending sound.

Kaerda struck the basin once.

Tassa's fire surged to meet it, not red, but a deep gold-white that hissed and cracked as it hit the corrupted stone. Bryn's shadows rushed forward in tandem, not to consume, but to shape—a veil against the backlash.

The forge screamed.

Darkness lashed out in a sudden wave. The light guttered. Pain bloomed.

Kaerda's grip faltered.

Nyv felt it first—the fire pushing too hard, the shadow tearing at their focus. She threw her hands wide, her voice cutting across the chaos.

"Resh akir!"

A brilliant wave pulsed from her, catching the heat, catching the pain. Element Bind shimmered through their bodies, soaking the backlash into her own magic and grounding it. Her legs buckled—but her circle held.

Kaerda grit her teeth and lifted her hammer again.

Bryn wavered, her jaw clenched. "Tassa—now."

Tassa's eyes flared.

She stepped forward, flame blooming not from her hands but her chest, her breath, her core. Light spilled from her like it had been waiting for years—not fire, but radiance made flame. The brilliance of it made the horde golem's treasure room seem dark in comparison. Her voice cracked as she screamed and drove it forward.

The forge ignited.

White and gold fire surged up the veins of the chamber. The shadow recoiled—but did not vanish. Bryn's hands swept wide, shaping the dark into a cage around the flame, wrapping it in purpose. Tassa pressed closer, her own fire anchoring it in place.

Kaerda struck once more—final, ringing.

The scream stopped.

The forge pulsed.

Then quiet.

Kaerda stepped back, smoke rising from her shoulders. Her voice was hoarse but steady. "It's done."

● ● ●

They didn't speak for a while. No one moved. The forge's light dimmed to a gentle ember-glow, warm enough to see by, soft enough not to blind.

Kaerda sank slowly to the ground, leaning against a fractured support column. Her breath came in slow, measured pulls. "We need time before I can shape anything," she said. "That... took everything."

Nyv silently pulled a small kettle from her bag and began heating water over the gentler edge of the forge. The scent of herbs and dry citrus soon filled the space. Tassa slumped down cross-legged beside Bryn and reached for her own satchel.

Kaerda accepted a steaming tin with quiet thanks.

For a few minutes, they sipped in silence. The only sounds were the clink of cups, the occasional flicker of flame, and Geoff's quiet breathing from where he curled against Nyv's boot.

Tassa was the first to speak. "We didn't just hold it back. We reshaped it. That was…" She shook her head. "I've never felt that kind of flow with anyone else."

Nyv nodded slowly. "We moved like threads in a weave. Every pull met with tension, but never resistance."

Bryn glanced around the firelight. "No spell could've done that alone."

Kaerda's voice was soft. "We did that because we were one motion. One accord."

● ● ●

After another quiet sip of tea, Kaerda looked to the forge, now glowing gently like the last breath of a star. "I want to shape something while this still holds. The forge is clean. It's listening. And I don't want this moment to fade without leaving something behind."

The others looked up.

Kaerda continued. "Nothing grand. Just something to bind us. To mark what we've done here."

Bryn reached into a small inner pocket of her coat. Her fingers lingered there for a long moment before she drew it out—a modest silver ring chased with violet etching.

"I want you to use this," she said quietly.

Kaerda looked at it, then to Bryn's face. "It's beautiful. Are you sure?"

Bryn nodded. "My mother gave it to me. A long time ago. Said it would find its way to the one who needed it most."

She set the ring gently in Kaerda's palm. "It found me once. I think now it should find all of us."

Kaerda closed her fingers around the ring, then reached into her own pack. From a side pouch, she withdrew a small shard of silver-gold metal—delicately faceted, its edges faintly warm to the touch.

"This," she said, holding it up, "was the tuning key from the hoard golem's vault. It still carries harmonic resonance from the enchantments woven into that lock—and from Tassa's flame, and Bryn's shadows, when we opened it."

She turned it in the light. "It's more than a key. It's a song remembered. A note that didn't fade. If we forge that into these tokens, we bring with us a memory of the moment we moved forward without violence."

Nyv looked down into her teacup, then slowly set it aside. "I don't have a token to add—not a physical one."

She placed her palm on the stone beside her. "But I still carry what the forge gave me during the ritual—the pain it meant to break us, and the strength I borrowed to hold us together."

She reached out, letting her fingers touch the ring and the tuning shard where they rested together in Kaerda's palm. A pulse of faint green shimmered beneath her fingertips, subtle but certain—life magic, grounded and real.

"I can give that energy to the blend. Transform what I took into something whole."

Kaerda met her gaze. "That will change the metal's nature."

Nyv nodded. "It should."

Kaerda turned toward the ruined vessel in the centre of the room. She stood slowly, her legs stiff, and crossed to the side where the copper-stone plating had fractured the least. With a small chisel from her belt, she carefully worked a wedge beneath one of the thinner seams and pried loose a piece the size of her palm. It came free with a soft metallic groan.

"This alloy was meant to contain a soul," she said quietly. "It failed, but the structure is intact. With what we've purged, what we've overwritten—it's stable now. If I fold it in carefully, it'll lend strength to what we make. And... remind the metal it has a better use."

She returned to the others, laying the soul-vessel fragment alongside the ring, the tuning shard, and where Nyv's magic still shimmered faintly in the air.

"That's enough to start."

Kaerda stood in silence for a moment, studying the assembled materials. Then she turned, stepped to the forge, and began her work.

She stoked the heart of the fire with care, coaxing the ember-glow into a sustained, golden heat. Tassa joined her without being asked, kneeling opposite and feeding measured threads of her flame into the basin, keeping the balance warm and steady.

One by one, Kaerda placed the materials into the crucible: Bryn's ring, the tuning shard, the soul-vessel alloy. As the metals began to soften, Nyv stepped forward and reached out, fingers spread. The faint green shimmer of her grounded magic entered the mix, and the colours within the molten pool shifted—violet, silver, gold, and pale green swirling into a new alloy never seen before.

Kaerda worked in silence, shaping the blend with careful hammer-strikes and divine guidance. When the first ingot cooled, she split it into four.

The first she rolled and curled into the shape of a cloak clasp, forming a spiral with a delicate hook, etched with soft flame motifs.

The second she shaped into a pendant, smooth and understated, inlaid with four faint glyphs—one for each of them.

The final ingot she halved and formed into two matching rings—simple, elegant, and bound by a mirrored design.

Kaerda set each finished piece aside with reverence. "They're not armour. Not tools. Just beginnings. They'll need refining still."

Kaerda handed the four items to Bryn, who had already set up her tools at one of the nearby tables.

Bryn offered a faint smile. "I'll refine them," she said. "But they're yours to start. The shape, the intent—it matters."

Kaerda nodded once. "The pendant felt right for me—quiet, but with weight," she said. "The clasp fits Tassa's flame—both things she keeps close to her heart. And the rings… they were always meant to be paired. I shaped them the way I see us."

Before she began her work, Bryn whispered a detection spell and passed her hands lightly over the items. Her eyes shimmered faintly as the magic responded. Traces of the ring's deep resonance, the tuning key's harmonic signature, and Nyv's nature-touched magic still lingered—woven through the alloy like threads in glass.

She paused, breath catching.

These weren't just symbolic tokens. Subtly, but undeniably, the alloy retained the magical echoes of their making. If separated, they would be able to find each other—like drawn notes in a chord.

This resonance wasn't from any spell she had cast—it pulsed with communal magic, the kind that had flowed through Nyv when she anchored them against the surge. Magic that belonged to all of them now.

Bryn began with the pendant and the clasp. She turned them gently beneath her lens, brushing fine soot away with a worn cloth, then whispered a quiet phrase as she conjured a faint shimmer of ritual magic.

At the centre of each token, Bryn etched the image of a single feather—its barbs long and tapering, the shaft curving ever so slightly as if caught in quiet wind. The top of the feather was sharp and smooth, tapering into fine detail, while the lower half deepened into a layered texture that suggested weight and purpose.

Near the upper spine of the feather, she had carved a spiral knot—its loops interwoven in perfect symmetry, a quiet echo of connection and motion. Lower still, set precisely along the central shaft, was a narrow-headed hammer, simple in design but grounded, its shape wrought from clean lines and balance. And at the very end of the feather, just beneath its curve, a single flare: a small orb of rising flame, etched not as fire consuming, but fire awakening—contained, deliberate, rising with purpose.

The entire pattern was shallowly engraved but deeply felt, each symbol shaped not to stand apart, but to flow into the next—feather, knot, hammer, ember—all part of the same form. Not decorative. Not symbolic. *Shared.*

She polished both pieces with a slow, circular motion until their surfaces caught the light fully—the etched motifs now gleamed with unmistakable clarity.

Without the others noticing, she inscribed the clasp and the pendant using a fine tool—so thin it shimmered like a wisp of thought. In delicate Elvish script, she carved the same line into both.

Before she moved on, Bryn brought the finished clasp to Tassa. She placed it gently in her hands.

"It holds," Bryn said quietly. "But it doesn't bind. Like your flame."

Tassa nodded once and fastened it to her cloak.

Then she stepped to Kaerda, offering her the pendant.

"Steady hands," Bryn said with a faint smile. "And a stronger heart. This carries both."

Kaerda accepted it solemnly and slipped the chain over her neck.

Then Bryn turned to the rings.

She worked slowly, letting the warmth of the forge and the residue of Nyv's magic guide her hand. The rings were already balanced, their mirrored designs perfectly shaped. With careful, ritual polishing, Bryn brought out the faint glint of violet in the silver—the soft green undertone where Nyv's essence had settled.

Once again, she etched the symbol of their Accord along each ring's outer surface: feather and knot, hammer and ember—each flowing into the next, not layered, but *woven*.

She then turned them carefully and inscribed the inside of each band with the same delicate Elvish script as the clasp and pendant. This time, she carved the words inward—meant not to be seen, but *felt*.

When she showed Nyv hers, she let her fingers linger just long enough for her to notice the inscription. "From me to you, this is more than a promise between members of a coven. It's a bond connecting who you and I are. Not what we can do," Bryn whispered. Her fingers lingered on Nyv's as she passed the ring over—not possessive, but reverent.

Nyv read the inscription, then looked up—her eyes bright with delight.

She took Nyv's hand gently. With care, she slid the ring into place on Nyv's finger.

Nyv said nothing. She smiled—wide and quiet.

Then, without ceremony, Bryn slipped the other ring onto her own finger.

"I've inscribed them all with the same words—words that represent our bond. Our Accord." Bryn said quietly to all of her friends.

Each woman read the inscription "What is felt need not be spoken."

Bryn looked once more at the items they now carried, the faint shimmer of residual enchantment still threading through them. She cleared her throat softly.

"There's something you should all know," she said. "When I examined the metal earlier, the magic didn't just linger. It held. The resonance from Nyv's spell, the ring, the tuning key—they've fused into something subtle, but enduring."

Kaerda tilted her head. "What kind of magic?"

"Location," Bryn said. "If ever we're separated, these will draw us back together. They resonate like notes in a chord. One sounds, and the others will feel it."

Nyv's brow rose. "You think that's me?"

Bryn nodded. "I think it's all of us. But the magic came alive when you grounded us. This—" she gestured to the tokens, "—is communal binding, whether we meant it or not."

Kaerda paused, glancing once toward the still-glowing forge. "Maybe... maybe the forge wanted to thank us. For setting it free."

The forge hummed once, low and warm. No longer broken. No longer angry.

Chapter 17 – The Threshold of Thought

The corridor descended at an angle too shallow to be natural, as if it had been carved not to guide footsteps, but to usher thoughts. The air pressed inward the deeper they went—still, but never silent. Sounds returned distorted, like echoes refracted through glass.

Nyv paused first. "This place is suspended, not buried," she said.

Kaerda ran her hand along the wall. "The stone isn't right. Too smooth. It's mirroring us."

Ahead, the path opened into a vast space—not a room, but a threshold. A half-formed battlefield lay beyond, shaped of cracked obsidian and fractured memories. Archways jutted at odd angles. Patches of the ground shimmered with scenes that shouldn't be there: Ravkari tundra, a molten forge, a circle of collapsed stone towers.

Tassa stepped through first. "These aren't places," she said. "They're thoughts."

Bryn's ravens circled tightly but refused to enter, or maybe they couldn't. One landed briefly on her shoulder, cawed low, and vanished in a ripple of shadow.

Nyv's place magic faltered—flickering, unreliable. "The leyline's here," she murmured. "But it's been bent into a loop. A closed thought."

They stepped together into the centre.

The ground shifted.

The battlefield shattered—not into dust, but into reflections. Each member of the Accord fell inward, into their own mind's conjured space. Not alone, but severed.

And waiting in each were shadows shaped like themselves—only twisted, and watching.

• • •

Bryn landed on her feet, but the space around her felt weightless, directionless—a void shaped like a shrine. The walls were made of black stone flecked with purple, like the temple where she had once heard the Queen of Stillness's whisper. But the flickering candlelight was gone. The alcoves were empty. There were no ravens.

Only silence.

Across the room, a figure stood. Her own face, but hollowed. Pale lips moved without voice. Shadows clung to her like mourning veils.

"You kept her silence so well," the illusion murmured, finally audible. "She doesn't answer you."

Bryn didn't move.

This was her deepest fear given form—not that the Queen of Stillness would rebuke her, but that she had never been seen at all. That the silence was not sacred, but hollow. That her entire purpose had been a misreading, a devotion to nothing. That her Queen's absence meant she had always been alone.

"She left you. Or maybe she never truly saw you." The illusion's eyes were mirrors. "You mistook absence for calling."

The words struck like needles, not because they were new—but because they weren't.

Bryn closed her eyes.

"I was never chosen to be safe," she said softly. "I was chosen to carry the silence forward."

Power did not surge in her chest. The illusion did not break. But the weight lifted, just slightly. The illusion wavered.

Bryn stepped forward. She could feel nothing beneath her feet, but her balance remained. The shadow-self began to retreat—not in fear, but in confusion.

She raised her hand and looked down at the ring.

The inscription within glimmered faintly, though no light reached it: *What is felt need not be spoken.*

She smiled.

"I was never alone."

The raven appeared—not from above, but from within. A flicker of black feathers burst outward as if pulled from her own ribs. It soared past the illusion and vanished into the unseen sky.

Bryn turned toward the direction it flew—and walked into the dark without fear.

As she moved, the shrine seemed to exhale around her. The walls pulsed faintly, not in menace, but in reluctant release—like a held breath let go. Her footfalls left no sound, but the echo of her resolve rippled through the illusion. Every step rewrote the space behind her.

She glanced back once—not at the illusion, but at the space where her shadow-self had stood. It was gone now, as if it had never existed. Or perhaps it had simply lost the power to shape her.

For a moment, she felt the faint brush of feathers across her shoulders. Not seen. Not heard. But known.

Then a corridor of violet light opened in the darkness—narrow and deliberate. It led not forward, but inward.

Toward the Accord.

● ● ●

Kaerda stood in a forge with no fire.

At first, she thought it was familiar. The curve of the walls. The way the workbenches were arranged. But there were no tools. No smoke. No sound.

The anvil at the centre was flawless—no chips, no burn marks. That was wrong. A working forge should bear scars, stories, even soot. This place had been scrubbed clean of purpose.

She stepped forward. Her boots echoed too evenly. The walls shimmered with a faint metallic sheen, like reflected heat—but gave off none. Her breath came too slow, like her lungs didn't belong to her.

Her reflection stared back from every angle—but not as she was. Her face was still, motionless. Her eyes glassed over. Her skin looked like polished steel.

She moved to the anvil and reached for her hammer. There was none.

Her hands were already closed.

Metal fingers.

She flexed them—and felt nothing. Not the cool metal. Not the friction of the air.

The illusion whispered in her ear, though no voice spoke aloud. *"You wanted strength. Now you don't need heart."*

She tried to speak, but her mouth did not obey. This was her fear—becoming a tool without a will. A thing of strength but no purpose. She had always feared that Durnach the Forgemaker saw only her forge, not the heart that wielded it. That all her craftsmanship was just function, not faith.

Only silence.

Kaerda closed her eyes.

And remembered.

The pendant—small, intentional, imperfect. Forged not by mandate, but by trust. Tassa's fire. Nyv's grounding presence. Bryn's touch of shadowed clarity. And her own hand—not divine, but dedicated.

She had created something not because she was told to—but because she believed they needed it.

And it had mattered. The four together were better than the one.

Her heart beat once. Then again.

A flicker of warmth returned to her chest, like the first glow of coals beneath ash.

She reached down—not with metal fists, but with intention—and seized the base of the anvil.

"I am not strong because I was made to be," she said aloud. Her voice returned, gravel-edged and true. "I am strong because I forge with others."

She lifted her right hand high and struck the anvil with her closed fist.

The sound that rang out was no echo. It was a call. A prayer.

The walls fractured. The mirrors cracked.

Light spilled through the seams.

And through the breach, she saw movement—three distant forms. One of them lifted a hand, silhouetted in violet and green.

Kaerda exhaled—her breath her own again.

She walked toward them.

● ● ●

Tassa ran.

The spiral of flame that surrounded her narrowed with every breath. Each time she turned, the corridor bent back on itself. Ash hung in the air like falling snow. The stone beneath her feet cracked with each step—not from her weight, but from her presence. The light flickered with an unnatural rhythm, more pulse than flicker—like a heartbeat panicked and erratic.

Everything burned.

This was her fear—unchecked, unrefined. That her fire, her magic, her very self was a curse. That she could not protect those she loved, only destroy them. That the power she carried wasn't divine, but ruinous. That one day, Bryn, Nyv, and Kaerda would each turn to ash in her arms.

The air shimmered around her skin with heat she couldn't control. Her breathing came shallow. Sparks danced from her fingertips no matter how tightly she curled them. The fire wasn't waiting to be summoned—it was already here, clawing out of her.

She saw a version of herself ahead, backlit by fire. This illusion smiled, teeth too white and too perfect. "Why do you pretend?" it asked. "You know what you are. Everything you touch, you ruin."

Tassa clenched her fists. Flames curled between her fingers unbidden.

The illusion stepped closer. "You didn't earn the fire. You were born from it. You can't shape it. Only survive it."

Tassa dropped to her knees. The heat pressed in from all sides, choking and feral. Bryn's face flashed in the blaze. Then Nyv's. Both burning. Kaerda's voice echoed like iron hitting stone—cut short. Her flame lashed out in all directions. The walls trembled.

Her voice was a whisper. "No."

313

She closed her eyes and reached inside—not for control, but for understanding. Not to silence the fire, but to listen.

The forge. The golden light.

She remembered Kaerda shaping the alloy. How her own fire hadn't consumed, but refined. How Bryn had trusted her, wordlessly. How Nyv had smiled when the clasp was set into place.

She remembered the clasp holding her cloak—the one Kaerda forged from the tuning key and Bryn's heirloom, the one that shimmered under Bryn's hand when she inscribed it. Not fear. Not restraint. Harmony.

This fire had never been wild. It had been hers.

Tassa stood.

She opened her mouth and spoke—not in Common, but in Draconic. The words were few. They didn't need to be many.

"Be still. I am the flame."

The spiral flared—then steadied. The fire narrowed, folded in around her like a cloak. Its edges no longer lashed, but coiled close, reverent.

The illusion hissed, retreating, its perfect face beginning to blacken and break like overbaked clay.

"I'm not broken," Tassa said. *"I'm tempered."*

The fire obeyed.

And as the last ember faded into golden light, she saw three others waiting, their silhouettes drawn sharp against the dark.

She walked toward them, her steps leaving no scorch marks on the stone.

● ● ●

Nyv opened her eyes to wind.

It wasn't cold—not yet—but it carried the emptiness of Ravkareth's farthest reaches. The tundra spread out in every direction, blanched of colour, without snow or sun. Just grey. Just stillness.

She turned in place. There were no tracks behind her. No voices. No Geoff. Not even the leyline beneath her feet. Her magic, which always hummed softly like breath in her bones, was gone.

A figure stood in the distance. Too far to see clearly. But Nyv knew its shape. Her own posture. Her own silence.

"You're not meant to stay," the illusion called. "You were always a guest. A visitor. A lonely child playing at being part of something greater."

Nyv stared.

This was what she feared more than death: to be forgotten. To have never truly been part of something. To believe herself loved, but be secretly pitied. To be the one who was let into the circle only out of mercy, not bond. A shadow trailing behind a coven she could never truly call her own.

The illusion stepped closer. "They're not your coven. They never were. The bond you felt? That was charity. Pity. They needed your magic, not you."

She looked down at her hands—empty. No wand. No scroll. Just the ring.

It shimmered faintly.

Nyv closed her eyes.

And whispered: "Kaerda."

The air warmed slightly.

"Tassa."

A hum, deep beneath her feet.

"Bryn."

The ring pulsed.

With each name, her magic stirred—not rising, but unfolding. Not summoned, but remembered.

She stepped forward.

The illusion snarled. "You can't leave. You have no place to return to."

Nyv walked past her. Not fast. Not defiant. Just certain.

The ring shimmered again. Words unspoken. Felt.

"*They needed ME.*" she thought defiantly.

She felt a pull—not like gravity, but like home.

And ahead, a light blinked violet and gold.

Nyv smiled.

And walked into it.

The air around her began to change—less like wind and more like breath. Each step echoed differently now, no longer flat and muted, but resonant, as if the ground beneath her recognised her passage.

She thought of the moments that had defined her magic—not when she fought alone, but when the Accord stood with her. Kaerda's forge-bound steadiness. Tassa's golden fire curving alongside her shields. Bryn's shadows dancing to match her movement without words.

Nyv whispered again, almost to herself. "We're not apart. Not anymore. They want me—she chose me."

The illusion behind her began to unravel. Threads of grey and shadow peeled away like dry silk, the false tundra dissolving into light. Her other self no longer watched. It had no eyes left. No voice.

She didn't turn back.

The ring pulsed once more, steady now—alive with magic that was not hers alone.

She followed the flicker of violet and gold, feeling her own heartbeat fall into rhythm with three others.

Toward the Accord.

● ● ●

They emerged from different directions, their footsteps silent, but synchronized.

Kaerda stepped through a cleft in the shattered forge-wall, still streaked with gold and ember. Bryn moved from the corridor of feathered darkness, shadow clinging to her heels like a memory not quite willing to let go. Tassa's flame parted like a curtain around her shoulders, gentle now, her cloak aglow with golden shimmer. Nyv stepped from a shimmer in the air itself, as if thought had opened for her.

They saw one another—and did not hesitate.

The battlefield did not welcome them. It twisted.

The illusory terrain warped into something new. Not individualized threats, but a unified mockery. The false versions of themselves reformed in the space ahead—twisted amalgamations of fear, failure, and pride.

Bryn's double stepped forward, head bowed, carrying a cracked relic of the Queen of Stillness. Kaerda's illusion moved with unfeeling precision, hammer raised, eyes blank. Tassa's shadow burned too bright, sparks flying wildly. Nyv's false self was already vanishing—fading at the edges like a thought denied.

The Accord slowed, but didn't stop.

They didn't speak.

Tassa moved in front of Bryn, one hand lifted—not to strike, but to shield. Kaerda took the left flank, shield raised. Nyv reached to Bryn's side and grabbed her hand.

Bryn gave the smallest nod.

"Now," she said.

Nyv lifted her hand.

"*Krén thîril.*"

Enhanced invisibility shimmered around them—not in silence, but in certainty. The magic swept outward, wrapping each of them in shared presence. The false battlefield flickered. The illusions twisted, staggered, and reached out as if to rebind the group, but their forms wavered. Their voices fractured into echoes of doubt that found no purchase. One by one, they faded—not with screams, but with silence.

They could not hold what they could no longer see.

Because what they had tried to divide... had rejoined.

The silence that followed was whole.

And through it, they walked—together, unseen, unbroken.

Toward the next threshold.

Chapter 18 – The Final Flight

The shattered spire rose like broken glass against a bruised sky, its jagged stairways of floating obsidian winding upward into stormclouds that pulsed with shadowlight. Lightning flickered at its peak—not natural, but deliberate, as though cast by a hand just out of sight.

The Silent Accord stood at its base, cloaked in the final traces of Nyv's communal enhanced invisibility spell. The land around them was scorched and silent, littered with fragments of shattered memory—glimmering shards that caught the light without reflection. The ruins beneath their feet whispered with voices long dead, echoes of an empire that had torn itself apart in pursuit of power.

For a long moment, no one spoke.

Tassa's eyes tracked the spire's peak. "Do you think he knows we're here?"

Kaerda answered without turning. "He knew before we crossed the threshold."

Bryn's gaze lingered on the fractured glass above, where lightning crawled through the clouds like veins in diseased skin. "The storm hasn't moved since dawn. It's waiting for us."

Nyv stepped forward, placing a hand on Chovee's javelin. Its glow was faint, but persistent—like a heartbeat buried beneath stone. "Whatever happens up there… we finish this. For Chovee. For the ones who couldn't."

Kaerda adjusted the straps on her shield. "And for those who still live. This ends with us."

They approached slowly, the silence pressing heavier with every step. The spire's base loomed larger than it had from a distance—a jagged ring of glasslike stone rising from the earth like the broken crown of a fallen god. The first stair hovered just above the ground, black and sharp-edged, gleaming with unnatural sheen.

As Bryn stepped onto it, the stone pulsed beneath her boot. Not a trap. A recognition.

"One way up," she said quietly.

Tassa offered a wry smile. "No complaints here. I've always preferred the high road."

They climbed.

The stairway cracked beneath them with every step, each platform floating slightly apart from the next. The gaps grew wider as they ascended, forcing leaps where once there had been bridges. Wind swirled around them in tight, suffocating spirals, filled with the scent of scorched metal and old ozone.

The higher they climbed, the more the world seemed to fall away. The desert and the ruin below faded to shadow, the horizon curling inward like a closing eye. Only the spire remained—an impossible tower, suspended by force of will alone.

Halfway up, they paused on a wider platform. From here, the full scale of the battle to come pressed into them. Below, remnants of their journey lingered: the broken trees, the half-buried ruins, the faint line of smoke where the forge had once glowed.

Kaerda exhaled, leaning slightly on her hammer. "Feels like we've been walking toward this since the day we met."

Bryn nodded. "Even before that."

Tassa glanced over the edge. "Do you think he'll try to talk? Or just... kill us?"

Nyv's voice was quiet but certain. "He'll talk. He wants us to understand why he wins."

"That's the mistake," Bryn said. "Thinking we care."

They resumed the climb.

The platforms narrowed again, bending in slow arcs, twisting higher into unnatural wind. At times, they moved beneath the group's feet, responding to unspoken intentions. Shadows flickered between the stones—not alive, but not entirely dead.

Bryn's ravens wheeled overhead in silence, wings angled into the wind. Even they seemed wary, circling with greater distance than usual. One cried out once, then fell silent again.

As they neared the top, the storm crackled louder. The air split in long, soundless pulses of lightning that lit the path ahead. And then—

A chamber opened before them.

Walls of translucent black rose in sweeping arcs, spiked with veins of lightning caught mid-strike. And in the centre, waiting beside a single broken throne, stood Vaelric.

He smiled as they entered. Not surprised. Not alarmed. Just... satisfied.

"You came," he said, almost reverently. "I had wondered how long it would take. But not if. Never if." He looked directly at Tassa when he said this.

"Especially you," he added, tilting his head. "Even before I knew your name, I felt it—the ember buried deep. You masked it with laughter, with riddles. But the flame beneath... it remembers. That memory is what drew me. What still draws me."

He smiled faintly, as though indulging an old secret. "Your path was always going to lead here. Some part of you has known that, even if you've tried to laugh it away."

He stepped forward, his presence calm, almost regal. The chamber shuddered faintly around him, like a held breath.

"You remember me as a wanderer. A guide. But even then, I was part of what brought you here.

"I watched your every step, measured your progress. That translation you couldn't have read alone. The enchanted map. The seed of suspicion planted just deep enough. You were never walking blind—not really. I laid the path because I knew you'd walk it. I'll admit—I was surprised when you managed to cleanse the forge. That place was meant to hollow you out, not strengthen your bond. But no matter. Cleansing it may have tempered your weapons, but it won't temper fate. The outcome remains unchanged. "

Nyv's jaw clenched. She didn't speak, but her silence sharpened the tension.

Vaelric turned to her first. "I always knew I would meet the one who carried golden flame—though I expected it to roar. But it was you I wanted to meet, Nyvana. Your discipline. Your fear. Your hunger to preserve. But then I saw the others—saw what you'd all become together. That changed everything."

His eyes swept across Kaerda, Tassa, then finally rested on Bryn.

"And you... You're the one who was never meant to last. A shadow clinging to memory. A vessel shaped by another's will. Yet here you are. Quiet. Anchored. Yours is the tone they've come to wear, and that... I didn't foresee."

He spread his arms, mock-gentle.

"I gave you help when you didn't know you needed it. I gave you time. And now, before the end, I give you one last offer. Join me. Stand beside what's inevitable. Vhal'turien refused me once, and paid dearly for it. But you—any of you—could still choose a different fate. There is power in understanding. In alignment. Why be ash scattered by the wind when you could be the storm itself?"

His voice lowered, coaxing. "You've seen what the world offers in return for sacrifice. You've lost friends. Family. You walk with the dead. Even your victories have cost more than they gave. Why not rise instead of fall? Why not survive... with me?"

He paused.

"But I know you won't."

His eyes drifted again to the javelin strapped across Nyv's back. The faint glow pulsed, subtle but steady. "I can feel it now—the thread that ties you here. That weapon isn't just steel and shadow. It's memory. Purpose. A vow made by the dead and carried by the living. You're not here for power. You're never here for yourselves. And that..."

He exhaled through a slow, bitter smile.

"You're here to save one soul. A noble effort. Personal. Contained. But the Heart doesn't work that way. It never did.

"I once tried subtlety. I gave the task to a Vaulmar Binder—clever, ambitious, obsessed with mastery over death. I let him approach the Heart, let him try to bind it with runes and ritual. He failed, of course—at your hands, no less Nyvana. He believed knowledge was enough. That power could overwrite sacrifice.

"Then I tried purity. A vessel without ego. The man with no mouth. A construct born of memory, but without voice, without self. He followed orders. He did not question. And still—he failed. You showed him that he lacked the fire that memory alone cannot provide.

"I've spent a long time learning from failure. That's how I know I'm ready now.

"You see, I don't want to break the cycle of life and death. I want to rewrite its language—make memory the mechanism. No more fear. No more forgetting. A world where death isn't a void, but a page already written and never lost.

"Vhal'turien thought sacrifice gave memory meaning. He was wrong. Memory is meaning. He just wasn't brave enough to claim it."

He looked across the Accord now.

"But you—you could be. You've felt it, haven't you? That pull. That ache. The sense that your choices are echoes. That you are being drawn into something you've already begun.

"Join me, and we will remake what comes next. Not for power. For certainty."

He let the words settle. Then, a sigh—less resignation than confirmation.

"But of course you won't. You've already made your choice, even if you haven't said it aloud. That's the thing about memory—it shows us not just what we've done, but what we *will* do. And your memories... they burn with defiance.

"Still, I wanted you to hear it. To know what you're refusing. When you fall, and you will, you'll know you were offered understanding and turned away from it."

"That is why you will never understand what's being offered. You still believe in sacrifice. In standing for someone else. Even now, you carry a fallen name like it still matters. You think defiance makes you strong. But all it does is delay the end. So yes, I offer understanding—before it ends. Before you lose. Because you will. You must."

He paused there as the smile widened.

"So many names," he said finally.

"But names won't help you now."

As he spoke, his body began to shift—too subtly at first to track, like smoke condensing into shape. His features warped, elongated, the illusion of humanity peeling away. Vaelric's form grew taller, broader, his eyes deepening into slits of stormlight. Wings, not yet fully real, flared behind him in shadows cast by no source. When he smiled again, it revealed a mouth full of gleaming, predatory teeth. Lightning pulsed through the black veins of the chamber as his presence thickened, pressing into their minds like a second heartbeat.

He stepped back toward the broken throne, now no longer appearing frail or mysterious, but vast. Terrible. Majestic.

Kaerda took half a step back, her breath catching. Even she, forged in stone and battle, had never seen a dragon of this magnitude.

Tassa's lips parted, awe flickering across her expression despite herself. The fire in her blood stirred, uncertain.

Nyv stood rooted. Her discipline steadied her spine, but her eyes widened—just slightly—as if reconciling the scale of what stood before them.

Only Bryn remained still. Her hair having loosened after the long climb, stirred gently in the unseen wind, her coat unmoved, her expression unreadable. The others felt the weight of the dragon. Bryn had already measured it—and moved past it.

"But you knew me best by the wrong one."

Bryn's eyes narrowed. "Mairadas."

The smile widened. "You do remember. Good. Memory is so slippery in places like this."

He raised one clawed hand—not in threat, but in declaration.

"You see yourselves as stronger together. But I have watched you, studied your rhythms. Your bond is impressive—yes. Even admirable. But it is also your crutch. Alone, you falter. Divided, you are smaller things. And so, I will show you yourselves... one at a time."

He let the words settle.

"This isn't punishment. It's revelation. I want to see what each of you truly is—without the others to steady your hand. Without your Accord to shield your weakness. I'll break your unity by showing you how little it matters."

The shadows surged. A pulse of blue light cracked the sky.

At the last moment, Nyv reached for Bryn's hand—unthinking, instinctual. Their fingers locked—not just in reflex, but in memory. The magic recognized it before they did.

The magic meant to tear them apart stuttered.

Far above, Mairadas' gaze narrowed—not surprise, but a flicker of something unreadable. The smallest crack in certainty.

"Curious," he murmured. "The bond holds stronger than expected."

Then his grin returned, broader. "No matter. Even unity has limits."

Bryn's shadow flared. Nyv's ward pulsed. The spell twisted, glitched. Instead of separating, they were hurled through the breach together, the force around them shrieking in protest.

● ● ●

Each member of the Accord was pulled away—

Bone-Anna and Geoff tumbled first, hurled from the chamber's edge as if discarded by unseen hands. They skidded across a slope of fragmented glass, landing at the outer rim of a warped battlefield that bent like memory.

Kaerda fell next, swallowed by a rift of molten light. The clang of her shield echoed as she vanished, drawn toward the purified forge as if summoned by flame and steel.

Tassa vanished in a spiral of shadow and fire, her scream muffled by distance as she was dragged into the Shadow Realm.

And Bryn and Nyv—together—landed hard on a field of ash and memory. The sky above them was half-shadow, half-light. A battlefield frozen in time. The javelin struck the ground beside them, its amber glow untouched by the fall—a memory, and a vow, refusing to be left behind.

Across it all, the dragon's laughter echoed.

"This is not a fight," Mairadas whispered, now everywhere. "It is a memory of what you failed to stop. Let us see what you make of it."

Bryn rose to full height slowly, her hand lightly squeezing Nyv's. "We hold the line."

Nyv's grip tightened briefly in return—wordless, steady. They had already chosen each other and chosen the Accord. Now they stood in that choice. Nyv squeezed back. "Together."

The words echoed the ones they'd spoken on the stairs—spoken before any of this began. What had once been prediction was now reality, and what had once been fear... had become foundation.

Above, the storm roared. And below, the final battle began.

Chapter 19 – The Silent Arrow and the Embered Glance

Bone-Anna landed in silence. No sound of impact, no grunt of effort. Just the whisper of fractured glass giving way beneath her skeletal frame. She rolled once, rose, and lifted her bow before the air had stilled. Nearby, Geoff the Newt lay on his back beside a shard of shimmering obsidian, his orange belly rising and falling. After a moment, he gave a soft hiccup.

The field was quiet.

Too quiet.

The battlefield they had landed on stretched outward in jagged arcs—ridges of black crystal and broken stone laced with veins of lightning. Towering, skeletal trees marked the perimeter, their branches crackling with flickers of stormlight. This was no natural place. It was a wound in the world. And it was watching them.

Somewhere ahead, the air pulsed with draconic energy—not full, not whole, but familiar. A lesser aspect of Mairadas waited—an early memory maybe?

Bone-Anna tilted her skull, listening. Then, wordlessly, she moved.

The air stirred.

Bone-Anna paused on a ridge of fractured stone, her skull turning toward a faint crackle that shivered across the lightning-veined trees. She didn't breathe. She never had. But something inside her ribcage pulled tight—like memory trying to speak.

Geoff the Newt skittered onto her shoulder, his claws surprisingly silent on her worn leather pauldron. His eyes blinked once, then narrowed. Together, they looked toward the source of the disturbance.

From a hollow at the far end of the battlefield, the ground cracked open. Something massive stirred beneath the surface, pushing up through layers of dead magic and crystalized storm. A shape began to emerge—four-legged, serpentine, sheathed in stormlight and skeletal plating. A lesser aspect of Mairadas, birthed from memory and shadow, not as large as they had seen Mairadas earlier and not truly alive, but terribly present.

The creature let out a hiss that trembled through the stone like a buried scream.

Geoff flared his frills and dropped from Bone-Anna's shoulder, landing low in a hunter's crouch.

Bone-Anna didn't hesitate. She knocked an arrow, the fletching a curl of blackened feathers, and loosed it in a single movement.

The arrow struck the creature's flank—no roar, no blood, but a flicker of light burst from the impact. The aspect turned its head slowly, storm-eyes narrowing on them both.

Then it charged.

Bone-Anna shifted her stance and fired again. Geoff darted right, weaving between glass shards like a streak of living shadow.

They didn't move together—yet. They simply moved.

The battle had begun.

The lesser aspect slammed into a ridge where Bone-Anna had stood a moment before. She was already airborne, flipping back with impossible grace. Her next arrow was notched mid-motion and struck the beast's shoulder with a sharp crack. Again, no blood—just that crackle of dissipated energy, like lightning dispersing across glass.

Geoff, now opposite her, lunged beneath the beast's arcing limb. He scrambled across the underside of the broken terrain, then leapt toward a jagged ledge. A burst of static struck the rock behind him as the aspect twisted to retaliate. Geoff hissed and dove again, tail lashing.

Their actions were clean, effective, even bold—but not connected. Bone-Anna loosed another shot just as Geoff triggered a distraction, but their timing was off. Her arrow landed, but didn't strike the exposed joint now revealed by Geoff's positioning.

Still, they held their ground.

Bone-Anna dropped low, evading a slam of the creature's tail that shattered a spire of black stone behind her. Geoff darted up its flank and slapped a tiny claw against a glowing sigil on its hide—just enough to disrupt its charge for a moment.

Neither of them acknowledged the other. They didn't need to.

And yet... they weren't winning. Not yet.

The lesser aspect slowed, as if recalibrating. Its next breath came heavier. Sparks flared from the cracks in its plating. It hadn't landed a blow, but it hadn't yet been threatened either.

It was waiting for them to slip.

They weren't losing. But they weren't winning, either.

Bone-Anna circled wide, her boots silent against the glass. She drew another arrow, this one tipped in something darker—venom, not from nature but memory created by her enchanted bow. The arrowhead pulsed faintly with a vitriolic sheen.

The aspect turned, tracking her with heavy, deliberate steps. She released—one, two, three arrows in rapid succession, each biting into a different joint. The creature slowed, slightly staggered.

She tilted her skull.

Kiting. That was the rhythm. If she stayed just out of reach, always retreating with precision and striking as she moved, it would follow. She could keep it focused. Distracted.

Behind her, Geoff caught on.

He darted to the far side of the battlefield and began to mimic her arcs, but tighter, sharper—scraping a claw across one ridge, knocking a stone loose on another. As the aspect turned toward him with a shriek of static, Bone-Anna loosed another arrow into the exposed flank.

The creature recoiled.

Not far. But enough.

A rhythm began—not perfect but growing. One led, one harried. Neither spoke, but the first beat of coordination had begun.

Bone-Anna reached for another arrow.

This time, she paused.

Above the battlefield, Geoff had scrambled to a shattered ridge. He looked down at the beast, then up to a loose formation of crystal spires hanging precariously above it.

With a sudden burst of energy, he leapt up the incline and slapped the ridge's edge with his tail. The stone cracked. A half-dozen jagged shards came crashing down.

The aspect shrieked as the rubble struck its shoulder and back, staggering it mid-turn. That gave Bone-Anna the opening.

Geoff had darted ahead again, but not randomly. He circled behind a jut of shattered glass and then skittered up its side, drawing the aspect's attention with a chirring sound that echoed strangely in the charged air. As the beast lunged toward him, it exposed its throat—a momentary gap in its armour.

Bone-Anna fired.

The arrow struck true, sinking just below the jawline. The creature staggered.

For the first time, it looked wounded.

Geoff glanced back, and Bone-Anna tilted her head just slightly—an acknowledgement, if not yet understanding.

The aspect roared and reared back to retaliate.

Bone-Anna reached for another arrow, but this one she didn't fire from where she stood.

In a motion both deliberate and new, she stepped—not with her feet, but with shadow.

The world folded.

She vanished from the ridgeline and reappeared atop a spire directly across the battlefield. Her bones hummed with the magic's aftershock. Her next arrow was already nocked.

Geoff dove low again, his movement perfectly timed to force the aspect to lift its head—and Bone-Anna loosed.

The shot slammed into the exposed plate behind its left eye.

The creature roared—not in fury this time, but in pain.

Together, Bone-Anna and Geoff advanced—not separate forces, but a single rhythm.

The tide had turned.

The aspect reeled, staggering backward through a wall of shattered crystal. It snarled—a grating, grinding noise like a thunderstorm collapsing inward—and dug its claws into the obsidian floor to regain balance. One eye flickered with unstable light.

Bone-Anna moved first. She didn't run—she glided from stance to stance, loosing arrows in precise intervals that struck joint, tendon, and plated seam. The poisoned barbs hissed as they landed, forcing the creature to shift its footing, to guard.

Geoff, now fully attuned to her rhythm, raced ahead and circled behind the creature's flank. With a calculated leap, he struck the same sigil on the beast's hind leg he had found before—this time, digging in his claws and scraping it until it sparked.

The lesser aspect faltered.

Bone-Anna loosed two arrows in rapid succession, one catching it in the spine, the second in the neck. Geoff launched himself from the beast's back, hit the ground, and rolled clear just as the aspect began to convulse.

The energy within the creature surged outward in arcs of violet-blue lightning. Bone-Anna and Geoff pulled back, ducking behind a fractured ridge just as the beast let out a final, unearthly shriek. The stormlight within it began to flicker, destabilize, and imploded.

With a sound like wind being inhaled by the void, the aspect collapsed into itself, reduced to shards of memory and fading light.

Silence followed.

Geoff stood atop a glass shard, blinking slowly. Bone-Anna lowered her bow.

The battlefield stilled.

Together, they had ended it.

From the air above the battlefield, something shimmered—faint at first, then sharp and brilliant. A portal unfurled in silence, outlined in golden flame. Its light cut through the dying shadows like dawn through stormclouds. It was unmistakably familiar—an echo of magic the Accord had seen before—but its presence here felt utterly out of place. It burned with warmth, not domination. Familiar, protective. Not his power—but hers.

This battlefield, this wound in memory, had not summoned it. Mairadas had not allowed it. Which meant it had come from elsewhere.

The Heart.

Somewhere far beyond this place, the will of Tassa Emberlin—perhaps even unknown to herself—had forced a gap in the enemy's grasp. It was not just magic. It was defiance made manifest.

And it was calling them home.

Bone-Anna turned toward it, her empty eye sockets reflecting its glow.

Before he moved, Geoff turned to the dissipating corpse of the lesser aspect and made an unmistakably rude gesture—tail flicked high, tongue stuck out with slow, deliberate flair.

Then, without ceremony, he strutted up Bone-Anna's leg and onto her shoulder, where he nestled against the curve of her collarbone as if he'd done it a hundred times. He blinked slowly. She didn't flinch. Somehow, she welcomed it.

For the first time, she turned her head and looked at him—not just a motion of recognition, but a choice to see. Once, she might have walked through without pause. But something within her—new, growing—chose to wait.

He looked back.

They stood there for a beat longer than necessary.

Then, in eerie unison, they stepped forward and entered the portal together— unhurried, unworried, and utterly certain it would take them where they were needed next.

Chapter 20 – Forge and Flame

Kaerda landed in silence, one knee pressed to cold stone.

She didn't stumble. Didn't breathe hard. She simply stood.

Around her, the air shimmered with heat—not wild, not natural. Controlled. Reverent. She recognised it before she understood it. This place was a forge, but not as it should have been. The fire burned low, steady, waiting. Its light flickered through dust-choked vents and veins of hammered brass set into the walls. Cracked anvil stones ringed the platform, some half-buried in ash.

She'd stood here before.

Or... someplace like it.

The layout was wrong. Too large. Too high-ceilinged. But the smell was the same. The rhythm of heat and echo. The sound of metal waiting to be moved.

She stepped forward slowly, her boots crunching over scorched iron shavings. One hand brushed the edge of a familiar tool rack. It had no dust on it.

The forge ahead pulsed once.

A memory, she realised—but not hers alone. The room responded to her like it knew her better than she knew herself. Like it had been shaped not just by the past, but by the future.

She drew her hammer from her back, reverently. The haft was worn smooth where her hands had gripped it across years. But here, under this light, it looked new again. She laid it down on the forge stone.

It hummed.

The same glow she'd seen when they purified the forge the previous day flickered beneath the coals. Blue-white flame, clear as glacier-light, edged in gold. She hadn't known what that glow meant then. She understood it better now.

This was the same forge.

Not rebuilt. Not restored. Remembered.

She wasn't reforging her hammer. She was forging it *again*—and the reason it had become her defining tool was because *this* moment had always happened. Even if it hadn't happened yet.

She pressed her palm to the anvil. It was warm—not with heat, but with memory.

Somewhere in the distance, metal rang. One strike. Then another.

And Kaerda began to work.

● ● ●

She moved like a memory unfolding.

Was she doing it now, or had she done it before?

The question didn't slow her. It didn't even need answering. In this place, time was shaped by will, not order. She simply followed the rhythm.

Every step toward the flame felt both familiar and new—her arms recalling motions before she'd chosen them, her breath in rhythm with strikes she hadn't made yet. She selected a set of tongs that hung just above her eye line, and when her fingers closed around the grip, they were already warm—as though they'd never left her hands.

The hammer's core, unshaped and inert, waited beside her. Not broken, not whole—just unfinished. It pulsed faintly, responding to the forge's low song.

She didn't question how it came to be there. The forge had remembered it for her.

Kaerda set metal to flame. The blue-white light responded eagerly, wrapping the ore in coils of heat that didn't burn—it revealed. She turned it, folded it, struck it. Each impact echoed not just across stone, but backward through time, like reminders.

Sparks rose with each strike—shimmering gold and silver, briefly forming silhouettes in the smoke. Not ghosts. Not illusions. Memories in motion. Tassa's silhouette turned, half-smiling. Nyv at rest, watching stars with a mask beside her knee. Bryn kneeling beside an unfamiliar altar. Geoff sitting in a pocket of Kaerda's coat, tail twitching.

She didn't pause to watch them.

She simply worked.

The hammer began to take shape again.

Not perfect. But destined.

A memory, yes.

But one that had almost learned to become real.

The flame dimmed.

Something massive stirred in the far dark of the forge's memory.

Kaerda set her hammer aside and turned.

The trial was here.

But Mairadas had miscalculated.

He had brought them here—led them through shadow and memory, believing their separation would weaken them. But in this place, this impossible forge born from time and devotion, he had given her the very thing he wished to deny: purpose, clarity, and renewal.

The hammer had been finished here not despite him, but because of him.

And that mistake would cost him. Kaerda already knew the truth of it. Mairadas already knew the truth of it.

The air behind her shuddered.

It emerged from the far end of the forge—larger than the memory-born wretch that had faced Bone-Anna and Geoff. This one was closer to truth, more defined in the shape of Mairadas himself. Plated in obsidian scales and wrapped in rivulets of molten light, its wings dragged through the heat-haze, casting flickering shadows that didn't match its form. It was too big for the forge room, but somehow it fit.

Its eyes burned with patient fury—not a mindless guardian, but a fragment of will that knew what it was guarding. The creature lunged.

Kaerda met it without hesitation.

The forge blazed behind her, sensing her moment. As the beast reared back, its eyes pulsing with molten hate, the flames flared in a sudden burst—white-gold and blinding.

The aspect reeled, shrieking, momentarily stunned by the searing light.

Kaerda moved.

She seized the newly-forged hammer and stepped into the creature's blind side. Her strike came from below the jaw, upward into the skull—clean, focused, final.

It took only one blow. There was no roar. No drawn-out death.

Just the sound of metal breaking stone, and silence.

The aspect collapsed in on itself, flickering with half-light and molten shadow before vanishing entirely.

The forge dimmed.

Kaerda exhaled once, then turned toward the open air. She placed her hand on the forge, reverently. A silent thanks passed from palm to flame—for its guidance then, and its grace now.

She knew it now—this was never a trial. It was the final blow to a plan that had unraveled the moment it believed her lesser.

The portal opened in golden flame.

It shimmered exactly as it was for Bone-Anna and Geoff in their landscape— out of place in this memory-bound forge, yet utterly familiar. A warmth not of fire, but of purpose.

This was not Mairadas's doing. It was defiance born of will—the will of Tassa Emberlin, carried through the Heart.

Kaerda didn't hesitate. She stepped through.

Chapter 21 – Split Soul, Split Field

A ripple of gold tore through the ashen air.

Kaerda emerged first, her boots landing with finality on the scorched ground. Behind her, Bone-Anna stepped from the golden-flame portal with quiet inevitability, Geoff perched regally on her shoulder. The light shimmered briefly, then folded inward, sealing the breach behind them.

No time had passed.

Bryn and Nyv stood exactly where they had been—watchful, grounded, unaware of the forge, the memory-battlefield, or the soul-forged awakenings that had just occurred. Their eyes narrowed at the unfamiliar portal.

Nyv tilted her head. "That wasn't shadow."

Kaerda nodded once. "It wasn't."

They didn't ask more. Not yet.

The five stood together now but Tassa was noticeably absent.

The battlefield, cracked and veined with shadowglass, responded. The ash underfoot swept into slow circles, as if drawn by the gravity of their bond. The wind died, then shifted. For a heartbeat, the world held its breath.

Nyv's jaw was tight. Geoff twitched once on Bone-Anna's shoulder, alert. Kaerda's hammer pulsed faintly with warmth. Bryn's ravens circled low, wings beating with unusual rhythm.

The pressure was building. Mairadas was close.

The ground trembled—not as a quake, but as if something immense had stirred beneath it.

Bryn's voice broke the silence, calm and steady.

"We hold the line."

Even as she spoke, Bryn's eyes narrowed. She was the first to see it—not just the battlefield's damage or the deepening veins of shadowglass, but the way the space itself was splitting.

Ahead of them, the air shimmered in a high, sweeping arc—a semi-transparent veil dividing the scorched field. On one side, ash and broken stone. On the other, shadows deeper than darkness, flecked with drifting gold. It was not a wall, but a boundary—between the physical and the soul, the material and the shadow.

Kaerda took a step closer. "Is that...?"

"Yes," Bryn murmured. Her voice was suddenly distant, focused.

She felt it through the token she wore—an echo of warmth and presence, unmistakable. The bond that linked their coven did not fade with distance or divide. It glowed when one stood alone, so the others would always know.

Tassa stood on the other side.

Just a silhouette at first, framed in flame and distance. But unmistakable. Facing something vast, something unseen from here. Her body shimmered, partially veiled in golden fire.

Bryn's breath caught. She looked at the others.

"She's on the other side," she said quietly. "And if we fall... she will too."

The battlefield had split.

And it was growing.

Not in motion, but in meaning—space folding outward, not like terrain expanding but like reality being rewritten to allow for what was coming. What had to come.

Bryn's gaze drifted upward. The ravens circled—but not all.

One had never returned. The loss had sat heavy in her chest for days, quiet but sharp.

Now, beneath the bending sky and the rippling ash, she felt it—not as grief, but as understanding.

That raven had not been lost. It had gone ahead.

Into memory. Into shadow. Into whatever this battlefield had become.

Its absence had become presence. A thread through time, tied now to this moment.

She closed her eyes. "You showed me the way," she whispered. "Thank you."

As the Accord shifted together—Nyv invoking her place magic, Kaerda slamming her shield into the earth, Bryn whispering her command through shadows—the battlefield held its breath.

And then, just beneath the clamour and clash, a tone emerged.

Faint. Harmonic. The metal of their rings and clasps vibrated with the resonance of something older than flame or fear. A melody born in the forge, remembered now not as music, but as unity.

Bryn felt it in her bones. Kaerda heard it in her shield. And Nyv, with her hand still lightly brushing Bryn's, knew: they were no longer fighting alone.

They were in accord.

And that sound—fragile but unyielding—was the proof.

The ash-field lengthened. The shattered ridges deepened. The sky bent, distorting to make room for something vast.

Bryn's breath misted. Not from cold, but from pressure.

Two dragons would face them soon—one in this world, and one in the next. The battlefield had to be large enough to contain the impossible.

And then—without fanfare, without roar—they arrived.

On this side, the dragon's massive form unfolded from the storm-choked sky. Scales shimmered with hues of dark cobalt and thunderlight, each movement rippling across the cracked ground. Its wings unfurled with glacial grace, eclipsing the fractured skyline.

They would have to win both sides.

● ● ●

Tassa's boots scraped against stone as she steadied herself.

The pull of shadowflame had tossed her here—somewhere beyond time, where the ground rippled like heat haze and the sky never settled on one shape. The moment the Accord had been torn apart, she'd fallen. Not physically. Soulward.

She straightened slowly.

The space was vast, quiet, and alive. Shadows drifted in patterns that responded to thought. Golden flame still lingered on her fingertips—leftover from the portals she had somehow willed open. She didn't know how she'd done it, only that she had needed to, and the Heart had answered. As it always seemed to, she thought in retrospect.

Somewhere behind her, she felt them arrive—Bone-Anna and Geoff first. Then Kaerda. She hadn't seen their battles, but she'd sensed the conclusion. Their survival. Their strength.

She wasn't alone.

But she was the furthest from safety.

The air grew colder—more still.

A presence stirred ahead, ancient and wide. It was not a shape yet. Just pressure.

On the shadow side, its mirror emerged—taller, thinner, carved of darkness and sorrow. Where the material form radiated power, this one exuded inevitability. Its eyes held no malice—only the certainty of dominion.

They were different, but the same. Reflections of one ancient being, split across realms, bearing down upon the Silent Accord.

Tassa exhaled slowly. "Alright," she muttered. "Let's dance, old shadow."

The pressure deepened.

● ● ●

The first storm-aspect rose from the earth like it had always been there.

A twisted fusion of lightning and bone, it cracked through the fractured ground in a column of screeching air. More followed—misshapen echoes of Mairadas, faceless but unmistakable, their forms built from wind-etched scale and shattered stone. They shuddered as they took shape, hollow mouths gnashing.

Bryn raised her hand. "Form up."

The Accord moved without hesitation.

Kaerda stepped forward, anchoring the front line, her old, but new-forged hammer glowing faintly with internal heat. Bone-Anna drifted to the flank, already drawing arrows from shadows. Geoff vaulted from her shoulder with eerie grace, scampering toward the high ground.

Nyv extended her hand toward Kaerda and whispered, "*Vheran kishel.*"

A translucent shield settled across her armour. The moment the barrier flared to life, a bolt of jagged stormlight lanced toward Kaerda's chest—faster than sight. The shield took the brunt of it, shattering outward in sparks and force, but Kaerda stood unmoved. The spell had done its work.

Bryn didn't speak. She raised her hand, and her ravens wheeled high, faster now—tracking something above. Something else.

Kaerda met the first storm-aspect head-on, her hammer breaking its clawed strike with a booming, radiant crack.

Lightning burst from the nearest construct, arcing toward the group.

"*Résh ákîr,*" Nyv intoned, and the shock met an unseen veil. Element Bind surged through the bond, blunting the strike for all of them.

Behind her, the Accord began to press forward.

Kaerda advanced deliberately, hammer spinning once before striking a second time—this time shattering a storm-aspect's arm in a burst of heat and thunder. She did not bellow or call. She simply moved with the force of the forge behind her.

Bone-Anna dropped to one knee, releasing a pair of arrows in fast succession. One shattered a creature's faceplate; the second pinned another's arm to the ground. Geoff scampered up its back and delivered a clawed jab to a weak joint in its neck, eliciting a surge of cracking light.

Nyv watched with the focus of a battlefield strategist. Her hands flared with latent power, but she did not transform and release the lightning she had absorbed—yet. Instead, she moved between Kaerda and Bryn, positioning herself where she could cast wide or ward tight, depending on the next threat.

Bryn still hadn't moved.

Her eyes followed her ravens as they circled higher. The dragon had already taken shape, massive and still—but something in its silence felt unfinished. Her ravens tilted in unison, spiraling tighter. It was about to act. She was waiting for it.

And until then, they held.

The Accord, five strong, advanced together through storm and bone. The field ahead trembled—but did not break.

● ● ●

"I was expecting more fear," Mairadas said. The voice didn't echo—it simply existed, folding around her from every direction. "But then again, you've always hidden well. Behind questions. Behind luck."

Tassa smiled faintly. "You hide behind power. That's the louder mask."

"You don't understand what I offer," he continued, circling her unseen. "A place. A name. The truth of what you are. You don't need them. They're not like you."

Tassa's gaze didn't waver. "No," she said. "They're not."

He paused. "You don't belong with them."

"No," she agreed again. "But they chose me. And I chose them."

"You could be fire incarnate," he said, voice softening. "Unbound. Risen above the broken faiths that chained your ancestors. You could rule what's left when the world forgets them."

"You think I care about ruling?" Tassa's voice was dry. "You really don't get me."

The shadows curled tighter.

"You hide behind luck," he repeated, slower this time. "But you're not lucky anymore."

Tassa's eyes flared gold.

"Who said it was luck?"

Heat rippled off her shoulders as golden light bled through the cracks in her skin. Her silhouette began to glow—brighter, deeper, more defined.

Power surged behind her ribs—nothing remembered, nothing borrowed. It was her own. Not inherited. Not given. Woken.

In the glow of her rising fire, Tassa saw something old—something not from her own life, but from memory passed down. Vhal'turien's memory. She saw Mairadas' betrayal not as myth, but as truth etched in agony. The moment the dragon who now mocked her turned on his kin, not in rage, but in calculation.

And Vhal'turien had trusted him.

That was the wound. That was the spark.

Tassa's breath drew in as if igniting from within. Flame gathered not from fury, but from understanding.

Now she understood.

Her feet shifted. Her shoulders straightened. Light pulsed along her spine in quiet defiance.

She wasn't changing.

She was becoming.

The soul of Mairadas stirred in the distance—but this time, it flinched.

Tassa raised one arm, and with it came a rush of molten light—not conjured, but released. Golden flame coiled around her limbs and spine, spiraling upward as her silhouette took sharper form.

"I remember," she whispered.

Then she struck.

Not with spell or staff, but with the weight of memory and flame. A spear of condensed fire shot from her outstretched hand—clean, focused, and true.

It pierced through shadow, striking Mairadas across the wing and shoulder. His roar echoed—not just in sound, but in feeling. Pain. Recognition.

It was the same strike he had once made against Vhal'turien.

Only now, it was returned.

● ● ●

On the material side, the battlefield changed.

The lesser constructs dematerialized, their forms collapsing into ash and wind, drawn back into the waiting will of something far greater. Mairadas was finished testing them. This was not a retreat of minions—it was the clearing of space. An unveiling. His power was about to strike in full.

Already the cracks across the battlefield were widening. Lightning surged beneath the surface. In the distance, coils of shadowlight twisted upward— summoning a storm-wrought form not yet given breath.

He was shaping something. Not constructs. A weapon. Something he planned to be overwhelming.

A pressure wave shuddered across the field—a shift in the air, the kind that comes before a god makes its move. The Accord felt it immediately: pressure deepening in the marrow, breath harder to draw, as if the world had grown heavier.

It should have come then—the storm-weapon. The final shape.

But something answered first.

The air shifted again, not with force, but with refusal.

From the mirrored planes of shattered pillars, from the warped glass ridges and scorched obsidian pools, shapes began to peel free—like silk tearing loose.

They stepped forward as echoes, then took form.

They were the grateful dead.

The souls the Accord had freed beneath the Pale Lanterns, now risen—not trapped, not lost, but changed. Each one moved with purpose, memory fuelling motion. Where once they wandered in illusion, now they hunted with focus.

One tore from a reflection like a spear, lunging into the twisting storm-shape with claws of glimmering light. Another burst from a puddle of shadow and slammed into a rising tendril of Mairadas's will before it could fully form.

Mairadas had meant to overwhelm.

But the past had not forgotten. And it would not be silent.

The battlefield reeled—not from what was summoned, but from what was remembered.

Kaerda surged forward into the chaos, her hammer crashing down beside a flickering spirit in perfect rhythm. Together, they struck one of the stormstuff tendrils mid-rise—a coil of raw, sparking magic that had begun to solidify into something weaponlike. Her blow didn't land on a creature, but on a forming force—breaking it back into wind and ash. It wasn't a battle line. It was a forge line.

Bone-Anna dropped to a crouch, loosing arrow after arrow into the unstable shapes that still trembled with potential. Her shots pinned down rising arcs of energy before they could harden. Geoff twisted beneath her volleys, clawing through shallow shadow-pools where Mairadas's magic still bled through.

Nyv raised one hand. Her palm still shimmered faintly from the absorbed lightning moments earlier, but she hadn't spent it. Not yet. She held position beside Bryn, watching the battlefield through narrowed eyes, every muscle poised. Her voice was quiet, steady.

"We have the line," she said.

And for a breath—they did.

Then came the second wave.

Not remnants, but reinforcements. A few of Mairadas's summoned shapes had escaped the disruption. From the fractured veins in the ground and the breathless sky above, they coalesced into new forms—larger, more stable, and far more dangerous than the aspects that had come before.

They moved with purpose, not instinct. Intelligent shadows plated in crackling cobalt scale, hulking and coordinated. Mairadas had shifted strategy.

Bryn's eyes didn't narrow. She had already expected this.

Her hand lifted, calm and deliberate.

"*Dúil pórth*," she whispered.

Six portals unfurled in silence, black-rimmed and vertical. They opened beneath the largest of the approaching forms just as they leapt. The moment their claws left the ground, they fell—not down, but away. Pulled sideways through the loop, suspended in the same motion that had made them dangerous.

Unlike before, these portals did not transport. They contained. They swallowed the aspects and banished them into nothingness.

The battlefield held.

Above them, the dragon shifted.

Mairadas's wings tightened, his body coiling with a measure more tension than before. A flicker passed through the veins of light beneath his scales—dimmed, for a breath.

His eyes, gleaming like shards of stormlight, narrowed.

A flicker of frustration. A note of rhythm disrupted.

He had expected fear.

What he found instead was memory. Resistance. Covenant.

Bryn lowered her hand without a word.

● ● ●

Tassa didn't chase the blow. She didn't need to.

Mairadas had recoiled. Not deeply—not with pain—but with something like memory interrupting instinct.

"Still not listening," he murmured, his form reassembling in pieces across the shadow horizon. "You think becoming more makes you strong. You're still tethered. Still hoping they'll win."

Tassa didn't respond at first. Her breathing slowed. Her hands lowered.

And then she smiled.

"I don't need to hope," she said. "They're already winning."

Golden flame spiraled off her form in soft, pulsing waves. It didn't burn. It shed. Shadow recoiled where it touched, not destroyed, but revealed. The soul-realm bent to accommodate her—where once it pulled, now it curved around her.

Mairadas lunged. Not with claws, but with pressure—raw will, pushing down like memory turned weight. Tassa sank half a step, then stood straighter.

Golden filaments laced through her arms. Her back arched slightly as two bright arcs of fire flared behind her—not wings, but the impression of them. Ancestral. Symbolic. A memory waking in her blood.

The shadow realm recognised her. And it bent.

Mairadas went still.

For the first time, he hesitated—not in fear, but in confusion. His eyes narrowed, not with dominance, but calculation disrupted. As if some script he had memorized no longer played the way he expected.

"You've changed," he said.

Tassa took another step forward. Flame trailed her heels like sunlight clinging to memory.

"No," she said. "I've returned."

The words hit like truth made solid.

"You are fire now," he said slowly, as if realising it too late. "Fire without restraint."

"Fire with reason," she corrected.

He snarled. "That makes you worse."

Tassa let the silence hold for a heartbeat. Then:

"Good."

"You wanted me to forget who I was," she said.

"I wanted you to survive," Mairadas snarled.

Tassa stepped forward once.

"I did."

She didn't charge. She didn't roar.

She burned.

And the world would come to her.

● ● ●

On the material side, the battlefield settled.

There were no more aspects. Mairadas had seen their failure. He would not waste more imitations.

What descended now was no echo.

The great dragon dropped from the sky, his wings folding inward like a closing trap. Where he landed, the ground split—not shattered, but parted with deference. Stone and ash peeled away from his presence.

The Accord stood ready. They did not retreat. They did not speak.

Kaerda raised her hammer.

Nyv's fingers crackled softly, the held charge beginning to rise.

Bone-Anna lifted another arrow, already nocked. Geoff flicked his tail, hunched and motionless beside her.

And Bryn stared at the dragon—not as an enemy, but as a certainty.

The time for tests had passed.

The final confrontation had begun.

Mairadas struck first—not with claw or breath, but with force. His wings beat once, a towering buffet of air meant to crush their stance and throw them back across the field.

It failed.

Nyv stepped forward, her white ponytail whipping like flame. Her fingers etched a tight sigil at her feet—drawing power from the place where they stood, magic ancient and Ravkari. The ground answered, anchoring not just herself, but all of them.

"*Válra thárán*," she whispered. The magic spread in threads of wind and earth, binding the Accord in communal grounding.

The wind passed. They did not move.

Mairadas roared—deep and primal, a sound of fury sharpened by disbelief. His wings flared wider, but the force of the scream could not reclaim the ground he had just lost.

Kaerda moved first.

Bone-Anna and Geoff broke left, their movements instinctive, unified—drawing Mairadas's eye with stinging precision and scattered distraction. Geoff darted in and out of flame-scorched rubble while Bone-Anna's arrows kept pace with his motion, each strike aligned with his leaps.

And then Kaerda was there.

She didn't speak. She didn't wait.

Her hammer, still echoing the memory of the forge, swung low and upward in a single, burning arc. The blow struck Mairadas beneath the jaw, not to shatter—but to demand notice.

● ● ●

Two realms. Two dragons. Two fights.

In the material realm, the Accord braced as Mairadas reeled from Kaerda's strike. The dragon's gaze swept over them now—not testing, but knowing. Bryn looked up as the clouds peeled apart, and in that brief split in the sky, she saw it.

Golden light. The shape of wings. A shimmer that didn't belong in this world—but she felt it in her bones.

In the Shadow Realm, Tassa roared.

It wasn't rage. It was declaration. Fire surged in a ring around her feet, and her silhouette burned brighter, the flame behind her now too vast to contain. Her enemy no longer looked down at her.

On the field below, Bryn and Nyv turned to each other. One nodded. The other breathed in.

Kaerda, Bone-Anna, and Geoff didn't need a signal. They had already moved. In this realm, the enemy had learned he could no longer look down on their combined power either.

The final stand had begun.

Chapter 22 – The Final Blow

The dragon did not hesitate.

Mairadas descended like a hammer of the storm—wings tight, jaws gleaming, eyes locked on the five who stood beneath him. There were no illusions now, no whispers or tests. Only strength. Only power.

Kaerda stepped forward first, her hammer already rising. The light of the forge still clung to her, heat trailing from her shoulders as if the memory of the smith's fire followed her into battle.

"For the Accord," she said—quiet, but unshaken.

The blow landed hard against Mairadas's foreleg. Not enough to wound, but enough to make him shift—acknowledging the impact.

Bone-Anna and Geoff were already moving wide. Arrows sang, sharp and rapid, finding soft seams beneath Mairadas's plating. Geoff darted through the rubble, his body a blur of motion.

Beside them, Bryn stood calm, one hand raised, her ravens circling tightly in formation. She whispered a word of power under her breath—*sîlú válën*—and lifted into the air. Shadows twisted beneath her boots as she rose, her coat billowing in the wind. Her gaze met Mairadas's, unwavering, as she ascended to stare him in the eye. Nyv broke away from the centre, moving to higher ground along the flank where she could keep the others in her field of vision. Her hands were free, fingers twitching as energy gathered between them.

Mairadas's tail whipped in fury, low and wide. Geoff, too close, was caught by the edge. His small body was hurled sideways, bouncing twice before landing still.

"Geoff!" Nyv called, her voice cutting through the roar.

But the lizard stirred, slowly—stunned, but not broken.

The dragon turned his gaze toward the rest of them.

Nyv moved lightning fast to the great wrym.

"Nyv!" Bryn called after her—sharp, protective. But she didn't try to stop her.

As she moved, Nyv pulled Shimmerstrike from its scabbard with one hand and summoned her Moonblade into the other. The air wavered around her as she

----

darted low across the battlefield, boots barely touching stone. She moved not as a soldier, but as a dancer—each step a line drawn in fury.

Geoff's pain echoed in her blood. And Mairadas would feel the cost.

She slashed beneath the dragon's foreleg, aiming not for a killing blow, but to maim—to hamstring the beast's terrible mobility. Sparks flew from the point of contact, shadowlight tearing where her blades met scale.

Mairadas recoiled slightly—not wounded, but marked.

And the battle began in earnest.

● ● ●

Tassa stood alone.

The shadows swirled around her like ink in water—dark, fluid, endless. Mairadas's soul loomed before her, vast and formless, more shape than body, more weight than substance. His eyes gleamed like distant lightning, and each movement sent a pressure wave through the stillness.

She held her ground.

Golden light pulsed at her feet, slow and deliberate. The wings behind her shimmered—still not full, still not flesh, but brighter with each breath.

"You cling to fire," the soul-dragon said, voice like thunder through sand.

"I carry it," Tassa answered. "There's a difference."

Mairadas lunged—not a motion of body, but of will. A line of thought like a spear. Tassa staggered back, pain flashing across her mind, not from fear, but from the magnitude of memory he hurled at her.

Vhal'turien falling.

The betrayal.

The cost.

And then another came.

Not a memory, but a reflection—Mairadas's soul bearing down with the weight of Tassa's *own* uncertainty. Every question she'd ever asked herself: Was she strong enough? Was she chosen, or merely lucky? The fire trembled at her back.

She nearly dropped to her knees.

But she held.

Breath drawn. Shoulders squared. Not defiant, not yet—just *unwilling* to fall.

"You're not the only one who remembers," she whispered.

And the golden fire did not fade.

● ● ●

The battle shifted.

Mairadas pivoted sharply, tail gouging a trench in the stone as he turned to meet Kaerda's advance. The dwarf's movements were slower now, deliberate—she had taken a wide arc, trying to draw his focus, and succeeded. A blast of heat met her halfway—scorching across her shield side. The metal flared red; Kaerda grunted but kept moving, shoulder lowered into the force.

Nyv rolled back from the edge of it, blades flashing. She wasn't done with them yet. Instead, she darted inward again, sliding beneath Mairadas's arc and driving her Moonblade up and across the thin membrane of his outstretched wing.

The cut didn't cripple—but it bled. Just enough.

The dragon staggered back with a shriek of frustration, wings drawing inward. Another arrow struck his ribs—fired from a position no one expected Bone-Anna could still reach.

Only then did Nyv fall back. Her Moonblade dissolved into starlight mid-motion, returning to the ether. Shimmerstrike she sheathed at her belt without a word. She turned, refocusing her stance—magic already beginning to gather at her fingertips once more. Her eyes found Bone-Anna on the ridgeline just as the next breath came.

The dragon exhaled—not fire, but concussive force, a wave of pressure and sound.

Bone-Anna didn't have time to move.

The blast struck her left side. Her femur cracked with an audible snap—more than a fracture. For a skeleton with no tendons and muscle to hold her leg together, it was as if her entire leg had been severed. She crumpled sideways, bones scattering and scraping against stone.

For a breath, she didn't move.

Then she looked down—not in shock, but with something like grim calculation. Her skull tilted, jaw twitching. A moment later, her arm swept sideways, reaching for her fallen bow.

She dragged it close with her good arm, propping herself up on one elbow, spine angling to compensate. Her eye sockets narrowed with eerie precision.

She wasn't giving up. She was adapting.

Above, Bryn's hand clenched slightly.

She didn't cry out. Didn't falter. But the quiet beneath her gaze deepened, her resolve settling like iron into ice.

Mairadas would not take another from her.

Geoff rushed to her side—still sluggish, but moving.

Kaerda roared and surged forward, hammer raised once more. Mairadas shifted just enough to avoid the full blow, but it clipped his shoulder—sparks flying. The beast's wing snapped wide in irritation.

From above, Bryn raised her hand.

"Nyv," she said.

"I see it," Nyv answered.

A rush of heat shimmered in the air around her hands—a raw build of elemental force coalescing as Nyv prepared her next strike. She didn't call on lightning. Not this time. She knew better than to feed a storm its own breath.

Above, Bryn's eyes narrowed in focus. Her hand began to draw a shape in the air, tracing slow, curved sigils as tendrils of darkness converged on her fingertips. A line of shadow leapt from her palm, lashing into Mairadas's shoulder—not to wound, but to *drain*.

Enervation.

The siphoned force flowed into her like ink spilled into water, and she turned her free hand toward Kaerda. A thread of that darkness pulled free again—now laced with heat and light—as Bryn redirected the dragon's stolen strength into the dwarven cleric.

Mairadas weakened. Kaerda straightened. The line held.

● ● ●

Tassa's steps slowed.

The fire no longer trembled at her back—it surged, pulsing with rhythmic force like a second heartbeat. She didn't understand it at first.

It had waited, ever since the vault—the coin the horde guardian gave her in silence. A gift for mercy.

The coin.

She reached for it—not with her hand, but with her will. The memory of the Horde Golem. The choice not to destroy it. The quiet reward it had given her.

It didn't burn. It *recognised*. And then it dissolved—folding inward, becoming part of the flame.

Tassa inhaled.

The wings behind her surged, no longer suggestion or shadow. They were flame. And they were hers.

Across the Shadow Realm, Mairadas faltered.

And for the first time, he took a step back.

● ● ●

Kaerda moved like a hammer reborn.

Strength flowed through her limbs—not just divine, not just borrowed. It was Bryn's precision, Nyv's fury, Bone-Anna's defiance. And now, it was Tassa's fire pressing forward in a realm apart.

She struck again, and Mairadas turned his full attention to her.

He rose onto his hind legs, wings fanning wide—and lashed down.

Kaerda saw it coming, but there was no time to dodge.

Mairadas brought both claws down in a raking strike, and Kaerda threw everything she had into her shield—divine magic flooding the sigils etched into its face, her voice rising in a half-heard prayer to Durnach the Forgemaker even as she braced. The blow connected like a falling mountain.

Her shield groaned, the runes flaring white-hot. The force drove her backward, boots plowing two deep lines in the stone. She didn't fall—but she bent, her shoulder buckling with the impact.

She gritted her teeth. Held the line.

And somehow—*survived.*

She grunted, staggered—but stayed standing.

The dragon's gaze narrowed, a smile coiling through him like heat through stone.

And that was when the Accord struck back.

Bryn glanced toward Nyv—only briefly—and Nyv gave the smallest of nods.

Their hands moved at the same time, as if rehearsed. As if this moment had already been decided.

Bryn's voice was quiet—almost too quiet to hear—but it carried.

"Now."

Nyv raised both hands, and Bryn reached inward.

There was no physical item drawn. No flourish. Just a soft pull of memory—a resonance in the four matching pieces of gear forged weeks earlier, deep in the memory-scarred forge. A shard of a soul vessel had gone into each piece, its origin long unspoken.

Bryn pulled it forward now.

A memory not her own—Mairadas's memory, woven into metal and worn by the ones who defied him.

Nyv felt it too. She anchored the space beneath them with Ravkari place-magic, tying the moment to reality.

356

And from the memory, a vision unfurled. The same scene Tassa witnessed in the painting days earlier.

A golden dragon—majestic, proud, turning in the sky.

A voice: "There is no room for weakness."

A bolt of lightning lanced forward, striking the gold from behind.

Mairadas's breath caught.

The smile faded.

He reared back—not from pain, but from the *clarity* of the memory. For a moment, the battlefield flickered.

He was no longer in control.

● ● ●

Tassa burned.

The wings were full now—fire and memory made form, curling outward with radiant purpose. Not shaped like those of a mortal or a dragon, but something older—something elemental. The air around her shimmered gold, ash lifting in spirals from the ground. With every step forward, the shadows parted as though ashamed.

Above and around her, the sky of the Shadow Realm split—not from violence, but from awe. Golden flame bled upward into the emptiness, and for a breathless moment, it was light without source. Memory without end.

And then came the roar.

Not from her mouth, but from her soul—a sound that carried the sorrow of betrayal, the fury of purpose, the truth of lineage. It echoed across the planes. And it was heard.

Mairadas recovered from the memory-strike across realms and surged toward her, fury rekindled.

He struck again—this time with focused soul-force, a blast sharp as guilt.

The gold ward activated.

A radiant shield formed midair, golden and complete, catching the blow and dispersing it into arcs of harmless light. The coin's last gift—the memory of mercy, held until the final moment.

Tassa stepped through the fading sparks.

She didn't speak.

She didn't need to.

The shadows around her pulsed, pressing against her flame. Doubt crept in.

And then—she remembered.

The javelin. The one Chovee once carried. How it had glowed when she approached.

How it had recoiled, not from her, but from what she carried.

She had laughed it off at the time. Called it silly.

But now…

Now she understood.

Chovee hadn't feared her. He had *seen* her.

Even in his troubled state between life and living, he had tried to warn her. Prepare her.

She gritted her teeth, flame rising in her chest. Not out of rage—but gratitude.

She was fire.

And her final strike was absolute.

From her chest, where the memory of the Heart had been kindled since the day they entered that chamber deep within the Velthorn Peaks, a golden flare ignited. Not summoned—but released.

It erupted like a sunrise forced through a needle's eye. A beam of radiant flame, forged from memory, grief, defiance, and lineage, surged across the battlefield of the soul. It struck Mairadas full in the chest.

The scream that followed was not pain. It was disbelief.

His form resisted for a moment. Then the golden fire bored through him, lasting longer than it needed to—burning not just flesh or soul, but *meaning*. What remained was not ash. It was **less** than ash.

A void where certainty had once been.

And then even that was gone.

Above the realms, Bryn's head turned—just slightly.

At the edge of her senses, she felt it more than saw it: a pulse of golden light, like a breath held and exhaled. In that moment, she knew.

Tassa was gone.

Not fallen. Not taken. Just… gone.

And the flame had chosen its own end.

Far beneath the Velthorn Peaks, the chamber where the Heart once waited now echoed with nothing at all.

● ● ●

Something changed.

The dragon's form on the material plane faltered. Not visibly at first—not in body—but in weight. In presence. The rage, the anchored power, the soul behind the fury… vanished.

Kaerda felt it in her bones. Nyv tasted it in the air. Bryn saw it in the slow ripple of the ravens above.

Mairadas was no longer whole.

Geoff moved first.

He darted toward a pile of broken stone, leapt onto a half-collapsed pillar, and let out a shrill, spiraling chirrup—a sound like wind winding through a canyon, rising in pitch until it became a note of focus.

The Accord turned to him.

He raised one tiny hand.

And the final strike began.

Nyv, guided by that note, launched flame—not in panic, but with surgical fury, driving heat into the cracks she and Kaerda had already opened.

Bryn cast a single large Shadowdrop, opening a shadow loop beneath Mairadas's hind leg. His foot dropped half a pace and found no stone. Balance broke.

Kaerda surged forward with everything left in her—the hammer lifted not for Durnach the Forgemaker, not for glory, but for Tassa.

And Bone-Anna, half-sprawled and missing a leg, loosed one last arrow with perfect timing. Earlier volleys had thinned as her injury worsened, but here, guided by Geoff's rhythm, she found one last shot. It sang through the air with eerie grace.

Geoff's chirrup crescendoed.

The arrow struck as the hammer fell. Bryn's shadow whipped upward to catch the light of Nyv's spell.

And Mairadas collapsed.

Not slowly. Not with grace.

Like a storm losing its shape.

Like a god forgetting its name.

● ● ●

The battlefield held its breath.

Mairadas lay dead, the gargantuan corpse of the dragon stretched across fractured stone and still-burning earth. The crackle of residual magic faded slowly. Nothing moved for a moment but smoke.

Kaerda lowered her hammer and staggered to Bone-Anna's side. "We need to splint this," she said, already reaching for strips of her own torn cloak. Her tone was clinical, but her eyes never left the jagged break in Bone-Anna's femur.

"I can repair it properly," she added, quieter. "I think I can forge something that fits."

Bryn descended in slow arcs, her flight spell dissipating as she touched down with the rest of them. Her gaze passed over the dragon's ruined body before resting on the others.

Geoff hopped down beside Bone-Anna and gave a satisfied chirp—less a cry of victory, more like a maestro's final tap of the baton.

It was done.

The Accord didn't speak right away. They stood among ash and silence, their chests rising and falling in the heavy stillness. No more attacks came. No more magic burned.

The adrenaline drained from them like the last breath of a long-held spell. Kaerda slowly sank to one knee. Bryn lowered her head. Nyv closed her eyes.

Even Bone-Anna, still half-prone, let her arm rest for the first time.

They had survived. Together.

Bryn's eyes flicked to the javelin.

The shadow that had clung to it like a stain—ever since Chovee's fall—began to dissipate.

"Look," she said, voice barely above a whisper.

They followed her gaze. The dark aura receded like breath into still air.

Nyv stepped closer, eyes fixed. "Does that mean... it's over for him too?"

The world around them dimmed. Just briefly.

● ● ●

Back in Ravkareth, snow is falling gently across old stone.

Chovee, whole and peaceful, sits cross-legged in meditation with a warm fire beside him. No shadow on his brow.

In the next room, Yeldanna. Her eyes widened as if struck by something distant and tender. She gasped—then smiled.

● ● ●

The Accord couldn't see it. They could only hope.

Bryn lowered her gaze. Nyv touched the javelin's haft, as if expecting it to speak.

But it was silent.

Epilogue – The Bond Unbroken

The dragon's corpse had barely cooled.

They stood at the edge of the battlefield, staring across scorched earth and silence. Mairadas was gone. The Accord remained—changed, tired, alive.

And stranded.

The spire had collapsed. It was unlikely they would return the way they came— there were no plants and druids. There was no path. No road. And Bone-Anna couldn't walk.

Kaerda crouched beside her, frowning at the jagged break. The bones were charred and fractured beyond a simple splint.

"We'll fix it," she said. "We need to get to the forge."

The spire's interior was fractured, but the stairs still held. Slowly—carefully— they descended through warped stone and lingering shadows, guiding Bone- Anna with makeshift support while Kaerda sketched repairs in her mind. The further they travelled, the more the echoes of battle faded, replaced by the familiar pull of memory-laced metal and reforged fire.

At the base, where the forge had once been reborn through their hands, they found it waiting—silent, intact, and ready.

Bits of shattered golems and broken husk-shells still littered the area. Kaerda began to gather pieces: core-threaded metal, slivers of imbued ore, and fragments of the same failed vessel that had almost contained a soul.

She worked quickly, precisely—every strike of her tools ringing with purpose. Bryn joined her, pulling from her own pouch the tools she'd once used to refine the rings, the pendant, and the clasp. She didn't speak—just polished, etched, and shaped alongside Kaerda.

Together, they forged Bone-Anna a new femur—metal and memory, bound by flame, shadow, and something older.

Kaerda affixed it and stepped back, Bryn re-invoked the same summoning magic she'd used to call the skeleton the first time, allowing the new prosthetic bone to become one with the rest of her frame. Bone-Anna stood.

The joint turned. Held. Accepted.

Bone-Anna stood still for a long moment. Her head tilted—not in confusion, but in thought. One hand flexed—she tapped her new metallic body part with her bony fingers producing a dull clunk. She nodded. Then her skull turned slowly, facing the far end of the ruin.

Kaerda followed her gaze. "What is it?"

Bryn stepped forward, sensing something beneath the surface—not magic, but memory. The same material that had failed to hold a soul... was now part of Bone-Anna. It remembered something.

The air ahead shimmered—not with heat, but with echo.

And the way home revealed itself.

Not all the way. But far enough.

The memory-thread carried them through the desert's edge—along forgotten paths once shaped by shadow and silence. Each step was guided by Bone-Anna's gaze and Bryn's attunement to the echoes around them.

At the boundary where the shadow-rich land gave way to hard earth and open sky, the memory faded.

They stood at the edge of the known, facing long miles ahead.

And began the walk home.

It took a few weeks to reach Estavar. The group stayed close to one another during the journey, leaning on each other through the exhaustion—Nyv and Bryn keeping particularly close.

They passed through smaller villages along the way—settlements that barely registered on maps, but where news travelled faster than the wind. People in those towns began to recognise the Accord by sight. Some stepped forward with hesitation. Others with reverence. A meal was offered. A barn cleaned. A room prepared without charge.

They accepted it all with quiet gratitude.

Word of the man with no mouth's fall had spread in the previous weeks and months. The world had shifted while they were away—less visibly, but unmistakably. People didn't know the details, but they recognised the ones who had helped bring him down. And they remembered.

When the towers of Estavar finally crested the horizon, the Accord said nothing.

They just kept walking.

They reached their home before nightfall on the seventeenth day.

It stood exactly as they had left it, tucked against the western wall of Estavar's quiet quarter. The herbs in Kaerda's windowsill had wilted. The forge had gone cold. The air held the smell of dust, not smoke.

It felt emptier without Tassa.

No one said it. No one needed to.

They stepped inside one by one, shedding packs, cloaks, and exhaustion. Bone-Anna took her seat near the hearth without instruction. Geoff climbed to his perch and coiled tightly, eyes half-lidded.

Bryn lit a lantern.

Nyv opened a window.

She glanced over her shoulder as the breeze moved past her. Bryn was already there, standing beside her, the lantern's glow soft against the sharp lines of her profile.

They didn't speak—not at first. But Bryn stepped a little closer, brushing Nyv's shoulder with her own. Nyv leaned into her.

"You still watching for signs?" Bryn asked, her voice low.

Nyv smirked. "Only the good ones."

Bryn smiled faintly. "Guess I count, then."

Nyv didn't answer. She just leaned, just enough, and let her shoulder rest against Bryn's.

Bryn turned slightly, kissing Nyv's cheek softly. Together, they watched the sky.

The feather mark on Bryn's skin softly shimmered, catching the last light of dusk. No words. No voice. Just a quiet, final affirmation: the Queen of Stillness had seen—and approved.

Kaerda leaned against the doorway, arms crossed, watching them all.

Together again.

Almost.

Kaerda cleared a space on the workbench, brushing aside metal filings and a half-finished hinge. She didn't look up, but they all knew: it was for Tassa.

Bryn concentrated on the ring she wore on her left hand—the Accord token forged from memory, purpose, and loss—worn as a bond and as a promise. It pulsed—once, faintly—and then stilled. A warmth, not heat. A heartbeat, not magic.

She closed her eyes. It wasn't a message. It was a pull—familiar and far. Not toward shadow. Not toward death. Toward flame. And she understood.

Tassa was alive.

Somehow, through flame and memory, she had survived. And the Accord's path—Bryn's path—now led toward Pyraestha, the Firelands.

Nyv, at the window, watched the horizon as the last light faded. Somewhere out there, flame still moved.

Geoff chirped once and looked to the east—not toward danger, but expectation.

The room fell quiet again. Not heavy. Not hollow. Just waiting.

"We're not done," Bryn said softly.

Kaerda tilted her head slightly, then nodded. "You know where Tassa is?"

Bryn nodded. "Pyraestha. That's where our tokens are pointing."

There was no argument. The others felt it too—Nyv in her ring, and Kaerda in her pendant.

Nyv stepped away from the window. "Then that's where we go."

Kaerda gave a sharp nod, already moving to clear her tools.

Bone-Anna, seated by the hearth, raised one skeletal hand—just a few inches, just enough.

Geoff chirped and leapt onto the table, spinning once.

Bryn turned toward them, but her eyes found Nyv. She reached out, fingers brushing Nyv's, and held on—lightly, but with intent. Nyv met the gesture without hesitation, her fingers curling around Bryn's in return. Whatever came next—they'd walk toward it together. "We will." Bryn replied. "But first... there's somewhere we need to stop."

The Compass of Her Heart

A Companion Tale to *The Silent Accord* told in the voice
of Bryn Lovas

They say memory clings to places. I used to think it clung to people, too—to their breath, their blood, the way their fingers linger on the edge of a book or the warmth they leave behind in a seat long after they've stood. But now, I've begun to wonder if memory is a kind of shadow, following not just people but choices.

This is a story about one of those choices.

The one I made to bring them home.

After the fire. After the storm. After Tassa was taken by her own flame and vanished into golden ash, we returned to Estavar. Nyv, Kaerda, Bone-Anna, Geoff, and I. Five of us remained, our number smaller but our bond no less complete. It wasn't closure. It was pause.

And in that pause, I knew it was time.

"You should meet her," I told Nyv one evening, as we sat together beneath the last lavender sky of spring. "My mother."

Nyv hesitated. Her fingers fidgeted with the strap of her satchel, eyes drifting to the horizon. "What if she doesn't approve? Of me? Of... us?"

I reached out, gently covering her hand with mine. "She will know how I feel about you."

She smiled back, the corner of her mouth quirking slightly. "And how exactly do you feel about me, Bryn?" she asked, voice soft but unmistakably teasing.

I felt heat rise to my cheeks, but I didn't look away. "I think you already know," I murmured.

Then, before she had time to react, I leaned over and kissed her cheek—light, deliberate, a whisper of truth made touch. Her smile deepened, but she said nothing. She didn't need to.

She didn't press further. She just kept smiling as we watched the evening sky. Hand in hand.

And so we went. All of us. And though I tried to carry myself with composure, I could feel the flutter of something restless beneath my ribs. I was going home—not just to the forest, but to her. To Nera. To my other home. After everything I had done in the Queen's name, after all the silence I had honoured and all the shadows I had shaped, I would stand once more before the one who taught me how to listen.

But more than that, I was bringing her Nyv. Not as a companion. Not as a fellow traveller. As something more. I was proud, nervous, even giddy. I wanted her to see Nyv the way I did. Not just the strength in her stillness, but the warmth hidden beneath it.

Kaerda packed her shield without a word. Geoff scurried between our boots, unbothered by the decision. Bone-Anna fell into silent step beside us before anyone even thought to ask. We walked east, then north. At some point during that first day, Nyv reached for my hand. I didn't hesitate. Our fingers laced together easily, and we walked like that for a while—quiet, steady, as though the rhythm of our steps had always belonged to one another.

Through quiet woods where the leaves turned silver in the moonlight and rivers whispered in a tongue older than birdsong. Morwen scouted ahead. The other ravens followed behind.

Nyv didn't speak often, but when she did, her words felt like the slow turning of earth: thoughtful, grounding. I think she was nervous. I don't know if it was about meeting my mother or about what we were becoming.

I watched her when she didn't know. The way her hand brushed against mine when we shared our rations. The way her gaze lingered on the places where shadow and sunlight met. There had been a moment, back in Tharniseth, when her voice cracked as she whispered she couldn't lose me. That moment hasn't left me. It walks beside me like another raven.

It took us three days to reach the grove.

The Lethvain Reach has no roads. Only memories. And if you know them well enough, they let you through.

And as we walked, something stirred in me—a feeling I hadn't known I'd missed until it returned. The smell of moss-damp stone and birch sap, the hush between bird calls, the way the earth gave just slightly beneath each step. I was home. Not just in place, but in memory.

I grew up in these woods. Long before I was chosen. Long before the Queen whispered through stillness and gave me Her mark. This forest raised me. Taught me silence before it became sacred.

There was a glade just west of where we walked—a place where the roots knot together in a way that makes a natural cradle. I remembered laying there when I was a girl, watching the clouds twist into shapes and pretending each one was a story. My father had brought me berries once, wild and sweet, and told me they were guarded by a squirrel who only shared them with children brave enough to sing their own name aloud. I did. Loudly. I remember his laugh. I remember the taste.

I had forgotten that memory until the trees reminded me.

My mother was waiting. She knew we were coming. She always knows.

As we neared the grove, Nyv glanced sideways at me. "What's she like?" she asked softly.

I smiled. "She doesn't look like me, not really. Taller, broader. Her eyes are the colour of dusk over frozen rivers. She's powerfully built—not muscular, but strong in the way deep roots are strong. She used to fight with her bare hands. Shadow monk training. Every motion she makes is careful, exact, like she already knows how the fight will end."

Nyv tilted her head, listening.

"She also carried a whip," I added. "Not for flair—she just liked the reach. Used it with the same control as her fists. Precise. Quiet."

Nyv smiled faintly. "Do you?"

I shrugged. "Not well. But you've seen the one I keep one in my pack. You've never asked about it. It's not to use. Just... for her. A tribute. A reminder."

Before I knew it, we were approaching the path that led to my childhood home. I'm sure Nyv could sense my excitement through the squeeze she gave my hand.

She met us at the edge of the path with a serene smile, and after a moment's pause, gestured for us to follow her around the side of the house.

"Come," she said. "Let's sit by the trees. We can speak properly there."

Before following, I tugged gently on Nyv's hand. "Give me a moment. I want to show you something."

I led her through the house in a quiet sweep—a simple tour, but rich in memory. I pointed to the low wooden bench near the hearth. "I used to sit there with my father and sort dried leaves for teas. He always swore he could taste the difference, even when I mixed them up."

I touched the doorframe with my fingers as we passed. "I scraped my shoulder there once, racing Kaerda's older brother. I was faster—but I didn't turn fast enough."

Nyv smiled softly as I led her through the back door, toward the trees.

Then, my mother greeted each of us in turn. Nyv first, placing two fingers against her heart. "You listen," she said. "That is rare."

When my mother smiles, it's as though the world holds still to listen. Her shadow is longer than her body, and sometimes it moves when she doesn't. She was smiling now.

Kaerda bowed with quiet respect, and my mother matched it with the reverence of one craftswoman recognising another. "Your forge burns steady," she said.

To Bone-Anna, my mother simply inclined her head. "Some spirits choose stillness. You have chosen purpose. And more than that, you have chosen *awareness*. That is no accident—and no small thing." Bone-Anna responded with the faintest motion: a slow, deliberate nod of her skull, as if acknowledging that she understood—and accepted—the weight of being seen.

And when Geoff peeked out from Nyv's collar, blinking slowly, my mother chuckled. She extended a finger slowly, letting Geoff sniff and crawl into her palm with surprising ease. "A quiet watcher. I see you, too." She scratched gently under his chin and added with a warm smile, "You have the look of someone who remembers more than he lets on." Geoff let out a low chirp of approval and curled contentedly into her palm for a few heartbeats before returning to Nyv's shoulder. It was, somehow, the most natural part of the evening.

Then Morwen landed on a branch just above us, silent and watchful. My mother looked up at him and gave a nod, solemn and knowing. "You've guided her well," she said. "Shadow's oldest feather. I remember your wings when I was her age." Morwen gave the faintest tilt of his head in return, then settled more deeply into the bough. It felt like a benediction.

Later, after stew and silence, we sat beneath the blackroot arch where I first heard the Queen.

My mom lit a lantern of featherglass. The glow didn't reach far, but it was enough.

"You carry her mark," my mom said to me, but her eyes were on Nyv. "And yet, your path is bound now to one who is not shadow-touched."

"No," I said. "But she listens. And she remembers. She makes me feel whole, like I belong."

My mom's eyes softened—not just with approval, but with something deeper. Recognition. The quiet joy of seeing a truth spoken plainly. She didn't speak at first. She simply reached out and rested her hand over mine, her warmth steady and wordless. As if to say, "*I know. I see it too.*"

Nyv looked at me then, and I could see the memory flickering behind her gaze: Estavar, the javelin, the first time our hands touched and lingered. Her presence was the first place I had ever felt I belonged without question. I didn't tell her that night, but I think I had already chosen her. The Queen hadn't said it aloud, but the silence She gave me when I asked was answer enough.

"And Kaerda?" my mom asked.

"Our anchor," I said. "Her hammer holds more than metal. She holds us."

My mom smiled then, proud and quiet. "Three remain. And three is a coven, if the bond is true."

It was then she asked me about the journey. I couldn't stop the words. I told her everything. How the Queen of Stillness had spoken to me—not once, but several times. How Her voice came not with thunder or fire, but in stillness, in silence, in moments when shadow remembered the truth. I told my mom how those moments had kept me steady, how they reminded me who I was, and who I wanted to be. I saw her eyes flicker at that—approval, not pride. Recognition.

Then I told my mom of the battle in the ruins near Velkhar, where the undead rose from beneath broken stone and forced us to face death before we understood what was rising. Of Tassa's fire and Kaerda's forge. Of Nyv's strength, hidden in discipline. Of the Vaulmar Binder. Of Vaelric. Of the dragon who had betrayed gold. Of Tharniseth and the broken mirror of memory. Of how Tassa fought alone and how we could not follow. Yet.

When I finished, my mom stood. Walked to the stone basin beneath the blackroot. Ran her fingers through its water.

"Pyraestha is not a place of chaos," she said. "It is a place of will. Flame exists to consume, but also to transform. If you go there seeking to retrieve something, be prepared for it to return changed. Or not at all."

Nyv stepped forward. "Then what should we bring?"

My mom turned. "Not what. Who. Your bond, if it is as deep as I believe, will hold more power there than any spell. Flame fears only one thing: memory strong enough not to burn."

My mom unwrapped a bundle from her cloak—a compass, bone and scorched gold.

"It only points when memory burns," she said. "And yours is already smouldering."

She pressed it into my hand. I felt the warmth immediately.

"It won't show you the way to Tassa," she continued. "But it will show you where your memory matters most. Where she last was, or where she will next be."

We slept beneath the trees that night. I did not dream. But when I woke, Nyv was sitting beside me, her hand resting near mine but not quite touching.

She didn't speak at first. Just looked at me, the weight of something unspoken pressing gently into the hush between us. Then she leaned forward.

Her lips met mine.

It wasn't tentative. It wasn't uncertain. It was quiet, full of knowing. A promise she hadn't needed to voice until now. Her kiss held memory—of shared battle, of wounds tended, of nights watched in silence. It held the truth of who we had become, and what we had never dared say aloud until this moment.

I froze for just a heartbeat. Then my breath caught—not from surprise, but from the feeling that I had been waiting for this all along. My heart didn't race. It settled. Like I'd finally stepped into the shape of something that had always been waiting to fit.

When she pulled back, her eyes searched mine—not for permission, but for understanding. And I gave it freely.

"Thank you," she said.

I didn't ask for what. Some things don't need to be spoken.

But I think I knew.

In the morning, the compass pointed east.

Toward Pyraestha.

Toward her.

And we followed.

Author's Note

This story didn't begin with a map. It began with a moment I missed—and flowered into a question that followed: What would someone give to come back?

Part I of The Silent Accord was written in response to a moment I missed—literally. I wasn't able to attend our regular Friday night Dungeons & Dragons game, a long-running campaign that featured the same group of friends playing in two parallel storylines. That particular night was a fill-in session while our Dungeon Master (a fantastic one) prepared the next chapter of the main storyline. The secondary campaign—our long-standing fallback—was the one we turned to whenever the main story needed a pause. This night's game was at the beautiful stage where the characters had history, the stakes were growing, and our DM was walking that careful line between challenge and fairness—making us feel epic, but never invincible.

That night, while I was away, one of the characters died. A close friend's character, actually—one whose story was tied to my character's in that game. He'd charged in, sword swinging, as he often did, and the dice didn't fall in his favour. There was no resurrection scroll waiting in a dusty pouch. No desperate journey to town to find a high priest. No long night around a fire debating what came next. Instead, the group stripped his body of anything useful and walked away.

When I read the game recap the next day, I was... conflicted. Part of me was shocked. Part of me wasn't. His characters are always bold, often to a fault—and it wasn't out of character for him to fall like that. Usually, his luck would keep his character from dying, but not that night. He rolled up someone new and just as foolhardy the next day and moved on. So did we. Mostly.

But I couldn't shake how it happened. Not the death itself, but how it ended. My character's story was tied to his. There was no resolution, no grief, no goodbye. So I wrote one—using new characters, a different setting, and a story that could hold the weight of what was left unsaid. Part I became my way of processing what had happened—not just for the character, but for the bond between them. A kind of narrative closure where the game had none.

Parts II and III came much later, and for different reasons. Writing became a way to slow down and exhale—to unwind from a job that often deals in crisis and noise. The Silent Accord became something quiet I could carry forward. A story about grief, and choice, and memory. A story where silence speaks louder than steel, and where strength doesn't always shout.

If you made it this far—thank you. For walking with these characters. For listening to what isn't always said. And for remembering what someone gave to come back.

— Robert

Acknowledgements

This book wouldn't exist without a missed game night—and the remarkable group of people I've shared a gaming table with for years. Thank you to Bryan, our Dungeon Master, for crafting worlds where choices matter and stories grow. Thank you to my childhood friend Gary, whose fallen character sparked the question that started all of this. And to everyone else at the table: Ryan, Don, Kevin, Anthony, Rand, and David—thank you for the laughs, the heartbreak, and the stories still unfolding.

To my wife, Robin—thank you for thirty-three years of quiet support, encouragement, and love. You've given me the space to dream and the strength to finish. To my daughter Sophie, whose curiosity and creativity inspire me daily—thank you for always being ready to listen, to question, and to imagine.

Thanks to the many hands, both human and artificial, who read early drafts, offered feedback, or simply asked how the writing was going. You helped this story find its voice.

And finally, to anyone who's ever needed a little closure, a little magic, or a reason to come back—this book is for you.

Rituals & Magic of the Accord

As recorded through battle, breath, and bond.

The Silent Accord's spellwork is not categorized by school or tradition, but by the shape of intent and the memory it carries. Each spell is an echo of the caster's lineage, training, and realm of origin—whether whispered through stillness, hurled from flame, or traced by ancestral hands. The following entries include signature spells and rituals used by Bryn, Nyv, Tassa, Kaerda, and others throughout their journey across Núvarien.

Auric Ember

Caster: Tassa Emberlin
Type: Attack
Command Word(s): *naulëth sülëar*
Casting Style: Always fire-based. Tassa has never used another element with this spell.
Spell Signature: A 4-inch orb of golden flame that ricochets after impact, typically hitting up to three additional targets.
Flair: The spell is visually described as radiant, inherited flame—a magic tied to Tassa's gold dragon ancestry and halfling legacy of luck.
Description: Tassa hurls a condensed sphere of golden flame, infused with the spark of her draconic bloodline. On impact, it bursts and may ricochet into nearby targets, searing them in fire guided by something older than luck. The flame remembers its path and answers only to her.

Awakened Will

Caster: Bone-Anna
Type: Evolving Trait / Cognitive Awareness
Casting Style: Exhibited through action and response—Bone-Anna follows strategy and emotional cues.
Spell Signature: A moment of hesitation, a purposeful choice, a coordinated defence.
Flair: Her awareness is growing. She does not speak, but she understands.
Description: As Bone-Anna journeys with the Silent Accord, she begins to exhibit signs of independent awareness and decision-making. Though silent, she understands tactics, can follow non-verbal plans, and defends allies on instinct. Her presence shifts from servitor to sentinel.

Counterspell

Caster: Nyv
Type: Reaction/Disruption
Command Word(s): núshtá këlím
Casting Style: Nyv interrupts spellcasting in real time, often without moving her feet.
Spell Signature: A subtle shimmer ripples outward from her blade or hand.
Flair: Her expression rarely changes—she simply ends the spell before it begins.
Description: Nyv's control is precise and absolute—magic dies at her word. When cast using Communal Binding, Shield protects the entire party from a single triggering attack.

Detect Magic

Caster: Nyv
Type: Utility
Command Word(s): náren vellûn
Casting Style: Spoken softly and deliberately, often as part of an ongoing investigation or ritual.
Spell Signature: A low glimmer washes across her eyes and hands, revealing the threads of enchantment layered around her.
Flair: Nyv uses this spell more like a lens than a beacon, tilting her head or reaching through magical auras to understand them.
Description: Nyv whispers to the Worldthread itself, drawing forth hidden enchantments and spectral traces. The world shimmers with latent power, each effect exposed in soft glow.

Dispel Magic

Caster: Bryn
Type: Disruption
Command Word(s): déshal nárú
Casting Style: Performed with quiet certainty and precise control, often following a brief moment of magical analysis.
Spell Signature: A sharp cut in the air, often through an open palm or downward gesture, followed by a dispersing shimmer.
Flair: Bryn's dispels carry the quiet authority of the Queen of Stillness— unmaking what was stitched into the world.
Description: A deliberate breath and a focused phrase tear magic from the world around her. Complex spells unravel, and hidden bindings fail in silence.

Echo Sense

Caster: Geoff the Newt

Type: Familiar Trait / Sensory Link

Casting Style: Passive and instinctive—Geoff reacts to Nyv's emotional and magical shifts without command.

Spell Signature: A twitch of his tail, a turn of his head—subtle, synchronized with Nyv's tension or focus.

Flair: Geoff is attuned not to magic alone, but to Nyv's presence, making his reactions feel like premonitions.

Description: Geoff can detect subtle magical vibrations and mimic Nyv's emotional or magical reactions with uncanny accuracy. Though he does not speak, his movements echo Nyv's intent, sometimes alerting others to unseen threats or emotional shifts.

Eldritch Blast

Caster: Bryn

Type: Attack

Command Word(s): márna rūvína

Casting Style: Delivered with practised calm—often one hand outstretched and eyes locked on the target.

Spell Signature: A bolt of force shaped like a raven erupts from her palm, trailing violet energy.

Flair: Bryn's blasts are more than raw power—they are guided messengers of intent, spectral symbols of her bond with the Queen.

Description: Crackling bolts of force shaped like spectral ravens spiral from Bryn's outstretched hand. Each strikes with the weight of her will—and the Queen's.

Element Bind

Caster: Nyv

Type: Reaction

Command Word(s): résh ákîr

Casting Style: Triggered the moment elemental energy strikes—her hand lifts, not in fear, but to embrace it.

Spell Signature: A shimmer of magic coalesces around her form, drawing the element inward in a spiral of muted colour.

Flair: The spell bends to her command like water to stone—absorbed, stored, and held for a retaliatory strike.

Description: Nyv absorbs elemental energy as if drawing breath—fire, lightning, or frost held within her frame, redirected with fierce economy. When cast using Communal Binding, Element Bind grants resistance to the entire party.

Emberforged Ward
Caster: Kaerda
Type: Defence
Command Word(s): *karun beldor*
Casting Style: Activated in the heat of battle by slamming her shield or striking her armour.
Spell Signature: A golden shimmer spreads across her armour or shield, inscribed with faint runes glowing like heated metal.
Flair: The ward hums with the tempered strength of Durnach the Forgemaker's forge—unyielding, radiant, and practical.
Description: A divine enchantment placed on Kaerda's shield or armour. Grants resistance to radiant and fire damage. Seen activated during major battles.

Enhanced Invisibility
Caster: Nyv
Type: Buff
Command Word(s): *krén thîríl*
Casting Style: Cast with a flick of the wrist and a low invocation, just before vanishing from view.
Spell Signature: The air shimmers briefly around the target before falling utterly still.
Flair: Even under duress, Nyv's use of invisibility is refined—woven with discipline and intention.
Description: An invisible veil cloaks the caster or ally completely. Even while attacking or casting, the target remains unseen—lost between breath and vision. When cast using Communal Binding, the entire party becomes invisible, even while moving or casting.

Fireball
Caster: Tassa Emberlin
Type: Area Damage
Command Word(s): nonverbal
Casting Style: Often hurled skyward from a single outstretched hand, with practised fluidity and a glint of anticipation.
Spell Signature: A golden sphere bursts high in the air before erupting in a

roaring inferno of flame.

Flair: Tassa's fire is not reckless—it is radiant and intentional, carrying the weight of her ancestry with every detonation.

Description: A golden ember arcs high before detonation, erupting in a wave of ancestral fire. Tassa's magic blazes not with rage—but with inheritance.

Fly

Caster: Bryn

Type: Movement

Command Word(s): *sîlú válën*

Casting Style: Cast with an elegant flick of the wrist and a spoken phrase, usually just before leaping into the air.

Spell Signature: Wisps of shadow spiral around Bryn's feet and shoulders as she rises smoothly into the air.

Flair: She doesn't soar—she drifts, calm and poised, as if carried by memory itself.

Description: With a whisper to shadow and thought, Bryn rises into the air. The world slows beneath her, her steps weightless, her sight far-reaching.

Flamekindle

Caster: Tassa Emberlin

Type: Ancestral Trait / Passive Enchantment

Casting Style: Always active—her fire spells take on their unique gold hue automatically.

Spell Signature: Flames burn golden, radiant, and do not flicker with wind.

Flair: Her fire is quiet until it strikes—burning brighter, hotter, and longer than most.

Description: Tassa's golden fire is never mundane. It resists being snuffed out by natural means and always manifests as golden flame—a trait passed down from her forgotten draconic ancestry.

Forge's Blessing

Caster: Kaerda

Type: Utility / Support

Command Word(s): *ánur meldán*

Casting Style: Performed with reverent care, often during quiet moments after battle or while preparing sacred tools.

Spell Signature: A warm light radiates from her palms, threading through metal or flesh like liquid gold.

Flair: Every motion is deliberate—Kaerda's divine magic is as much craft as prayer.

Description: Used to repair damaged gear and grant temporary resilience. This spell restores what's broken—be it armour or resolve—with the steadiness of Durnach the Forgemaker's hand.

Forgebound Endurance

Caster: Kaerda

Type: Divine Blessing / Passive Resilience

Casting Style: Always present. She simply continues working or standing without pause.

Spell Signature: None—only a quiet determination and refusal to fall.

Flair: Her resilience is not supernatural in appearance, but it is unmistakable in practice.

Description: Kaerda does not sleep during vigils and rarely tires. This blessing from Durnach the Forgemaker allows her to endure long hours of labor, travel, or battle without faltering.

Glacier's Path

Caster: Bryn

Type: Area Damage

Command Word(s): *éhtë foróchél*

Casting Style: Cast with a commanding phrase and extended arm, often used at range to disrupt enemy formations.

Spell Signature: A crashing wave of jagged glacial stone erupts along a straight line, tearing through terrain and enemy alike.

Flair: The spell echoes like falling ice across stone—ancient, mournful, and devastating.

Description: A thunderous rift of glacial stone tears forward from her, scattering enemies in a howl of ancient cold. It is the path of ruin—and warning.

Hallow

Caster: Bryn

Type: Ritual / Area Sanctification

Command Word(s): *tharell ónatha*

Casting Style: Cast slowly over hours within a sacred boundary, usually accompanied by a candlelit vigil or shadow-marked sigils.

Spell Signature: A faint ring of glimmering shadow expands outward, followed by a breath of silence as the area settles into sanctified stillness.

Flair: The magic feels heavy with purpose, as if the Queen herself watches from beyond.

Description: A sacred ritual granted directly to Bryn by the Queen of Stillness. Used to consecrate a location, repelling undead and forming a barrier that cannot be crossed. This divine magic requires uninterrupted casting and leaves a lasting mark of the Queen's favour on the land.

Hammer of Judgment

Caster: Kaerda

Type: Combat

Command Word(s): *grond thalan*

Casting Style: Invoked mid-strike, Kaerda channels Durnach the Forgemaker's fury through her weapon with a firm step and divine exhale.

Spell Signature: Her warhammer glows with radiant heat before discharging in a concussive burst on impact.

Flair: The spell knocks enemies back not with rage—but with the righteous clarity of Kaerda's faith.

Description: Kaerda's hammer glows with divine energy and knocks back enemies. Described in combat scenarios as a radiant knockback effect, especially potent against undead and fiends.

Heat Metal

Caster: Tassa Emberlin

Type: Control / Damage

Command Word(s): *brásk élën*

Casting Style: Cast with a clenched fist and sharp glare, Tassa channels focused flame into metal with purposeful wrath.

Spell Signature: The metal glows red-orange, smoking and distorting in waves of heat, often forcing enemies to drop weapons or armour.

Flair: Her version of this spell burns cleaner and hotter—refined through instinct and an echo of something older.

Description: Tassa focuses her flame into an enemy's armour or weapon, heating it to an agonizing degree. The metal glows orange, forcing enemies to drop it—or suffer repeated burns.

Queen's Mantle

Caster: Bryn

Type: Defence / Obscurement

Command Word(s): *gwâth thúrîn*

Casting Style: Activated mid-battle with a calm breath, as if donning a familiar cloak.

Spell Signature: Shadows surge outward like flame, cloaking Bryn's form in moving darkness that lashes at attackers.

Flair: The spell is both protection and punishment—a gift from the Queen of Stillness that burns those who dare approach.

Description: A swirling cloak of dark flame coils around Bryn, shielding her with the Queen of Stillness's sanction. Those who breach it suffer not just pain—but judgment.

Ravenflock

Caster: Bryn

Type: Divinely Granted / Companion Swarm

Casting Style: Always present unless banished; ravens swirl to aid her focus or strike with intention.

Spell Signature: Ten spectral ravens orbit Bryn, sometimes spreading wide to scout or striking with precise coordination.

Flair: These ravens are not illusions or familiars—they are soul-guides, entrusted by the Queen of Stillness.

Description: Bryn is accompanied by ten spectral ravens from the Shadowfell. They assist in scouting, enhance precision in battle, and allow her to see through their eyes. If one falls, she can summon another. They are ever-present manifestations of her divine bond.

Rite of Resonance

Caster: Bryn

Type: Ritual / Item Attunement

Command Word(s): nonverbal

Casting Style: Performed in quiet focus with fine tools, Bryn traces runes and shadow-thread across the item's surface.

Spell Signature: The object pulses faintly with dim silver light, resonating with past intent and magical memory.

Flair: This ritual feels like unearthing a whisper from the past—it is not cast, but revealed.

Description: A meditative process using soot, tools, and shadow-weaving, this rite reveals magical harmonies bound within crafted items. Bryn uses it to unlock or attune enchanted objects, often uncovering links between maker and bearer.

Sanctifier's Pulse

Caster: Kaerda

Type: Utility / Empowerment

Command Word(s): *núrôn tâl*

Casting Style: Activated through stillness and breath, often in sacred or reforging moments.

Spell Signature: A radiant pulse expands outward from Kaerda's hands, reinforcing surrounding divine effects with golden resonance.

Flair: The magic does not command attention—it deepens what's already there, lending strength in silence.

Description: Used during sacred forging or moments of ritual reinforcement, this pulse of divine energy stabilizes unstable magic and bolsters the spiritual integrity of enchanted items or sacred sites. It amplifies nearby divine effects and imbues constructs or weapons with holy resonance.

Seidra's Grasp

Caster: Nyv

Type: Control

Command Word(s): nonverbal

Casting Style: Cast with a gesture and a focused look—Nyv speaks no words, letting the spell form through will alone.

Spell Signature: Red-gold spectral chains lash outward and bind a humanoid target's limbs, glowing faintly in the dim light.

Flair: This spell evokes Nyv's Ravkari ancestry, silent but forceful—a magic born of discipline and heritage.

Description: Nyv conjures spectral chains of red-gold light that lash toward a humanoid target, binding their limbs and locking them in place. Draws from her Ravkari battle-magic tradition.

Shadowdrop

Caster: Bryn

Type: Battlefield Control

Command Word(s): *dúil pórth*

Casting Style: Spoken low with a guiding hand, often while targeting multiple enemies across a wide field.

Spell Signature: Ink-black portals bloom beneath foes, pulling them into a suspended demiplane where time slows and sound ceases.

Flair: Bryn's mastery over this spell allows her to use it both as displacement and as containment—turning her control of space into a tool of delay, disruption, and collapse.

Description: Opens swirling portals of shadow beneath up to six enemies. Those caught are cast into a pocket realm, stunned and removed from battle. In advanced forms, Bryn alters the portals to drop enemies from above, collide them midair, or pin them in planar stasis—turning the battlefield into her design.

Shadowlight Vision

Caster: Bryn
Type: Detection / Utility
Command Word(s): nonverbal
Casting Style: Cast with stillness and a narrowed gaze, often while scanning the air or space ahead.
Spell Signature: A soft ripple of lightless shadow crosses her vision, allowing hidden forms to emerge in her sight.
Flair: Bryn sees not with her eyes alone, but with the edges of the world— where silence holds secrets.
Description: Bryn peers through shadow's veil, revealing that which clings to the edge of light. The unseen becomes silhouette, flickering in defiance.

Shatterwake

Caster: Bryn, Nyv (shared spell)
Type: Destructive Puls / Kinetic Disruption
Command Word(s): rakae
Casting Style: Spoken with sharp intent, hand thrust or palm open toward the ground. When cast together, Bryn and Nyv synchronize their release, amplifying the wave's resonance.
Spell Signature: A moment of breathless stillness, then a concussive shockwave cracks outward from the ground in a tight arc—splintering bone, shattering skulls, and fracturing brittle stone.
Flair: The magic resonates within the body before it ruptures outward. When cast in tandem, Bryn's controlled focus and Nyv's place magic weave the pulse into devastating harmony, their bond amplifying its reach and force.
Description: Releases a thunderous pulse of force that fractures bone and splits armor, traveling along the ground in a circular shockwave. Effective against skeletal forms, brittle constructs, and clustered enemy lines. While raw in its basic form, Shatterwake's true power lies in synchronized casting—where multiple invocations of *rakae* cause the waveforms to align and intensify, magnifying destruction across the field.

Silverstride

Caster: Nyv
Type: Movement

Command Word(s): nonverbal

Casting Style: Cast with a single step forward and a sharply spoken phrase.

Spell Signature: A burst of mist and a crackle of static as Nyv vanishes, reappearing up to thirty feet away.

Flair: Her teleportation is quiet and sudden—like wind slipping through a gap in stone.

Description: Nyv briefly shimmers, disappears, and reappears elsewhere in a blink. When cast using Communal Binding, she can teleport the entire party up to thirty feet in coordinated motion.

Veilstep

Caster: Bryn

Type: Racial Ability / Teleportation

Command Word(s): nonverbal

Casting Style: Used instinctively—Bryn steps lightly into a shadow and emerges elsewhere without warning.

Spell Signature: Her form briefly shimmers with trailing black mist, vanishing into shadow and reappearing up to thirty feet away.

Flair: This ability is not learned—it is inherited, born of her Shadowbound bloodline and shaped by the Queen of Stillness's realm.

Description: Bryn can teleport up to 30 feet through shadows, appearing silently in a new location within line of sight. She uses this for swift repositioning, escape, or stealth—disappearing and reappearing like a whisper carried on the dark.

Veilstep (lesser)

Caster: Bone-Anna

Type: Divinely Granted / Teleportation

Command Word(s): nonverbal

Casting Style: Executed in eerie silence—Bone-Anna gestures or moves as though pulled by unseen strings.

Spell Signature: Her body distorts briefly in silhouette before vanishing, reappearing elsewhere with a soft burst of shadow.

Flair: Where Bryn's Veilstep is graceful, Bone-Anna's is uncanny—more haunting than heroic, as though reality yields to her unfinished state.

Description: Bone-Anna can teleport up to 30 feet through shadows. Though she does not speak, this ability manifests instinctively in combat. It is part of her undead nature, refined by time with the Silent Accord.

Shared Resonance

Caster. Nyv & Bryn
Type. Communal Binding / Bonded Trait
Casting Style. Emerges between them during heightened emotional or spiritual states.
Spell Signature. A faint shimmer connects them and spreads outward to the rest of the party.
Flair. Their bond awakens ancestral magic neither could wield alone.
Description. After their bond was acknowledged, Nyv and Bryn unlocked Communal Binding—a Ravkari power usually shared only between the Seidra allowing defensive and utility spells to affect the entire Silent Accord. This shared resonance is subtle but profound, connecting magic to emotion.

Shield

Caster. Nyv
Type. Reaction
Command Word(s). *vherán ákîr*
Casting Style. Cast in an instant, often mid-step or mid-parry, with a single spoken word and flick of the hand.
Spell Signature. A shimmering translucent barrier flares into existence, just long enough to deflect the blow.
Flair. Nyv's shields are instinctive—a response of will and practice rather than thought.
Description. A flash of will manifests a ward that halts blade, bolt, or flame. It is the swift promise that she will not fall.

Silent Mimicry

Caster. Geoff the Newt
Type. Behavioural Ability
Casting Style. Not cast—this behaviour is ever-present, emerging in moments of focus or danger.
Spell Signature. Geoff mimics Nyv's gestures or stance with eerie timing.
Flair. Some believe he's just well-trained. Others suspect something far more magical.
Description. Geoff mirrors Nyv's posture and reactions with precision, often anticipating her next move. This ability deepens their bond and occasionally causes enemies to mistake his movements as part of spellcasting.

Soulfire Aegis

Caster. Kaerda

Type: Defence / Reaction

Command Word(s): *góndrël vákór*

Casting Style: Activated instinctively in response to an overwhelming blow.

Spell Signature: Her armour's runes flare white-hot, deflecting force with a halo of radiant steel.

Flair: The spell feels forged rather than conjured—its power shaped in fire, faith, and resolve.

Description: When struck by a devastating blow, Kaerda's divine ward ignites. Her shield and armour shine with radiant light, absorbing a portion of the attack and anchoring her in place. The Queen's favour may shield Bryn, but Kaerda stands on strength alone.

Spiritsight

Caster: Nyv

Type: Racial / Sensory Ability

Casting Style: Passive trait, triggered in moments of danger or intense magical focus.

Spell Signature: Subtle—Nyv's breath slows, and she visibly senses fluctuations others cannot.

Flair: Her awareness is elemental, tied to wind and pressure—answers found in silence.

Description: A latent trait enhanced by Ravkari training. Nyv can hold her breath indefinitely and instinctively senses changes in magic and emotion through atmospheric shifts.

Spiritsworn

Caster: Nyv

Type: Defence / Area Control

Command Word(s): *válra thárán*

Casting Style: Performed with arms outstretched and voice steady, calling to the unseen spirits of her Ravkari ancestors.

Spell Signature: Ethereal figures swirl protectively around her in a slow, silent storm, striking enemies who step too close.

Flair: The spirits are not summoned—they arrive of their own accord, drawn by her conviction.

Description: Nyv summons Ravkari ancestors from memory and magic. They encircle her like a storm—shielding allies, striking intruders, and whispering truths from the past.

Voice of the Forge

Caster: Kaerda

Type: Inspirational

Command Word(s): górn êkhá

Casting Style: Spoken with unwavering clarity, often following a spiritual test or moment of revelation.

Spell Signature: Her words echo with divine cadence, cracking illusions and bolstering the will of allies.

Flair: Kaerda's voice channels Durnach the Forgemaker's strength—not thunderous, but immovable.

Description: Used to break mental or emotional domination, freeing herself or others from illusion or despair. The invocation steadies the spirit and burns away doubt with truth forged in faith.

Walking With the Dead

Caster: Bryn

Type: Ritual / Utility

Command Word(s): nonverbal

Casting Style: Performed in stillness and reverence, requiring a copper coin placed beneath the tongue of each participant.

Spell Signature: A veil of quiet shadow settles over the group, dulling sound and cloaking their presence.

Flair: The dead sense nothing—the group becomes silent echoes walking beside graves.

Description: A solemn rite that cloaks the party in the Queen's shroud, rendering them undetectable to undead for one hour. As long as no spells are cast and no attacks made, they move through haunted lands unseen, as living ghosts among the dead.

Wavebind

Caster: Nyv

Type: Control

Command Word(s): êlûn vârïs

Casting Style: Cast with an open hand and whispered command, drawing the tides through gesture more than force.

Spell Signature: A rising column of water spirals upward from the ground, lifting and restraining enemies in its grasp.

Flair: The magic is tidal, unhurried yet overwhelming—Nyv calls it like a tide, not a weapon.

Description: Summons a rising column of water that lifts and restrains enemies within its surge. Used both for crowd control and to disrupt battlefield positioning, the spell feels more like nature answering than power exerted.

Spells Listed by Command

Command	Spell Name	Translated From
ánur meldán	Forge's Blessing	"blessing of the forge"
brásk élën	Heat Metal	"sear the iron"
déshal nárú	Dispel Magic	"unravel the binding"
dúil pórth	Shadowdrop	"repeat the portal"
éhtë foróchél	Glacier's Path	"spear of frozen flow"
êlûn vârïs	Wavebind	"path of moonlight"
góndrël vákór	Soulfire Aegis	"bind the magic"
górn êkhá	Voice of the Forge	"rend the core"
grond thalan	Hammer of Judgment	"seal the voice"
gwâth thúrîn	Queen's Mantle	"shadow veil"
karun beldor	Emberforged Ward	"anchor truth"
krén thîríl	Enhanced Invisibility	"hidden by pact"
márna rûvína	Eldritch Blast	"forceful rupture"
naulëth súlëar	Auric Ember	"flame reborn in wind"
núrôn tâl	Sanctifier's Pulse	"reveal the hidden"
núshtá këlím	Counterspell	"unweave intention"
náren vellún	Detect Magic	"reveal the unseen"
rekae	Shatterwake	"release the force"
résh ákîr	Element Bind	"absorb the strike"
sîlú válën	Fly	"slip through the space"
tharell ónatha	Hallow	"grasp of spirit"
válra thárán	Spiritsworn	"guardian spirits"
vherán ákîr	Shield	"deflect the strike"

Loom of Núvarien

A world shaped by silence, bound by memory, and carried forward by flame.

Every thread spun in this world—be it spell, name, god, or place—emerges from the Loom. It does not explain itself. It does not unravel cleanly. But those who walk its edge—the Accord among them—have gathered what can be known.

The world is not written in chapters, but in threads—some knotted in ritual, some frayed by silence. The Loom of Núvarien holds the world in tension, each strand a breath, a name still spoken or nearly lost.

What follows are the strands we can still follow: realms, rituals, deities, magic, and memory, recorded not to master the world, but to move within it.

The Loom does not end here. It only frays where we stop looking.

Woven Ember Cosmology Simplified

As spoken to initiates of the Accord, and remembered by those who walk between realms known within the cosmology as 'strands'.

The world of Núvarien is not round, but woven—held aloft between memory and silence, fire and unraveling. Its structure is layered, sacred, and ever-shifting, seen not only with the eyes but with the soul. This simplified cosmology offers a glimpse of the realms above and below the world-disc, and the tensions that shape magic, gods, and the fate of all who walk the threads.

Núvarien

The name of the world-disc itself. It is flat, circular, and suspended between elemental and metaphysical tensions. The disc has two faces:

- Verdance – The upper face of the disc, home to forests, rivers, life, and waking memory.
- Umbraveth – The lower face of the disc, a shadowed mirror where forgotten things drift and memory moves backward.

Each side of the disc is influenced by realms above and below. These realms are not geographic, but cosmological—planes of thought, magic, or resonance.

Strands Above Verdance

- **Aetherim** – The sky-path of breath and story. This is where wind-spirits and ancestral whispers dwell.
- **Pyraestha** – The realm of sacred fire and transformation. It tests, reforges, and remembers through flame.
- **Stillmere** – A luminous sphere of silence and timelessness. From here, the Queen of Stillness watches.

Strands Beneath Umbraveth

- **Aetherim** – The wind path continues below, but its direction reverses. It carries forgotten names downward.
- **Narmarien** – A deep oceanic realm of memory submerged. All that is unspoken drifts here in sorrow and quiet weight.
- **The Deep Unweaving** – The spiral of unmaking. It is where meaning dissolves and the pattern fails.

These strands are felt in magic, story, and dream. Spells resonate differently depending on their origin and alignment with these planes. The Silent Accord's journey moves through many of these layers—sometimes knowingly, sometimes only through the thread of memory.

Woven Ember Cosmology Diagram

Places in Núvarien

The Silent Accord takes place exclusively on the Verdance (Material World) side of Núvarien.

The Banished City
Once known as Tharniseth, this city was exiled into Umbraveth by Vharion the Final Warden. Its people, now called the Banished, returned altered and devoted to Nhalis, the Veilmother. Their return was flawed, and the city eventually collapsed.

Estavar
A lakeside city known for quiet resilience, artistry, and the long shadows cast by its past. The Silent Accord once called it home.

Lethvain Reach
A sacred and silent forest touched by shadow and memory. Some say the trees remember.

Merishan
A crossroads realm shaped by trade and compromise. Its people are pragmatic, diverse, and often caught between greater powers.

Ravkareth
A cold, wind-hardened land in the north, home to the Veilwardens and Seidra witches. Known for its deep-rooted traditions, elemental magic, and fierce cultural memory.

Tharniseth
The true name of the Banished City. Cast into Umbraveth to spare the world. Its name is rarely spoken aloud, and even then, only in fear or reverence.

Vaulmark
A powerful nation ruled by the Vaulmar Binders, whose magic bends soul and law alike. Once a land of scholars, now cloaked in firelit ambition and ritual might.

Veltharyn
A fallen empire obsessed with perfection. Their magic could alter truth, identity, and history—until they unraveled beneath their own unattainable ideals.

Vharask Dunes

A sun-bleached expanse of ruin and whispering wind. Once dry earth—now scarred by the fall of ancient cities.

Threads of Practice

Observed and recorded by Accord spellcasters, seers, and lorewardens

Magic in Núvarien is not divided by school, but by source, intention, and the thread it touches. Some magic flows from the Worldthread, the great lattice of memory and naming that sustains Verdance and echoes through Stillmere. Some is drawn from the Witherlace, where pattern frays and silence unspools meaning, binding itself to the secrets of Umbraveth and Narmarien. Others cast between—through the Veil—using concealment, inversion, or reflection to shape the world unseen.

Each caster within the Silent Accord draws magic differently. What matters is not how a spell is cast, but where its thread begins.

Worldthread
Different cultures bend the Worldthread to their needs: the Ravkari use it to empower communal and place-bound magic through emotional and ancestral connection; the Vaulmar manipulate it for rigid control, binding, and destruction; the Velthari once shaped it in pursuit of perfection, altering identity and memory itself.

- *Communal Casting*
  Unlike solitary spellwork, some traditions in Núvarien rely on shared intent. When casters are bonded by emotion, ancestry, or oath, their magic can resonate and amplify. The Ravkari Seidra perfected this art; when their circle stands as one, even silence becomes a spell.
- *Seidra Magic*
  A place-bound, elemental form of casting rooted in Ravkareth. Its strength lies in location, emotion, and communal bond—especially powerful when shared among trusted companions.
- *Bonded Magic*
  A rare ancestral ability unlocked by Nyv, allowing certain protective spells to affect the entire Silent Accord. Represents the deepest form of magical trust and kinship.

Witherlace
Often associated with Nhalis, the Veilmother, the Witherlace unravels memory, identity, and emotion—offering power at the cost of truth. It flows in shadows, between names, and beneath silence.

- *Echo and Burden*

  All magic in Núvarien leaves something behind. Whether cast through the Worldthread or the Witherlace, each spell bears the echo of the caster— emotional residue, flickers of memory, or ancestral traces. To cast too often without rest is to become frayed at the edges.

The Veil

The unseen boundary between the physical and the spiritual, the remembered and the forgotten. Magic in Núvarien often flows most powerfully along this veil—crossing it, binding to it, or breaking through it. To those who walk its edge, silence is not absence—it is conduit.

Magic Modalities

Magic in Núvarien flows from two great forces— the Worldthread and the Witherlace.

The Worldthread is the luminous structure of memory, naming, and restoration—woven through places, people, and the sacred stillness.

The Witherlace is the frayed edge—born from forgetting, distortion, and the pull of unmaking. Every spell, enchantment, and ritual arises from the tension between these two.

Yet beneath them lie finer distinctions: modal threads that define how magic behaves, feels, and acts. These threads are not schools, but intentions—woven expressions shaped by realm, ancestry, and purpose.

In the world of Núvarien, magic flows not from elemental schools or rigid classifications, but from modal threads—conceptual expressions of magical behaviour drawn from the Woven Ember cosmology. These threads define the intent, structure, and resonance of magic. Each spell weaves itself from one or more of these modalities, shaped by the caster's will, origin, and alignment with memory, silence, or transformation.

Binding Magic

- *Purpose:* To stabilize, connect, preserve, or restore.
- *Common Uses:* Shields, healing, consecration, soul-tethering, defensive enchantments.
- *Realm Affinity:* Núvarien, Stillmere, Aetherim
- **Examples**: Shield, Soulfire Aegis, Sanctifier's Pulse, Hallow
- *Philosophy:* "To bind is to remember the shape of things."

Veil Magic

- *Purpose:* To conceal, obscure, distort, or protect through deception.
- *Common Uses:* Invisibility, misdirection, spatial folding, battlefield redirection.
- *Realm Affinity:* Umbraveth, Deep Unweaving, Aetherim
- **Examples**: Enhanced Invisibility, Queen's Mantle, Shadowdrop, Silverstride
- *Philosophy:* "What is veiled is not absent—it is waiting."
- *Purpose:* To reshape, empower, or transmute.
- *Common Uses:* Elemental spells, flight, radiant attacks, altered states.

- *Realm Affinity*: Firelands, Núvarien
- **Examples**: Auric Ember, Fly, Hammer of Judgment, Flamekindle
- *Philosophy*: "Change is the only truth that burns clean."

Echo Magic

- *Purpose*: To reflect, respond, or call upon memory and resonance.
- *Common Uses*: Ancestral summoning, communal magic, dream-vision, spirit-sensing.
- *Realm Affinity*: Aetherim, Núvarien, Umbraveth
- **Examples**: Spiritsworn, Echo Sense, Shared Resonance, Awakened Will
- *Philosophy*: "What was once spoken still listens."

Unmaking Magic

- *Purpose*: To undo, sever, disrupt, or nullify magical constructs.
- *Common Uses*: Spell negation, disenchantment, magical cancellation.
- *Realm Affinity*: Deep Unweaving, corrupted Umbraveth
- **Examples**: Counterspell, Dispel Magic
- *Philosophy*: "To end a pattern is not evil. It is clarity."

Reflection Magic

- *Purpose*: To receive, reveal, or observe without altering.
- *Common Uses*: Divination, magical detection, attunement, passive insight.
- *Realm Affinity*: Narmarien, Stillmere
- **Examples**: Detect Magic, Shadowlight Vision, Rite of Resonance
- *Philosophy*: "Not all magic must act. Some must witness."

Control (Composite Modality)

- *Purpose*: To restrain or direct without destruction.
- *Often Paired With*: Binding or Veil
- **Examples**: Wavebind, Seidra's Grasp
- *Philosophy*: "Power without cruelty is mastery."

Factions and Deities

As recognised across Verdance, Umbraveth, and the realms beyond

The world of Núvarien is shaped not only by magic and memory, but by those who walk its threads—mortal and divine alike. Some gods forge, some unravel. Some speak in silence, others in flame. Just as the realms above and below echo with tension, so too do the loyalties and beliefs of those who dwell within them. This section offers a brief account of the known powers, their followers, and the subtle war between purpose and forgetting that runs beneath every oath, every faction, and every act of reverence.

The Banished

Former citizens of Tharniseth, exiled into the Umbraveth by Vharion the Final Warden. Altered by their time beyond the veil, they returned changed—servants of Nhalis, the Veilmother, and bearers of forgotten magic.

Durnach the Forgemaker *(also called the Flamefather)*

Durnach the Forgemaker is the divine force of creation through fire, revered by Kaerda of the Silent Accord and by all who shape the world with purpose. His domain lies within Pyraestha, the sacred realm of transformative flame above Verdance. It is said that his forge is not a place but a presence—that wherever metal meets conviction, he is there. Through Kaerda, his strength endures in every act of patient craftsmanship, in every blow struck to build rather than to destroy. Durnach's fire does not consume; it tempers. He is not the god of invention, but of intention.

Dragons

In the Woven Ember Cosmology, dragons are not simply beasts, but living embodiments of memory, flame, and will. They are thought to have emerged where the realms of Pyraestha (sacred fire) and Stillmere (timeless silence) once touched. Emberstone dragons carry the fire of purpose. Ashbound dragons carry the fire of hunger. All dragons remember—and some remember too much.

- ### Ashbound
  Dragons of hunger and distortion. These arise where Narmarien brushes against Umbraveth, their fire corrupted by sorrow or loss. They burn not to shape, but to consume.
- ### Emberborne
  Dragons of purpose, memory, and creation. Dragons of purpose and

----

remembrance. These beings emerge from the confluence of Pyraestha and Stillmere. They carry the fire of creation, guided by memory and ancient will. Many believe Vhal'turien, the First Gold Flame, is Emberborne.

Elunara, the Waking Bloom

Elunara, known as the Waking Bloom, is the gentle divine force of healing, renewal, and memory restored through living things. Her presence is rooted in Verdance, where breath, growth, and balance shape the world above. She is honoured not through temples, but through gardens, rest, and the quiet rituals of care. Where Nhalis veils, Elunara reveals—though never with force. She grants renewal through stillness and quiet blooming, returning strength to those who falter. The temple where Bryn recovered is one of her oldest sanctuaries. Her followers are gardeners of soul and soil, bearing witness to life's return.

Ithiruun, the Thread-Eater

Ithiruun, known as the Thread-Eater, is the nameless hunger that stirs in the depths of the Deep Unweaving. Unlike other divine forces, Ithiruun does not speak, create, or remember. It devours meaning, consuming not only spells and names, but intention itself. It is said that those who fall too far into oblivion do not meet death—they meet Ithiruun. The Witherlace frays where Ithiruun's hunger touches the world, and even Nhalis is said to pause when her unraveling nears its edge. Scholars fear it. The Silent Accord does not name it twice.

Nhalis, the Veilmother

Nhalis, the Veilmother, is the cosmic force of shadow, secrecy, and unraveling. Her presence pulses from the depths of Umbraveth, and her whispers spiral down through Narmarien into the Deep Unweaving. Patron of the Banished and feared by truth-tellers, she feeds not on death—but on what is forgotten: memory, identity, and names left unsaid. It is said she weaves in reverse, unmaking as she goes. Her touch is felt in the Witherlace, the fraying thread of magic that distorts pattern and undoes shape. Her name is never spoken twice in the same tongue.

Queen of Stillness

An ancient and enigmatic force, the Queen of Stillness walks not among the living or the dead, but the moments between them. Her presence radiates from Stillmere, the luminous realm of silence and timelessness above Pyraestha. She is neither worshipped nor feared in the traditional sense—her influence is felt in silence, in final choices, in memories left unspoken. Her ravens are not omens of doom, but vessels of remembrance, gathering pieces of what would

----

otherwise be forgotten. She does not command armies or demand temples; those who serve her do so through memory, reverence, and quiet resolve. Her chosen, like Bryn Lovas, are not bound by death—they are carriers of memory, marked to walk the thresholds others avoid.

Seidra
A title for witches within the Veilwardens. Deeply bound to the land and its spirits, each Seidra is a keeper of story and storm, trained in elemental and place-bound magic.

The Silent Accord
An adventuring party bound by shared grief, trust, and purpose. Comprising Bryn, Nyv, Kaerda, and Tassa, the Accord walks between myth and memory—carrying each other through flame, shadow, and silence.

Thalra, the Drowned Light
Thalra, the Drowned Light, is the mournful daughter of Nhalis and the silent tide of Narmarien. Where her mother unravels, Thalra remembers—dimly, deeply, and without voice. She is the presence behind sorrow, the echo of every name that sinks beneath the waves. Unlike the Queen of Stillness, who guards memory with reverence, Thalra lets it drift. She does not preserve, she endures. Oracles say she weeps not for what was lost—but for what will never rise again. Her touch is felt in grief too quiet to name, and in the rituals of letting go.

Vaulmar Binders
Arcane practitioners from Vaulmark who wield forbidden magics of binding, domination, and memory erosion. Ritualistic and powerful, outside their own lands they walk the line between law and tyranny.

Veilwardens
A sacred order of witches from Ravkareth who preserve the balance between elemental forces, ancestral spirits, and the quiet spaces where magic listens. Often misunderstood, always vigilant.

Vharion the Final Warden
A mythic figure of arcane sacrifice, Vharion cast the city of Tharniseth into the Umbraveth to protect the world. Remembered with reverence, fear, and the silence that follows a necessary loss.

The Whirling One
The Whirling One is a capricious, elusive force said to ride the currents of Aetherim, the sky-path of breath and story that winds above and below the

world-disc. Neither god nor demon, this being is wind given will, voice given shape. Some believe it to be the first breath of Núvarien itself, still wandering. Its influence is found in gusts that carry forgotten names, in whispers heard between dreams, and in songs that refuse to die. The Whirling One is not worshipped, but remembered through oral tradition, wind-flutes, and sky-written runes. Place-magic and spoken spellcraft often echo its pattern.

Myths and Customs

These fragments of belief, tradition, and legend are known throughout Núvarien. Some have faded into silence. Others may yet return in stories still to be told.

The Binding Accord
A legend older than the Silent Accord, telling of a group bound not by blood, but by choice. Said to be the first example of communal magic, their legacy endures in Ravkari tales about those who choose each other over power.

The Chain of Names
A mystical theory originating in Ravkareth: that every soul is anchored to the world by its name, and to forget a name is to sever that tether. Among Seidra, names are guarded, layered, and rarely given freely.

The Doctrine of Stillness
A whispered belief held by some among the Shadowbound and Veilwardens. It teaches that stillness is a form of reverence—that true understanding of death, memory, and magic comes not through mastery, but through silence.

The Return of the Banished
Centuries after their exile, the Banished returned from the Umbraveth—altered, diminished, and loyal to the Veilmother. Their return was flawed. Without a tether to the land that had moved on, the city collapsed, and its survivors scattered like memory in a storm.

Ritual Forging
A devotional act among followers of Durnach the Forgemaker. Tools, weapons, and even simple items are shaped not only for use but with spiritual intent. Among Kaerda's people, forging is both creation and prayer.

The Severing
The act by which Vharion the Final Warden banished the city of Tharniseth into the Umbraveth. Though spoken of as a single moment, some scholars believe it was a process—an unraveling of place, name, and purpose that took days or even weeks. No one who remained in the city survived.

Veilfasting
A rite of magical solitude performed by Veilwardens when approaching a threshold—of knowledge, of power, or of grief. The caster remains isolated and silent for days, speaking only when what must be said cannot be withheld.

Lexicon of Threads and Names

As gathered and preserved by the Silent Accord

The following entries have been assembled by the Silent Accord and their allies to preserve the language, realms, and truths woven through Núvarien. These are not all the names that exist—only those remembered. Some hold power when spoken aloud. Others are better whispered only in dreams. Treat them with care, for in Núvarien, to name something is to thread yourself into its memory.

Aetherim – The breath-path of Núvarien, a realm of wind and story that winds above and below the world-disc. It carries names, whispers, and ancestral echoes.

Ashbound – A lineage of dragons shaped by sorrow and unraveling. Born where Narmarien touches Umbraveth, they consume rather than transform.

Binding Magic – A modality of magic that stabilizes, connects, or restores. Used in shielding, consecration, and memory preservation.

Communal Binding – A Ravkari magical trait awakened through shared conviction. It allows spells to extend across individuals bound by trust or covenant.

Deep Unweaving – The lowest realm beneath Umbraveth, where memory and meaning dissolve. Ithiruun stirs in its depths.

Dragons – Beings formed from the tension between flame, silence, and memory. Divided into Emberborne and Ashbound lineages.

Durnach the Forgemaker – Also called the Flamefather. A divine force of sacred creation through fire, rooted in Pyraestha.

Echo Magic – A modality of magic that reflects or responds through memory, resonance, or ancestral link.

Elunara – The Waking Bloom. A gentle force of renewal and balance, honoured in Verdance.

Emberborne – Dragons of sacred fire and memory, born of Pyraestha and Stillmere. Their flame is purposeful.

Ithiruun – The Thread-Eater. A force of oblivion in the Deep Unweaving, where it devours intention and unravels meaning.

Miaradas – A shadow dragon of the Ashbound, born of sorrow and unraveling where Umbraveth brushes Narmarien. He does not hoard gold but silence, and her breath unravels memory itself.

Magic Modalities – The classification of magic by behaviour rather than school. Includes Binding, Veil, Transformative, Echo, Unmaking, Reflection, and Control.

Narmarien – The submerged realm beneath Umbraveth, filled with quiet grief and unspoken memory. Thalra, the Drowned Light, resides here.

Nhalis – The Veilmother. A force of shadow, secrecy, and unraveling. Her domain pulses from Umbraveth into Narmarien and the Deep Unweaving.

Núvarien – The disc-shaped world where all stories begin. It is suspended between silence, memory, and flame.

Place Magic – A Ravkari tradition practised by Veilwardens like Nyv. It draws strength from environment, history, and unspoken presence.

Pyraestha – The sacred realm of transformative flame above Verdance. A realm of trial, legacy, and reforging.

Queen of Stillness – A silent force who watches from Stillmere. She governs stillness, memory, and final moments.

Reflection Magic – A modality of passive revelation. It reveals what already exists without altering it.

Shadowlands / Umbraveth – The lower face of Núvarien, where memory drifts and reflection deepens. Governed by Nhalis.

Shared Resonance – A magical bond formed between members of the Silent Accord, most notably Bryn and Nyv. It allows certain spells to affect the group as one.

Silvarien (see: Verdance) – The upper face of Núvarien, where growth and memory unfold in sunlight. Governed by Elunara.

Stillmere – The celestial realm of starlight and silence above Pyraestha. Home of the Queen of Stillness.

Thalra – The Drowned Light. A daughter of Nhalis who resides in Narmarien. She holds sorrow without undoing.

Transformative Magic – A modality of magic that reshapes or alters through flame, force, or elevation.

Umbraveth – The mirrored underside of Núvarien, ruled by Nhalis. Also called the Shadowlands.

Unmaking Magic – A modality of magic that disrupts or erases existing structure, such as counterspell or dispel.

Veil Magic – A modality of magic that conceals or distorts through shadow, secrecy, or deception.

Veilstep – A short-range shadow-teleportation used by Bryn and Bone-Anna. It draws on Umbraveth's tension.

Verdance – The upper face of Núvarien. A realm of balance, growth, and living memory. Also known poetically as Silvarien.

Whirling One – A windborne force tied to Aetherim. It is remembered in breath, story, and motion.

Witherlace – The fraying thread of magic linked to shadow and unraveling. It corrupts structure where meaning decays.

Pronunciation Guide – The Silent Accord

In a world shaped by memory and silence, names carry power, and words—when spoken—echo through shadow and flame. This guide offers readers a way to speak as the Accord speaks, and to enter the story not just in thought, but in voice.

This guide provides phonetic pronunciations for names, places, spells, and key terms used throughout The Silent Accord trilogy and related works.

Characters

- **Bryn Lovas** – /brin/ (rhymes with "thin") /LOH-vahs/
- **Nyv Vojta (Nyvana)** – /niv/ (short 'i' as in "give") /VOY-tah/
- **Tassa Emberlin** – /TAH-sah/ /EM-ber-lin/
- **Kaerda Flintward** – /KARE-duh/ /FLINT-werd/
- **Bone-Anna** – /BOHN-ann-uh/
- **Dalebar** – /DAYL-bar/
- **Geoff the Newt** – /jeff thuh newt/
- **Mairadas** – /MAIR-uh-dahs/
- **Yeldanna** – /yel-DAH-nuh/

Places

- **Candlecut Hollow** – /KAN-dl-kut HAH-low/
- **Estavar** – /ESS-tuh-var/
- **Lethvain Reach** – /LETH-vayn/
- **Núvarien** – /NOO-vahr-ee-en/
- **Pyraestha** – /peer-AYTH-uh/
- **Ravkareth** – /RAHV-kah-reth/
- **Shadowlands** – /SHAD-oh-landz/
- **Vaulmark** – /VAWL-mark/
- **Velthorn Peaks** – /VEL-thorn/
- **Verdance** – /VUR-dans/

Magic & Terms

- **Communal Binding** – /kuh-MYOO-nuhl BINE-ding/
- **Durnach (the Forgemaker)** – /DUR-nahk/ (epithet: /FORJ-may-ker/)
- **Queen of Stillness** – /kween uhv STILL-ness/
- **Ravkari** – /rahv-KAR-ee/
- **Seidra** – /SAY-drah/
- **Shadowbound** – /SHAD-oh-bound/
- **Vatra** – /VAH-truh/
- **Veilstep** – /VAYL-step/
- **Veilwarden** – /VAYL-wohr-den/
- **Witherlace** – /WITH-er-lace/
- **Worldthread** – /WORLD-thread/

Spell Incantations

- **ánur meldán** – /AH-noor MEL-dahn/ (Forge's Blessing)
- **brásk élën** – /BRASK EH-lehn/ (Heat Metal)
- **déshal nárú** – /DEH-shahl NAH-roo/ (Dispel Magic)
- **dúil pórth** – /DOO-eel POR-th/ (Shadowdrop)
- **éhtë foróchél** – /EH-teh for-OH-kel/ (Glacier's Path)
- **êlûn vârïs** – /EH-loon VAH-rees/ (Wavebind)
- **góndrël vákór** – /GON-drell VAH-kor/ (Soulfire Aegis)
- **górn êkhá** – /GORN EH-khah/ (Voice of the Forge)
- **grond thalan** – /GROND THAH-lan/ (Hammer of Judgment)
- **gwâth thúrîn** – /GWAHTH THOO-reen/ (Queen's Mantle)
- **karun beldor** – /KAH-roon BELL-dor/ (Emberforged Ward)
- **krén thîríl** – /KREN THEE-reel/ (Enhanced Invisibility)
- **márna rūvína** – /MAR-nah roo-VEE-nah/ (Eldritch Blast)
- **naulëth súlëar** – /NOW-leth SOO-lee-ahr/ (Auric Ember)
- **náren vellûn** – /NAH-ren VELL-oon/ (Detect Magic)
- **núshtá këlím** – /NOOSH-tah KELL-eem/ (Counterspell)
- **núrôn tâl** – /NOO-rohn TAHL/ (Sanctifier's Pulse)
- **résh ákîr** – /RESH AH-keer/ (Element Bind)
- **sîlú válën** – /SEE-loo VAH-len/ (Fly)
- **tharell ónatha** – /THAH-rell OH-nah-thah/ (Hallow)
- **vherán ákîr** – /VHEH-rahn AH-keer/ (Shield)

- **válra thárán** – /VAHL-rah THAH-rahn/ (Spiritsworn)

This guide will continue to expand as the world of *The Silent Accord* grows.

About The Silent Accord

For those who turn to the final pages before the first—and for those who have just closed the cover and find themselves still listening.

Some stories are told in fire.
Others, in silence.

The Silent Accord is not a tale of chosen heroes or ancient prophecy. It follows four women—each carrying memory, loss, and a quiet hunger for meaning—as they navigate a world fraying at its edges. They do not raise banners. They do not chase destiny. But through shadow, ruin, and remembrance, they form a bond stronger than either oath or origin.

Bryn, who listens to the silence between words and calls ravens from the dark.
Nyv, whose blades and binding magic defend more than the living.
Tassa, all fire and laughter with the echo of something ancient in her breath.
Kaerda, who shapes salvation on an anvil and speaks best through steel.

Together, they do not seek to change the world. But they refuse to let it end unchallenged.

This is a story of stillness and strength.
Of love that is quiet, of memory that resists erasure.
Of what it means to carry one another—when the names are forgotten, and the thread begins to fail.

Thank you for reading!

If you've walked this journey through *The Silent Accord*, thank you.

This story was written for those who believe that strength can be quiet, that memory can shape magic, and that the bonds we choose matter as much as the ones we're given.

If the story stayed with you, I would be deeply grateful if you shared your thoughts in a review on Amazon or Goodreads. Even a few words can make a meaningful difference—it helps other readers decide whether this is a journey they too should take.

Your voice helps keep the story alive.
Your words help others find their way to the Accord.

I'm already at work on the next book in this series. I look forward to continuing the journey with you.

Thank you for being part of this.

— Robert

About the Author

Robert Stewart is a writer and public safety leader with almost three decades of experience in public safety communications, dispatch operations, and paramedicine. His work has spanned some of Canada's largest communications centres and included national-level advocacy for front-line call takers and dispatchers. He holds a Bachelor of Arts in Psychology with distinction from the University of the Fraser Valley in British Columbia, along with advanced certifications in project management, quality improvement, incident command, and communication centre leadership.

The Silent Accord is his first novel—an original high-fantasy epic about memory, silence, and the bonds we choose. Blending mythic worldbuilding with emotional depth, his writing explores resilience, identity, and quiet defiance in the face of overwhelming forces.

Robert lives in Manitoba, where he currently leads 9-1-1 operations for a diverse and expansive region. He shares life with his wife Robin—his partner of 33 years—and their daughter Sophie, a bright and creative nineteen-year-old who shares his love of stories. When not writing or working in public safety, Robert can be found in his shop working with wood and resin, printing and painting models of never-to-be used fantasy miniatures, and trying to shoo their calico cat off his workspaces.

P.S.

If you wish to speak of the Accord, you may write to **queenofstillness@gmail.com**. If you have found a flaw or a forgotten thread within these pages, let it be known—so that the story may remain whole.

Silence does not mean absence. I listen, even between the words.

www.ingramcontent.com/pod-product-compliance
Lightning Source LLC
Chambersburg PA
CBHW072001110726
47910CB00005B/1611